A
DARK
SACRIFICE

Also by Madeline Howard

The Hidden Stars: Book One of the Rune of Unmaking

* A *
DARK
SACRIFICE

BOOK TWO
OF THE RUNE OF
UNMAKING

*

MADELINE HOWARD

An Imprint of HarperCollinsPublishers

A DARK SACRIFICE. Copyright © 2007 by Teresa Edgerton. All rights reserved. Printed in the United States of America. No part of this book may be used or reproduced in any manner whatsoever without written permission except in the case of brief quotations embodied in critical articles and reviews. For information address HarperCollins Publishers, 10 East 53rd Street, New York, NY 10022.

HarperCollins books may be purchased for educational, business, or sales promotional use. For information please write: Special Markets Department, HarperCollins Publishers, 10 East 53rd Street, New York, NY 10022.

FIRST EDITION

Eos is a federally registered trademark of HarperCollins Publishers.

Designed by Nicola Ferguson

Library of Congress Cataloging-in-Publication Data has been applied for.

ISBN: 978-0-06-057592-2
ISBN 10: 0-06-057592-1

07 08 09 10 11 OV/RRD 10 9 8 7 6 5 4 3 2 1

This book is dedicated
to the memory of
my dear mother,
Eleanor Waller,
who is much missed,
and
to the swordsmen, magicians,
and sorceresses
who helped create video magic
in the winter of 2006,
and
to Jack and Ethan Johnsen,
who came to us like a miracle
in a dark time.

SYNOPSIS–
THE HIDDEN STARS

✴

Silüren uilédani amffüriandem—All things are changing under the moon.

The first book of *The Rune of Unmaking* told of a world in a perilous state of flux. A century had passed since a disastrous conflict between the wizards of Alluinn and the mages of Otöi ended in their mutual destruction. The death of a thousand magicians sent a pulse of energy through the entire world of matter, altered the course of the moon, and ushered in an age of change and mutation. Two great empires, north and south, fell in a single hour, throwing the world into a state of anarchy that lasted for decades.

And then, unlooked-for, came an era of peace and prosperity.

Few guessed what was ahead when a new young queen was crowned on Phaôrax. Ouriána had ensnared her entire realm in webs of dark sorcery before even a shadow of a threat touched the minds of a new generation of wizards in their stronghold on the island of Leal. Proclaiming herself the Divine Incarnation of the Devouring Moon, she appointed twelve priests to perform her rites. They were men to begin with but magic twisted them; in their scarlet robes and changed appearance they came to be known as the Furiádhin, the Mutated Ones. From Ouriána's great temple at Apharos the smoke of sacrifice rose to the heavens.

Not content with being worshipped as a goddess in her own kingdom, Ouriána manufactured a claim to the vacant throne of the northern empire, declaring war on all who opposed her. Leading the opposition were the High King Réodan, on Thäerie, and the wizards of Leal.

The war dragged on for years as Ouriána's magician-priests led her armies to victory after victory. Those who resisted her had but one hope, an obscure prophecy that out of Ouriána's own house and bloodline would come the one capable of overthrowing her rule and restoring peace. But the self-styled Empress-Goddess cast over her twin sister, Nimenoë, a curse to render her barren. For although Princess Nimenoë never joined Ouriána's enemies, she could not be counted among the Empress's friends.

Despite the curse, Nimenoë eventually did conceive a daughter, though at the cost of her own life. Present at the birth on Thäerie were three wizards. Well aware that Ouriána would want the infant killed, they agreed that Éireamhóine, the more powerful of the three, should take the baby on a winter journey across the wide northern continent. Once he reached a place of safety, he would raise the child in secret, until she came of an age to fulfill the prophecy.

But Ouriána, by means of her dark arts, had learned of the child's birth and the wizard's plan, and sent six Furiádhin in pursuit. High in the mountains of the Cadmin Aernan the priests did battle with Éireamhóine. That battle and its deadly consequences were felt by wizards and magicians across the world; everyone was convinced that Éireamhóine, Luenil the nursemaid, and the infant princess were dead.

Nineteen years of resistance passed, but Ouriána's victory seemed inevitable. In order to put heart into his allies and discuss new strategies, King Réodan summoned them to a council at the wizards' Scholia on Leal.

King Réodan's council was electrified by the arrival of a wandering wizard who revealed that he had seen a young woman in the far northern kingdom of Skyrra who was undoubtedly the lost princess, the child of the prophecy. The Skyrrans knew her as Winloki, niece to their king, Ristil, but the wanderer was able to present convincing evidence that she was indeed Nimenöe's daughter.

In order to recover the princess, the council decided to send a secret embassy—an embassy so small it would never attract Ouriána's attention—to inform her of her true name and destiny, and convince her to return to Thäerie. Present among them were Sindérian, a young healer, and Faolein, her father, a wizard of repute. They were joined by the half-Faey prince Ruan, among others.

The travellers set sail, hoping to make most of their journey by sea, but after an attack by a water-dragon their ship was so badly damaged it was all she could do to limp into the nearest port—which happened to be in unfriendly territory. From that point on, perils beset their entire journey north. Faolein was bespelled out of his own body and into the form of a falcon. Thinking him dead, Ouriána set trap after trap for Sindérian, which the wizard's daughter somehow always found a way to escape. Half convinced that someone or something more powerful was protecting the young healer, the Empress, in a rage of frustration at being thwarted where she had expected little resistance, wove a greater spell: an intricate curse called an *aniffath*. What made an *aniffath* so powerful—and insidious—was its ability to keep on growing and changing to suit the circumstances.

Meanwhile, hundreds of miles away in Skyrra, King Ristil fought a war of his own against the barbarian Eisenlonders. His adopted niece, Winloki, ignorant of her own origins, had grown into a beautiful, headstrong young woman and a gifted healer. Her desire to use her skills on the battlefield had been continually thwarted by King Ristil's determination to keep her safe at home. But Winloki was equally determined. Taking the place of another young healer, she secretly joined an army led by Ristil's son Prince Kivik, who was heading east to unite with a larger force. By the time that Kivik and his kinsman Skerry (who had been betrothed to Winloki in a childhood pact) discovered her presence, it was too late and too dangerous to send her back.

A clash with Eisenlonders soon taught Winloki that war was an uglier business than she had ever imagined. Kivik's troops, unable to locate the armies of the King's Marshalls, fought skirmish after skirmish, suffering great losses in doing so. It was beginning to look like the expedition was doomed.

Seeking a safe haven, they arrive at Tirfang, only to discover that it is already occupied by refugees and besieged by ice giants and the bearlike *Varjolükka*. Breaking through the siege, Kivik and his people reached the fortress, but were then trapped inside. Only Winloki seemed to realize that.

A
DARK
SACRIFICE

1

*

Voices of ice giants, thundering, tremendous, boomed in the distance.

Prince Kivik shivered and wrapped his patched green cloak more closely around him. The western sky had cleared, allowing the sun to shine out brightly, but a wicked, bitter wind blew down from higher peaks to the northeast. Gritting his teeth at the thought that this killing cold—unexpected, unseasonable—was likely to continue, he leaned across the pitted white stones of the parapet.

From his present vantage point, high on the outer walls, he could see a wide swath of snowy ground below the fortress and before the gates, where the enormous footprints of giants and the bearlike *Varjolükka* coming and going were pressed deep into the drifts. And even though he could not see them, he knew that a host of fierce white bears and blue-haired giants would be somewhere very near, patrolling the valley floor just beyond the range of his vision, or lurking in pinewoods along the valley walls, maintaining this siege that kept him and his men confined inside the ancient fortified city like rats in a trap.

Standing there with the wind lifting his light brown hair, King Ristil's son felt a familiar rage and frustration building inside of him. Before him lay the muddy chaos of the snowy fields, littered with the frozen bodies of men, horses, and things that were neither beasts nor men, behind him a vast landscape of towers, spires, parapets, balconies, peaked roofs, and cupolas, all arrayed in a glittering, improbable armor of ice.

Far in the distance, he spied a bright splash of color, green and gold, against the white glare of snow. For a moment he felt his spirits rise, thinking it might be some vanguard of his father's armies. But as they advanced, growing ever sharper and brighter, Kivik could just make out the indistinct forms of five—no, six men riding their horses at breakneck speed down the throat of the valley. He felt his hopes sink, a cold lump begin to form in the pit of his stomach. These were his own scouts, sent out many hours earlier under cover of darkness.

But what madness, he wondered, *could have possessed them to return in broad daylight, when they risk being seen by the giants and the skinchangers?* Then he saw what followed in pursuit: two of the *Varjolükka,* moving along at an incredible speed considering their ungainly, bearlike bodies, gradually narrowing the distance between them and the scouts.

Turning sharply on his heel, Kivik moved swiftly toward the stairs, meaning to alert the men who minded the gates. He had descended only two or three steps when a murmur of voices and a rattling of chains down in the gatehouse told him that the guards had seen everything, were already preparing to throw the gates open. Realizing he had no other help to offer, he returned to his vantage point by the parapet, to watch the race and shout encouragement at the riders.

As always, it disturbed him to see how the were-beasts moved: the way bones and muscles slid beneath the skin; the uncanny action of the limbs, apparently clumsy but deathly efficient, as if magic rather than sinew held everything together.

On came the men, their green cloaks whipping in the wind; on plunged the frantic, wild-eyed steeds, their flanks gleaming with sweat. Only when they drew near enough for Kivik to see foam flying off their bits did he realize that at least two of the horses were not so much *running* as running *away*, terrified to the point of madness by the proximity of the *Varjolükka*. It would not take much to spook them into throwing their riders.

"Hold on," he whispered around a hard knot in his throat. "Hold *on*!"

To his horror, a grey mare near the rear of the pack stumbled. By sheer force of will, it seemed, her rider just kept his seat, gripping with his knees while he fumbled for his sword. Before he could yank the blade more than halfway out of the scabbard the skinchangers were on him. Man and mare disappeared under a snarling pile of dirty white fur and bloody muzzles. The grey screamed once and then was silent.

Kivik spotted his cousin Skerry (the one dark head among so many shades of blond) twisting around in his saddle to see what was happening. He began to rein in, as if to go back and render assistance, but a glimpse of the carnage was enough to convince him it was already too late. Skerry gave his sorrel gelding its head, and the big red horse flew across the field.

Not far behind, the bear-men left what remained of the scout and his mare in a tumbled, bloody heap and went lurching after him.

With a last desperate rush, Skerry and the others reached the gatehouse and disappeared inside, only moments before the iron gates slammed shut in the very teeth of the enraged *Varjolükka*. Rising up on their mighty hindquarters, the were-bears bayed their fury to the skies.

A short time later, just long enough to cool down the horses and stable them in an alley of makeshift stalls in the outer bailey, the cousins met by the second gate.

"Another man lost," Skerry ground out between clenched teeth. With his red nose and wind-bitten ears, he looked every bit as chilly and miserable as Kivik felt.

The Prince nodded wearily. The tally of his dead grew longer and longer as the days went by. Twice he had gathered together some of his hardiest fighters and attempted a sortie out through the main gate; twice he and his men were beaten back. Though the numbers each time seemed to favor him, the axes and war hammers of the giants, the immense strength of the were-bears, somehow prevailed. He and his band of stalwarts had been forced to retreat back through the gate, staggering under the weight of wounded and nearly lifeless comrades they carried in with them. Reckoning up his losses now, he found them much too great to justify a third attempt.

Nor, Kivik decided, would there be any more scouting parties. "Even if we *could* break the siege," he said, continuing the thought aloud, "even if we could, where would we go?

"More to the point," he added as he and Skerry left the

windy outer ward for a smaller, more protected enclosure where the Prince and his officers had set up their tents, "what of the refugees who followed us here, the hundreds we found waiting for us when we arrived? Where can *they* look for safety if we leave them here undefended?"

With a sigh of frustration, Kivik ran a hand through hair grown shaggy and unkempt. Now that the excitement was over, he was once more keenly aware of his own dirt and discomfort, of unwashed skin itching under steel byrnie and quilted padding, in places he could not reach to scratch. He tried to remember the last time he had been warm enough, or clean, or had slept in a real bed. Between that time and this stood the memory of a thousand mischances and miscalculations, a thousand horrors.

A wild, inhuman ululation came carried on the wind, raising the fine hairs at the back of his neck. As he paused to listen just outside the entrance to his tattered green pavilion, the sound echoed from ridge to ridge along the valley walls, then came back again, slightly altered and in a different key, from one of the high eastern peaks where clouds still gathered, black and swollen with snow.

The giants are exchanging messages with their own kind farther up the mountain, he thought, all the blood in his veins rushing backward toward his heart. "What mischief are the creatures plotting now?"

"I can't imagine them trying to storm the walls while we still outnumber them," answered Skerry, following him into the dank, ill-lit interior of the tent. "Though when their friends from Eisenlonde arrive, I think we should be prepared to defend our position."

"Defend this fortress which ought to be impregnable, yet somehow never is?"

Skerry shrugged. "We needn't hold it for very long. The hawks we sent out with messages, some of them *will* get through. And then it can be only a matter of days before your father comes with the army he's been raising to relieve us."

But Kivik did not feel nearly so confident. When King Ristil would arrive was a matter of sheer conjecture, but the Eisenlonder barbarians, being so much closer, were certain to turn up first. Along with more of the ice giants and the bloody skinchangers, unless he was much mistaken.

Yet somehow his greatest fear was of the citadel itself. The Old Fortress at Tirfang, it had a bad name: witches built it, raised it by magic, infecting even the ordinary materials in which they worked—stone, timber, and slate—with their dark sorceries. It was not a place of safety, not of long-term safety anyway; Kivik was well aware of that. It had not proved so for the ancient witch-lords, or for anyone since. No one in a thousand years had successfully defended it. The seven great encircling walls, the seven mighty iron gates, they still stood, but the flesh-and-blood defenders had always died.

"We can't really know what happened here five hundred or a thousand years ago," offered Skerry, as if reading his thoughts. An ice-edged wind swirling through the courtyard shook the flimsy silk walls of the pavilion, blew a wintry gust in through the open doorflap, and then moved on. "It would be a great pity, would it not, if we defeated *ourselves* with our own superstitious fears, all for the sake of some old tales which might not even be true."

Yet when it comes to these old tales, how do you tell the true from the false? Kivik wondered, rubbing at a cheek grown bristly with red-brown stubble. As recently as two years ago, he might have dismissed frost giants and *Varjolükka* as purely imaginary, but now he knew better.

The long hours of the day dragged on, bright, chilling, implacable. The constant glare of sun and ice made Kivik's eyes burn; the cold ate at his bones, making old wounds and battle scars ache. *Like a greybeard,* he thought with a wry grimace. *Not a man of barely twenty-four years and half a hundred battles.* Yet to feel the sharp edge of cold was good; already, some of those who let themselves grow numb and drowsy had died.

By the next morning, when the Prince and Skerry set out to take a tour of inspection around one of the inner wards, the sky was mostly overcast and spitting snow.

Just like the other six courtyards, this one had become a squalid clutter of patched tents, ramshackle little sheds, shacks, byres, chicken coops, huts, hovels, and shelters more primitive still: hastily erected out of scavenged wood and fragments of stone; backed up against the bailey walls wherever possible; gathered together elsewhere in tipsy congregations that seemed to stand merely because every single one was relying for support on the others around it. A dark smoke, from hundreds of tiny cookfires, hovered over everything. Someone had dug a trench down the middle of the yard, and it was already half full of filthy ice and raw sewage. Piglets squealed, goats bleated, hens cackled; the cacophony was almost as bad as the stench, which was considerable. It was worse than the squalor of the most despicable slum; it was the way, maybe, that thousands of people displaced from their homes were forced to live now, throughout Skyrra.

It was war—just one more toll of the war, to be paid in the

coin of human misery, Kivik reflected angrily, and it made no sense, not any of it, because *the war itself* made no sense. They had been attacked, savagely, mindlessly, relentlessly, and they did not know why.

To make matters worse, for all the hardships the refugees were prepared to endure, they had fled their homes pitifully ill-equipped to deal with this murderous cold—which no one could have expected in what ought to have been the middle of summer.

Yet from the first they might have found snugger quarters. Much of the fortress appeared inhabitable—the tall houses in the outer wards, the massive central keep, the lower floors of the soaring white towers—but no one had summoned the courage to venture inside. In truth, it took all the courage that most of them could muster just to pass through the gate-houses from one yard to the next, convinced as they were that the witch-lords, though dead, still lingered on as a malignant presence.

In one of the hovels, an old woman began to cough, a deep, racking, bone-shaking cough that went on and on and on—reminding Kivik that spectral sorcerers quite aside, these deplorable living conditions were, of all dangers, the most immediate. Already the smoke and damp were rattling in too many chests; more deaths would come of that if this freakish weather did not break.

A small figure made its way toward him across the crowded yard, bobbed an awkward curtsy, and shyly pressed something into his hand.

Gazing down at the child, Kivik experienced a pang of deep distress. A little maid of ten or eleven, she was dirty and emaciated, with fair hair ragged and snarled. He opened his fingers to see what she had given him.

It was exactly what he expected it to be, a wooden charm, crudely carved and brightly colored, strung on a leather cord. He owned dozens, probably hundreds, of these primitive talismans, presented to him by his father's subjects. Yet he thanked her gravely, as was his custom, and slipped the braided cord over his head, so that the charm hung at chest level over his mail shirt. The little girl rewarded him with a tremulous smile, took two steps backward, then whirled and ran off.

In my charge, all of these people. A fierce protective instinct flared up inside him as he watched her go. *Under my protection.*

He slid a sideways glance in his cousin's direction, and Skerry's words of the day before echoed in his mind: *"It would be a great pity, would it not, if we defeated ourselves with our own superstitious fears ..."* Then he thought of those ugly black storm clouds the giants were accumulating higher up the mountain.

He came to a sudden decision. "Summon all my captains together," he told Skerry. "I've a plan to discuss with them."

I wish I'd held my wretched tongue, if anything I said gave you this mad idea!" Skerry protested a short while later.

They were seated inside the tattered silk pavilion along with a handful of Kivik's surviving officers, gathered around a meager fire of sticks and straw. Though the other men muttered and shook their heads, they seemed content to let the Prince's young kinsman voice their concerns.

"Granted that the danger may be—probably *is* purely

imaginary. But what if it isn't?" said Skerry. "You are far too important to us, and we dare not risk losing you when one of us could just as easily go in your place. I'm quite willing. I *should* be the one to go, since it was I who gave you the idea, at least indirectly."

"I would never," answered Kivik, flushing to the eyebrows, "order anyone to do anything I feared to do myself. No"—he threw up a hand, demanding silence, when Skerry looked like he might argue further—"my mind is made up, and I certainly don't require anyone's permission. Nor have I asked you all here to debate the matter; I simply wish to inform you of my decision. I am determined to spend the night alone inside the central pile of the fortress, and if—*when* I emerge in the morning alive and unscathed, it's more than likely the people will take heart, follow my example, and move indoors out of the weather."

The men were silent, no doubt considering the consequences should he *not* emerge unscathed, if some ancient evil still dwelling within those walls were to deal him a swift and appalling death.

And for all that he strove to put on a brave face before the others, Kivik could not quite shake off his own dread. As a lad, he had listened far too closely to far too many ghost stories told by his nursemaids and the servants at the Heldenhof. He could remember most of those tales, in every ghastly detail, far too well.

Yet whatever might happen, it had to be better than slowly freezing to death out in the courtyards, knowing that shelter behind stout stone walls was available all along, that only his own cowardice left him wretched and shivering in the cold outside.

"At least let me go with you," said Skerry. "To share the adventure—if there *is* an adventure."

"No. I suppose there must be other perils in old ruined buildings, besides supernatural ones. You are my second-in-command and will have to take charge if anything happens to me." Nor was Kivik prepared to place his closest friend in unnecessary danger so soon after the last time.

Skerry made a wide gesture, indicating the other officers gathered in the tent, seasoned warriors all: men with grey in their hair and beards, yes, grim and battle scarred, but still hardy, still battle ready. "Any one of these men could lead in my place: Regin, Deor, Haestan, Roric. Any one of them more experienced, more worthy than I."

"More experienced than either of us," sighed Kivik. "But the people might lose heart without a prince of our house to rally them—and they've suffered so much already."

Unfortunately, that was not the end of the argument. Deor, Haestan, and some of the others were moved to state their opinions, and because he was accustomed to listening (if not to yielding), Kivik let them say whatever they would. Finally, he agreed to allow two guards from among the ordinary fighting men—*volunteers,* he insisted—to spend the night inside the building with him.

"Though whether I take two men or two hundred," he grumbled, fingering the wooden charm, "I don't see what difference it could possibly make if the spirits of any dead witch-lords turn up to challenge me."

2

✶

The doors of the central keep stood open at the top of a flight of dank stone steps, inviting the Prince and his two young guards, Berin and Nali, to step inside. Kivik paused on the last stair, trying to remember if these massive doors, riddled with wormholes and scarred by wind and rain, had been open or closed the first time he saw them—trying, with no more success, to convince himself that it did not *mean* anything either way.

He turned back to take a final look at the world outside. Above the eastern walls, a waxing moon sailed high in a sky of clear, cloudless blue, but the westering sun, turned dim and milky behind a sheer veil of falling snow, made it appear there were two moons in the heavens tonight: one silvery white, one palest gold.

Ought I, he wondered, *take this for an omen?* Little serpents of fear ran down his spine. In all the old tales that ever he heard, the moon was far from friendly to men, being envious, changeable, and above all mischievous—then what *could* a double moon mean but a doubly unlucky influence?

A damp wind circling the courtyard caused the guards' torches to flare and throw off sparks. Nali cleared his throat; Berin made a nervous gesture, rattling his sword inside its sheath. Realizing that his own hesitation was making them anxious, Kivik advanced on the doors.

He felt a momentary disorientation crossing the threshold, a head-spinning impression of sound and color, a blaze of light and heat, but it all passed so quickly into shadows and silence he thought he had imagined it. Then he was in a dim, confined space, breathing dust and darkness, until his men came in with their lights, the shadows fled, and a chamber he had believed no larger than a cupboard changed into a guardroom of more than ordinary size. Ancient weapons clad in rags of cobweb hung in ordered ranks along one wall. Across the room, a barred metal gate like an iron jaw had rusted in place halfway between floor and ceiling.

Motioning the two boys to follow after him, he headed toward the gate, his progress across the room stirring up wraiths of dust that lingered on the air a moment or two longer than seemed quite natural. Something crunched underfoot; when he looked down to see what it was, his stomach twisted into a hard knot. One boot rested on a disarticulated hand still clutching a weapon gone green with corrosion. When he lifted his foot, the tiny finger bones crumbled away to a fine, ashy powder.

He gritted his teeth and continued on. A few more determined strides took him under the gate and into a hall so vast its farther limits disappeared into darkness. By torchlight, it was just possible to make out the nearer walls to right and left, where soaring arches led on to other spaces—large or small he could not tell, though his mind conjured up further immensities.

After a brief hesitation, he chose an opening at random and led the way across the hall, through the arch, and into a chamber less lofty and imposing but still of considerable size. Three long tables spanned the length of the room, covered in a filmy lacework of cobwebs. A dull glint of tarnished metal under the spiders' weavings, a reflection off a clouded gemstone, these bore witness the tables had been richly laid with silver chargers and jeweled cups, but either the guests had never arrived or had fled the revels early: at the head of each table sat a mummified figure in filthy, decaying silks; the other chairs and benches were empty.

A flicker of movement drew Kivik's attention up to the ceiling, where a swarm of busy spiders translucent as glass went scurrying away from the light as fast as their brittle-looking legs could carry them. They had spread their woven nets from beam to beam, and hundreds of tiny lizards, no bigger than his smallest finger, were trapped in the meshes.

He realized that his palms were sweating, despite the dry chill. "This room is by far too large and drafty. Let us look for more intimate quarters."

From the banquet hall, they passed into a maze of corridors and interconnected chambers. In one, vines and thorny roses had crept in through a window, filling up most of the space, creating an impenetrable barrier. In another, a white fox started up from a bed of rotting tapestries, where it had been napping nose to tail. Those who had lived in these rooms obviously had a taste for the grotesque: statues half man and half beast stared out at them from deep niches, watching their progress from chamber to chamber; door handles mimicked the heads of imps, apes, gargoyles, and hobgoblins.

Other rooms dazzled the eye with treasure, spilling out of open coffers, scattered across the floors, heaped up in glittering piles: a fortune in gemstones and fine enamels; watery pearls the size of hen's eggs; jars and phials and pitchers of marvelous design spilling a dust of jewels and precious metals—all of them tumbled together, broken, or otherwise spoiled. Gold, silver, and platinum had been mingled and fused with baser materials. Chalices, brooches, diadems, shields of beaten metal were pitted, stained, and corroded, eaten away by rust and verdigris, discolored by salts. Banners and hangings of unparalled richness had grown shabby and faded with age.

Yet along with the treasure there was a charnel house of bones. A skull on a bedpost glared at them with eyeholes sealed by cobwebs; mice squeaked from a nest inside a hollow rib cage. A skeleton like old ivory sprawled on the floor, one arm reaching for a diamond necklace; another, suspended by the neck from a silver chain, swung back and forth in a faint draft.

But these were not—they could not be—the bones of the witch-lords, who had lived and died here a thousand years ago. There were abundant stories of ill-fated attempts to take and hold the fortress in practically every century since the witches met their mysterious end. Kivik's own uncles-and-cousins-many-times-removed had not been immune to the lure of riches here, and they had—in their greed, or their desire for adventure—led many a simpler man to his death in the process.

In whose dust are we leaving our footprints? he wondered.

And he felt a little prickle of guilt for choosing such young boys to accompany him when older, more seasoned men had offered to come instead. In his stubborn refusal to bring any man who might speak his own mind—who might ask inconvenient questions and undermine his resolve—had he not, perhaps, done these boys an injustice?

Nali could not be much more than sixteen; redheaded Berin looked even younger. Farmers' or tradesmen's sons he reckoned them, not bred up as he had been for battle and the slaughter of men. In less perilous times no one would have expected them to take up arms. As it was, they had already seen and done things no sixteen-year-old boy should ever have to face. He had been thoughtless to include them in the exploration of what was little better than a tomb.

"Do not touch *anything*," he said out loud. "Take *nothing* away with you. The treasure here is cursed." The boys nodded wordlessly.

A barrel-vaulted passage like a long gullet brought them abruptly into an enormous kitchen. After so much ruined grandeur elsewhere, the homely squalor of the place came as a shock. Marble had given way to damp stone flags. An unwholesome moisture dripped from walls of unfinished stone. Fireplaces capable of consuming whole trees were black with soot, and spits the size of wagon axles red with rust. The room looked as though it had been subjected to a whirlwind: shards of broken crockery lay on the floor, mixed in with the bones of men and animals.

"It's the ogre's kitchen—the old hag's larder," Berin said in a hoarse whisper. Nali's face had turned a sickly white, as though all the blood had drained away.

Kivik wanted to say something reassuring, but the words stuck in his throat. His eyes moved uneasily from a rack of monstrous forks, ladles, and choppers to the immense iron ovens, gaping open like hungry mouths, then on to a stew pot large enough to cook an entire ox, hooves, horns, and all. And he had to admit to himself, if not to the boys, that it was precisely the setting for the more gruesome sort of nursery tale: the place where evil crones cooked up ghastly messes and four-and-twenty children were baked in a pie.

"The cooks here must have been drunkards or slatterns," he said sternly. It was a feeble effort, but the best that he could do.

Next to the kitchen they discovered a small, windowless room behind an iron grating, which might have been used only for storage but looked suspiciously like a cage. After that, a little more exploration of pantries and sculleries was more than sufficient. They were not sorry to leave those regions behind.

Ascending and descending what seemed like a hundred winding white staircases, Kivik had the occasional giddy sensation of time running backward or standing still. Once, he glimpsed the owl-eyed moon through a high, round window; only minutes later he entered a room where rows of long casements flooded every corner with brilliant sunlight. Corridors branched, ran together, or turned back on themselves, spiralling inward; sometimes they ended at blank stone walls. By now he was most thoroughly lost, could not possibly have retraced his steps back to the courtyard if he tried.

All along, he had been expecting a close, musty atmosphere, but if anything the air smelled fresher the farther they ventured into the building. No, not precisely *fresh*, but a light, pleasing fragrance floated on the air, not flowery but sweet. It was most like an herb-infused honey wine that Sigvith, his stepmother, and his little half sisters brewed in their stillroom, he decided, and yet not exactly the same. It reassured him with its homeliness, but there was something about it that disturbed him, too. Sometimes he thought he heard a faint, sweet music, troubling to the ear, though he could never tell from which direction it came or identify the instruments.

If I were to fall under a spell, he told himself, *it might happen just this way.* That he was already deep in enchantment never occurred to him.

An anteroom cluttered with broken furniture led into a large bedchamber, one that showed signs of occupation within the last century. There was a four-poster bed not much worm-eaten, with hangings not much decayed. When, out of curiosity, he drew back the velvet coverlet, a cloud of dust motes rose and spun in the torchlight, igniting like a thousand tiny suns. The mattress underneath had been reduced to an unpleasant mass of mildewed rags and feathers, but once he restored the worn velvet covering to its former position it seemed the most comfortable resting place he was likely to find.

He made a swift decision. "I vowed to sleep within these walls to prove that it was safe," he said, doffing his cloak. He had seen nothing more threatening than old bones—yet there were night terrors that attacked a man sleeping, and those he must test as well.

The guards set to work immediately to make the room more habitable: stopping up holes in the shutters with scraps of cloth they found on the floor, gathering up broken sticks of furniture in the antechamber and piling them on the hearth. When Nali thrust his torch into the stacked wood, a cheerful blaze sprang up, altering the whole aspect of the room.

With a little assistance, Kivik began to remove his plate and mail armor. Unthinkingly, he removed the wooden charm as well. Then, in his shirt, leather breeches, and hose, he stretched out on the velvet coverlet. Berin stationed himself at the foot of the bed, Nali by the door. Thanks to the fire, the room was already comfortably warm; in truth, it had become so in a surprisingly short time.

He had wondered whether sleep would really be possible, but already a delicious drowsiness was stealing over him, and he could scarcely focus his eyes on the ragged bed-curtains. There were pictures worked in faded embroidery, so dim he could hardly make them out. Maidens were turning into owls—or perhaps they were owl-headed witches wandering in a midnight wood—and there were roses, hundreds of perfumed roses like the ones that had invaded some of the rooms, only these had teeth. He was still trying to work out what it all meant when sleep overcame him.

He woke, or thought he did, some hours later, to find the room wonderfully changed. Instead of wood, a pile of jewels was burning on the hearth, bathing the room in light of the intensest colors. Where things had been shabby and dusty before, all was clean and orderly. It was a moment before he realized, with a jolt, that Berin and Nali were missing.

He knew his own people too well to imagine they had deserted him willingly. But what could have happened to them?

He knew himself a light sleeper, knew he could never have slept through any kind of struggle.

Climbing out of bed, he buckled on his sword belt, wrapped himself up in his cloak, and went off in search of his guards. The antechamber and corridor outside were illuminated by a soft glow, as from dozens of wax candles. In the way of dreams, none of this seemed strange; instead he found it oddly reassuring. All around him there were moving shadows, though the light was steady and seemed to come from all directions at once.

Farther down the passageway, he caught just a glimpse of someone disappearing into a cross corridor. He hurried to catch up, and once he rounded the corner he had a clear view of her, drifting (there was no other word for it) along the passage far ahead of him. Yet, though he lengthened his stride and quickened his pace, though she appeared to move no faster, he could not overtake her, or even narrow the distance between them.

After an immeasurable time of fruitless pursuit, she led him back to the banquet hall. Like the bedchamber, this room was wonderfully altered. Webs, spiders, and lizards had all been cleared away, and a great host had gathered there, as if in expectation of some high festivity. The pale-skinned, violet-eyed witch-folk were only a small part of that varied throng. There were werewolves and Varjolükka; bogwalkers and frost giants; the Folk of the Sea and of the Higher Air; things winged, horned, and hooved. And every one of them—man, woman, and beast— was splendidly robed and jeweled for the feast. Wherever Kivik looked, rings of topaz, opal, and garnet glowed on taloned hands; a string of amber beads encircled a hairy neck; diamonds like tiny stars glittered in luxuriant locks of mermaid green.

At first, the beauty of the witches delighted him. Never before

*had he seen such loveliness united with such rare grace of form
and movement. Yet gradually he began to feel there was something deadly, something subtly abominable simmering just
below the surface, something that made them as unnatural in
their own way as the beast-men. The more he gazed, the more he
detected hints of an inhuman severity bordering on cruelty, here
in the malice of a frigid pair of eyes, there in the scornful twist of
an otherwise perfect pair of lips.*

*Then he began to hear their voices inside his mind—recog-
nized in those voices a faint echo of the sweet, troublous music
that had enchanted him before—and it seemed to him then that
their faces were not evil, not cruel, but merely sorrowful.* We
were betrayed, *they told him,* by the same master who led us
on from wickedness to wickedness, and then sacrificed us to
his own ambition. Whatever wrong we did, we have repented
many long years. You need not fear us. Indeed, we only wish
you well.

*Yet a little burr of doubt continued to prick at his mind. Can
the dead lie? He could think of no reason why not—nor any
reason to doubt them either.*

*Someone was pressing him to drink from a massive goblet
rough with unpolished gemstones; he could not see a face, but
the hand on the stem was covered in brindled fur. He thought
he ought to refuse, he intended to refuse, but his hands seemed
to move independently of his head. He raised the cup to his lips
and took a sip of the clear, strong wine. The flavor was full and
rich—but it left a bitter taste on his tongue.*

He woke with a start, lying on his back in the four-poster bed.
Raising his head from the velvet coverlet, he found Berin and

Nali still standing guard in the exact same places they had been when he first drifted off. How long had he slept? It could not have been very long, or the boys would have changed their positions, if only a little. Yet what a long and strange dream it had seemed to be!

Despite the brevity of his nap—and in spite of the lingering aftertaste of the dream wine in his mouth—he felt wonderfully refreshed. Indeed, he felt warm, safe, comfortable right where he was, all these things for the first time in many weeks. Nevertheless, he rose and armed himself with the help of his guards, then led them back through all the mazes of the many-corridored keep.

Though the plan of the place had puzzled him before, he had no trouble finding his way back to the guardroom and the door to the courtyard. Somehow, the mazes had resolved themselves as he slept.

Outside, it was full daylight, the sun dazzling off new-fallen snow, but the cold struck him forcibly and the wind tore through him in an icy blast. He no longer had any doubts about moving into the keep. It was folly, he told himself— worse, it was *madness*—for his people to remain outside in their makeshift shelters.

As he moved through the outer wards of the fortress with the news of his safe return running on ahead of him, he met up with Skerry and their cousin Winloki standing with heads close together, as if caught in the midst of some private conversation. He greeted them cordially, amused by nearly identical expressions of relief he saw on their faces at finding him whole and sane after his night's adventures—after all, he had never been in the slightest danger.

But his amusement faded as he took a longer look at Winloki. Because she had changed; how she had changed! Unlike Skerry, whose gaunt face he had grown accustomed to in stages, seeing him every day, the alteration in her was far more dramatic. There was little left to remind him of the confident, high-spirited girl he had known in Lückenbörg. Her red-gold hair was pinned up in untidy braids; her gown of healer's grey was threadbare. Dark smudges of exhaustion discolored the skin under her eyes. The long, arduous trek to Tirfang, the privations that she as much as anyone had suffered since, had worn away so much of her beauty that Kivik felt his heart turn over in pity. He promised himself that somehow, someday he would make it up to her.

In the meantime, there was much to be done, and the sooner started the better for everyone. "Tell Thyra and the other healers, you can choose any room in the keep that you like to serve as an infirmary," he told her. "I want all of our sick and wounded moved inside immediately."

3

✳

The road was dusty, weary, and long, winding up one
gentle rise and down another, across broad grasslands
under the glare of the noonday sun. Despite the heat
Sindérian's headache had finally subsided, from a pain that
threatened to crack open her skull to a dull throb, a slight
blurring around the edges of her vision.

The falcon that was her father—that had been the wizard
Faolein—flew on ahead. At her side walked Prince Ruan, alien
and inscrutable as ever, while the guardsman Aell brought up
the rear. Her stomach growled with hunger; mornings came
far too early during summer in these northern lands, and it
had been a long time since breakfast.

"We might," said the Prince when they reached the top of
the next rise, "like to stop and rest a while in the shade of those
trees." He indicated a little copse of oak and ailum nestled in a
hollow west of the road.

Sindérian swung around to look at him, a motion that sent
sharp pains shooting through her head. She was beginning to

recover after being beaten against the rocks when their boat sank two days ago near the coast, but it took a long time for a head injury to mend, even when one happened to be a wizard and a healer.

She frowned at Ruan, as much in puzzlement as in pain. It was not like him to suggest a pause so early in the day; the inhuman vitality he had inherited from his mother's people, the Ni-Féa Faey, made him always eager to keep going, to press on despite weariness, pain, or tired feet.

Not, she thought irritably, *that he is likely to have experienced such a thing as tired feet in the whole of his life!* His unflagging energy—along with a certain shine that never seemed to wear off no matter the hardship—was particularly insufferable at moments like this.

"Your face is the color of whey, and you look utterly spent," he said. "A rest now may save trouble later."

Sindérian wanted to say no. Despite the warmth of the day, despite weariness and headache, she felt a suffocating sense of urgency. They were, after all, in a race with Ouriána's minions to reach Lückenbörg, and the price of arriving too late threatened to be disastrously high. But as she wavered indecisively the falcon flew back and landed on her shoulder, cocking his head and regarding her with a fierce golden eye. It made for a startling contrast when her father's mild, gentle voice spoke inside her head: *Be wise, Sindérian, and do as he suggests. A short delay now could make for a swifter pace after.*

With an impatient gesture, she agreed. They could not afford to make mistakes born of haste, and a brief rest in the shade of trees would be very welcome.

Sitting in the long, cool grass under an oak, Sindérian drew in a deep breath, savoring complex odors of earth and growing things. There was, she believed, something particularly healing about the air here. *A green smell in a green land.*

Aell handed her a leather flask, and she took a long drink of water, then passed it on to the Prince. Resting her back against the rugged bark of the trunk, she allowed herself to relax, let her eyes close. Neither sleeping nor dreaming, she reviewed the events of the last few months, watched them pass like so many vivid paintings behind her eyelids.

It had begun at the wizards' Scholia on Leal, with that thunderbolt of an announcement that Nimenoë's daughter still lived. The Princess Guenloie, subject of a hundred prophecies, born to be Ouriána's bane and the salvation of her foes, had been discovered alive and grown to young womanhood. A small party had been chosen to travel north to the realm of Skyrra, where the girl had been seen, a secret embassy meant to enlist her aid in their ongoing battle against the Empress and to bring her back home to Thäerie, the place of her birth.

Already, the journey had been long, difficult, and full of unexpected obstacles. Perhaps worst of all was the voyage from Arkenfell, which ended in disaster and left them as they were now, travelling on foot through a foreign land, destitute except for those things they wore or carried with them. At least Prince Ruan had been able to sell the brooch from his cloak, in one of the tiny towns along the coast, and he had used a handful of ivory coins to buy the water flasks and a small amount of food.

A windstorm of wings fanning against her face brought Sindérian out of her thoughts with a jolt; perhaps she had been dreaming after all. Opening her eyes, she saw Faolein under-going a new transformation: flesh and bone turning malleable as wax, stretching here, condensing there. In a very short time, a bird of a kind she had never seen before, something between a goshawk and a kestrel, was preening its feathers in the grass at her feet.

But why this, and why now? she asked. Something that felt like a shard of ice lodged in her throat. Even knowing the thing was impossible without far more magic than they possessed between them, she had hoped against all hope that this change would see her father back in his own shape again.

We have travelled far beyond the usual hunting grounds of the peregrine, he answered. *I believe I may be more at home in these lands as a northern sparrowhawk.*

There was movement on her left, a soft grunt as the Prince and Aell left their seats on the ground. Ruan glanced down at her with a thin smile and a slight lift of the eyebrows. She nodded, accepted the clasp of Aell's warm, calloused hand, and allowed the man-at-arms to pull her up from the grass to her feet.

They were four now who had so long been five, because Jago had been lost with the boat, Jago who had been a stal-wart, if generally silent, presence throughout the long jour-ney and would be sorely missed. Sindérian knew that her own grief was trivial compared to what the Prince and Aell must be feeling after all the years and battles they had shared with the tall, taciturn guardsman. If they could mask their grief with a stoic resignation, even use the loss to spur them on rather than weaken them, then so could she.

She drew in a deep, steadying breath, pushed back a strand

of dark hair. "I am better for the rest," she declared. "Let us go swiftly now."

They set off again at a much brisker pace than they had used before, and the hawk flew circles around them as they went.

By necessity, they travelled very light. When they came to a farm, a village, or a settlement, the people were kind, if inclined to be wary, but in the end the farmers and villagers had little to spare, whether to sell or to give.

"They say they've sent great stores of food and other necessities to the capital for the troops that are mustering there," the Prince reported, after an unsuccessful attempt to buy supplies. And in none of the places where he asked could he find anyone willing to sell him horses to speed their journey—not a shambling old carthorse or a wild, unbroken colt—though he offered all that remained from the sale of the brooch, and his beautiful and costly golden torc besides.

"Between the King's levies and the stock they need for farming and breeding, they simply haven't a nag to be spared—and that is that!" muttered Sindérian. "If we mean to reach the capital, we will have to continue on foot."

And so they did, day after day, pacing out the dusty miles of the roads leading north, gradually making their way from the wide meadows, placid rivers, and reedy lakes of the Autlands into the more densely settled country of the Herzenmark, where vast fields of young wheat and rye rippled in the wind. At night they slept walled around by knee-high grasses; by day they developed blisters and wore out the soles of their boots.

Sometimes a farmwife would offer them fresh curds or buttermilk, and sometimes they were able to buy flat, hard loaves from a village baker. This bread, made with seeds and split peas mixed in with the salt and buckwheat, proved difficult to chew, but it always disappeared before it had a chance to go stale. Otherwise, eggs, cheese, onions, and an unknown root vegetable that flourished in great abundance were the staples they lived on. All of them except Faolein, who naturally hunted, living on field mice and small, careless birds.

And everything considered, the travellers had a much kinder welcome in Skyrra than any they had received in Arkenfell—which was as surprising as it was convenient. In one place after another, it was easy to see that women and girls were carrying on most of the work of farming and herding, with the help of some grey-bearded ancients, very young boys, and a handful of men who had returned from the wars lamed, blind, missing a hand or an arm. Occasionally, patrols of grim-faced warriors rode by at a brisk pace, proving that the western marches had not been left entirely undefended.

Yet for Sindérian and her travelling companions this was a peaceful and pleasant time, far removed from the dangers that had dogged their footsteps through Mere, Hythe, and Arkenfell. And the days were so long and bright, the skies so enormous in that broad green country, sometimes the travellers felt giddy with light. None of them had ever been so far north, and the northern summer with its short, warm nights was an astonishment.

One night, she sat up late studying the sky for portents, a thing she had not dared to do since her first night in Skyrra. There were signs in plenty of conflict and turmoil, particularly among the Hidden Stars—those mysterious bodies and ever-changing constellations that only the magically gifted can see—signs, too, that events were hastening on to some terrific conclusion. She feared those events were leaving her far behind. With her wizard's sight she watched as a celestial army charged across the sky: crystal-white warriors blazing with light, mounted on fiery rainbow steeds, but their banners were the colors of blood and smoke. For the space of a heartbeat, she thought she could hear the distant hurly-burly of their progress; then all was silent except for the breeze whispering in the grass.

"What do the heavens tell you?" asked Prince Ruan out of the darkness.

"What do *you* see?" she countered. Even after all these months, King Réodan's grandson remained something of a mystery. He was a riddle and a contradiction: half Man, half Faey, and yet paradoxically something else as well that was neither one.

"I see the same stars that you do; I see battles and skirmishes," he answered. "But not being a wizard, a magus, or an astromancer, I have no idea what they mean."

"Nor do I," she said with a rueful shake of her head. It was not much use, after all, to know that great things were happening and not know what or where. "There are days when the Sight is more a burden than a blessing."

A long time followed during which neither of them said anything. Sindérian shifted her weight on the ground, relieving a cramp in one leg. "Guenloie—" she began at last, then fell silent.

Again came his surprisingly deep and melodious voice out of the night. "What were you going to say?"

"There is no guarantee that Guenloie will believe anything

we tell her, no guarantee that she will consent to go back with us. Why should she care for *our* troubles, when her people are suffering, too?"

The grass rustled as he moved a little closer. Now she could see a pale, moonlight-colored blur where his face was, catch the glint of his odd turquoise eyes. "We are here to persuade her, are we not? And you most of all. Wasn't that the reason you were chosen?"

And that, she realized, was the very heart of her fear. That *she* might fail, when others had already suffered and sacrificed so much. How could she bear it, with so much at stake? Except then Sindérian remembered that she was not likely to have to bear *anything* for very long. She was under Ouriána's curse, and therefore under sentence of death.

The next day they walked until early evening before setting up a camp. As night deepened and the sky went from dark blue to a fathomless starry black, flames like the tongues of dragons started up in the darkness to the northeast. Sindérian guessed there was a large settlement somewhere up ahead, greater than any they had passed so far, and men were lighting torches up on the walls. Then Faolein swooped down, landing on his accustomed perch on her shoulder, back from a short flight scouting ahead. *A few hours' walk in the morning and you will reach Lückenbörg.*

She drew in an unsteady breath, hope and fear warring inside her. In Lückenbörg, she and Guenloie would meet again. A bond had been forged on the first day of the little princess's life, and all down through the years Sindérian had felt that connection tugging at her, even when everyone said—and she half believed it herself—that the child was dead. *"Look to your foster sister. She has need of you,"* Faolein had commanded that terrible night when death had followed birth in swift succession. And she had obeyed, taking the infant into her heart even as she lifted her out of the cradle and hushed her crying. But would Guenloie—who was now called Winloki—experience that bond, too?

Sindérian felt a knot of doubt twist inside of her. She had not known how many hopes she was building around that recognition until this moment, on the brink of learning the truth.

They set out walking a little after sunrise in the grey haze of morning. Soon, they had abundant company on the road. Wagons rumbled by; horsemen cantered north and south, raising the dust. Shepherds and pigherds and gooseherds converged from intersecting lanes and pathways, driving their flocks before them. Old women carrying baskets of cabbages, onions, and turnips wandered in out of the fields and tramped on toward the King's city.

Presently they came to immense earthworks, and not long after that to a timber palisade extending for at least a mile east and west. In the center of the wall a pair of tall wooden gates stood open, and through that gateway a great traffic could be seen constantly coming and going.

To the east of the gate there stretched a vast encampment where the muster of the westlands had already assembled: riders, archers, foot soldiers, armorers; men who drilled with spears, pikes, axes, and short swords. On the opposite side was another camp of lesser size, where men of Arkenfell and Mistlewald had pitched their tents and affixed their woven banners to long, sturdy poles. It seemed that Skyrra did not stand alone after all—though help had not come in quite the numbers that must have been hoped for.

Down through the centuries, the city of Lückenbörg has always resembled a market town far more than the capital of an ancient kingdom, its unpaved streets crowded three seasons out of the year with traders, trappers, dogs, donkeys, and towheaded children. They build the houses there with steeply pitched roofs and stout wooden shutters to shed the snow and keep out icy winds during the bitter northern winters, but to visit the city in summer, as Sindérian and her fellow travellers did, was to see it colorful with many small gardens. She could glimpse fruit trees and wicker beehives behind or between many of the houses, and wherever she looked, window boxes seemed to be overflowing with the hardy northern flowers that grow so swiftly while the sun still shines.

Yet she felt her heart sink at the sight of so many groups of somber-looking people living in tents, frail little shacks, or overturned wagons on every open patch of ground. The first outriders, she feared they might be, of a great army of the dispossessed gradually moving toward Lückenbörg from the east.

Once she and the men had familiarized themselves with the plan of the town and its thirteen separate wards divided by high wooden walls, once they had learned the direction of the Heldenhof, their next task was to buy some clean, whole garments. There was no denying, Sindérian told herself ruefully, that her own appearance was by far the worst; linen, homespun, and wool never wear so well as steel and leather. However, the Prince and Aell were looking a little threadbare, too, and they meant to present themselves at the doors of the palace as persons of quality rather than beggars and vagabonds. They bought what they needed (somebody's castoffs, but in good condition) from stalls in the marketplace, and then found an inn willing to provide rooms and baths for the afternoon.

Sindérian met the men in the innyard an hour later. Thanks to a bath and clean clothing she felt wonderfully refreshed. Unfortunately, her altered appearance brought on one of the Prince's long, cool, assessing glances, as he took in the color of her linen gown, the dull green cloth of her cloak.

"You are in mourning again," he said with a slight lift of his arched eyebrows.

"I never put it aside intentionally," she retorted, blushing in spite of herself.

Nevertheless, said Faolein's voice in her mind, *six months is a long time to wear black when there was not even a formal betrothal. When was the last time you even thought of Cailltin of Aefri? Do you wear this now to remind yourself—or to remind Prince Ruan?*

But to this she had no reply, being unsure of the answer.

Her companions also sported new cloaks and footgear—in Ruan's case, a pair of high, mouse-colored boots and a long mantle of dull red velvet. While all this finery had exhausted the money from the brooch, he still had his costly golden torc, which he had resigned himself to sacrifice if the worst happened and they were forced to wait for days or even weeks before gaining an audience with the King.

Although that would be disastrous, Sindérian said to her father as they headed for the Heldenhof. *If we are left waiting too long, our mission will fail. Ouriána's priests could arrive at any time.* Yet how different it all would have been if Faolein were there in his own body, and in his customary purple robes—for who would deny entrance to a Master Wizard of the Scholia on Leal?

You are our wizard now, he told her. *It is for you to find a way.*

The Heldenhof was less like a palace than a jumble of two- and three-story timber houses all joined together, a rambling yet somehow graceful structure, with wooden balconies, outside staircases, and deep projecting eaves. The doorposts and window frames were carved with a whole menagerie of fabulous beasts, and whenever a puff of wind gusted down the lane, what looked like at least a hundred fanciful weather vanes and lightning rods spun around and around.

But it was no small matter, as Sindérian and her friends soon learned, for visitors to enter the King's house without a summons from the King himself. The builders who first raised that venerable old pile had diverted a stream to either side, effectively isolating the palace in the midst of running water, and the only way to cross it was by means of a wooden bridge, guarded by men in armor of silver mail who barred the way with long-handled axes.

Prince Ruan, however, was not intimidated. He approached the guards with his light, confident step. "Let King Ristil be told that Anerüian Pendawer of Thäerie and Sindérian Fael-lanëos of Leal bring greetings from the High King Réodan and the Nine Master Wizards," he said, introducing Sindérian with a flick of his hand. "Let him be told, too, that we ask leave to enter and speak with him directly."

But the guards, though visibly impressed by his lordly air, had not been instructed to receive unexpected visitors, no matter how exalted or how far they had traveled. Nor could even one of them leave his post to carry a message inside.

The Prince retreated, in a blazing state of frustration, his narrow jaw set and his lips compressed in a thin line, while Sindérian and Aell trailed soberly after him. It seemed they had no recourse but to wait at the far end of the bridge until someone who *did* have the right of entry happened to pass by and agreed to act as a messenger.

And so they waited, hot and prickly in the sunlight, as the day wore on. They waited so long that Sindérian finally left the bridge in disgust and retreated to the other side of the street, where she sat on the edge of a wooden porch, chin on fist, simmering with impatience.

A donkey cart went by, and a woman driving a flock of goats. Someone in an upper story opened a pair of brightly painted shutters. Weathercocks gyred in the wind. From across the lane, Prince Ruan glared at her, as if he would say as Faolein had, "You are our wizard now. It is for you to find a way."

But truly, she thought, what way was there? She could hardly force an entrance by magic, or conjure up a messenger out of thin air to carry Prince Ruan's greetings. She *might* cast a spell that would put the guards into a sound sleep, but even that relatively harmless procedure was unlikely to win them any friends once they were actually inside: embassies do not come in like invading forces.

She chewed on a ragged fingernail and glanced sideways at her father where he perched on the porch beside her. He might enter the palace easily enough, fly in through an open window with the guards none the wiser. And while he had not the power to speak with anyone once he arrived inside, he *could* carry a written message, supposing someone capable of reading it could be found. . . .

She was just opening her mouth to suggest a trip to the marketplace, to sell the torc and buy paper and ink, when there was a little commotion on the street. A group of fine ladies in silks and velvets rode up on beautiful high-stepping horses, with a swarm of servants and attendants following immediately behind them.

With a glare and a shake of her head for the Prince, Sindérian waited for the riders to dismount, then stepped forward and made a deep obeisance before a severe-looking, fair-haired woman who appeared to be the highest in rank. "My companions and I are envoys from Thäerie and Leal. We have arrived here after a long, perilous journey, bringing messages of great urgency for the King. In truth, our errand here is so vital," she added earnestly, "that even an hour's delay in bringing these things to King Ristil's attention might prove fatal. Will you help us?"

The recipient of all this eloquence was frowning doubtfully when another woman, somewhat younger and a good deal comelier, gave a smile and a friendly nod in Sindérian's direction. "But I know this lady, do I not?" Pulling off her riding gloves, she beckoned the young wizard to advance a little closer. "Yes, I *do* know you, though I don't distinctly recall the place or the occasion."

Sindérian herself hardly knew what to say, until Faolein's voice spoke with quiet conviction inside her head: *It is Luenil.*

Even then it took a moment before that name had any

meaning. Then a fragmentary memory surfaced. *Luenil— Guenloie's* wet nurse?

She is called Sigvith now, answered Faolein. *It is easy to see that she has risen in the world since the last time we saw her. Nevertheless it is the same woman.*

Sindérian blinked and cast her mind back more than nineteen years. Yes, there was a strong resemblance—but more than that, she knew that her father was infallible in the matter of names. It was his great gift. Gathering her wits, she sank into another curtsy. "Lady, we *have* met, but it was so long ago I scarcely dared hope that you would remember."

Luenil (or Sigvith) smiled again, an expression that brightened her whole face and made her appear many years younger. The resemblance, elusive before, was now unmistakable. "Then you are very welcome here. If you and these friends will follow us inside, I will try to arrange an audience with the King."

And so, under the aegis of no less a person than Ristil's queen, Sindérian and her companions entered the Heldenhof, a turn of events that left her head spinning. "You managed that very cleverly," Prince Ruan hissed in her ear as they crossed the threshold. "But how did you do it?"

Sindérian shook her head and gave no answer. She was not altogether certain herself how this fortunate meeting could possibly have occurred—and even if she *had* known, this was hardly the time for complicated explanations.

4

*

Reluctantly at first, Kivik's refugees began to move indoors and find quarters for themselves in the ancient buildings. A pair of bedraggled old women hunkered down in a pantry inside the keep; a blind woodcarver, his daughter, and five skinny grandchildren settled in a nearby scullery; before the day was over, a dozen more had trickled in through the worm-eaten doors. In contrast, the fighting men, more accustomed to obeying orders, packed up their gear immediately and took up residence in the seven gatehouses, an old barracks, and a row of houses in the outer bailey.

Over the next two days, more and more of the dispossessed gathered up their scanty belongings, their blankets, cooking pots, and rough bits of crockery; deserted the rapidly diminishing city of tents and hovels; and joined their relatives and neighbors indoors. Kivik did not deceive himself as to the reason, which was a certain habit of loyalty more than any conviction that the buildings were really safe, and he was more grateful than he could say for their show of faith.

But this *time their faith will be justified,* he told himself. *This time I've chosen well for them.* It never occurred to him to wonder at his own confidence, or to ask how a single night inside the keep had banished all his doubts.

One evening at sunset, he decided to join some of the men who patrolled the battlements on the outermost wall. After climbing a long, windy stair, he discovered Skerry already there ahead of him, stationed by the jagged parapet wall on the south side, looking out across the valley with an expression of intensest concentration on his face.

Waving the others on, Kivik walked over to join him, curious to discover what held his cousin's attention so completely that it kept him standing there in a gale, which, if it were any stronger, might have blown him right off the battlements.

For a time neither spoke. They had been friends for so long that they sometimes divined each other's thoughts by a hundred small clues of stance and expression, so that words were unnecessary.

Down below, the snow was ruddy with sunset. If he listened carefully, Kivik could hear the quarrelsome evening voices of the crows in the pinewoods. Higher up the mountain, rocks crumbled in the cold, setting off a minor avalanche. Between the woods and the fortress a company of ice giants was stamping around in the drifts, performing some species of maneuver. In the wan light, their immense, rough-hewn faces, every shade of grey from almost black to a muddy ashen hue, looked craggier than ever; their uncanny blue hair took on a faint purple cast.

Kivik shifted his weight from one foot to the other, threw a corner of his cloak over his shoulder to keep out the wind.

No amount of gazing at the giants could make them less fearsome. Their size alone was enough to terrify, their prodigies of strength and ferocity, their unfathomable power over the weather. Though they had never attempted to attack the fortifications or batter down the gates, they gave a vigilant impression of watching the fortress as closely as those inside watched them. They appreared to be waiting for something.

The Prince scowled. A parley was impossible, for there was no way of communicating with them. Perhaps worst of all was how little he and his people knew about them. He wanted to ask: *Why did you attack us? What are we to you? A year ago you were only a legend. Why do you make common cause with the Eisenlonders and the skinchangers against us?*

But he and they had no common language. Their speech was no more to him than the booming of the wind, the cracking of stones up in the heights; he imagined that any words of his would be as the squeaking of mice or the twittering of birds to them. A wizard might speak to them, perhaps, but not a prince of Skyrra.

"I think," said his cousin, coming unexpectedly out of his reverie, "that I am learning to recognize some of them. That old fellow there: I have an idea he is one of their chieftains."

Kivik's scowl turned thoughtful. Compared to the other giants, the one Skerry pointed at was positively gaunt and stooped—if still many times the size of the biggest man in King Ristil's army—and his hair was the color of blue smoke. An elder, he might be, or a clan patriarch, supposing the creatures even knew such concepts. "Anyway, he seems to keep the others in order."

The giants began to disperse, heading off in several directions: some toward the woods, some toward the mouth of the vale. One of them, with an aspect wilder and keener, and his sapphire hair caught up in a great horse's-tail by an iron ring, heaved up his war hammer and proceeded to reduce a pile of boulders into tiny fragments, roaring hugely all the while. So far as Kivik could see, his action served no other purpose than to flaunt his strength.

"And that one?" he asked. Merely to look into those eyes was like sinking into a well of dark water, wickedly cold and deep.

"A brute and a bully. I've seen him come to blows with several of the others. See, now, how the old one snarls and shakes his head, as though rebuking the braggart for his swagger?"

Kivik would have preferred to refuse the obvious conclusion but it clamored for his attention anyway. It gave him an odd sinking feeling to think of the giants as distinct personalities, with friendships and rivalries, antipathies and loyalties.

They were an ancient, mysterious race, the ice giants. *Skørnhäär*, that was an old name for them—whether Eisenlondish or some other foreign tongue Kivik did not know—a difficult word to get the mouth around. For years almost past counting there had been very little reason to call them anything, everyone believing they had been driven beyond the boundaries of the world ages past by southern wizards, or else bespelled into an endless slumber. He wondered if someone would make a new word for them now they had returned, and how they named themselves in their own language. In no way akin to humans, according to all the old accounts they were self-aware, rational, emotional, and therefore capable of barbarisms unknown to the animal kingdoms.

The silence on the wall turned prickly with things unsaid. "You don't care to think of them being like us in any way," Skerry observed wisely.

"Do you?"

His cousin thought for a moment, then grunted a negative. Kivik could almost read his mind: as giants, the creatures were formidable; as Men, they were monstrous.

"Like or unlike, they will probably grind our bones for bread readily enough," he said glumly, "if they ever find a way to breach these walls."

Skerry did not answer, but the sky flung down a stinging spatter of snow that burned where it touched bare skin.

Once everyone had accomplished the move indoors, a giddy enthusiasm broke out. Inside the keep and the adjoining towers, some of the braver souls took the ragged banners and tapestries off the walls, hanging them inside doorways and across shuttered windows to keep out drafts. Inspired by the broad marble fireplaces and deep circular fire pits, they started felling trees in the gardens and courtyards, where they had barely found the courage to gather deadfall before, until every room where people congregated had its own roaring fire. Farmwives and herdsmen brought their livestock in with them. Soon, sheep and goats were seen wandering in the splendid high halls; geese, chickens, and other small fowl mingled with the human inhabitants in the snugger antechambers, wardrobes, and closets.

An odd winter-holiday atmosphere began to spread, even though it was the wrong time of year, even though no one had anything to celebrate. Yet the merriment was infectious. What if they *were* on short rations and often went hungry? They had shelter, fires, fellowship; they were surrounded by the wonders of a magical, long-ago age. No one was willing to believe that the food might run out entirely before help arrived.

And perhaps, Kivik told himself with a thin smile, there was a kind of wisdom in making the most of the fires and comfortable surroundings while they still could. Who could predict how long this peaceful interlude would last? He thought of the giants and were-bears outside the walls, he thought of the Eisenlonders—they *were* coming, and no amount of optimism among the refugees and camp followers could banish his certainty of that.

So while the halls resounded with a cheerful stir of activity and the people made merry with the little they had, the Prince made certain that his men continued to keep a careful watch from the battlements, and that those in the barracks spent a large portion of each day in mock swordfights, sketching out plans of the outer fortifications on bits of parchment, and otherwise preparing for the inevitable siege.

But there was someone at Tirfang who shared in none of the gaiety, someone who wandered through the cursed fortress like one in a bad dream.

A strange mood was on the princess Winloki, an intimation of evil that grew each day. She was always starting at noises or at scurrying shadows that nobody else heard or saw, and things seemed to be constantly, inexplicably going awry, though none but she recognized a steadily worsening pattern: Food stores spoiled despite the cold. Wounds went bad that had seemed to be healing. Small objects disappeared the moment she turned her back on them.

Caught between fear and frustration—and angry because of the fear—she even found herself quarreling with the oldest and most experienced healers, Syvi and Thyra.

"We should use only the simples and potions we brought with us from Lückenbörg," she cried out one day. "Everything we brew *here* turns to venom!"

Startled by her outburst, Thyra dropped a glass phial, which shattered on the hard stone floor. "You acccuse me of poisoning our patients, Princess?"

"Not you—the Old Fortress." Yet Winloki could see that her words were utterly wasted. There was puzzlement and disbelief on the older woman's face—Thyra, who not many days past had been as terrified as anyone of entering the buildings.

Wherever Winloki went, she was always aware of some lingering residue of monstrous passions, ancient cruelties, and blackest sorceries. Yet altogether worse, because more palpable and encroaching, were the shadows: shadows milling about, clawing their way up the walls, shadows clinging to doorways and windowsills or hanging from the lofty ceilings like giant bats. Sometimes, where the shadows were deepest, there was a glint of blood-red eyes.

At times she was convinced that she was *breathing in* shadows. As the days passed, she began to feel starved for light, parched with the lack of it, as though she could never get a sufficiency. The great hearth fires seemed weak and anemic in the presence of her need, she felt so steeped in shadows. When that need was greatest, she took brisk walks through the courtyards, hoping to catch a glimpse of the sun struggling through the clouds. If it chanced to break through she lifted her face, letting the light beat against her skin, drinking it in.

In a pond in the courtyard a child had fallen through the ice and very nearly drowned. He said that a water nixie had pulled him down. But when his grandfather and another man plumbed the pool (it was not, after all, very deep), all that they found was pebbles, mud, and the roots of water lilies. Nevertheless, Winloki was inclined to credit the nixie.

She did what she could to warn the others of their peril, cautiously at first to avoid starting a panic, and then more directly. Every hint, every warning was received with polite incredulity. Even Skerry, who ought to have believed her—knowing the peculiar intuitions of which she was sometimes capable—even he returned nothing but the same infuriating silence he had used since they were children to outlast her more determined efforts to have her own way.

But can't you see? she wanted to shout at him, folding her arms across her chest as if to contain all the anxiety and frustration brewing inside of her. *Don't you know that this is different?*

He did not and would not. In truth, she sometimes wondered how she could ever have pledged herself to marry a man capable of such determined blindness. Then he smiled at her and brushed his fingers across her face, and she knew that even though he did not believe a word she said—even though he thought her whimsical, unreasonable, possibly delusional—he remained steadfast in his devotion, which was either heroic or heroically stupid. She preferred to think the former.

But none of this brought Winloki any closer to being heard, much less heeded. On the day she realized that the refugees were beginning to make use of the fortress's perilous treasures—ploughmen eating moldy bread off dishes made of silver and onyx, their daughters wearing combs of opal and ivory in their hair—she very nearly gave up trying.

She spent too many hours lying sleepless in her make-shift bed, listening to a black wind that always seemed to be blowing during the brief hours of twilight and darkness. And when she did sleep, tales told by her nursemaids came back to haunt her, until her dreams became a web of nursery-tale horrors: golden apples spiked with venom; innocent stepmothers forced to dance themselves to death in red-hot iron slippers; the slimy amphibious suitor who changed into something infinitely worse once he was admitted to the maiden's bedchamber. A silver spinning wheel shone in the dark behind her eyes; it went round and round like a millstone grinding corn, but it was crystals of ice that came out of the mill and fine blowing snow.

Most confusing was the presence of two women who came to her often as she dreamed, out of no tale that she could remember, yet strangely familiar. They were alike in form and feature, yet so different in expression, one mild, one fierce, that she never had difficulty telling them apart. The first wore stars in her sunset hair; the other a diadem of moons. Each seemed to require something of Winloki, a word or a deed or an answer of terrible significance—though sleeping or waking the Princess could never quite puzzle out what that something might be.

And so it went, day after day and night after night. If others would not see the truth, it was up to her to take steps to protect them. While daylight lasted, she gabbled half-remembered charms she had picked up over the years from servants at the Heldenhof. She hunted up bits of charcoal in the fireplaces and fire pits, and used them to scribble runes on thresholds and windowsills. *Rüadin* for rowan, a specific against witchcraft. *Tysa* for mint, often used in healing. *Tiné. Dair.*

"Only it's no use," she cried out in a sudden fit of nerves, flinging down her piece of charred wood. "These aren't even Wizard's Runes, just the names of plants." It *was* no use. She had only the dimmest idea of what she was doing, that and a natural gift which had never been trained.

Hopeless, she thought, glaring down at her broken fingernails, flexing her thin, charcoal-smudged fingers, *hopeless and worthless.* What use was it to *see,* if having seen you could still do nothing? The magical arts had been declining in Skyrra for more than a hundred years, ever since the north severed ties with the south. Even healers were not what they had once been, their gifts steadily diminishing, and the indigenous runestone readers had all but disappeared. So much had been lost, so much knowledge, so much skill, and yet the enemy Eisenlonders kept *all* their black arts.

Too late, the shadows whispered, in a deep, throaty murmur coming from a place just over her shoulder. *Already too late; they are almost here.*

Winloki clapped her hands over her ears, but it did no good. The whispers only continued.

5

✳

The day everything changed began with an excited milling down among the beast-men and *Skørnhäär*, who
had already gathered in numbers much greater than
usual outside the gates. Giants trumpeted to each other across
the valley. White bears rose up on their haunches and sniffed
the air. A snarling and a growling started up, so terrific as to
freeze the blood of the men stationed on the outer fortifications.

Then one man with keener eyes than the rest spotted, very
small in the distance but still unmistakable, the vanguard of an
Eisenlonder army, their bronze armor shining dully in the weak
sunlight, their wolf's-head banners snapping in the wind.

Word spread very swiftly through the fortress. Messengers
went running to the barracks, to Kivik's apartments, and to
the armory. Meanwhile, a hum of excitement travelled even
faster than the messengers could sprint; before very long the
news was being gabbled from person to person among the
refugees and camp followers.

Skerry first learned what was afoot when a young guard came tumbling down a stone staircase by one of the gatehouses, almost knocking him over, so eager he was to spread the word: "The enemy has been sighted. They are almost here."

He helped the youth to right himself, asked a few sharp questions, and sent the boy on. Then he went off with a great swinging stride through successive gateways and yards, then into the keep, arriving at the quarters he shared with Kivik only to discover that his cousin was already gone.

The Prince had *been* there, only moments before, a bewildered Deor told him, but after issuing a great many rapid orders he had disappeared. Skerry was not yet ready to give up the search. Moreover, he had an idea where Kivik might be found: the same place that he would have gone in his kinsman's place.

Hastening down a hallway near the infirmary, he met Winloki hurrying along in the opposite direction. "Something terrible has happened. All day long, I've had a presentiment. And the shadows—the shadows have been practically in a frenzy."

"Nothing has happened that we haven't been expecting," he told her soothingly. "The Eisenlonders are coming, but we have no reason to suppose they'll attack immediately, not after a long march through the mountains. Even when they do, it's likely to be a long siege."

Casting a harried look back over her shoulder, Winloki continued on her way, leaving Skerry to go his.

He climbed a spiralling staircase in one of the towers, up to a breezy, roofless chamber at the top that offered an unobstructed view of the entire valley. As he had expected, Kivik was already there at one of the tall windows, watching the forward edge of the Eisenlonder army: a dark mass moving slowly yet inexorably toward the Old Fortress.

An hour later, they had still not seen the end of it. Horsemen and foot soldiers continued to flood into the valley. Those who had already arrived had set up a camp just out of arrow range—and a careful distance from their gigantic allies.

"So many of them. How can there be so many?" Kivik finally spoke in a dull voice. "It seems that for every man we've killed this last year a dozen more spring up out of nowhere to take his place."

Skerry nodded grimly. "Whatever they say back at Lückenbörg, there were *never* such numbers in all of Eisenlonde. They *must* be hiring mercenaries; nothing else makes any sense."

"Mercenaries," Kivik said bleakly. "Let us say that most of them *are* mercenaries, for the sake of argument. Then how have the petty lords and chieftains of Eisenlonde found the coin to hire so many? Are there gold mines in that godsforsaken part of the world that nobody knew about?" He put his back up against the wall between the windows, folded his arms across his chest. "Or have they rich friends, friends who are somehow, for some unknown reason, our real enemies? Are the barbarians hiring mercenaries, or has someone bought *them*?"

Skerry struggled to think of a logical answer. Slowly at first, ideas seemingly unrelated began to link up, to grow connections—finally creating a picture that, if it still eluded complete comprehension, at least made a coherent whole.

"Perhaps not enemies of Skyrra," he said. "Perhaps *someone else's* enemies. People in a place where a child was born with such extraordinary gifts, it was decided to spirit her away for her own protection and entrust her to strangers in another country."

"Winloki." Kivik caught his breath; then he nodded, one short, sharp movement of his head. "We both know, though it's supposed to be a great secret, that she's not truly our kin—nor even likely to be Skyrran, but of southern stock instead. And that ring, the one with the queer symbols that she wears sometimes, it's no heirloom of *our* house."

In truth, there were many strange things about their young cousin-by-adoption: that she was capable of healings even the oldest, most experienced healers could never hope to accomplish; that she had other odd, unpredictable abilities even she did not understand. What they did *not* know, because they had never been told, were the exact circumstances surrounding her birth.

"But who . . ." Kivik groped for words. "Who could be powerful enough, ruthless enough, to involve two countries in a bloody and senseless war, all because of a nineteen-year-old girl who doesn't even know who she is?"

Skerry shook his head. "Someone who does know, only I can't even hazard a guess who that could be." Then his eyes went wide; he felt all of the blood drain out of his face. "Unless—unless it might be someone who keeps half of the world at war. Someone who has been sending out her armies and conquering other kingdoms for longer than either one of us has been alive. And all of it, they say, for mere vanity and greed!"

"Phaôrax?" The very name seemed to darken the air, though it was a name seldom thought or spoken in the north. "But that's so far away, it's almost impossible to imagine such a distance."

It was an immense distance. The island where Ouriána, the

self-styled Empress, self-styled goddess, ruled might as well have been on the moon or at the bottom of the sea, it seemed so far removed, so inaccessible. Skerry gave a little mirthless laugh, shaking off the thought. "We are building theories out of sand, snatching fantasies out of the air. It's too incredible."

But then another thought struck him. "Whether or not any of this could possibly be true, I think it wisest to say nothing to Winloki. She's been so odd lately, so skittish." He did not mention meeting her near the infirmary, or what she had said then; it was all of a piece, anyway, with the way she had been behaving for so many days. "If she took it into her head that she endangers the rest of us just by being here, she might do something reckless, something foolhardy."

Unfortunately, they both knew that where Winloki was concerned, that possibility always existed, even under ordinary circumstances. She had a good heart, but she was headstrong and prone to act on impulse. On the other hand, neither was she a fool.

"Although there is no saying that she won't eventually make some of the same guesses we have," Skerry continued. "She may have done so already, which would certainly account for her extraordinary behavior." His fingers curled, reflexively, into a fist.

Kivik nodded glumly. "With that in mind, I will assign guards to watch her for her own protection." His scowl deepened. "In fact, I will double—no, triple—the number she had on the journey here, just to be safe."

Far removed from Kivik's airy vantage point in the tower, down in the mazes and the firelit chambers of the fortress below, his people were reacting with excitement, fear, and anticipation.

In the outer bailey, a martial atmosphere prevailed. The fighting men were energetic, almost eager, finding relief, after such a long period of idleness and uncertainty, in the familiar preparations before a battle. They polished their swords until they gleamed, sharpened spears, mended their gear. Messengers came and went, relaying the Prince's orders. Even the horses in the stables caught some of the excitement, growing restive and nearly unmanageable.

Elsewhere, his gaunt host of refugees gathered together in uneasy congregations, exchanging news when they had it, speculating when they did not. Whatever spell the fortress had cast over them before, it was unravelling now that the jaws of the trap had closed and no one could escape. Sometimes they tried to bolster their own spirits, muttering about the towering height of the outer fortifications or reminding themselves and each other of the mighty gates, murder holes, and arrow slits.

"There's seven great walls they have to get through or over," someone would say. Or "A warrior of Skyrra is worth three from Eisenlonde." Not one of them had been up to the ramparts to see for themselves; they could not know that the men of Skyrra were outnumbered by a great deal more than three to one.

Meanwhile there was great activity among the camp followers, those weathered and sinewy women who had seen battle before, even if their position at the rear driving the heavy wagons had usually spared them actual involvement. They fletched arrows, tested bows, put their knives to the whetstone.

In the infirmary, Thyra and her healers began to cut up linens and roll them into bandages, grimly sacrificing the last of their chemises and undergowns. So the preparations went on into the evening and all through the night.

At dawn, there were signs of sluggish movement in the enemy encampment. While the Eisenlonder camp stirred back to life, two separate companies of ice giants went stalking across the fields in the early morning light and disappeared into the forest. Crows screamed in the pinewood; there was a roaring, a rending, and a crashing of many trees falling at once; the air filled with the scent of murdered pines.

Shortly thereafter the first group of *Skørnhäär* returned, dragging some of the tallest trees behind them. Stone axes rose and fell, and in a remarkably brief time the logs were bare of branches. Then the giants began building ladders, splitting some of the discarded limbs for rungs, chopping them into smaller segments, and hammering them to the frames. In the meantime, the second company emerged from the woods and set to work stripping branches, too.

In the gatehouse, Kivik had gathered his captains together in a small candlelit room within the thickness of the walls, to study plans of the fortifications and add the final touches to their plan of battle.

They did not take long to reach an agreement. Because the great encircling outer wall was miles around, there could be no question of defending every part of it. Some sections, however, rose much higher than others, particularly to the north, where the ramparts reached such incredible heights it did not seem possible the enemy would even attempt to scale them. Therefore, men would be concentrated at strategic locations on the east and west walls, and especially on the south, which was by far the most vulnerable.

"Particularly here by the gates, where the assault is likely to be most fierce," Kivik was saying, when a rising clamor of voices came in through the arrow slits along one wall. His curiosity thoroughly aroused, he led the captains clattering up to the roof, to see what had occasioned such excitement.

They had no need to question the men stationed on the battlements; the cause of their uproar was there for Kivik and his officers to see as soon as they arrived at the parapet. "But what do you suppose it *is* that they are building?" asked Skerry.

For the ice giants had stopped making ladders and were working on something more complex and mysterious: a construction made out of logs whose purpose neither the Prince nor any of his men could readily identify. The Eisenlonders were busy too, digging what appeared to be postholes near the camp, mining the slopes just below the woods. At the same time, one of their chieftains, a great yellow-haired lout, went riding back and forth astride a white horse, shouting orders to the toiling giants.

"So they *can* speak to the *Skørnhäär*—some of them can, anyway," Kivik said under his breath. "But in what language? What sort of speech could they possibly have in common?"

"They may speak with them," Skerry answered, "but even so, they dare not approach too near."

It was true: the Eisenlonders continued to give their formidable allies a wide berth. Wherever the great stony figures went, the barbarians left a broad circle of empty space around them. "I don't envy them their new friends," commented

Roric, scratching at his beard. "The bloody skinchangers are bad enough. But it must be cursed cold down there with the cursed giants."

Kivik could only agree. Only the lightest scattering of flakes was falling over the fortress, yet the sky continued to pour down snow and sleet on the Eisenlonder encampment. Even keeping as much distance as possible between themselves and the giants, the men down there had to be suffering agonies of cold. Nor would wolfskin cloaks and gaudy woven blankets offer much protection from Winter personified. Already many of the barbarians appeared half frozen. Their cloaks were heavy with ice and their faces almost as blue as the giants' hair.

"May they all suffer frostbite," growled Deor, shaking a fist.

Though Kivik eventually released his captains to their various duties, he and Skerry lingered on the gatehouse roof, eager to learn what the giants were building. Already, the creatures had placed eight stout logs upright in the postholes, packing in enough dirt to hold them in place, then added to each of these supports a cross-member, somewhat smaller in size, that rested inside deep slots cut into the tops of the uprights. Next, they began lashing wooden arms to the beams—whose purpose was finally revealed as some kind of axle.

"Siege engines," said Skerry, his face gone blank with astonishment. "They are building trebuchets!"

Kivik, too, was momentarily confounded. Like any young prince, he had naturally been thoroughly educated in warfare, taking lessons alongside his brothers and his cousins. In the course of those studies he and Skerry had both seen drawings and even models of similar machines. But no siege weapons had seen use in all of Skyrra for hundreds of years. They were part of a past, a way of life, intentionally abandoned after the worldwide cataclysm known as the Change. Kivik strongly doubted that any of the ordinary fighting men were capable of recognizing these engines, though the barbarians were building them right under their noses.

But neither, he thought uneasily, *have the Eisenlonders ever displayed any such arts of war.* Until quite recently they had been best known for cattle raids, thievery, and avoiding pitched battle, their tactics—if you could call them that—consisting of lightning-swift strikes and surprise attacks. Yet there before him was evidence of a sophisticated kind of warfare unlike anything the barbarians had known or used in the past.

Kivik felt the hairs rise at the back of his neck. Not for the first time, he was aware of unknown forces and agendas at work, far beyond anything within his experience. "Say that the Eisenlonders taught the giants how to build these machines— but who taught *them*?"

To this Skerry had no reply, either busy with his own thoughts or else absorbed in watching the preparations down in the camp, where the Eisenlonders had taken over from the giants and were attaching ropes and a sling to each of the tre- buchets.

Kivik's mind went back to some of the more fantastic ideas they had mooted last night. It made no sense, he told himself, that the Dark Lady of Phaôrax should have gone to such lengths simply to capture or kill Winloki, when nothing could have been easier than sending emissaries to Lückenbörg months ago, years ago, to swoop down and abduct the girl.

Yet who *else* had the power or the will to stir up a war like this one, and yet take no visible part?

"Maybe," he said slowly, "maybe we have arrived at the right conclusion, only the wrong way around. We know Ouriána has been expanding her territories for all these decades, but we never imagined she would ever be a threat to *our* lands, because the distance between us was so impossibly far, and most of all because she never sent her armies farther north than Rheithûn."

The ideas were coming swiftly. It astonished Kivik how clearly he saw things now—how wretchedly blind he and others around him had been before. "All this time we believed ourselves safe, were certain she would be satisfied gobbling up the old Empire lands, and that once she had done so, her hunger for conquest would be sated. But *why* did we think so?"

He answered his own question. "Because it was comfortable, because it was convenient. Yet if her armies had ever ventured into Arkenfell, or even into Weye, we would have recognized our danger readily enough! Then, at the very least we would have made firm alliances with Mistlewald and Arkenfell, perhaps with her enemies on Thäerie and Leal. But if she strikes at us *now*, using the Eisenlonders as her puppets, if she strikes now while the kingdoms of the north are fragmented, disorganized, not even capable of recognizing our true enemy—"

Kivik drew in a long breath and let it out. As things stood now, Ouriána might swallow all the kingdoms of the north at a gulp and be in a position to attack the coastal principalities of Hythe and Weye from the north and south at the same time.

As if it were a sign, the sun disappeared behind a bank of clouds, casting a deep shadow over all the valley.

By late morning the air quivered with tension. Knowing that the first assault would begin very soon, the defenders assembled in force up on the ramparts. Their helms and shield-bosses gleamed with a cold light; their swords and spears gave back a deadly glitter. On the valley floor the enemy stood ready, rank upon rank, and a murmur rose up from the horde, like the sound of the sea.

Kivik passed among his men, speaking such heartening words as were customary before a battle. Behind a feigned cheerfulness, a reckless air of courage, he managed to conceal his own misgivings. And the men responded: backs were a little straighter and heads rose a little higher wherever he went.

Down by the trebuchets, the giants had harnessed the largest of the *Varjolükka* to the dangling ropes, and the purpose behind all the digging on the slopes was no longer a mystery. The Eisenlonders had been mining stones, stacking up great piles of rocks and boulders by the siege engines, ready for use.

At a signal from the man on the white horse, giants by each of the machines took up several large stones and dropped them into the slings. One by one, the loaders aimed and roared out their orders, bear-men rose up on their hindquarters and heaved on the ropes, and the wooden arms swung, slinging the first deadly missiles high into the air, speeding toward the fortress. Up on the walls, men scattered before the deadly barrage of falling stones.

Under the covering fire of the trebuchets and a rain of

arrows from the Eisenlonder archers, other giants began to haul the long siege ladders forward. With the use of long forked poles, they pushed the ladders upright, angling them against the walls until they were lodged so firmly between the battlements that the defenders were unable to shake them loose.

As the giants drew back again, a lone trumpet sounded; a great noise went up from the barbarian host. Then the front ranks swept toward the foot of the wall and began swarming up the ladders. The battle had truly begun.

At the beginning, the men of Skyrra were able to cast down most of the ascending Eisenlonders as swiftly as they climbed up. But the numbers of the enemy were just too great. Before very long they had forced a way from the ladders to the parapet, from the parapet to the wall-walk, pressing the defenders hard.

Again and again, Kivik flung himself into the middle of the conflict. No prince of Skyrra had ever hung back during an engagement. In truth, when the battle fury gripped him, it would have been impossible for him to hold still. He moved from one point to another, wherever the fighting was most heated, shouting out encouragement to his men, slaying every Eisenlonder who came in his way.

In the noise and confusion of battle, his heartbeat accelerated, while everyone around him seemed to slow. He no longer felt the cold. Sweat dripped down from his forehead into his eyes and he dashed it away with a thoughtless gesture. When one shield shattered, he snatched up another and kept on fighting without a pause.

Through the corner of one eye, he could see Skerry fighting along beside him. His cousin's style was altogether different, each stroke aimed methodically, precisely, so that his opponents fell back steadily. A hail of arrows came pattering down, glancing off the stones, and Skerry ignored them. A sword flashed and he swung up his own, hardly breaking a sweat. When a barbarian lunged in his direction, Skerry capably finished the man off.

Kivik adjusted his grip, which had grown slippery with somebody's blood, then took a mighty swing at a convenient head. The barbarian flung up his sword to block, and the blades locked. Kivik pushed with all his might, forcing the man to take two steps backward; then, as the swords disengaged, he aimed a swift downward cut to the knee. Somehow the blow landed higher than he intended and was absorbed by the skirt of a chain mail tunic.

Kivik ground his teeth. There had been a time—when he was young, very young—when he had firmly believed that a man fought only for honor and glory, that winning a battle was less important than how it was conducted. All this had changed: he fought now for the survival of his people and had no time for the conventions of combat. Ruthlessly, and with a lethal absence of compunction, he took every advantage he could. So when the barbarian swung, Kivik ducked, blocked with his shield, and moved in closer. Pursuing his advantage, he heaved up his sword and drove the pommel down, with all of his strength behind it, on his enemy's helm.

Momentarily stunned, the Eisenlonder stood immobilized. Seizing the moment, the Prince planted his heater shield against the other's buckler and pushed, sending the man backward over the inside parapet wall and hurtling ninety feet to the yard below. Kivik did not even stop to watch him fall.

As he turned, a rain of stones fell on the walkway almost at his feet. He leaped sideways, but not quickly enough to avoid an explosion of sharp pebbles as stone met stone and several of the rocks cracked. One fragment hit him just above his eye, drawing blood. He hardly felt the sting.

Somewhere in the press of battle he had lost track of Skerry. There were bodies everywhere, Skyrrans and Eisenlonders alike, and he could only hope that his cousin's was not among them. When he brought his sword crashing down on the helmet of an opponent, the blade, which was already notched, shivered into splinters. He tossed it aside, caught up a bloody axe from the slackened grip of a dead barbarian, and hewed to right and left.

There came a brief lull, one of those welcome moments in the ebb and flow of battle when it was possible for Kivik to catch his breath. The men around him had beaten back a flood of opponents and managed to upset one of the Eisenlonders' ladders. Those on the bottom rungs who had survived the fall were struggling to erect it again.

Then one of the captains—Roric or Haestan, he could not be certain which—gave a breathless whoop of joy, and somebody else flung out an arm, pointing. At first, Kivik saw nothing but a blur of wings above the field of battle, then he realized with a lift of his heart that it was one of his own messenger hawks sent out days before. Taking this for an omen, someone behind him gave a hoarse cheer.

A flight of arrows from archers down on the field went singing through the air. The bird turned, describing a beautiful curve across the sky, and by some miracle avoided being hit. Kivik held his breath. Then another flight went up, more accurate than before. One arrow clipped a barred grey wing, another struck full in the feathered breast. There was a brief flutter, and the hawk dropped like a stone.

It landed in the ranks of the Eisenlonders, where whatever messages it had been carrying were lost.

6

✳

It was a hot summer night on Phaôrax, and a ghastly full
moon shone down on Ouriána's capital city of Apharos—
that city of spires and steeples and dagger-pointed towers,
comfortless and cruel to all but a favored few. The air hung
heavy and breathless in the narrow streets; no hint of wind
stirred the banners hanging limp outside the nobles' tall houses
or the trees in the palace gardens on the promontory. Even the
waters of the bay were sluggish in the heat, and the hundreds
of ships and boats tied up by the docks could scarcely be seen
to rock. Yet a slow, simmering excitement continued to build
as the night wore on.

For this was the eve of the *Faldhalüra*, the Rites of the
High Summer Full Moon, and the city was electric with the
knowledge that shortly before daybreak the Empress herself
would walk barefoot through the streets, on her way to bathe
in the sea and call up prodigies and portents for the coming
year.

By an hour before sunrise, crowds of early risers had gathered outside the New Temple, eager to catch a glimpse of their goddess-incarnate and bask in her presence.

A bell clanged somewhere within the precincts of the temple: once, twice, three times. Breaths bated, hearts trembled, as a door of beaten brass swung open. A thousand sighs went out together when Ouriána appeared in the opening and stepped down to the rough cobbles.

She wore only a white linen shift that left her arms uncovered from wrist to elbow, but her beauty shown out more splendid and terrible than ever. Without crown, scepter, or necklet to set it off, it was somehow more primal, the response it evoked more visceral. Her skin glowed and her unbound hair was a curtain of silken fire hanging past her knees. Her eyes were like gates into unfathomable mysteries; few dared to meet her gaze as she passed.

Like a sphinx or a leopardess she stalked through the city, and crowds of eager worshippers fell in behind her.

They followed her from the temple to the south gate, then outside the walls and along the shore. For a time, rounding the promontory, the footing grew rocky and difficult. While Ouriána flowed on ahead, unscathed and oblivious, those who followed stumbled often, scraping toes and knees, bloodying their palms on the shingle in their eagerness to rise and not lose sight of her. At last they came out on an isolated stretch of beach where pearls, old coins, and bright bits of jade sometimes washed up, offerings from the sea to the Empress-Goddess.

The moon was a great ivory globe veined with crystal, hovering just above the silvery water. From the perspective of those watching, it looked as if the gap between moon and sea had narrowed to inches, that any of the larger breakers coming in might drench her pale face with spray. With exquisite timing, the Empress had arrived at the precise moment for the rite to begin.

A hush fell over the crowd. One slow step at a time, Ouriána waded out into the water until she stood knee-deep in the little wavelets, her linen skirts soaked in brine and her long red hair floating like kelp behind her.

Just as the rim of the moon touched the ocean, the Empress lifted her arms and called out three words in a thrilling voice. The sea turned as clear as glass from horizon to horizon, then the waters went roaring out with a terrible rush and hurry. They reached the lowest tidemark and still continued to sink, until it looked as though the moon were drinking down the sea.

Those watching felt a shock of horror, never doubting that the moon *would* swallow the ocean dry without their goddess's intervention. And Ouriána, standing aloof and implacable, looking out over acres of wet sand, allowed them to experience that terror to the fullest. She inhaled their fear and awe like incense, she drank it in like wine.

A sense of great forces striving for mastery crept over the waiting throng. The earth seemed to pant beneath their feet, the cosmos to reel around them. At any moment, they believed, the stars might go out like windblown candles, the foundations of the earth crumble and send them all tumbling into the void. And still the sea retreated, farther and farther, until none could see its nearer edge. Some wept or cried out for mercy; no few threw themselves facedown in the sand and lay there shuddering.

Then Ouriána raised her arms again. It was impossible to hear what she said over the distant noise of the waters, but for a timeless moment the night went utterly still. Then the tide came rushing back as quickly as it had gone out, crashing on the beach in a froth of white foam and a cloud of spray—not one eyelash farther than the previous tideline.

The people set up a quivering but enthusiastic cheer. The rite had been successful, their prayers and offerings had been found acceptable, and by the grace of Ouriána they were spared for another year.

By the time the Empress finally waded back to shore, day was breaking in the east. The crowd parted reverently to let her pass. Her bath in the sea had changed her profoundly. No less beautiful, she had such a freshness about her that she might have been born that very morning. Her face was bright with a savage innocence; her eyes had taken on an astonishing luminescence. And all along the beach, men and women reached out to touch the sandy hem of her gown, a damp tendril of her hair—hoping to be renewed as she had been renewed, to be lifted above the sorrows and the cruelties of their daily existence, if only for an hour.

On the other side of the city, Maelor woke with an aching head, a dry mouth, and a queasy stomach, after a typical night of little sleep and feverish dreams. Bleary-eyed, the old astrologer shuffled about the shabby attic room with its dusty clutter of mystical odds and ends, preparing himself for the day ahead. For all that he was such an abstemious man, it was not surprising if people sometimes mistook him for a drunkard.

He splashed water on his face, nibbled a hard rind of

cheese, finger-combed his straggly hair and beard. Squinting sideways, first out of one eye and then the other, it seemed to him that the strands of hair dangling to either side of his face had grown thicker and darker, that his beard was less wispy than it had been the night before. Reality had become fickle of late, constantly shifting and reshaping itself, capable of endless permutations. Unfortunately, the changes never seemed to last very long.

Despite his pounding head and ringing ears, today of all days seemed touched with magic, a day that offered amazing, even miraculous possibilities. He was at a loss to explain it, not even certain whether these new sensations were symptoms of further mental deterioration or of returning sanity. Indeed, the question had perplexed him for many years, whether *he* had been mad all of this time, or if it was *the world around him* that limped and hobbled along utterly disjointed and disconnected.

But as the morning was already well advanced, he shrugged off these speculations as fruitless, shoved some small items into the capacious pockets of his tattered robe, and left the room. First locking the door behind him, he descended, by way of a rickety staircase, six long flights to the street below. On every landing, armies of cockroaches scattered at the sound of his footsteps. Once outside, he set off at his usual ambling pace for the marketplace, where he spent the better part of each day juggling balls, performing minor tricks of conjuring, and (when circumstances favored him) scribbling the occasional horoscope on scraps of paper.

The neighborhood where Maelor lived was all dirty, narrow streets coiling uphill and downhill like angry snakes, and even

more squalid alleys that wriggled and squirmed between rows
of aging houses. Bits of ragged laundry hung drying from
upper-story windows. Cats of all colors prowled in the refuse
below. Half wild and half domesticated, most of these cats
were more bone than fur—but lean and feral or sick and lethargic, the one thing they all had in common was *hunger*.

As the old man walked, the air trembled and objects shifted.
Sometimes he thought he could see right through the eroding
stonework and into another, fairer Apharos, a city gracious
with gardens and filled with birdsong. In that city there were
many cats, too, but so sleek and well fed it was unlikely they
ever bothered the fat grey mourning doves strutting on the
roofs. And everywhere he looked there were statues: glorious
winged figures in marble and alabaster, poised as if ready to
leave their weight of stone behind, spring into the air, and take
flight.

He had not walked much farther when the vision faded,
leaving him stranded in the Apharos he already knew, the city
of dingy houses, crumbling stone, and parched earth. Another
man might have wept at the change. Maelor simply ambled on.

After about another quarter of a mile the street began
to skirt the edges of another district, known as the Thieves'
Market or Under-City—though in point of altitude it was no
lower than most parts of Apharos, and more elevated than
some. It had earned that name by virtue of its shady com-
merce and unsavory dealings, its business mostly conducted
in a complicated warren of cellars, tunnels, and caves, under
the ruins of what had once been villas of the high nobility
and the ancient Temple of the Seven Fates. Only a few broken
walls, the foundation, and the cellars of that imposing edifice

remained, and it was said that Ouriána's malice had hastened the process of dissolution; there were many still living who could remember when the temple and the houses were still in use. The present inhabitants were thieves, smugglers, pirates, and rogue magicians, whose occupation of the ruins the Empress appeared to tolerate, if not actively encourage. Yet none of those violent and predatory men had ever accosted Maelor, and today they allowed him to pass, as they always did, unmolested. His reputation preceded him: everyone knew that he never carried anything worth the effort of stealing, extorting, or swindling.

At intervals, his visions continued. Some of them were terrifying, like the imps and hobgoblins he saw dancing on the roofs or gnawing with sharp teeth at the foundations of buildings. Other things were clearly hallucinatory, as when sounds became solids and all the colors sang, or the sky turned to glass and a single enormous eye peered through.

But most of what he saw and experienced that day struck him with all the force and poignancy of memory. So far as he knew, he had lived in the city for only ten years. There was, however, a large portion of his life about which he knew nothing at all. Had some part of that life been spent in Apharos? Should he know some of these people he saw drifting by him, as insubstantial as ghosts? Those redheaded twin princesses, who looked hardly old enough to sit in the saddle, riding along together on identical fat white ponies caparisoned like chargers? That dignified old lady on a grey palfrey who stopped at nearly every corner to distribute alms? If he did remember them, those memories were incomplete, devoid of names and a common history.

From the Thieves' Market the old man came into a more prosperous part of the city. In that neighborhood the buildings were considerably newer, but no more pleasing: all flint, granite, and limestone, all hard angles and pointed roofs, no softness, no comfort, no grace anywhere; it was all just as hard as Ouriána's heart. The only touches of beauty were in the dozens of statues and fountains bearing her likeness.

Indeed, it was a setting deliberately fashioned for the Empress to rest in like a rare jewel. Her architects, masons, and stonecarvers created nothing beautiful that was not in her image, while every icon of the older religion that preceded her cult had been decapitated, mutilated, or hammered into dust.

Maelor paused where two streets crossed while a procession passed. Although they were only a straggling line of limping, dazed-looking worshippers, just now coming home from the early-morning ritual, the magic that was on the day transformed them: they became acrobats and maskers of an old-style *samhrad* celebration, clattering through the streets with all the noise and good-natured merriment that bells and pennons, streamers and tambourines, could possibly provide. The old man watched them, his head swimming and his heart thumping like a drum, until they were out of sight. He waited until his mind grew quieter and the dizziness passed, then staggered on his way.

Where several lanes ran together like the spokes of a wheel, something loomed up: a statue in white marble, a magnificent winged woman with a swan's great pinions and a crown of light, rising in splendor to scatter blessings over the city. For one heart-stirring moment, she was the reality, everything else illusion. Maelor's pulse pounded so hard, it seemed that his veins must burst—but then he blinked and the figure changed. After all, it was only another statue of Ouriána, this time in the guise of a siren, with the leathery wings of a bat and a slippery mermaid's tail.

And so, in his slow and meandering fashion, the old man came at last into the great market square down by the docks. On any other day, odors of fish, salt water, and rotting garbage mingled with scents of oranges and lemons, spices, boiled sweets, and sizzling meats served straight from the skewer; today, however, was a day of fasting from sunrise to sunset, and the food stalls were deserted.

Yet the square appeared no less crowded and busy. On the contrary, carpenters hammered at temporary stages; merchants of the cloth guilds erected tents; and everywhere Maelor looked, extra stalls were being squeezed in between the more permanent booths already there. All this in preparation for the more riotous festivities that would begin at nightfall and continue on through the following day.

The old man hunkered down in his accustomed spot and sat dreamily watching the activity around him, at first too engrossed to set out his conjurer's props and astrologer's tools. He took everything in with equal delight, from the knife grinder pushing his wheeled grindstone across the square, to the card readers and crystal-gazers in a blue silk pavilion directly opposite him, for he was as curious as a child and just as easily amused. Leatherworkers, potters, and glassmakers were already hawking their wares. A cohort of temple guards marched by in their sinister dark armor, and palace officials moved from booth to booth and tent to tent, collecting fees. Over by a dry fountain, a group of penitents in coarse black homespun was preparing to walk barefoot over burning rocks.

But as the sun rose higher and the day grew hotter, things began to mutate again. Maelor blinked and one of the female penitents became a rope dancer in gaudy satins and velvets; across the way, a one-legged blackbird perched on the fortune-tellers' tentpole transformed into the phoenix of legend, brilliantly feathered and wreathed in gorgeous flames.

The old man wrinkled his narrow brow. If this went on much longer, anything might happen: dung change to gold or cobbles to carbuncles; a wretched old mountebank be translated into a genuine magician. And with that thought, just for a moment, the old fire tingled in his veins. Runes and charms rioted in his brain; patterns, symbols, strictures, spells to chain the elements and calm the raging winds, all these were his. A name—possibly his own, lost these two decades—struggled to take shape in his mind.

Then the bells in the New Temple began their midday clamor, and the bright, entrancing images rapidly faded. The knowledge went out of him like a smothered flame. He was only Maelor the mad astrologer again: a dirty, hapless, bewildered old man, sitting in the dust of the market, hoping to earn a handful of coppers by juggling balls or performing a trick or two.

Yet a faint memory of power still surged in his blood, and all that long day he carried off his illusions with remarkable panache. He conjured butterflies and flowers out of the air. The balls that he tossed glittered like silver moons and golden suns. He even stole fire from a fire-eater and swallowed it down, scarcely singeing his beard in the process.

Finally, drunk on those dregs of power, he made a pageant

for the people in the square, a story acted out by phantoms he crafted out of light and shade, color and air.

It was an epic tale of knights and maidens, kings, queens, and princes, in the great city of Apharos long ago. They had been noble and courageous, those lords and ladies of another age, and after Ceir Eldig in Alluinn foremost in learning in all the Empire lands. They loved bright colors, rich fabrics, strong wines, and all things beautiful and finely crafted. They were impulsive, magnanimous, high-handed; they could be dangerous when provoked. But if their virtue was no greater than their pride, at least it was no less, and none of their faults were mean or petty ones.

Then Maelor went on to tell of the lesser folk who lived in that long-ago city—common by birth but extraordinary in their attainments. They had been wizards, scholars, and alchemists, merchants, craftsmen, soldiers, and poets. They fought wars; they built great ships and sailed in them to all the lands of the known world; when they sinned they sinned largely, then regretted and made their amends afterward with much the same fervor. And if their aspirations had been larger than their hearts, at least their hearts had been large enough to aspire so nobly. When he had finished, there was not a man or a woman in the marketplace he had not moved to tears, not one in whom he had failed to awaken a hunger for past glories.

And it was his most successful day ever. When he left the market in the late afternoon, his pockets jingled with so many small coins that he should have been a target for every footpad and pickpocket in the Under-City, had they only known.

But unknown to Maelor himself, reports of his afternoon conjuring would begin to reach the temple in another day or two, and his name inevitably come to the attention of the Empress.

7

All things were well ordered and well founded at the
Heldenhof. Wooden floors had been polished to a
sheen like water, walls were bright with murals and
woven hangings; there was a wholesome smell of beeswax, of
stillrooms, and of rose leaves set out in open jars to keep the
air sweet.

Yet Sindérian could not help noticing, as a pair of aged
manservants led her and her companions through dim, cool
rooms and up two and a half flights of stairs, that the palace
was strangely quiet. She thought she could hear muffled voices
and footsteps coming from other chambers—and once the
click, clack, thump of a loom, faint with distance—but they
met no one along the way except for an ancient harper. It was
emptier here, perhaps, than it had been in happier times.

As they climbed, the broad wooden staircase grew narrower and narrower, steeper and steeper. At last the servants
brought them into a sunny room at the top of the house and
left them there alone. Sindérian felt a sharp twinge of disap-

pointment. Had she really expected the King would be there? Clearly, they were meant to wait in this room until he granted them an audience.

She studied her surroundings. Wide casement windows, thrown open to catch the breezes, flooded the room with northern sunlight and brought with it the sounds of stable-yards and mews, the fresh scent of gardens. There were two small tables cluttered with maps and sheets of parchment, a rug of woven grasses, and some elaborately carved oak chairs and benches; these were the only furnishings.

Walking over to one of the windows, she gazed down on a rambling landscape of shingled roofs. Far below, pigeons were feeding in a stone-flagged courtyard. Directly opposite her window, a lightning rod with green glass globes swung back and forth in the light breeze; otherwise there was nothing else on the same level. That last half-flight of stairs had brought them up to the highest room in the palace. It came to her then that this might be a place where King Ristil conducted the private business of governing his kingdom, far from prying ears.

Yet, there was no telling how long it would be before the King arrived. Maddeningly, Prince Ruan declined to take a seat (which kept Aell standing, too), but Faolein perched on a rack of antlers over the door, and Sindérian defiantly chose one of the chairs and sat down to wait.

Hours later she was still waiting. She divided her attention between watching the Prince pace the floor with an increasingly violent and restless motion, and keeping her eye on a stream of sand trickling through an hourglass up on the mantelpiece.

Already, she had risen from her seat twice to turn the glass over and start the sand moving again.

"After all," she said, throwing herself back down in the chair a third time, and making a mighty but ineffective effort to mask her own impatience, "if it were not for an amazing stroke of luck we might still be waiting *outside* the palace. Here, we know that King Ristil will see us *eventually*."

Ruan's only reply was a motion of the shoulders; whether he intended to convey something by this action or was merely fidgeting she was unable to decide.

An hour ago, one of the guards from the bridge had turned up briefly and whisked Aell away to some barracks or mess hall in order to feed him. Sindérian fervently wished that it had been otherwise, not because she grudged the man-at-arms his meal, but because she thought, on the whole, he would have made a more peaceful companion than the Prince.

"At least," she ventured once more, "any shred of doubt we had that Winloki and Guenloie are one and the same has van—" She broke off abruptly when brisk steps sounded outside, and a lean, big-boned, fair-haired man entered the room, closing the door behind him.

He wore a plain golden circlet and a heavy golden chain; his garments were of good cloth, neither rich nor splendid; but there was a certain authority in his bearing and manner that left no room for doubt: finally, they were in the presence of the King.

Sindérian sprang from her chair and sank down into a curtsy. Prince Ruan's bow was not very deep, just saved from insolence by its grace and elegance. It had been a long time, maybe, since he had gone down on one knee for anyone less exalted than his own grandfather. Faolein only ruffled up his feathers, staring at King Ristil with his round, yellow eyes.

"You find us in the midst of councils of war." The King motioned Sindérian and Ruan to be as they were before, likewise taking a seat for himself. "Otherwise, you would never have been kept waiting so long. My second son, Prince Kivik, is trying to hold a perilous position at Tirfang in the Drakenskaller Mountains, and we have been mustering a great host to ride to his rescue. It leaves tomorrow at first light."

At the names "Tirfang" and "Drakenskaller" Sindérian sat bolt upright in her chair. A series of images burned in her brain like cold fire: A long white road. A fortress with high, glittering walls. A cache of deadly jewels. Yet how could the mention of things she had never seen, places she had never been, conjure up such vivid and terrifying pictures?

"I have been told your names, and who you are," King Ristil went on. "But I can only guess what brings you so far in such perilous times."

Sindérian took in a deep breath and came straight to the point. "Nineteen years ago a wizard of my order was travelling in the north with an infant in his care. Both were lost. Yet we have reason to believe they may have come here."

A frown touched the King's face and then was gone. "I have been expecting you, or messengers like you, ever since Aethon of Sibri was here last autumn. But of course I have known for much longer that someday someone from Thäerie or Leal would come asking questions about a wizard and a child."

"Then Éireamhóine *was* here?" A glance flashed between Sindérian and her father. "Then how . . . That is, why did no one know? Wizards have been searching for him all these years.

The Nine Masters themselves have concentrated so much of their thought and will on finding him that any mention of his name, were it only a whisper, should have reached them long ago."

"But in this case he came late at night and few people knew of it." Ristil was silent for a time, creasing his brow, perhaps dredging up memories that would have grown dim after so much time. Finally he spoke. "Nineteen years ago, we admitted visitors far more readily. The wizard arrived one night between midnight and dawn. Only the guards who had escorted him in knew that he had come, and I swore both men to secrecy afterward. To me, Éireamhóine was already well known, for he had visited here often when I was a boy, and I was shocked to find him so changed. In truth, I hardly recognized him at first, he appeared so wild and strange. And what the guards did *not* know, because he revealed it to me alone, was that he had carried an infant in with him, hidden under his cloak.

"When the guards left us," the King continued, "he allowed me a glimpse of the child: a tiny but most beautiful little girl. He was confused in his mind and rambling in his speech, so that it was a long time before I had the whole story from him or heard how he had been separated from the nursemaid in the Cadmin Aernan, how difficult it had been caring for the child afterward."

Leaning forward in her chair, Sindérian opened her mouth to ask about Luenil, but then thought better of it and subsided. Prince Ruan, who had finally settled on a bench by the windows, shifted his jewel-bright gaze in her direction, as if he were aware of things unsaid though unable to divine their meaning.

After another pause, the King took up the story again. "Éireamhóine told me that his powers were waning, were almost spent. When the last spark was gone, he knew he would not be able to protect the child. Even worse, he was unsure if any of the Furiádhin had survived the avalanche, afraid that one or two might be following him, still intent on destroying Nimenoë's daughter. He thought that his company endangered the child, as even a ruined wizard must attract Ouriána's attention sooner or later. And so he had made up his mind to leave her with some trustworthy person, then lose himself in some distant part of the world. Pehlidor he said, or perhaps he might travel south, where the Dark Lady and her servants would never expect him to go. He asked me to take the child under my protection, and after thinking the matter over I consented."

"That was generous—but very dangerous!" Sindérian could only marvel at the courage that had prompted him to accept such a perilous charge for the sake of people half a world away.

He gave a slight shrug of his broad shoulders. "I had my own reasons for doing so. We remember the Old Alliance here in the north even if we no longer honor it. And of course, Ouriána of Phaôrax is nobody's friend. But most of all, I agreed to take the child because—by a coincidence so great as to be miraculous—my own sister had just given birth to twins only hours before, under this very roof."

As he spoke, Ristil began idly shuffling through the stacks of parchment. "You will understand that it was necessary to bring my sister into our confidence. When Éireamhóine told her his tale, she sat up in bed and cried out that we should

not turn the baby away—no, not if it were the spawn of dragons!"

"But by that time Guenloie would have been older than the
other two children by many months," said Sindérian, her dark
eyebrows twitching together. "How could anyone mistake her
for a newborn infant?"

"Éireamhóine thought there was some strong magic protecting the child, keeping her small—easily hidden, easily
overlooked—while the journey and the danger continued.
She grew as the other children grew after she came here.

"And it was not many months," the King added, with a
faint smile, "before people began to notice that Winloki, as we
named her, was a most precocious infant, walking and talking at a very early age, long before her supposed brother and
sister."

"And Éireamhóine? Have you seen him since?" Sindérian
asked eagerly. "Do you know where he is now?"

"No," said the King. "But your wizards should be looking for a bewildered old man, not the Éireamhóine of former
days."

Ristil sighed, put down the papers he had been handling. A
pair of lines between his eyes deepened. "The child that he left
behind came to be as dear to me as my own daughters. Yet I
have always known, my sister has always known, that a higher
destiny awaited her elsewhere, and that someday she would
leave us."

Sindérian's hands closed on the arms of the chair; she
leaned forward in her seat. "Then as you are already resigned
to losing the Princess, may we see her? May we tell her how
sorely she is needed in the south?"

Again the shadow of a frown passed over the King's fair, strong-featured face. "I wish that I could grant you that favor, but Winloki is not here," he said gravely.

Stunned, Sindérian sat back in the chair—fearing the worst, fearing they had come too late. She forced words out from a suddenly dry throat. "Not here? But where—"

"She is, or was, at Tirfang with my son and his men. But the messages we received from the Drakenskallers are now many days old. The Old Fortress may already be under attack, may already have fallen. I can't even tell you if she is still alive."

Sindérian and the Prince sat rigid and speechless with shock and disappointment, absorbing the news. Faolein fluttered down from his perch and landed on the back of his daughter's chair. Although she was aware of him, no thoughts passed between them; it seemed that *he* had no words either. Up on the mantelpiece the last few grains of sand slipped through the neck of the hourglass.

Prince Ruan was the first to break the silence. "I've heard tales of the Old Fortress at Tirfang. They call it invincible; they say that it never has and never could be taken by force."

"So they say," the King answered grimly. "But they also say that the fortress itself is perilous and unchancy, that those who have tried to defend it have always failed. It's as if the place breeds treasons and misfortunes like a disease." Then his shoulders went back and his chin came up; his light eyes blazed. "Be that as it may, I will not abandon my son—neither to the ghosts of Tirfang nor to the Eisenlonder barbarians. And so, against the advice of all my counselors, I will take my place at the head of the men who ride out tomorrow.

"If you wish," he added, "you may ride with me. But be

warned, it is a long journey from here to the Drakenskaller Mountains, and even moving with all speed we may come too late."

It was the most they could do to thank him and accept his offer of horses, still reeling as they were from the destruction of their hopes.

Dinner in Ristil's spacious, high-raftered hall was simple and hearty: fish, game, and rabbit; bread and plenty of honey; hot soup and blackberry tart. A modest, sensible repast for a royal household. Servants came and went swiftly and efficiently, setting tables with fine linens, lighting tall white candles, tossing herbs into fires to make the smoke sweet.

The Queen was there at the table, gracious and smiling, along with her bevy of small sons and daughters, and there were so many of Ristil's sisters and nieces present that Sindérian hardly knew how to keep them all straight. They ate from plates and bowls of thick-walled pottery, drank from beakers made of heavy glass, pale green and palest blue. It was, on the whole, a subdued gathering. Behind an outward display of quiet good cheer, it remained perfectly obvious that all were thinking of loved ones in danger at Tirfang.

After the meal, Sindérian and the Prince were separated. A serving woman led her to a small, clean chamber in an upper story. There were hides on the floor, a bright woven blanket on the bed, and a green bronze dragon with a fire in his belly and the light shining out through his eyes and mouth.

The woman indicated a pile of gifts the Queen had sent up for Sindérian's use on the journey ahead: a change of clothes and some clean shifts, a boxwood comb, soap, and two pairs of thin woolen stockings. There were also packets of healing herbs—only such simples as any good housewife might keep, but welcome nevertheless.

Sindérian felt tears sting her eyes as the kindness she had received in this place suddenly overwhelmed her. Not since Brill had she experienced such disinterested and unaffected generosity from people who had such heavy troubles of their own.

Whatever happens, may this house be safe, she thought fiercely. *Let the good they do here come back to them threefold.*

And when she was alone again, she began to work a spell of protection, dribbling wax from a burning candle onto the floorboards, sketching out the runes *tarien* and *dünadh,* pulling threads from the hem of her gown and weaving them into intricate knots. Finally, she whispered a *béanath,* a charm of blessing:

Dioho nélo ani ashladi anaëllen dénes nadath,
Dioho ansiansé altheönad angen,
Mûr dei deinnar dioho dir aldeinad ran.

It might not be much in a world at war, in an age of terrors; yet she hoped it would do them some good, however slight.

It was the dark hour before dawn when the same servant came back in with a light to rouse her. Sindérian had not undressed, so it was only the work of a moment to bind up her hair and pull on her boots. Meanwhile, the woman packed up the Queen's gifts in a leather pouch. Then it was back through the halls and out to a courtyard, where she found the Prince and Aell already waiting for her.

More servants, carrying candles in earthenware pots, appeared to light their way across the bridge through a series of small private gates in the walls dividing the town, then out through the main gate, to the Skyrran camp. Faolein stretched his wings, launched himself from Sindérian's shoulder, and flew on ahead.

Outside the great wooden palisade, both camps were astir with activity. By the light of hundreds of lanterns and torches, tents were taken down, folded, and packed away, and men were milling about on a thousand last-minute errands: dowsing campfires, inspecting their gear, tightening girths and adjusting saddles, loading up wagons. It seemed like they would never be ready in time, yet Sindérian knew from experience that they probably would. It was all so familiar: the brassy glint of armor by firelight, the smell of horses, leather, sweat, and excitement. She might almost have been back in Rheithûn before the fall of Gilaefri.

As the King had explained the evening before, he had divided his army into two unequal parts. The greater part consisted of more than a thousand riders, including the troops from Mistlewald and Arkenfell. These were men prepared to travel swiftly and with tight belts. In addition to what could be carried by a train of lightly burdened packhorses, they took only such food and water as they could individually carry with them, and they wore their shields and spears strapped at their backs. A smaller force, made up of foot soldiers as well as cavalry, would be escorting the heavily laden supply wagons at a necessarily slower pace. Neither party expected to meet up with the other until they reached the fortress in the mountains.

Amid all this movement and confusion it was difficult for Sindérian and her friends to locate King Ristil. They found him just as the first streaks of lavender and gold were painting the sky—and they might not have met up with him then, were it not for Prince Ruan's keen eyes. Surrounded by his captains and esquires, the King was grim and businesslike in armor of silver mail, and a sword with a golden hilt was strapped at his side.

"You three will ride with me in the vanguard," he told them. At his command, two grooms and a stable boy led forward the horses he had personally selected for their use, already harnessed and saddled.

By the time the rim of the sun was burning the eastern grasslands to gold, everyone was mounted and ready, awaiting the King's pleasure. Somehow, the milling crowds had resolved into an organized, disciplined force. At a sign from the King, horns blared, banners were raised, and the first troops set off. At the last moment, Faolein swooped down from a clear sky and established himself on his daughter's saddlebow.

Riding along on the elegant black mare the King had chosen for her, glancing back over her shoulder at the equally fine gelding that would carry her during the second leg of the journey, Sindérian felt an uncommon lift to her spirits. To be not only mounted but well mounted, to be riding out in the cool of the day—

Then an idea that had troubled her during the night came back to plague her, and her high spirits tumbled abruptly. For it was entirely possible—worse, it was more than likely—that she and her companions had arrived at Lückenbörg in advance of Ouriána's priests *simply because the Furiádhin had never been going there at all.* They had, as she knew very well, ways of learning things that were not altogether natural, not altogether right, methods that might have revealed to them weeks ago where the Princess was to be found.

And with that kind of knowledge, they might be *anywhere* on the road to Tirfang. They might already be so far ahead, it would be impossible to catch up to them.

After three days of hard riding, changing horses as necessary, King Ristil and his travel-stained and sunburned army reached a region of bony hills at the foot of the mountains, where they set up a camp in a rocky field between great tables of cracked stone.

Beyond the hills rose the gaunt peaks of the Drakenskallers, but the middle slopes—which ought to have been green at this time of year—were oddly and ominously white. All along, Sindérian had been testing the winds for omens. Those from the north and east brought ambiguous and confusing messages. At the same time, the stars continued to predict tumults and prodigies. The sight of those white slopes did nothing to allay her fears.

There had already been two short but fierce skirmishes with Eisenlonders along the way. Fortunately, in each case the advantage of surprise, strength, and familiarity with the terrain favored the Skyrrans, and their numbers had not been greatly reduced. But there were also encounters with hundreds of refugees, all of whom had news and stories to tell, and these encounters served to impress upon the King and his men how badly the war was actually going.

Not one of them, perhaps, had truly understood that the

Haestfilke had become like a desert, emptied of its inhabitants. Because relatively few of the dispossessed had managed to reach the capital, it had been easy to believe that the numbers Kivik and the marshals reported were greatly exaggerated. That illusion was difficult to maintain when a slow but steady stream of the hungry and the homeless came straggling down the road.

On this first evening in the foothills, some of the scouts brought another party of ragged women and ill-fed children into camp to speak with the King. They found him seated on a camp stool nursing a sprained wrist, where a blow had fallen during the last skirmish and been deflected by his vambrace. The news they carried with them was particularly grim: several days earlier and some eighty miles to the east, an Eisenlonder army of incalculable size and strength had been seen heading into the mountains, their destination unquestionably the Old Fortress at Tirfang, where Prince Kivik was known to be holed up with his men.

Ristil took care to show nothing of what he was feeling, either to the refugees or to his men; he kept a well-schooled face throughout the recital. But he spoke privately with Prince Ruan afterward. "The road from the east is longer and more difficult than the way we go, yet with such a start I hardly see how they could have failed to arrive at the Old Fortress by now. Meanwhile, *we* have at least another three days' ride ahead of us."

But with the mountains so near, the King instructed his falconers to send out a goshawk, one of Kivik's own messenger birds, trained to return to the place it had last been released. If the Old Fortress was already under siege, he thought it might help to stiffen their resistance if they knew that help was on the way, and what numbers he was bringing with him.

He watched the goshawk rise into the air, circle in the sky, take its bearings, and go winging off toward the peaks. Then he went back to the campfire and rejoined his captains. "An early night and an early rising," he announced, as cheerfully as he could.

Nevertheless, he had a sharp misgiving that sleep would elude him this night.

8

✳

With savage glee, the barbarians tore the dead bird apart, strewing the ground with its feathers and blood.

In the sudden silence up on the wall, Skerry materialized beside Kivik. "Let them gloat while they still can," he said, raising one hand in a fierce gesture. "At least we know our own messages were received, or else why was the bird flying back to us? We know that help is coming."

"Yes, but how soon—and how many men?"

At that moment, another wave of Eisenlonders came scrambling up the ladders and fought their way past the men at the parapet. Kivik and Skerry both waded in, shouldering a way through the press, hammering blows to right and left. A barbarian took a swipe at the Prince's head; he flung up his shield just in time and received a jarring blow that he felt all the way up his arm to his shoulder.

The battle raged on. The sun burned like an ember in the grey sky, and sleet continued to fall. It seemed to Kivik that he had been fighting for an eon, for an eternity, yet the sun had progressed only a little past noon. A sudden outcry brought him running back toward the gatehouse, forcing his way with shield and axe.

The giants had created a battering ram out of a tree trunk and two wagons, and were using it against the great double-sided gate. Timbers groaned and iron hinges screeched, but the gate that had never failed in a thousand years held. Kivik arrived on the walkway above the gatehouse just as the ice giants rammed again. He felt the shock through his feet, heard the protest of wood and metal below.

How much longer can it hold? he wondered. Forever, according to the legends, but his faith in the magical impregnability of the fortress was rapidly fading in the face of this determined attack.

He rallied his men, shouting an order to pick up some of the larger stones from the trebuchets and drop them on the giants. As soon as the ram rumbled into action and those who operated it came within range, the stones rained down. Most of them bounced off the giants' thick hides, doing little harm, but one rock larger than the rest landed directly on a giant's head and sent him toppling. The men cheered. The *Skørnhäär* roared and positioned the ram for another rush.

"More stones and bigger," Kivik called out to those behind him. "And send me some of the archers from the west wall."

Even in the inner wards, there was no avoiding the tumult and uproar of battle. Some of the refugees made a show of indifference, trying to carry on as usual, observing the rhythms of their everyday lives. Young children shrieked and played noisy games while their mothers bustled about the kitchen, boiling up cauldrons of very thin porridge, brewing unnourishing soups out of snow, chicken bones, and the occasional beetle or spider for flavoring. The blind man in the pantry amused his grandchildren by deftly constructing slingshots and whittling out wooden tops.

But in other parts of the fortress a sickness was spreading. Already weakened by the dwindling food supplies, many were sinking under the added burden of fear and uncertainty. *Or perhaps,* thought Winloki, *they are finally succumbing to a subtle malignancy in the fortress itself.*

Like her fellow healers, she tried to be everywhere at once. By midafternoon, dozens were burning up with fever; others had simply collapsed. She had nothing to give any of them but wormwood and clavender, which she dared not dispense with too liberal a hand, reckoning most of them too frail for a violent purge. In the infirmary casualties came in so quickly that before long there was no place to put them. At Thyra's suggestion half of the healers moved to an outer courtyard, where they set up tents and cots just inside the second gate. It was there that Winloki spent the next several hours, digging out arrowheads, slapping on poultices made of cobweb, and binding up shattered limbs.

"You ought to take care, Princess," Syvi admonished her as they worked side by side trying to keep the most desperate cases alive. The more experienced healer was herself pasty-faced and hollow-eyed, yet she knew her limits and had never been known to exceed them. "You don't eat, you don't rest—you ought to know the danger in draining too much of your strength. If you collapse or die, what good will you be to any of these men?"

Winloki answered absently, agreeing to eat a bite and take a nap eventually, a promise she had no intention of keeping—or of breaking either, it passed so quickly out of her mind—and went on applying tourniquets, cauterizing wounds, and working spells to stop the flow of blood.

Most of the day had already slipped away before she realized that one man or the other seemed always to be following her, that some familiar faces were turning up again and again as she moved between the tents.

"My cousin has ordered you to *guard me!*" she accused the boy Haakon as he helped her to lift an unconscious man onto a cot. By this time she was dripping with sweat and bloody to her elbows—she who used to pride herself on the neatness and dispatch of all her healings. "Did you suppose that I wouldn't notice? I may be distracted, but I'm not yet blind!"

Over by one of the tent poles she spotted a man with a hard, sober face trying to look inconspicuous. If Haakon and Arvi were there, she had little doubt there were other guards lurking in the vicinity. "Truly," she said under her breath, but loudly enough that they both might hear her, "it seems there are *better things* you might be doing!"

The youth blushed and ducked his head. "We do as Prince Kivik bids us, my lady. Your danger may not be immediate, but when and if it is—"

"Danger?" Winloki gave him an incredulous look, though all the time her hands were busy cleaning, bandaging, rubbing on salve from an iron pot. "Why should I be in more danger than anyone else? It ought to be *less.* Surely even Eisenlonders respect the sanctity of healer's grey!"

Arvi abandoned the imperfect concealment of the tent pole and came over to stand beside her. Not so long as ten days ago he had been carried into the fortress as cold and stiff as a frozen corpse, after one of the sorties. It had taken all of Winloki's skill, all the power of the runes on her ring, to bring him back again. "I suppose there must have been healers in some of those settlements we saw, the ones that were levelled and burned," he said. "Where are they now? It's certain we never met any among the refugees."

The din, which had receeded while she worked, broke out afresh. Men swore or vomited in pain; some of the more serious cases babbled and begged for relief. Winloki pressed the heels of her hands to her temples, willing the pounding to cease. Yet she had never been one to give way or to ask for protection, and she was not about to do so now.

"If the barbarians *have* been slaughtering healers, you ought to be guarding Syvi, Thyra, and all of the rest of them—I can look after myself."

As if in answer, she heard the crash of a ram, followed by wild horns blowing. A volley of rocks overshot the walls and landed not far from the tents, striking sparks off the marble pavement.

All this time, the gates had continued to hold, though one side hung slightly askew on twisted hinges. A party led by one of Kivik's captains began to build a barrier of carts and wagons just inside, an added precaution should the gates finally fail. It must have been a powerful magic the witches had woven into the fabric, or the timbers would have split long ago.

For Kivik up on the wall-walk, exhausted after hours of fighting, it seemed that his movements had slowed, that every movement he made required an infinite effort. The only thing

keeping him alive was a similar lethargy on the part of his opponents.

He had discarded his shield as much too heavy, had been
forced to abandon the axe when it lodged in an enemy's skull
and refused to come loose. He was fighting two-handed, using
a sword that somebody tossed him when he lost the axe. There
was a hard ache in his chest, and pain stabbed at him with every
breath; he thought that some of his ribs must be broken.

It hardly mattered by now, because he knew he was going
to die. The battle had continued too long; no skirmish in the
field had ever lasted for so many hours. His men were dropping from sheer exhaustion, but the numbers of the enemy
were constantly refreshed. He fought by instinct rather than
conscious thought. When two men tried to engage him at
once, he sidestepped to avoid a blow, raised his sword, and
struck and struck again. Blood fountained, turning to ice in
the freezing air, landing with a faint rattle on the stonework.

Then, unexpectedly, lightning leaped across the sky; thunder crashed and roared. The snow stopped falling—not gradually, but suddenly, unnaturally. Kivik watched in a daze as
all of the snow that was in the air rose up with a *whoooosh* in
a great turning cloud and went whirling away into the sky. A
hush fell over the fortress and the enemy camp below.

In that moment of dreamlike clarity, he forced his way to
the parapet and gazed out across the valley, watching the approach of three gaunt figures in scarlet cloaks who rode at a
headlong pace through the ranks of the Eisenlonders.

The air still crackled with the promise of lightning. On
they rode, these phantoms in red, their white hair lifted by
the speed of their passage, and the dark mass of the barbar-

ian host gave way before them. So pale they were, their faces frozen to a heartless immobility, that Kivik nearly mistook them for the ghosts of dead witch-lords come back to claim their own.

One of the specters lifted a withered hand, and a spiderweb of purple lightning flashed across the sky. The concussion that followed shook the wall under Kivik's feet, knocking him over; others, not so lucky, were thrown from the ramparts. He could hear them screaming all the way down.

Then a section of the fortifications close to the gate began to sway. Those who could flung themselves to safety where the ramparts stood firm; those who could not sent up a wail. Bits of mortar and fragments of flying stone went racketing and tumbling as the wall that had never been breached in a thousand years crashed down, taking more than a hundred men with it.

9

*

They were a day and a half riding through the foothills, a shapeless landscape of dry grasses and rough stones. By noon of the second day King Ristil's army began their ascent of the mountains. At first the way was easy, the road leading through grassy uplands where the slope was gentle. Later, they came into a forested region of birch, alder, and hawthen, where it was necessary to slow the pace. There the ground was steep and rocky, and the trees came right down to the edge of the road, causing the way to narrow until no more than six or seven men could ride abreast. In the disciplined confusion of re-forming the line, those to the rear had a long wait before they were able to fall in and follow after the leaders.

Riding along beside the King, Sindérian finally found an opportunity to ask him the question she had been longing to ask since their first meeting. "You told us," she said, "that Éireamhóine was separated from the Princess's nurse in the Cadmin Aernan. Yet I'm *certain* I recognized her at the Heldenhof—and more than that, she knew me, too!"

All along King Ristil had maintained an appearance of un-ruffled serenity, but Sindérian was healer enough to sense the taut nerves, knotted muscles, and clenched jaw beneath his outward display of calm. She knew that he had been think-ing of his son and adopted niece, that behind that unclouded blue-eyed gaze a thousand fears were gnawing at his mind. But now he smiled at some pleasant memory, and his whole aspect brightened.

"The answer to that is such a remarkable story, I wonder if you would even believe it." He laughed and shook his head. "And yet—why not? No doubt you've heard more incredible things at your school for wizards on Leal.

"My tale begins more than two years after the wizard brought Winloki to Lückenbörg. It was that time at the end of winter when it first becomes possible to cross the Cadmin Aernan, and a large party of merchants was travelling from Hythe to sell their goods in Arkenfell and Skyrra. Strange things are often seen and experienced in those mountains, as perhaps you know, but none more amazing, I think, than the sight that met these travellers as they neared the summit: a beautiful young woman encased in a block of ice. One of them said that she looked like an enchanted princess sleeping in a crystal coffin; another said no, she resembled a mermaid or a water nymph, floating just under the surface of the water. He almost believed he could see her long brown hair moving in an invisible current."

Caught up in his own story, the King had relaxed. His jaw unclenched; some of the rigidity was gone from the muscles in his neck and shoulders. "They thought it would be a fine thing to take the frozen maiden with them, as a kind of curio.

So they loaded the block onto a sledge, covering her up with their furs and woven blankets to keep the ice from melting, and made their way down from the Cadmin Aernan, through Arkenfell, and across the waters of the Necke to Skyrra. Spring is slow to arrive in the north, but by the time they came to the channel the ice was already slowly melting.

"*I* first saw her at a village not far from the coast, where I used to keep a hunting lodge. By then, very little of the ice remained. The crystal coffin had become a crystal shroud, a thin skin of ice clinging to her own skin. Still, she was a wonder! She looked so fair and so perfectly lifelike, I knelt down beside her to take a closer look. You will be thinking," he added, with a faint reminiscent smile, "that I woke the lady with a kiss."

Sindérian nodded. That was *exactly* what she had been thinking.

"I believe I had some such notion, but there was no need. Hardly had my knees touched the ground when the last of the ice melted away. Then all of her lovely color came back, she opened her eyes and sat up on her couch of furs, with the water pouring off of her and all her clothes and hair streaming wet.

"All memory of her life until that moment was gone," he continued. "She could not remember her name, or where she had been before the mountains, or even what it was that brought her into the high reaches of the Cadmin Aernan. I insisted that she travel with me back to the Heldenhof, and there—because she was in a sense newborn—she was taken to the nursery and cared for along with the children, until she grew stronger."

"And you never guessed who she might be?" Sindérian said, with a skeptical quirk of her dark brows.

Ristil's chestnut stallion shied at something in the road, but he controlled it with a sure hand on the reins. "I suspected she was the girl that Éireamhóine lost between Hythe and Arkenfell. The wizard told me he cast a spell of protection in the last moments before the avalanche hit them. A spell wrought in haste, he said, and he hardly dared to imagine it had been successful, but still there was a chance, a small chance . . ."

The King shrugged. "I could hardly proclaim the truth to the world without telling the tale of the wizard and Winloki. And as for the young woman herself, it seemed to me that she had *chosen* not to remember. Éireamhóine had told me enough of her unhappy story; I hadn't the heart to revive those bitter memories."

"And you fell in love with her and married her."

A cold wind came down the mouth of the pass and lifted his bright golden hair. "My sons loved her long before I did. The death of her child—from which I believe she suffered deeply, even without remembering the cause of her pain—the fact that *they* were still mourning their own mother, these things seemed to strike a chord of sympathy between them. It was my eldest who gave her the name of Sigvith, while she was still with them in the nursery. But I was not far behind Arinn and Kivik in learning to love her. She was so beautiful and good, what did it matter to me who or what she had been before? If I hadn't already two sons, perhaps my jarls and thanes would have protested more vigorously when I announced I would marry her. But in the end, they were more than reconciled, for as you have seen she is as kind and gracious as she is beautiful."

Sindérian nodded thoughtfully, remembering Luenil as she

had been at seventeen: bitter, sorrowful, defiant—reckless of her own safety. It was pleasant to have seen her as she was now, in comely, prosperous, graceful middle age. This one time the Fates had been kind.

Leaving the mixed forest of the lower slopes for the cliffs and gorges, the woods of pine, spruce, and fir farther up the mountain, was like riding from summer through winter's door.

It began with wisps and rags of vapor, and the sun making rainbows through shimmering veils of mist and cloud. Then the mist thickened into a fog so dense it muffled all sound. As the fog grew colder and colder, moisture froze on Sindérian's eyelashes and hair; her face began to feel like a mask of ice. At the first intimation of sunlight up ahead, she drew a deep sigh of relief.

But when she finally emerged from the fog it was into a cold flurry of snowflakes. And the deeper the army rode into the mountains, the heavier and heavier fell the snow, until soon they were forced to plough a way through high drifts blocking their road.

"No, never before at this time of year, not within memory," the King said in response to Prince Ruan's question. "But there may be ice giants somewhere about, and it's said that they make their own weather."

Whatever the cause, the weather grew worse. A great wind came skirling through the mouth of the pass, hurling sleet and snow into their faces. For Sindérian, swaddled in a borrowed blanket over her cloak, there were times when the men and horses just ahead of her appeared as nothing more than bulky grey shadows. Then lightning flared and a barrage of thunder rolled down the mountainside, setting the horses dancing and fighting at their bits. She felt the shock of it carried on the air even before she heard it.

Not a natural storm, she decided, every hair on her head tingling. Far from any ordinary clash of the elements, she believed she could sense a conscious intention behind every last snowflake and freakish turn of weather. But the tempest soon passed, all but the shrilling wind and a light fall of snow. In the woods to either side of the road, icy pine needles rattled in the blast, and the horses were so dashed and buffeted by the gale, which seemed to come at them from every direction at once, they could make little progress.

The sun dipped toward the horizon; a slip of dirty yellow moon came up. Though no one wished to stop any longer than necessary in such miserable conditions, it was obvious that the horses could not go on forever. When the King finally called for a halt, the riders began to set up camps under the trees and to search the area for pinecones and seasoned wood. A hundred communal fires sprang up in the shadows, snapping and sputtering, struggling to stay alive in the falling snow. Soon, a hundred tin kettles were hard at work boiling up water for soup or comfrey-root tea.

Finding a place near one of the fires, Sindérian settled down with her back to a fallen log and her legs drawn up to her chest inside the blanket and cloak. After a while her teeth stopped chattering. The horses made a kind of wall screening their riders from the wind, and a layer of dead pine needles made a damp cushion that was better at least than sitting on the ground. Just outside the circle of firelight, Faolein landed on a snowy branch overhead, where he fluffed himself up and drew in his head until he was nothing but a round ball of feathers.

It seemed to Sindérian that she must have dozed off for a time, because the next thing she knew a dim light was sifting through the branches, and she was surrounded by the groans and faint curses of men heaving themselves up off the ground, brushing themselves off, and gathering up their things.

She lifted her head from where it had been pillowed on her knees and rose stiffly to her feet. Stamping her boots in order to bring life back to her frozen limbs, she looked to the left and right, wondering what had become of her father during the night. The sparrowhawk was nowhere in sight. When she cast her thought out in search of him, she made only a tenuous contact. He seemed to be well but far away, higher up where the air was more rarified.

Reassured by the thought that it would hardly be possible for *him* to lose *her* so long as she travelled with such a vast host, she headed out of the trees, with both her horses following behind on a leading rein. When she reached the road it was to walk out into a sleety sort of drizzling rain.

All around her riders were mounting up, getting ready to ride. So it seemed that she had somehow slept through breakfast—or perhaps there had been no breakfast at all. She adjusted the hood of her cloak and took the bay gelding by the bridle. As she swung up into the saddle, a cloud bank to the east parted, and sunlight erupted like a fountain of gold above the peaks.

By noon, the sky was a brilliant, cloudless blue and the weather had turned distinctly sultry. Ice and snow melted into slush, the way grew slippery, and the entire line slowed to a walk.

Long before evening, everyone was mired in a river of mud. The footing had become so treacherous, it was necessary to dismount and wade through the muck, leading the horses. Toiling along with a hand on each bridle, Sindérian tried to avoid the places where the mire was deepest, but her skirts were already soaked with muddy water halfway to her knees.

But at least, she reflected sourly, she had the satisfaction of knowing that Prince Ruan, trudging along immediately ahead of her, looked scarcely better off. If he walked with a lighter step than anyone else, if he rarely struggled to keep his footing, the horses he led still saw to it that he was splashed with his fair share of the mud. His hair hung down in damp strands like tarnished silver, and when he looked back to see how she was faring, she saw he had a long streak of mud on one side of his face.

By the time that Faolein returned, landing so softly on the black mare's saddle that she never heard him, Sindérian was so intent on finding the best footing for herself and the horses that she failed to even notice his presence until his voice spoke inside her head. Then she glanced up with a scowl, to meet the sparrowhawk's inscrutable golden stare.

Ask to speak to the King. I have news for him—and not of the best.

Sindérian's request was relayed to the King, passing by word of mouth from one person to the next. She knew when it reached the front of the line because someone shouted out an order and all progress stopped. She expected an answer to be relayed back to her, but Ristil himself came striding through the filth, flanked by two of his captains.

Resting herself against the gelding's solid flank, she repeated everything her father told her, as quickly as the words passed from his mind into hers.

I have flown as far as the Old Fortress, said Faolein. *There has been a great battle there: a section of the outer wall has been reduced to rubble, the second gate is broken, and the courtyards are filled with bodies.*

"If the Eisenlonders are in possession of the fortress, all of *our* people will be dead." King Ristil seemed to age before Sindérian's eyes; the lines in his face deepened and his shoulders drooped. "The barbarians never take captives and they slay without mercy. My son, my niece, young Skerry—everyone will be dead."

"Perhaps not all of them are dead," she replied after a swift consultation with her father. "When Faolein was there, the Eisenlonders had not reached the innermost courtyards. It's true that both sides are greatly diminished, and the fighting is sporadic, but *someone* was defending the third gate."

A silence fell as everyone looked to the King to see how he would react. Very pale and set of countenance, he stood staring down at the ground. "We will continue on," he said at last. "There may only be a handful of our people left, and we may come too late to save even them. But either way—"

His chin went up and his eyes acquired a steely glint. "Either way, we will still ride there with all speed—if only to bury our dead."

IO

✳

The city of Xanthipei in Mirizandi—gorgeous, corrupt, glamourous—baked in the heat, dazzling with light and color, stinking like a midden. If rebellion was also stewing there, Prince Cuillioc had not detected so much as a whiff under the pervading ambiance.

On the palm-tree-lined streets the usual traffic of sedan chairs, elephants, camels, and sweating pedestrians was no less boisterous than any other day, no less varied and brilliant in its exotic reds, tangerines, yellows, and aquas, even if it did move a little more sedately under the broiling rays of the sun. Parrots molted in silver cages; dancing girls shimmered on open-air stages in the bazaar; brothels and opium dens did their usual brisk business. In short, the people of Xanthipei—so easily and improbably subdued by the Pharaxion invaders—carried on much as always, while Prince Cuillioc, his household of twenty knights and one undersized page, his fighting men billeted throughout the city, and his mob of generally contentious Pharaxion nobles had melded so completely into the Mirazhite way of life, the Prince sometimes wondered who, exactly, had conquered whom.

So when a woman's shrieks ripped through the air one day as he attempted to while away the tedium of a hot afternoon, sipping chilled wine in the shade of a fig tree and playing a game of three-sided *chaet* with two of his knights, he was slow to react. He had drifted so long in the dream of luxury and vice that was the Mirazhite capital, the woman's first screams produced only a feeble sensation of curiosity. Only when sounds of a vigorous struggle and a babble of angry voices followed was Cuillioc shaken from his customary afternoon torpor. Abandoning his shady nook, he set off in the general direction of the commotion, and those of his attendants who were not too sleepy (or too far gone with drink) went straggling after him.

It was the twenty-first day of a stupendous hot spell in Mirizandi. Day by day, the swamplands adjacent to the city were drying up; in many places they were already more mud than water. Sometimes crocodiles crawled out of the ooze and waddled through the outlying neighborhoods, scattering the people and stampeding the livestock; occasionally, someone or something failed to move fast enough. No one dared to meddle with the creatures, for fear of a powerful cult that held them sacred.

Along with the heat, summer brought forth a prodigious burst of growth in the gardens of the Citadel. There was, Cuillioc considered, something vaguely monstrous about all this vegetable exuberance: the immense sulphur-colored lilies under his bedchamber window that scented the air with a cloying perfume; the fast-growing creeper that put forth flowers the color of red-hot iron and swallowed up arbors, pergolas, and colonnades so completely that no evidence of the structures beneath remained; even the feverish haste of lemons, oranges, and apricots, which brought forth starry white blossoms and sun-colored fruits at the same time, and in such unnatural abundance.

Yet the same heat that made the plants respond so wonderfully had a very different effect on the Prince and his people. The thirty-six men-at-arms who formed his garrison at the Citadel had grown lethargic, putting off their battle armor, wrapping it up in silk, and storing it away in cedar chests to keep it from rusting in the humid climate. Even his troublesome courtiers seemed content to idle away the unbearably hot days in the palace gardens, waited on by deft, silent, ever-smiling Mirazhite servants, and to spend their nights in wine shops and pleasure houses, or in the erratic pursuit of some ultimate experience of voluptuous decadence out on the streets, at the beast shows, or in the rituals of the so-called mystery cults.

When Cuillioc woke in the mornings with the fumes of wine still in his head, he vowed to do better. He needed, above all, to remember he was a soldier of the Goddess, the sword in her hand, the instrument of her will. Yet somehow the weeks crawled by in a glut of heat, idleness, and stale, stale pleasures, and all of his best intentions amounted to nothing.

By the time the Prince arrived at the place where the screams had originated, the incident was already over. Nevertheless, it had served to stir up his blood and pique his curiosity, if only a little, and he was inclined to investigate.

Cuillioc glanced around the sunny courtyard. It seemed unusually crowded for the hottest part of the day. He spotted several of the demure, dark-eyed servants; a handful of men from the garrison; a number of his Pharaxion nobles, sweating in their satins and rich brocades. No one seemed willing to meet his eyes. He finally singled out the one person likely to know what it was all about: the minor lord he had appointed as his palace chamberlain.

He could, when he chose, be most thoroughly the Empress's son: glaring out of the same green eyes, staring down the same straight, aristocratic nose. He could draw himself up to his full height, which was by no means paltry, and cause men like the chamberlain to wilt beneath his gaze.

"Your pardon, Great Prince," was the quaking response. "I regret the matter came to your attention." The man wiped his forehead with a bit of silk. "The situation is simply this: three of your men have been keeping women here, slaves from Oméia and Chalézia they purchased from the pleasure houses. Now one of the women is dead and the others are found to be dangerously ill. Of course I had them removed immediately, lest the contagion spread. What you heard was only their protest at being cast out into the streets during the heat of the day. There is no—"

He was interrupted by the arrival of a grim little procession. The deformed priest Iobhar limped into the courtyard, mumbling prayers and liberally suffusing the air with incense, and two gaunt figures dressed in black sackcloth followed after him, carrying the dead woman in on a litter. Those they passed drew back hastily, crooking their fingers in the ancient sign against misfortune.

Cuillioc frowned in the fierce southern sunlight. "What is the meaning of this?"

The acolytes, Maël and Omair, stopped moving at once and put down the litter, but Iobhar, white-faced and ghastly in his crimson robes, continued to hover ghoulishly over the corpse. "This woman died in an advanced state of wickedness," he intoned portentously. "Therefore, we perform a rite of purification to cleanse the premises."

The Prince raised a skeptical eyebrow. "Until the rest of us stop *living* in an advanced state of wickedness, I don't see the use."

Iobhar bared his yellow teeth, hissing out something under his breath. Three or four courtiers tittered appreciatively until Cuillioc cut the laughter short with a quelling glance, feeling faintly ashamed of himself for having provoked it.

Still, it was hard to see how the transgressions of a single slave woman—who did not even sin of her own free will—could amount to very much. A foreign slave at that, he noted idly, of a much darker hue than the warm-skinned natives, with a curious undertone to her lips and fingernails, which in death had turned an ugly blue-grey.

Sudden vertigo overcame him, standing there in the glaring sunlight. He sat down abruptly on a low marble wall encircling a fishpond choked with water weeds. At the sight of all the pale, flabby, perspiring faces gathered around him, Cuillioc felt more and more queasy. *Too late,* he thought. *At the very least too late for any of the men who consorted with those women.* He wondered how many might already be ill.

On the other side of the courtyard, the chamberlain was conducting a low-voiced conversation with two of the servants. The Prince summoned him back with a peremptory gesture. "I wish to know more about whatever it was that killed this woman. It might be anything: a plague, a murrain, a putrid fever. We know nothing of diseases that breed in this climate!"

"I promise you, Great Prince, you have *no* need for concern," the chamberlain answered hastily. "The servants have just been telling me they recognize the symptoms, and it is *a slave's disease only.* They say many are afflicted during the summer months, and most of those die, but it *never* touches the free citizens, not even those of the lowest class."

Dabbling his fingers in the tepid water, Cuillioc caught a glimpse of something stirring below in the dark tangle of roots and stems. He leaned a little closer. Beneath a scum of dead insects floating on the surface, he spied three great carp, their armored scales gleaming bright orange, deepest indigo, and bloody crimson. In the ceaseless motion of their spotted fins and gossamer tails they appeared to be fanning themselves. Yet even the fish, he observed wryly, could obtain no relief. They were as glassy-eyed and enervated by the heat as he was.

Glancing up from the carp pond, he met the enigmatic gaze of the furiádh priest. "You are older than I by half a century, Iobhar, and you've seen more of the world. Have you ever heard of a disease like this one—so particular about who it strikes down?"

"I have not," answered Iobhar, bowing his white head in elaborate humility. "It's true that whenever there is an epidemic in a great city like our own Apharos, the ill-fed, the unwashed, and the ill-housed suffer the soonest, suffer the longest. But once any disease takes hold in the city, men and women of the highest rank are no more likely to be spared than anyone else. I find it difficult to imagine how it could be any different here."

"That is what I thought, too." With a languid gesture, Cuillioc motioned to one of his knights. "Find me a doctor of physick, Gerig. Discover, if you can, who is the finest physican in all Xanthipei, and bring him here to the palace to speak with me."

With the excitement apparently over, the Prince returned to his shady spot under the fig tree and sat down again by the ivory game board. Studying the position of his playing pieces, he reached out absently for the silver cup he had left behind earlier. Finding the goblet almost empty, he put it aside with a grimace of disgust.

What *business* had he addling his wits for weeks on end with the strong southern wines, he asked himself sternly. Then he remembered a cooling drink they made here called *julla*, which seemed to be nothing more than rose petals and lemon juice added to cold water, and he thought that a man of sense might choose that beverage instead. He signaled to his page, the nameless urchin he had snatched from the galleys almost on a whim.

But by the time the boy stood before him, half sheepish and half defiant, Cuillioc had already changed his mind. He found himself wondering: was the water here safe? And he was suddenly appalled by his own negligence, for that was a question he should have asked weeks ago. If the usual conditions of war hardly applied here, that was still no excuse for such abominable carelessness.

"You have been in the kitchens," he said to the boy. "Where do the cooks get the water they use in preparing our food? Are there cisterns in the palace? Are there wells?"

The urchin answered with a shake and then a nod of his head. He never spoke when he could avoid it; he was that wary of losing his place and being sent back to the galleys. When he did speak, it was only to parrot those things he heard in his capacity as the Prince's spy. Of his own past, of his present doings, he said not a word, and no amount of kindness could win his confidence—nor could any amount of scrubbing or feeding, apparently, make him more pleasing to look at. He was as unlovely in the wrinkled silks of his newfound prosperity as he had ever been in the direst extremes of poverty. Yet, oddly, Cuillioc trusted him, if only because the boy's best interests were so intimately linked with his own.

When the boy remained silent, one of the Prince's opponents spoke up from across the *chaet* board. "I've seen the servants soak leaves of some foul-smelling herb in their water before they drink it. If it tastes as bad as it smells—" He shuddered dramatically.

"It's the same spice they put on everything they eat," added the other player, a knight named Brihac. "Everything they cook in the bazaar reeks of it."

But Cuillioc was scarcely listening. That the water came from wells inside the Citadel was all he needed to know. He sent the boy to the cellars for a cup of the rose-scented *julla,* then returned his attention to the ivory game board.

The game went so slowly that after a time his attention began to wander. Stifling a yawn, he glanced around the garden. In the branches overhead he recognized a small green bird that sometimes raided crumbs from his breakfast table. She was beating her wings and darting about, trying to attend to the needs of a nestful of newly hatched youngsters. By his count, this was the third family she had attempted to raise since early spring, and if she seemed a little desperate in her efforts to provide for her brood it was hardly surprising—all of the previous fledglings had died before they left the nest.

All at once, Cuillioc's drowsy sense of well-being fled, and again he felt nausea clutch at his stomach. In the midst of this superabundance of life there was too much death, too many fatalities to be quite natural, like the slave woman earlier, like the baby birds who died before they even learned to fly. Even the drowned dragonflies floating in the gilded basin of the nearest fountain filled him with a sudden sense of dread.

Something had changed. When the old lethargy threatened to take over again, this time Cuillioc found the energy to fight it off. It was as if all the vessels in his heart had shriveled and narrowed in the heat—but now they expanded with a fresh flow of blood.

This change, however, was not an altogether pleasant one. He spent all the rest of that day in impatient anticipation, waiting for the young knight Gerig to produce the physician. When evening brought neither Gerig nor the doctor, the Prince dined with a very poor appetite and went early to his bedchamber.

As he stood by an open window listening to insects creak in the hot, humid darkness, he cast his mind back, reliving the events of the summer, from the time he first landed with his sixty galleys of war, twelve hundred fighting men, and that viper's nest of ambitious minor nobles, backstabbing place-seekers, and petty schemers, which his mother the Empress-Goddess had seen fit to inflict on him—whether to bolster his perceived inadequacy or to punish it, he could never be certain.

He had begun wisely, that much he knew, by sending his scouts out to the rice fields, rain forests, and primitive little villages surrounding the city on three sides. The scouts all returned with similar reports: the farmers and villagers were just as complacent and superstitious as the city dwellers, and far less equipped to fight off an invasion.

Cuillioc remembered asking himself: *If the treasures of Mirizandi are to be so easily gained, why has no one ever invaded before? What do the kings and princes of Nephuar, Cenuphar, and Opidäia know that we never learned on Phaôrax?*

Surely it had been sensible to choose to investigate? To seek the answers to all such questions before he went blundering off with his army into the fields and forests, or gave up the thick walls of the Citadel for some other position of unknown strength? But then came the heat—so relentless, so intense—and all of his zeal had melted away.

Idiot. Witling, he scolded himself now. *You knew all along that conquering this city was only the means to an end. Mirizandi and her people are nothing to Ouriána—or at least they've no place in her immediate plans, except as a source of wealth to pay off her mercenaries fighting in the north. She wants to control those fabulous mines that rumors place somewhere in the interior.*

How could he have forgotten any of this, particularly with Ouriána's priest always on hand? All during that wasted summer the only exception to the general torpor and stagnation had been Iobhar, haunting the dim corridors and shady gardens of the Citadel like some irksome spirit in his heavy red robes, exhorting the Prince to action.

Cuillioc felt sick at heart when he considered what a tale the furiádh priest would have to tell when they returned to Apharos. He often thought he saw contempt in that bloodless face, disdain in those brass-colored eyes. Priests, warriors, magicians—the Furiádhin were not even human anymore, they were so steeped in sorcery, and it was useless to try to read their emotions. Yet this much he knew from experience: Iobhar hated anyone the Empress had ever honored with a scrap of her affection. He would do her son every injury and disservice he possibly could.

And now he need not do *anything*. To simply tell the truth would be enough.

Crossing the room with a purposeful stride, Cuillioc took a handful of rolled parchments from a shelf and carried the maps over to the bed.

Unfurling the first one he traced with his forefinger each of the features his scouts had sketched in: the city here; the indented line of the shore; a village; a long stretch of forest and swamp; the nearest cities, Persit, Meraz, and Pira. And all of the plans he had made before, the tactics he had devised with the help of these same maps and somehow forgotten, they all came swarming back into his brain.

In a sudden fervor, he fell to his knees by the bed and performed the rituals of homage to the Goddess. For the first time in weeks he left nothing out, went through all of the hymns and chants without hurrying through a single passage.

When he was finished he felt somehow cleaner and curiously exalted.

The knight named Gerig was out all night, ranging through the city, first pursuing rumors of a highly skilled and revered physician, then pursuing the man himself. He finally caught up with him just after daybreak.

But when the physician arrived at the Citadel, solemn in dark green robes and a five-cornered black hat, he had nothing much to tell, beyond what the chamberlain had already passed on. "It is the Summer Fever, a disease that crops up only in the slave quarters. I can assure you, Great Prince, there is no reason for you to feel the least alarm."

They were in one of the dim, thick-walled audience chambers. If there was any flicker of emotion in those jet-bead eyes, it was there and gone before the Prince could even be sure that he had seen it.

"How can a disease know a free man from a slave? How did *this one* gain such a fine discrimination?"

"There are many mysteries of the human body we do not comprehend." The doctor continued to speak with that same unnerving calm. "But of course there are many theories: that the disease arises from an excess of the melancholy humor, that it comes of a derangement in the animal spirits. Others say—But I hardly think these abstruse speculations would interest you. Only know this: we who have lived in this city all of our lives have no fear. Why, then, should you?"

After he dismissed the physician, Cuillioc turned to Iobhar. At his request, the priest had stood in the shadows as a silent witness to the whole conversation. "A very smooth and plausible liar, I think, but a liar nonetheless."

"He is lying about something," Iobhar agreed. "Yet I believe he spoke truly when he said the citizens have no fear for themselves. We know how people react to even the *threat* of an epidemic illness. They have a hundred different ways of warding off contagion—with fumes and smokes, talismans and philtres—though few of those measures succeed. I have seen nothing like that here. The inhabitants do seem to be convinced this Summer Fever cannot touch them."

The Prince changed positions in his chair. "And should we, because of that, be just as certain of our *own* safety?"

"I would not advise it, Great Prince. For your own protection, I suggest you remove yourself and the noble lords of your household out of the city, at least until we know more. You might go to your flagship. The winds blow inland, and the air will be purer out on the water."

Cuillioc studied the furiádh in a tight-lipped silence. The effects of yesterday's uproar were still with him, stirring up his sluggish blood; his thoughts were more lucid now than they had been for many weeks. And first among those thoughts was an impression that Iobhar had been uncommonly helpful, unusually forthcoming with what he knew and what he guessed.

Sweat gathered in the palms of the Prince's hands, and he could feel it trickling down his sides; early as it was, it promised to be hotter than the day before. He was not quite certain which disturbed him more: the idea of Iobhar as his friend and counselor, or as his undeclared enemy. Weighing one thing against the other, he decided he would rather have one of the sacred crocodiles crawl into bed with him and declare undying friendship than form even a temporary alliance with the priest.

Nor could he dismiss the all-too-likely possibility that

Iobhar and his Pharaxion nobles had fabricated an elaborate hoax in order to further some convoluted scheme. They had been quiet far too long. Certainly, he could not imagine any one of them balking at the murder of a slave; most of them had connived at much worse. The only trustworthy men in the Citadel were those of his own household.

But if there were plots, it would be better to pretend that he had no suspicions. So with his most guileless smile, he thanked the priest for advice he had no actual intention of following. To leave the city in Iobhar's charge? He was not such a fool as that.

"If I may make a suggestion, Great Prince. Your little rat of a page seems to be cultivating friendships in the kitchen, and indeed all through the servant's quarters. Perhaps you should instruct him to question his friends about the disease."

Cuillioc turned the idea over in his mind, trying to uncover the hidden snare. Never had Iobhar made a suggestion that was not part of some scheme. Yet after a long period of examination Cuillioc could only conclude that this time his own advantage and Iobhar's marched hand in hand.

Accordingly, he did as the priest advised, sent for his page, and gave him his instructions.

11

✴

The sun dipped behind the mountains, but King Ristil would brook no delay. Dusk lasted long at this time of year, and he was determined to keep his riders moving.

So great was his desire for speed that they rode for a time under the stars. More than once, those who rode to the fore nearly came to grief riding too close to the edge of a sheer drop, or barely missed tumbling into some deep chasm when the road turned and the land fell away. They were saved each time by Prince Ruan's keen night vision. At last the King said they might stop a while and rest the horses. Everyone dismounted and sat on the ground; they lit hundreds of little fires, but no one slept.

At the first tint of purple dawn above the peaks, they were up and riding again. The weather remained clear and bright; melting snow formed thousands of tiny rills and rivulets running along beside the road. They travelled all through that day with the fewest possible stops to breathe the horses, and took their meals in the saddle, when they even thought to eat. So swift was their progress that those who rode in the vanguard reached the valley under the pinewood shortly before nightfall and saw the Old Fortress rising up ahead of them in the fading light.

It took Sindérian's breath away: her first glimpse of the ancient fortified city, piled stone upon stone, level upon level, to such incredible heights. Every stone shone with a pearly luster; every roof tile was afire in the sunset. Yet something that might be a memory, or a warning, or an omen, hovered at the edge of her thought.

As they approached the walls, a deadly silence hung over the entire valley. Even the birds had fled—even the carrion eaters, and that was strangest of all. Sindérian had seen battlefields before, but never anything like this. Wherever she looked there was desolation: hundreds of bodies left to rot; immense wooden siege engines, broken and abandoned, looking like nothing so much as gibbets waiting for someone to come and be hanged.

All the horses began to jibe and balk. From his perch on her saddlebow Faolein bated and screamed like a wild hawk, protesting something large, dead, and covered in dirty white fur lying directly in their path. Steering the black mare in a wide circle, Sindérian glanced over her shoulder to get a better look. It lay stretched out on one side, with an arrow piercing a bizarrely elongated throat.

"Skinchanger," she said under her breath.

"*Varjolükka*," answered one of the King's men. "Our horses can never abide them, alive or dead, but the barbarians teach their own beasts to endure them."

She saw just ahead a gaping hole in the fortifications, and all around where the wall had been there was great debris of shattered stone and pulverized rock. When they reached the outskirts of the wreckage, horses shied again, this time from a gigantic, sprawling man-shaped figure pinned in place by a pile of stone blocks and the splintered remains of a ladder.

Worst of all was a pervasive smell, a taint, infinitely worse than anything rising from the decomposing bodies, with a stomach-churning familiarity about it that Sindérian could not immediately place. Then she did remember; the muscles in her abdomen clenched, and sweat broke out on the palms of her hands. It was the stench of blackest magic, and the last time she had encountered it in such strength was on the road from Gilaefri after the fall of Cuirarthéros.

So it was true, just as she had feared even before the thunderstorm: Ouriána's priests had arrived here first.

Weaving a path through the rubble, Sindérian and those who rode with her came at length into the outer bailey. White marble walls rose sheer on either side; buildings stared blindly into the yard with dark, shuttered eyes. And everywhere was the *drip, drip, drip* of melting ice falling on marble pavements.

Here, someone had at least made an effort to pile up hundreds of the bodies as if for burning, until the work of gathering so many must have proved overwhelming. Following after the King, the first riders passed under the arch of a broken gate and into a second yard, then into a third, and each was the same: silent buildings and piled corpses. Meanwhile, shadows were steadily lengthening and it grew darker and darker between the walls.

Circling the third enclosure looking for a way into the next, Sindérian heard a faint rattle of chains, followed by the sound of timbers scraping over gravel. An inner gate began to open slowly, a foot at a time. Lantern light flashed from within as someone peered out, and a moment later the gate swung wide.

A crowd of gaunt-faced men, followed by women and children like pale ghosts of famine erupted into the yard. Most came silently, but no few wept unashamedly as they fell to their knees before the King. Visibly moved, Ristil swung down from the saddle and walked among them, dropping a comforting hand on a man's shoulder, a light caress on a child's hair. Their hands reached out eagerly to touch his cloak as he passed; men and women cried out his name, followed his every movement with hungry eyes.

Sindérian felt her throat close up and her eyes sting—how could he bear this tide of suffering, sorrow, and loss?

"Haestan," said the King, stopping before a man with grizzled hair and a scarred face. "It *is* Haestan? You are one of Prince Kivik's captains." The old warrior nodded. "Then you will tell me what has happened here, and if my son is alive."

With his grey head sinking under the King's regard, the old man answered in a voice roughened by grief. "Highness, our losses have been heavy. Most of the men who came with the Prince from Lückenbörg are dead. Your son is alive and so is Lord Skerry, though both suffered many wounds. But—" He choked on the words, shuddered, and went on with an effort. "But our Lady Winloki is gone."

"Gone?" Ristil seemed to sway, then quickly regained command of himself. "*Where* has she gone?"

"No one knows where. The Princess was stolen away from us. But perhaps—it may be—Prince Kivik would wish to tell you more of this himself."

"Yes," said the King. "Yes. I am eager to speak to my son. Take me to him at once."

Prince Kivik's tale—after an emotional reunion with his father—was so convoluted and full of strange twists, he was more than halfway through before Sindérian and the rest began to make sense of it.

They were seated with the Prince and his cousin by one of the cavernous fireplaces in the keep, sipping a thin broth of uncertain origins out of cracked wooden bowls. After many digressions, he finally came to the point in his story where the wall near the gatehouse shattered in a burst of light and sound. "And then I saw them picking their way through the rubble. They weren't Eisenlonders, nor dead witch-lords as I first thought, but creatures I had never seen before, all in red robes, like to men in form—but *not* like them either."

"In truth, they were Furiádhin," said Sindérian, putting her bowl aside. With the first pangs of hunger dulled, she had no desire for more of the bitter broth. "Accompanied, no doubt, by their acolytes and temple guards."

Kivik frowned and shook his head. "I never imagined that Ouriána's priests might look like that." Then he shrugged, a movement that brought on a little grunt of pain. She suspected cracked ribs or a broken collarbone.

"And yet it is the only thing that would make any sense of what happened next. One of the *Skørnhäär* came striding in after them, stepping over bodies and broken walls. We both saw that much"—he and Skerry exchanged a bleak, frustrated glance across the room—"but we didn't know what they were after; even if we *had* guessed, we thought that Winloki was safe in the infirmary behind six more gates. And in the confusion of organizing an orderly retreat, getting our men down from the walls and across the outer ward to the second gate, fighting every step of the way, we never knew until afterward that our cousin had been abducted."

Skerry took up the story from that point. "Somehow the giant knew where to find her. Those who saw everything said that he led the strangers straight to the healers' tent, where she was working. A dozen men rushed to defend her but it was no use; the riders and the ice giant just trampled them down. Then one of the creatures—the Furiádhin—snatched her up onto his horse, and away they all went as they had come, back through the gap in the wall."

His jaw was bruised and his left arm in a sling. Like everyone else who had been holed up in this place for weeks, the two Skyrran princes were knife-blade thin, as haggard as ghosts, but there was also an unnatural pallor, an unsteadiness to their movements, which spoke of illness and injuries beyond the obvious ones Sindérian could see. They were probably on their feet at all only in stubborn defiance of their own healers.

Skerry balled up his good fist and slammed it against his thigh. "By the time we heard about any of that we were penned up inside, and we had no way of following after her—supposing we were foolhardy enough to try and carve a path through thousands of Eisenlonders and hundreds of the bloody giants and skinchangers."

"But how, in the end, did you contrive to kill so many?" asked Prince Ruan, leaning forward in his chair. "Or where did they go?" Aell looked equally intrigued by those same questions.

Kivik shook his head again. "Some of them left that first night, and I don't know why. Otherwise, they killed each other as often as not. Once they were inside the walls this cursed place proved to be no more lucky for them than it had been for us—and more quickly fatal."

Sindérian could well believe it. Even now there were evil spells at work here. Around the edges of the room darkness wavered, something shifted. In a far corner, a shadow vaguely resembling a rat sat up and chittered at her. No one but she seemed to notice—except perhaps Prince Ruan, who flared his nostrils and narrowed his eyes when the chittering was loudest.

"All day yesterday," Kivik was continuing, "they divided their time between scaling our walls and fighting among themselves—and rather more often it seemed to be the latter. There were three different groups of them, so far as I could tell: the giants and skinchangers; the Eisenlonders; and those others we've been fighting this last year whose language we never understood. The trouble seemed to begin when the *Skørnhäär* and the *Varjolükka* took offense at something the Men did or said. They killed fifty or a hundred—just squashed men flat or tore them to pieces—and then loped off." He grimaced at the memory. "That was the last we saw of them. But afterward, it seemed that the barbarians split into many warring factions and bloody battles kept breaking out between them."

"Impossible, after all the things we've seen, to doubt that

there *is* a curse on the fortress," added Skerry. Unshaven and ill kempt, they had little of the prince or lord about them. Everything they wore, everything that was not made of metal, was patched and mended, right down to their scuffed leather boots. "Though why we survived it so long, and why it turned on our enemies in the end, I don't understand."

Sindérian thought that she knew. *Blood will have blood,* that was one of the oldest and cruellest laws of magic, and however civilized and learned magicians and wizards became, it still held true. The Eisenlonders and their allies had initiated the violence here, and it was for them to pay the heaviest price.

"However it happened, the last group of them staggered off this morning, nursing their wounds. Either they knew that you were coming," said Kivik, looking toward his father, "or they finally realized the Old Fortress had a deadly influence on them."

"We would already have formed a rescue party to go after Winloki, long before this," Skerry added, "but whether to head north, south, or east, to go farther into the mountains or back to the flatlands again . . ." His voice trailed off in frustration.

There is only one way the Furiádhin will be taking her, said Faolein, leaving his place on Sindérian's shoulder, walking sideways down her arm, and balancing on her wrist. *They will be riding south by the easiest way, at least until they come to the sea.*

Sindérian thought the same. "They will—they *must*—head south and eventually west, toward Phaôrax," she told the King. "They have no reason to go east to Eisenlonde, and they have no more use for the Eisenlonders, now that they have the Princess."

Skerry drew in his breath sharply. His eyes moved from

Sindérian's face to the hawk, and then back again. She thought he was probably finding it difficult to make sense of things—particularly those things he had been told about her and her father. "That was the cause of it then, the entire bloody war—because Ouriána of Phaôrax wanted to abduct Winloki?"

"I think . . ." Sindérian hesitated, turning the idea over in her mind, then went on. "I think you may have been the victims of Ouriána's mistake. She has her seers and astrologers, a certain degree of Foresight herself. She must have been conscious of a threat in the north, and until she learned that Winloki was alive—"

"She thought *we* were the threat? The whole Skyrran nation? Or that we would *become* a threat as she moved her armies north through the coastal principalities?" Another glance passed between Skerry and Kivik; it seemed the idea was not entirely new to either of them. "But this can't be the end of it. There are too many old grudges between Eisenlonde and Skyrra. The barbarians won't turn around and meekly go home, just because that woman on Phaôrax has suddenly lost interest in stirring them up."

"No, it won't end here," Sindérian agreed regretfully. "There are some things that, once started, can't be so easily stopped."

An uneasy silence crept over the gathering and lasted until Prince Ruan asked the one question on every mind. "But can we really believe the lady is still alive? She's been in their power for two days already. They tried to kill her once before, when she was only a helpless infant. Would they hesitate to do so now?"

Another message passed between father and daughter.

"They tried to *capture* her before," said Sindérian. "What they meant to do to her afterward we only guess. And whatever Guirion might have intended *then,* this time it is Camhóin-hann, the High Priest, who has her. He is wiser by far than any of the others—and therefore infinitely more dangerous. To kill the daughter of Nimenoë is not something he would undertake lightly, nor something he's apt to attempt while still on Skyrran soil.

"If indeed Camhóinhann intends to harm her at all," she added at her father's prompting, "it may be that Ouriána has reserved that task for herself."

"But can we rely on that being so?" said the King, wrinkling his brow. "Can we be certain that he will, in any case, not harm her immediately?"

"No. That is far from certain. Any rescue party would have to leave soon."

Ristil hesitated; he seemed to be weighing matters very carefully. "We almost killed our horses getting here," he said with a shake of his head. "Nor have we provisions enough to start a thousand men on the road again, not until the supply wagons come."

"But small parties travel more swiftly than large ones," Kivik offered eagerly. "And our horses here are well rested. If Skerry and I took a handful of men and went on ahead—"

The King interrupted him with a look like a thunderstorm. "Neither of you look capable of sitting a horse. And even if you *were* able to ride, what do you believe such a small number could accomplish against three of Ouriána's priests? By all accounts, their powers are terrible."

"We will go, too." The words were out of Sindérian's mouth

almost before she thought them. "My father, Prince Ruan, Aell, and I—we will go with Prince Kivik. If we can't stop the Pharaxions, perhaps we can at least delay them until you and your army arrive. And it sometimes happens that a small party can manage by luck and ingenuity what a greater army never could by mere force.

"As for your son and Lord Skerry," she added with a glance in their direction, "no doubt your healers here have exhausted their strength trying to help so many. But if you will let me try what I can do, it's possible they may be able to ride by morning."

After the King gave his consent, Sindérian transferred Faolein from her arm to Aell's, braided back her hair, and pushed up her sleeves.

She made each young prince lie down in turn on a bench by the fire. Then she made a careful examination, feeling with a combination of touch and intuition for broken bones, flesh and nerves stretched past their limits, animal spirits failing, and blood running thin. In this way she learned that Kivik had three cracked ribs and Skerry a broken arm, in addition to many gashes, scrapes, and bruises between them. As she had expected, in each case there had been a great loss of blood.

Having determined so much, Sindérian began to set her charms: drawing the runes *quornü, rühas, craich,* and *güwelan* in water and ashes, pouring thought and intention into battered flesh and broken bones, along with as much of her own vital and animal spirits as she dared, to compensate for the loss of blood.

"*Omaro gürdath maren, oma gürdath onés,*" she chanted under her breath as she worked the final *shibeath* on Skerry. "*Diohach séo güwelean nésoma!*"

Already exhausted by long days in the saddle, short rest, and less sleep, she was white and trembling by the time she had finished. She took two steps away from the bench, and her bones turned to water, her knees buckled, the world went spinning away into a grey void. She would have fallen if Prince Ruan had not somehow anticipated her swoon and moved in quickly to catch her.

"That was not very wise," he hissed under his breath when he had helped her back to her former seat by the fire. "One day, you will go too far."

It was now near midnight and far too dark, under the withered moon, to think of riding out. That meant there was time enough for rest and to eat a scanty meal.

After they ate, one of the healers took Sindérian through the maze of stone and shadows that was the keep, and finally into a tower room where she could sleep.

Strange thoughts danced in her brain, a procession of fey, bright images: wicked queens, bone-grinding ogres, owl-headed witches. *I have seen this place, this fortress, before,* she told Faolein as she sat down on the small makeshift bed. *I dreamed of it long ago. It was different, as things often are different in the way of dreams, but still too like to be mistaken.*

And was it a good dream or an ill one? her father asked.

Sindérian shook her head, uncertain how to answer. *Neither good nor bad. But I dreamed that dream on the day after the night the Princess was born, and I can't help thinking we were intended to meet here, she and I.*

Neither said so, but they both knew what that meant. If the meeting had occurred as it was fated, everyone might have been spared much trouble and grief. As they had *not* met, no good could come of it.

In the small hours of the morning those who had been chosen for the rescue party headed for the stables, where horses and provisions were already awaiting them. A cool dawn wind swirled through the courtyards, causing the torches that some of them carried to flicker wildly.

Striding along beside the two Skyrran princes, Sindérian felt stronger after her short sleep. Dismay at arriving too late had given way to her native stubbornness—which always had an invigorating effect. Her mind was so busy with thoughts of the days and challenges ahead, she was taken by surprise when Prince Ruan abruptly reached out and clasped her by the wrist, drawing her away from the others.

His handsome face was pale and oddly intent. "You have some plan you chose not to reveal to the King—when do you *not* have a plan? But this time the risk is too great. It's not too late to change your mind, wait here with the King, and follow after us later."

Sindérian stopped walking. "Do you think I am afraid to share in the danger?"

"No, I think you are careless of your own safety—and therein lies the peril. I think there is something you have been hiding from the rest of us, ever since we almost drowned in the Necke." His grip on her arm tightened; his suspicious frown deepened. "'By luck and ingenuity,' you said. You have a courageous spirit, but even with the greatest luck in the world, what do you think you can do to hinder three Furiádhin?"

She shook back her long, dark hair, made a dismissive gesture. "Éireamhóine faced six of them, and killed three."

"*Éireamhóine* had nearly five times your years and experience, and by the King's account he paid dearly for those three deaths. If *I* were killed or maimed, who would suffer for it except myself? My grandfather has more than a dozen grandsons. And King Ristil has other sons besides Prince Kivik. But you have gifts that would be sorely missed."

"Then let me use those gifts! Let me not waste them," she said passionately. "And you seem to forget that Faolein will be with us."

"I forget nothing. But Faolein seems to have lost the power to do anything beyond changing his shape—and never back to the one he had before, the one best able to help us."

Unable to endure his steady, unnerving gaze, Sindérian slipped out of his grasp. The others, after hesitating a moment to see if she and Ruan would follow, were getting too far ahead. Fearing to lose her way in the maze of yards, she gathered up her full skirts in both hands and hurried to catch up with them.

"It's true my father can no longer make the signs or speak the words," she tossed over her shoulder, "but every spell and charm he ever knew is still with him. You saw what I was able to do in Arkenfell under his instruction. If Faolein goes, then so must I, to serve as his hands and voice."

Drawing even with her, the Prince strode along at her side, still scowling ferociously. "It is not for me to tell you what to do. The wizards of Leal are the High King's allies, not his subjects. But if you were my sister or my cousin—"

"If I were your sister or your cousin," she retorted, "you still wouldn't have the power or the right to change my mind!"

12

✳

For a night and a day they travelled at a punishing pace—priests, acolytes, temple guards, and their angry, confused, and terrified prisoner—without sleep, without food, stopping only briefly to rest the horses or to perform their accustomed rituals at moonrise and moonset. At night, the Furiádhin conjured up eerie spinning globes of green luminosity to light the way down dangerous mountain roads. By day, they raised the hoods of their crimson cloaks and rode with their faces in shadow, protecting their moon-pale skin from the sun.

Winloki sat up as straight as she could in the saddle, tear-less, defiant, determined to show neither weakness nor fear. She had passed beyond exhaustion into that waking dream-state where the body no longer knows it is being pushed beyond its limits. Her captors had bound her so securely to the saddle there was no danger of her falling off during this wild ride over sometimes rough terrain—they had also, more ominously, manacled her hands. Thin silver bracelets encircled her wrists, joined together by a fine but exceedingly strong silver chain.

Otherwise, they had done her no violence, handled her no more cruelly than the conditions of their headlong pace required. Yet she was sick and terrified with the knowledge that violence must be coming, perhaps as soon as their first stop to eat and sleep.

And always she was aware of the silver bracelets lying smooth and chill against her skin. The chain was long enough to allow some freedom of movement, but a potent magic in the bands themselves thwarted her every attempt to work her own spells, whether to heal muscles bruised and aching after so many continuous hours in the saddle, or to try to escape. She had been worrying her tired brain for hours trying to come up with a reason why such elaborate precautions would be necessary. *These creatures, so terrible, so powerful, what need have they to fear me and my untrained gift? Why cuff me and constrain me like a thief or a murderer?*

When she finally realized what it might mean, the blood rushed into her face in a burning blush and the rest of her body turned cold. She knew stories—stories told in whispers, stories overheard, never intended for the sheltered ears of a princess—about the cruelties inflicted by violent and wicked men on female prisoners. At the same time, there was a widespread belief that no healer need ever endure rape, because the man who attempted that outrage would find himself assaulting a corpse.

Could something so simple and horrible be the real reason behind her abduction? Or was it—considering the extraordinary nature of her captors themselves—likely to end in some *worse* violation she could not even imagine? These thoughts, when she allowed them, left her dizzy with horror.

Oh yes, she knew herself well enough, knew the extent of her gifts well enough, to be certain that she *could* take her own life rather than face torture or degradation—but the bracelets robbed her of all choices, whether to live or to die. And whatever these men intended, be it rape or worse, she was helpless to prevent it.

They had followed a descending track since morning, leaving the pinewoods behind, riding through country that was harder and chancier: a region of rockslides, chasms, plunging waterfalls, and a scattering of shrubs that had somehow rooted themselves in what looked to be solid stone. Shortly before nightfall, Winloki's mysterious abductors finally stopped to set up a camp in a little alpine meadow of thin, dry grasses beneath high cliff walls.

While the guards saw to the horses, the acolytes pitched tents made of the same coarse black cloth they wore themselves. She sat neglected astride her horse, gritting her teeth, trying not to droop in the saddle, until one of the men remembered to untie the ropes holding her in place and lifted her down with surprising gentleness.

As soon as her feet touched the ground, the world swung around her; she turned light-headed and giddy. It was only pride that kept her upright. A swarm of black-robed figures closed in, ushering her over to a place where the ground sloped, and one of them indicated she was to sit. Then she could finally let her legs give way, sink down in the rough brown grass.

The crowd parted before one of the hooded priests. His ankle-length scarlet robes were split for riding; he was booted and spurred, belted with a sword and two long knives; yet she thought he had an austere look about him that suggested a cloistered, meditative life rather than battlefields.

He offered her a drink from a leather flask. Too parched to refuse, Winloki warily accepted, holding the bottle in both hands, taking an experimental swallow. The spirit was so potent she almost choked, but it satisfied her thirst, with an unexpected taste of honey and herbs.

There had been ample opportunity by now, just by watching and listening, to learn some of their names, to learn a little about the men who held her prisoner. Camhóinhann, Dyonas, and Goezenou: those were the three Furiádhin, more horrible in the flesh than imagination had ever painted them. The others were their acolyte-servants, or else guards attached to their temple in Apharos and by extension to the priests.

This one, who silently accepted the flask when she handed it back to him, was Dyonas. Inside the blood-red cowl his face, with its fine, sharp features, was bleached of color; his flat metallic eyes had no more humanity than ice or wind. And if, under the heavy layers of his clothing, his figure appeared boyishly slight, she did not for that reason make the mistake of thinking him weak or effeminate. No, he was as thin and bright as a new dagger, and likely to prove every bit as lethal. In truth, he had the look of a man who would die on the rack, who would perish in flames, before he would yield a point so trivial that no one else would take it for an inviolable principle. On either side of his forehead were short, polished ivory horns.

As soon as he walked away, the questions began to hammer in her brain. Why had *she* been singled out from among so many? Or if she had been their object all along, what could they *possibly* want from her that they were willing to come such a distance to find her? So far, nothing she had seen or heard, none of the bizarre and terrifying tales she remembered about Ouriána of Phaôrax and her monstrous priests, provided any answers.

Before long, all but two of her attendants drifted off and busied themselves with various tasks about the camp. In the field beyond the tents, the Furiádhin had gathered together a few of the black-robed acolytes and appeared to be holding a low-voiced council, darting occasional glances in her direction. *They are deciding what to do with me,* she thought. *Or much more likely,* when *they will do it.*

Her fingers twisted in her lap, weaving charms as her lips formed the words, though by now she had little hope any of them would be effective. Again and again she made the signs, whispered the spells; again and again her charms refused to take hold. The silver bracelets were very light and delicately made—they hardly weighed more than air—but they did their work remarkably well.

When the discussion across the way came to a close, Winloki braced herself for the worst. Just as she had feared, they all walked over to the knoll and regrouped around her.

"Are you hungry?" asked the one called Camhóinhann. His voice was so deep and compelling, so filled with strange music, it sent shivers along her skin. When she stubbornly refused to answer, he spoke again: "Or is there anything, Lady, that you require for your comfort?"

Winloki could hardly return his glance. *This one,* she thought, *is a hundred times more terrifying than Dyonas.*

Just to look at him made her bones tremble and her heart quake. He was so tall that he towered head and shoulders over every man in the camp, and for all that he was so wasted and thin, a large frame gave the impression of great physical strength and power. His face, too, was striking: neither hideous nor handsome, yet with an indefinable something about the features or the expression that suggested both. Most of all, she thought he was someone who could sway others by the sheer force and magnitude of his personality—and Winloki knew with every fiber of her being that she did *not* wish to be influenced by him in that way.

She shook her head, unwilling to let any word escape from her dry, scratchy throat, fearing some tremor or crack in her voice might be mistaken for cowardice. There *were* a great many things that she "required for her comfort," her freedom first among them, but pride forbade that she make any request, accept any favor, no matter how trivial.

When the others began to drift away to take up their several duties elsewhere, Camhóinhann remained, staring down at her with unsettling pupiless eyes. "If you wish to avail yourself of the privacy of those bushes over there, you may feel free to do so," he suggested quietly. "No one will disturb you."

It was but one more indignity, she raged inwardly, that she should require permission for something so natural—something so private. She wanted to say no; the word trembled on her lips. Rebellion was strong, defiance was strong, but nature was stronger still. She started to rise, then flinched back involuntarily when a lean white hand reached out to help her.

"You have no need to fear me," he said, bending down to remove, by some trick she could not see, the chain from the silver cuffs. "I mean you no harm. Nor will anyone here offer you any indecency. The bracelets are meant only to prevent you from injuring yourself."

Winloki glared up at him in surprised indignation. "Am I to suppose, *against all reason,* that I am *not* your prisoner?"

"You are our captive, certainly, but an honored one," he answered gravely. "As for my companions and I, no doubt we appear monstrous enough to you, but we are priests and votaries of the Devouring Moon, essentially celibate."

With that vaguely ominous word "essentially" echoing in her mind, Winloki walked past him and into the screening shrubs, where she did what she needed to do. Emerging from the bushes afterward, she spotted a little rivulet running downhill over the rocks and started in that direction. Almost immediately, guardsmen and acolytes surrounded her once more, escorting her over to the water, where she washed her hands, then back to her former place on the slope.

She sat down again, wrapping her skirts around her legs, brushed back her tangled hair, and inhaled deeply. After subsisting so long on the stingy air of the heights, she had almost forgotten what it really was to breathe.

Almost immediately, Camhóinhann returned and chained her wrists together again. "Perhaps you are ready to eat now?"

Coming to the disheartening conclusion that she only punished herself by refusing—and discomforted *them* not at all—Winloki nodded. Within moments a cold meal appeared, consisting of meat, cheese, cakes, and fruit (such a feast, indeed, as she had not known in weeks) offered to her on a wooden platter by a kneeling acolyte. She ate sparingly, only enough to keep up her strength. The idea of sharing their food robbed her of appetite, and the little that she did eat sat uneasily in her stomach.

Meanwhile, a thin nail-paring of a moon had appeared in the sky and it was time for the evening rite. Wavering between guilt and a reluctant fascination, she realized that it was impossible for her not to watch. Though she cared nothing for their atrocious religion, or for their "goddess in human form," she could not help being intrigued by their rituals.

As one man, all of the priests and acolytes dropped to the ground in a profound obeisance, with their arms outstretched and their faces in the dirt. Minutes passed, during which the worshippers remained moveless, silent. But Winloki could feel that *something* was happening, something that raised the hair at the back of her neck, made the nerves jump beneath her skin. Finally, as if in response to an unheard signal, they all rose together in a single movement, and Dyonas began to sing in a clear, high voice.

The words of his song were strange to her, and yet oddly familiar. It was as though he spoke in a language that she *ought* to know, but only halfway understood. Winloki closed her eyes, let the impressions wash over her. A great weariness and disgust began to press down on her, a crushing sense of futility.

She seemed to see a vast landscape as of all the world spread out before her: hills and mountains, oceans and rivers—and everything she saw was hideous, ill formed, wounded past healing. The moon rained down vapors, the skin of the earth cracked; men spread out across the face of the land like the lesions of a disease.

The entire race had degenerated: they were worse than vermin, less than apes, lower than the creeping things of the earth. The weak battened on the strong, the sick infected the well. Thousands suffered and died who should never have been born at all.

But then some quality in the words or music changed, and her sense of futility and despair began to lift.

She was in a place of burning gums and incenses, of hot, heavy perfumes. Skyrrans built no temples or fanes, yet something, some inner voice or the hymn itself, told her that this was a temple dedicated to Ouriána, goddess incarnated.

Upon the high altar, fires of purification and regeneration were burning, consuming the sins and sorrows of a suffering world, and praise for the Goddess rose to the heavens on the smoke of a thousand sacrifices. What was ill made (said Dyonas's song) would be unmade and created anew. Let the ignorant, the cowardly, the misguided beware. It was not in their power to prevent the inevitable; their efforts at resistance only prolonged the agony. All must pass through the fire, either to perish or be transformed.

Finally, the hymn soared into sublime regions of felicity and hope.

Winloki found herself alone in the blue-black dome of the night. Stars flashed like diamonds. The moon was a fiery crystal egg, cloudy but translucent, and she could see a luminous amorphous shape inside, as of something struggling to be born. Then there was a sound so loud it shook the firmament, it fractured the sky. A cold wind blew in from some place of dark vacancy beyond the stars. The egg cracked, and a younger moon emerged, brighter than the sun and more glorious. Its birth was more than a sign, more than a portent; it was a promise and a pledge: pres-

ent pain would give way to future bliss. No life would be wasted, not one drop of blood shed in vain. After the violent purgation would come a New Age, when men would live as gods.

As the last notes lingered on the air, Winloki discovered that she was weeping, though with what emotion—anger or fear or hope—she was not even certain.

The rite was over and darkness was swiftly gathering when one of the acolytes approached her to say that a tent had been prepared for her use. Three guards escorted her across the campsite. On a sudden impulse of curiosity, she lingered for a moment outside the tent, studying the faces of her guards— hoping that they, who were solid and human and ordinary, might offer some clue as to what awaited her, might be easier to comprehend than the ghastly priests or the grim and aus- tere acolytes.

They were strapping young men, hardly older than she was herself, and they blushed like girls under her steady regard. As hard as she looked, Winloki could find nothing sinister about them, not for all their glinting, dark armor or their array of weaponry. If there was anything, *anything* to set them apart from the Skyrran soldiers she had lived with, healed, and (far too often) watched die in these last terrible months, she could not find it.

A movement on the other side of the camp drew her at- tention. It was the third priest, Goezenou, standing where a shaft of moonlight illuminated his hawk-nosed, lantern-jawed face. Too many times, during the course of the last day and night, she had noticed him watching her, not with the same disinterested vigilance as the others, but as though he wanted something *from* her. The guards caught sight of him at the same time she did, and all three turned taut and watchful. One of them stepped between her and the furiádh, as if to shield her—or perhaps to prevent her from seeing something not meant for her eyes.

Whatever he meant by it, the gesture came too late. She had already met the full force of a glance so intense and disturbing it made her feel violated. If ever she had looked into the face of raw, unadulterated evil, she had just done so now.

She ducked quickly inside the tent and sank down on the ground, breathless and queasy, trying to regain control over herself, to quell the bone-shaking shudders of revulsion.

At length, the sickness passed, and she began a listless examination of her surroundings. Gradually it dawned on her that the tent was not without its luxuries: a bed of heather and somebody's beautiful fur-lined cloak to serve as a blanket; a lantern; a folding stool; a flask of wine and a silver cup; a basin of water and a cloth to wash her face. It was evident that someone had taken considerable thought for her comfort. But who had it been? And just how long and how far could she count on that someone's goodwill?

All through the night, lying restless and half awake, listening to footsteps or the clink of armor, a word passing between the men standing guard just outside, she had ample occasion to torture her brain with questions. If only the King and Elf-hael had told her about her own origins, so many, many things that bewildered her now might have made perfect sense!

Yet more than anything else, she wondered if there were *any* chance she might still be rescued. Her heart sank with the knowledge that it was almost impossible that any of her people at the Old Fortress had survived. *I saw Haakon and Arvi die,* she remembered. *The battle was already lost.*

And no matter how she arranged events in her mind during that seemingly endless night, no matter how she tried to make them add up to some other outcome, she always came back to the conclusion that everyone was dead: Skerry and Kivik. Thyra, Syvi, and the other healers. All the refugees who had suffered so much and struggled so hard to win through to safety. The Eisenlonders, who took no prisoners, who spared no lives, had slaughtered them, every one.

At dawn, a different set of guards came into the tent to wake her, escorting her outside so that others could take it down. They gave her a folding stool to sit on and, with the same bashful courtesy she was beginning to expect, brought her a cold breakfast of bread, water, and dried fruit. She had scarcely finished eating when the three priests and all eight acolytes surrounded her again.

"There is something we should have attended to before this, but other matters took precedence," said Camhóinhann, his great shadow falling over her, his broad shoulders blocking out the sky. "You have a ring made of bone with a runic inscription. Perhaps no one told you: it belonged to your mother. We know the ring was on your hand when we took you out of the fortress, and I must ask you to give it to me now."

Winloki was bewildered, and then uncertain how to reply. On the night of her abduction, during a brief pause to change the horses, she had removed the ring and concealed it when no one was looking. She had never imagined it could have any special significance for her captors, had certainly never guessed they would know more about it than she did; she had merely deemed it too valuable to lose. Now that it seemed so important, she was more eager to keep it than ever. She considered, briefly, if a lie would avail her anything.

"No," said Camhóinhann, reading her face, or reading her silence, all too easily. "If you told us you had lost it, we would be obliged to search you. We prefer to spare you that indignity—but don't allow yourself to think we would hesitate if you make it necessary."

Again Winloki felt Goezenou watching her. Turning her head to meet his gaze, she intercepted another naked and disturbing glance—one that told her as clearly as words that *he* at least would welcome the opportunity to lay hands on her.

Blushing furiously, she reached up under her hair, found the lock at the base of her skull where she had anchored the ring, and untied the knot. With a mutinous look, she held out her hand, palm uppermost, offering the ring to Camhóinhann.

He reached out to take it, but before his fingers touched the ring his hand wavered and his face convulsed. He staggered back with a great cry of pain. All the lesser priests and acolytes reacted at the same time: hissing and cringing, raising up their cloaks to cover their faces. Even Winloki was shaken by the violence of their recoil.

Several minutes passed. Then it was Camhóinhann, as if by some great effort of will, who recovered first.

"It seems that you must keep it after all," he told her. "Hold it, and keep it safe. *We* dare not take it, and it is far too rare and valuable a thing to be entrusted to one of the temple guards."

13

✳

Prince Cuillioc woke in the middle of the night with the scent of smoke tickling his nose and a burning sensation in his lungs. *Bonfires,* he thought groggily.

But he came back awake a short time later at the sound of swift footsteps outside in the antechamber. Still heavy with sleep, fighting the weight of it, he had succeeded only in propping himself up on his elbows when the door flew open and two of his knights, Gerig and Brihac, burst into the room. "Great Prince, our galleys are burning! They've set fire to our ships."

Pulling himself up into a sitting position, Cuillioc shook the red-blond hair out of his eyes. "What—all of them?"

"At least a third, perhaps as many as half." As he spoke, Gerig moved around the room, lighting the oil lamps, closing the shutters to keep the smoke out. "It's still very dark, and there's little to be seen from this side of town."

By now, Cuillioc was most thoroughly awake. "What have we done to put out the fires?"

"Steps have already been taken to save as many ships as possible. Our men billeted down by the water claim to have the situation well in hand. But—"

"But with our ships fired," said the Prince as he threw off the covers and left the bed, "the next thing we can expect of the natives is an open rebellion. To stop that we will need to take swift action."

He could be decisive in a crisis like this one. Striding over to a table where pen, ink, and paper were waiting, he tore a sheet into several pieces, wrote out instructions on each one, and called for men to act as his couriers.

He dressed in haste, careless of which garments were handed him. Opening a chest at the foot of his bed, he began lifting out pieces of armor—corselet, gorget, vambraces, cuisses, greaves—and passing them one by one to Gerig or Brihac, who discarded the protective silk wrappings before placing them on the bed. But all the time his mind was busy.

"The galley slaves!" He stopped what he was doing and uttered a furious oath. "Those poor wretches chained to their oars in the middle of that holocaust—"

"Your concern for criminals, traitors, and prisoners of war is somewhat misplaced," said a familiar, flat voice. It was Iobhar, standing in the open doorway.

"Do not grieve yourself," the priest continued, sketching a brief genuflection. "Perhaps you've forgotten: rather than leave so many in idleness all of these weeks, we brought most of the slaves ashore and put them to other work."

With a curt nod of thanks for the information, the Prince turned back to his armor chest, took out the dragon-crested helm, and passed it on to Brihac. "So the Mirazhites finally show some backbone and lash out against us. But did they truly imagine there would be no reprisals?"

Iobhar took several limping steps into the center of the room. "I take it the natives depend on us to be in a panic—and for the most part too helpless to retaliate. Things are beginning to happen very swiftly now. I've spent much of this night with the garrison, where most of the men are violently ill, and every hour brings new cases. Moreover, I've received word that dozens of your men throughout the city are stricken as well. Some have already died. It seems the Mirazhites timed the burning of our ships very carefully."

Cuillioc could hear shouting down in the streets, a buzz of consternation passing from room to room inside the Citadel. He forced himself to stand still as the two knights began to arm him—but all the while he was cursing himself for a fool. Cities like this one *bred* contagion. Why had he lingered so long in Xanthipei?

"It seems that we are all dying," Iobhar went on in his passionless voice, "every Pharaxion in the city. In truth, we have been dying for months, without even knowing it."

"Dying of this Summer Fever, which only kills slaves?" Lifting his arms so that Gerig could buckle the breastplate in place, the Prince gave a bitter laugh.

"There is no Summer Fever. The physician lied to us—just as you suspected all along. He also failed to tell us that we have been living on poisons ever since we first set foot on the soil of Mirizandi: imbibing them with every bite of food and sip of drink, taking them in with the air, soaking them in through our skins."

There was a clatter of metal on the tiled floor as someone—Cuillioc did not look to see if it was Brihac or Gerig—dropped a heavy piece of armor. "The Mirazhites have been secretly trying to kill us with *poisons*?"

"For the most part we have been killing ourselves just by being here," said Iobhar, slipping his hands inside the sleeves of his scarlet robe. "The land generates poisons, breathing them out in vaporous exhalations, contaminating everything and everyone. The birds and beasts seem to have made some internal accommodation, though many of the young ones die, but the human inhabitants can survive only by eating of a powerful herbal elixir. Combined with this medicine, the noxious vapors produce a pleasing sensation of lightness and well-being; without it, they have a slow but deadly effect. By the time that the more dramatic symptoms appear, death can follow in a matter of days—or hours."

Cuillioc caught his breath. So many things that had baffled him before were starting to assume new meanings: the waking dream of his first weeks in Mirizandi, his weakness and lethargy since. Even the fact that his scheming courtiers had been so strangely quiescent since the slaughter of the hostages. "Those leaves the servants stew in their own drinking water—the spice you can smell all over the marketplace—*that* is the elixir?" His eyes narrowed. "But then—how did you come to learn so much, Iobhar, and all of it so quickly?"

"Most of this comes from your little guttersnipe page. He has been asking questions, gathering information, just as you instructed."

Knowing how the urchin feared Iobhar, Cuillioc was frankly incredulous. "And he came to *you* instead of to me?"

"I met the boy on my way up from the barracks and convinced him to speak. I apologize for any rough handling, but it seemed expedient." The furiádh stretched his pale lips into a hideous grimace, which may have been intended as an ingratiating smile. "Even as I questioned him, the boy was alternately burning with fever and shivering with an ague, and I feared he would not be able to give sensible answers for very much longer."

In that sticky heat Cuillioc felt a cold horror, right down to the marrow of his bones. "No wonder the natives never took arms against us. Why *should* they exert themselves, when they had only to welcome us into their city and we were doomed!"

He felt sick with humiliation when he thought how they had gulled him, exploiting his ignorance, blinding him and his men with pleasure—yes, even inviting his contempt. Yet it boggled the mind to think that an entire city could keep such a dangerous secret for so many months, and not one of them speak out.

"In fact, the poison is slow and subtle; it takes many months to kill," said Iobhar. "And it sometimes happens that visitors who leave the country soon enough eventually recover. But the Mirazhites were not content to remain silent and leave us to perish in our own time. The grocers, wine merchants, and all the others who supply the Citadel have been sending us foods and wines in which the poison is particularly concentrated. Meanwhile, the grains and fruits the servants eat are far more wholesome, besides being sprinkled with the herbal elixir. It was unfortunate for the slave who died—and for those other trulls your men brought in from the brothels—that they were eating the same food as the garrison. Foreigners themselves, they knew no better. Naturally, with a woman's weaker constitution, one of them was the first to succumb. Which," the priest added, "undoubtedly alerted those in the city that the crisis was near. When the first cases appeared in the barracks they would have known it was time to act."

Waving his helpers aside, Cuillioc picked up his gilded vambraces and began to strap them on. "But the boy?" he asked, picturing that thin, wiry body, which no amount of feeding could ever fill out. "He should have succumbed long before the women did; what kept *him* alive all of this time?"

"He has been taking some of his meals with the native servants, where he surely ate of the herb without even knowing it. Ironically, had he stayed with the galley slaves it would have been healthier. No one has been making a concerted effort to hasten *their* deaths.

"As for my acolytes and me," Iobhar added with a self-satisfied smile, "our abstemious habits have undoubtedly served us well."

Cuillioc (still busy with the arm guards) remembered how little the furiádh had seemed to suffer in the heat, and he wondered if it was even possible to poison someone whose very blood seemed to be two parts venom and the third part malice.

"But for yourself and so many others . . ." Iobhar spread his hands wide, allowed his voice to trail off. There was no need to say anything more. They had all been eating and guzzling like pigs, and were going to suffer for it.

The Prince closed his eyes, muttered a prayer to his mother, knowing all along that she would not hear him, would not help him if she did; she had so little patience with incompetence and failure. No, it was up to him to find a way out of this trap, and more than a thousand lives hung in the balance.

He opened his eyes, made an effort to reorder his thoughts. "You said that some who leave these cursed shores live. Unless the situation at the harbor has grown worse since that first report, about half of our ships remain. The galley slaves will have to take their chances, whether the Mirazhites mean to poison them or claim ownership after we are gone—we'll never find room for them now. The men-at-arms can row." Cuillioc reached for his sword belt and girded it on. "If we act swiftly, while some of us still have strength, we may get as far as Nephuar or the archipelago—depending on how the winds favor us."

He cinched the belt in place. "We may all still die, but any chance is better than none."

It had not cooled much since midnight when Cuillioc finally prepared to leave the Citadel and set out for the docks. With so much smoke in the air every breath tasted like red-hot ashes.

After hours spent receiving reports, making hurried plans, and sending out orders, it was time to see for himself that all the wheels had been set in motion for a swift departure. Just inside the gate leading out to the street, he met Iobhar, accompanied by his two haggard acolytes, Maël and Omair. The priest asked for a word aside, and Cuillioc consented.

"It has occurred to me, Great Prince, that it would not be wise to tell the rest of our people too much," said Iobhar when they had moved out of earshot of the others. "It would be difficult to hold them back from a wholesale slaughter if they knew that every man, woman, and child in the city had connived against them. Alas, this is no time for revenge. When we are whole and strong again, when we can lead a great force out of Phaôrax to strike quickly, punish them for their perfidy, and leave just as swiftly—"

"I leave it to you to think on revenge," Cuillioc interrupted him. He knew beyond any doubt that even if he should be one of a handful to survive, he would have no place in any future army sent back to Mirizandi. Another commander who had failed so spectacularly could expect to pay with his life; as Ouriána's son, he merely faced humiliation and disgrace, but it would be years before she trusted him with another command, if she ever forgave him at all.

Striding through the dark streets toward the place where the galleys were moored, with the remaining knights of his household in attendance (eight had been stricken and two had already died), Cuillioc felt his eyes smart and his throat burn, the smoke was still so heavy. Sometimes torches flared in the reek and shadowy figures hurried past. Each time his hand moved toward the hilt of his sword as he braced himself for trouble, but each time a closer look revealed that these were his own men, sent out earlier to seize supplies of food and water.

Even supposing anyone survived so long, Cuillioc knew that his crippled armada would be several days at sea. And thus the wicked conundrum: whatever privations the rest would have to endure, those who were strong enough to row *must* eat and drink to keep up their strength, though they took in more poison in the process. After torturing himself over that question for the better part of an hour, he had finally arrived at this uneasy compromise between conscience and necessity, sending out his armed scavengers to raid the larger houses, to pillage the cookshops and food stalls in the bazaar—to go anywhere that food might be gathered quickly and in sufficient quantities—reasoning that those things the people kept for themselves would be at least more wholesome than the supplies they had sent to the palace.

So now his men went from house to house, forcing a way in, emerging shortly afterward with whatever they could carry off, then loading their plunder onto one of the donkey carts they had commandeered earlier. Otherwise, the streets were silent and empty. The inhabitants had been mysteriously quiet ever since the ship-burning.

He arrived at the docks without incident, walking into a scene of milling confusion. Torchlight burned on the waters of the bay and wherever puddles of sea-spray had formed on the marble piers. The air stank of wood smoke, boiling tar, and burnt rope, but it was beginning to clear.

Squinting in the bright light, the Prince took charge. Before very long, he had managed to organize things so that a steady stream of people and supplies was being loaded aboard the remaining galleys in a more or less orderly fashion. At the same time, he sent out men in rowboats to clear away the wreckage of scorched timbers and other debris lest it foul the oars when it came time to depart.

Yet it was a delicate balance to keep everyone moving, to convince them of the urgency without starting a panic. Perhaps he was aided by the effects of the poison, which made so many of them docile, too dull-witted to ask the sort of questions that would create an uproar.

The eastern sky was glowing like a furnace, turning the waters of the bay to molten copper, before they had finished loading.

The rising sun found them still hard at work, none of the ships ready to depart.

During a momentary lull in the activity on the docks, Cuillioc paused to listen, conscious of an increased hustle and bustle in the adjacent streets, a noise that overwhelmed even the clamor of seabirds.

He turned to get a better look, and an extraordinary sight met his eyes: richly dressed merchants mounted on camels; princes and nobles of the city seated in howdahs atop great elephants or riding in gorgeous zebra-drawn litters. Advancing in stately procession, they skirted the wharves, heading for a short stretch of beach following the curve of the bay. Once they reached the beach, they settled down to wait on the sand, with no other purpose, so far as he could see, but to watch the invaders depart.

"They think us a spectacle arranged for their amusement," hissed a voice behind him, and Maël, the older of Iobhar's acolyte-servants, moved past, shaking a bony fist at the growing crowd on the beach.

Cuillioc nodded grimly. He had a sudden bloody vision of what would happen if he sent a hundred or so able-bodied men in among the spectators—a thought he entertained for only a moment before letting it go and turning back to his task. Although the provocation was extreme, he was neither vicious enough nor foolish enough to order a massacre.

The morning light, at first so gentle on the skin, had hardened and become crueller by the time the last of the sick and dying were carried aboard the galleys, the oar ports opened, and the oars slipped into place. Then everyone waited for the Prince to give the final order.

Cuillioc boarded his flagship, followed by the priest and his attendants. It was his misfortune that Iobhar's galley had been destroyed in the fire, that courtesy demanded he be offered a place on the Prince's own. Yet it was likely to be a brief voyage, Cuillioc consoled himself with grim humor, and it hardly seemed possible that Iobhar's presence could make things any worse than they already were.

He took a last look around him, searching for familiar faces, counting heads, making certain that all the surviving members of his household were present and accounted for, that none of his attendants, sick or well, had been mistakenly left behind. One face was missing.

"Does anyone know if my page came aboard?"

No one did know, and a quick search of the ship failed to locate him. Cuillioc ran a hand through his hair, torn between the danger of any further delay and those same odd impulses that had caused him to take the young thief under his protection in the first place.

"Would you risk the lives of so many, merely to go back for a little gutter-rat your mother's laws have already condemned?" asked Iobhar. He had previously drawn up the hood of his cowl to protect his white skin from the sun; now he lowered it, leaned closer, and pitched his voice so low that only the Prince could hear him. "He hardly looked capable of lasting the night when I saw him. Yet on the very small chance he has survived this long, his friends in the Citadel can do more to keep him alive than we can.

"Perhaps," he added carelessly, "they will even choose to do so."

Aware that the furiádh spoke good sense, Cuillioc reluctantly gave the order to loose the chains and raise the gangplank. In a few moments more, the oars had been raised and the drumbeat began. Slowly, and not at all smoothly, because the rowers were so inexperienced, the oars fell and rose, fell and rose, and one by one the ships slipped away from the quay, their shadows running before them.

Cuillioc now had the leisure to take note of his own condition, to recognize that he himself was far from well. The day was warm—only moments before he had been sweating—but now his teeth were rattling inside his skull and he shivered inside his padded armor. Even when someone produced a lightweight cloak and he gathered it around him, the shivering continued. His world was beginning to fragment, separating into a series of brief, bright moments with blanks in between, and it grew increasingly hard to keep track of consecutive events.

Deciding it was too much effort to go so far as his own cabin, he found a place to sit on the deck, with his back to a water keg. Resting his head against the barrel, he closed his eyes. The rusty-hinge voices of the gulls slowly faded, and he slipped into a quiet, dark place.

A movement of air across his face brought him abruptly back. Stumbling to his feet, he was astonished by how distant and tiny the domed roofs and crazy leaning ziggurats of the city had already become. While he dozed, the flagship and two other galleys had reached the mouth of the bay and were about to cross into the light-drenched waters of the open sea. He had been roused by a strong breeze blowing across the bow from the southwest.

Up on the bridge, the ship's master shouted an order to raise the sail and ship the oars. At the same time, men on board the two galleys just ahead and directly behind performed the same actions. When the great squares of scarlet silk began to fill with wind, Cuillioc felt heartened in spite of himself.

He inhaled deeply, savoring the brisk salt air. Even the motion of the ship felt good—and why not? Island born and island bred, he had been taught to regard the great ocean-sea encircling the world like a serpent biting its own tail as his second home. In truth, he felt easier out here with the wind and the waves than he had ever felt in his mother's palace at Apharos.

Perhaps, he thought, *I need not die after all.* If the air of Mirizandi was pure poison, might not the fresh ocean breezes serve as a powerful medicine? Already he felt stronger.

Then someone near the prow of the ship gave a shout. As heads turned in that direction, other voices rose as well. Cuillioc swerved around to look too.

A pair of ships had been sighted to the south, past a ridge of high cliffs forming a partial barrier between the restless waves of the ocean and the placid sapphire waters of the Bay of Mir. As the galley left the cliffs behind and Cuillioc gained a wider view, it seemed to him, for a dizzying moment, that the whole surface of the water, north, west, and south, was covered with sails: sun yellow, tiger orange, peacock blue. A great fleet of two-masted feluccas and xebecs, along with more formidable vessels of three, four, and even five masts, was closing in from both sides—and every deck on every ship was crowded with armed men whose shields and weapons flashed white fire in the sunlight.

In that incredible proliferation of masts and sails, it was difficult to get any clear idea of the number of enemy ships.

One thing only was obvious: Cuillioc and his thirty-eight galleys were vastly outnumbered.

"But where have they *come* from?"

"In all probability from Persit and Meraz," answered Iobhar, appearing beside him. "Though how they managed to exchange such swift communications with Xanthipei remains a puzzle. One can almost admire their cunning," he added with a snarl, "how well they have executed the entire plan from first to last."

And suddenly, Cuillioc was able to see the whole complicated plot with bitter clarity. *Everything* that had happened was part of the scheme: The slow months of poisoning. All of the beguilements and distractions that kept him and his men in the city until the time was ripe. Followed in due course by the swift events of the night just past, beginning with the fiery destruction of almost half of his galleys, and yes, even the hour when the servants became willing to tell his little page everything they had kept secret for so long.

The timing of each individual step had been calculated with the *utmost precision,* all meant to bring him and his ships out on the water at this present time, in their present weakened state, *just to provide sport for the Mirazhite navy.*

Even for people as indolent as these there could be little amusement, and certainly no glory, in cutting the throats of invaders while they lay sick and dying in their beds, but in attacking ships manned by the walking dead, doing battle with a fleet crippled and in disarray—it seemed there was glory enough.

Yet, oddly, the Prince felt a surge of gratitude. "I would never have expected this last favor," he said under his breath.

There was a flutter of scarlet cloth, and the priest's white face rose up directly in front of him. "Favor? I do not think I understand you."

"No? Then I will explain. Instead of slinking back home in humiliation and defeat, we've been given the chance to make a good end." He started toward the bridge in order to take command while the battle lasted, but Iobhar slipped around him to block the way.

"Perhaps you've forgotten, Great Prince: I can summon a wind that will enable us to outrun the fastest ship in the Mirazhite navy. They have cut off our galleys inside the bay—but this ship, and possibly the ones just ahead and behind, may yet escape. Not so romantic, perhaps, or so compatible with your peculiar idea of honor as going down with the rest of the fleet, but it would be wise—it would be expedient."

Cuillioc flashed him a look of contempt. "No," he said, stepping around the priest and continuing on toward the bridge, so that Iobhar was forced to follow if he meant to hear the rest. "They have given us an opportunity to die like men, and I'm not minded to refuse." Nor was he willing to take two or three ships back to Phaôrax to serve as scapegoats for the entire debacle. He owed his men much more than that.

"They may have chosen us for their *sport,* but I intend to give them a *battle* they will long remember! We stay and fight. In the name of Ouriána—for the honor and glory of Phaôrax."

14
*

By dint of much clumsy maneuvering and a fair degree of luck, Cuillioc's inexperienced oarsmen managed to ram one of the Mirazhite vessels, and Iobhar's sorcery accounted for another, consuming it in a cold, unearthly fire, before one of the enemy ships drew near enough to cast out grappling hooks and catch the Prince's galley in a virtual death grip.

Then there was an exchange of missile fire, in which the taller ship had all of the advantage. Arrows, lances, and rocks rained down on the galley, while Cuillioc's men, retaliating with slings and crossbows, could scarcely see their targets. Even in the first few minutes the slaughter was tremendous, and it might have ended swiftly had not the glittering Mirazhite warriors, eager for glory in hand-to-hand combat, leaped down from their own ship to the deck of the galley.

Then the Pharaxions, fueled by desperation, overcame their weakness and the blood flew in every direction. The Prince himself seemed to be everywhere at once, hair flying, sword running red. One man after another fell before the fury of his onslaught, and all around him the deck was littered with the bodies of men he had killed.

Reckless of his own safety, determined to account for as many of the enemy as possible, he nevertheless knew that he could not last much longer. With the tide in his veins alternating between fire and ice, his pulse pounding like a drumbeat in his ears, he could feel his strength failing, his movements growing heavier and slower, his cuts and thrusts less and less accurate. Sometimes it felt as though the sky was falling down on him, the whole weight of it threatening to crush him. Already several men had gotten past his guard and landed glancing blows. Blood trickled into his eyes from a gash on his forehead, and his whole left side was wet and burning under his armor and padding.

Up on the bridge, Iobhar and his acolytes had been defending themselves with greater success. Omair and Maël waged a furious battle with swords and round shields, for the poison had not much affected them as yet, and the priest fought with chanted spells as well as a long knife. The knife was the lesser weapon, and whoever suffered the touch of his left hand died shrieking.

Suddenly, in the midst of dispatching a tall Mirazhite warrior, Iobhar became aware of dark shadows gliding one after another across the wooden deck. Risking a brief skyward glance through eyes watering with the smoke, he caught sight of a great flock of wyvaerun passing immediately overhead. He had no time for more than a bare glimpse; two more men (refusing to profit from the example of their fellows) closed in on him from either side. But now as he slashed and ducked he was chanting a new spell.

In the sky overhead, the wyvaerun began to wheel about. Minutes later, a dozen of the snake-bird hybrids came plummeting down in a rush of dark wings, striking with beaks, claws, and scaly prehensile tails. For a moment the sun went out like a windblown flame. As the Mirazhites were beaten back, three of the creatures, many times larger than the rest, descended on the furiádh and his servants, hooked their iron claws agonizingly into flesh and muscle, and rose into the sky, carrying Iobhar, Omair, and Maël with them, lifting them back into the searing light.

On the galley below, Prince Cuillioc finally fell beneath a shattering blow from a two-handed axe and moved no more.

Most of that day passed in a delirium of pain before the wyvaerun set the priest and his acolytes down, none too gently, on a barren stretch of shoreline, then soared back into the sky to rejoin their flock.

They left their passengers torn and bleeding, almost more dead than alive. Maël was unconscious and fell in an awkward heap, where he remained for many hours, while Iobhar and the other acolyte lay panting and moaning on the hot sand. Only at moonrise, with the heat of the day beginning to fade, did they recover enough to look to their own welfare, ripping their outer garments into strips to serve as bandages, then lurching painfully to their feet to search for water. Of the three, the furiádh had suffered by far the worst, for the skin of his face and hands had been scorched by the fierce southern light while he dangled in the air helpless to cover himself.

"The Empress has spared our lives by sending her winged messengers to save us," said Omair hoarsely, out of a dry, cracked throat. "But they have handled us cruelly."

Iobhar knew from experience that while the sunburn would fade, his own hurts would never truly mend; the marks would be there always, nor would he ever be entirely free of the pain. "Consider yourself fortunate," he said, baring yellow teeth in one of his unpleasant smiles. "You now bear the stigmata of the Goddess."

They had no way of knowing whether they were still in Mirizandi or safe in Nephuar, but there were no signs of human habitation along the shore, and inland it was dense rain forest concealing any villages there might be nearby. When they finally discovered a spring of sweet water not far distant, Iobhar decided to remain in that spot, set up a camp of sorts in the shade of the exotic vegetation, and remain there for as many days as it took to regain their strength. In any case, the moon was waxing and would be full in another two nights.

The interval was an uneasy one. By day, birds and monkeys made an ear-splitting din in that dense tangle. During the deep indigo nights the sounds were fewer and more ominous: yelps and screams, occasionally accompanied by the rank stench of some large predator. So little they knew of these southern lands outside the cities that it was impossible to reckon the dangers.

On the night of the full moon, Iobhar limped alone through the forest, heading for the shore. Fireflies hung in the dark under the trees like sparks from a furnace, but when he came out into the open, the beach was drenched in cool white moonlight. It was a clear sky, but the stars seemed faint and tremulous compared to that tremendous moon.

Removing a silver disk from a pocket in his robe, he placed it reverently on the sand, so that the glory of the greater disk might be reflected in its smaller counterpart. He had lost a flask of oil blessed in the temple on Phaôrax, but because the moon and the tides were so intimately linked, seawater would serve in its place.

Scooping up a palmful of water from a tidepool like a sheet of black glass, Iobhar allowed it to drip from his hand onto the metal disk. Gradually, the silver clouded over, then began to shimmer with unwholesome purple light.

He sensed the presence of the Goddess, like heavy perfume, even before her face appeared on the disk. Though her image was tiny, the priest could see that her face was drained of color, her eyes intent and electric with tension. Her fiery auburn hair seemed to crackle. *There was a battle at sea,* said the voice inside her head. *I saw it in one of the Dragonstones, though only dimly.* All *of our ships were lost?*

I fear so, said Iobhar. *We were greatly outnumbered. There was no other possible outcome.* He hesitated, cringing at the thought of what he must tell her next, but knowing that Ouriána's wrath would be a hundred times worse if the news came belatedly and from other lips. *And, I grieve to inform you, Prince Cuillioc is dead. He fought bravely, his enemies fell in great numbers, yet even so valiant a man could not hope to prevail against so many.*

There was a long, nerve-racking silence before she responded. *My son is dead?* A shudder passed over her, then there was another lengthy silence, during which the furiádh squirmed uneasily.

Prince Cuillioc is dead, she said at last, *and yet* you, *Iobhar, were spared?*

He had prepared himself to answer the question in advance, but now that the moment had arrived, all the words he had planned nearly deserted him. *Before I left for Mirizandi, you told me that the one thing you could not tolerate was another failure from Prince Cuillioc, another humiliating defeat.*

Her eyes narrowed, and he could almost hear the hiss of her indrawn breath. *And so you arranged for him to die a hero's death?*

Oh no, Radiance, he protested, panic beating in his breast. *I arranged nothing. Let us say, merely, that I did nothing to prevent a heroic death from overtaking him. Did I mistake your meaning? Have I done wrong?*

A third time Ouriána was terrifyingly silent, while Iobhar waited in agonizing suspense for her reply, and her image wavered like the moon seen through water.

No, she said finally. *No, you have not done wrong. In truth, the reason I sent you with him to Mirizandi was because I knew you would not be deterred, as another might, by sentimental attachment to the Prince, from doing what needed to be done.*

She heaved a great sigh. Squinting at the disk, the better to see her face, Iobhar was startled by an expression he had never seen there before—not grief precisely, but a kind of angry perplexity, as if she, who was always so sure, so unshakable, did not quite know what she ought to be feeling. *And yet my son is dead.*

Iobhar bowed his head in mock sorrow. *Many have lost sons in the war, Radiance. Fathers, brothers, lovers—many have died, and women and children have mourned them. Your great sacrifice sanctifies their smaller sacrifices.*

Yes, she replied bleakly. *All are sanctified by the death of my son. You say—you say that he died well?*

In truth, he died most heroically, Iobhar said unctuously. *Died as he lived, valiantly, honorably.*

Then, said the Empress just before her image began to fade, *I must arrange for him a hero's funeral.*

15

✳

Sindérian was growing hardened to a swift mode of travel, to taking her sleep in snatches and eating most of her meals cold. Besides, it suited her desire for speed.

Three days and the better part of two nights of hard riding brought the company under Prince Kivik's leadership out of the mountains and into the foothills, where the grass grew sparse and coarse on rocky slopes. At a place where the road divided, they found unmistakable signs that retreating Eisenlonders had marched off in one direction, roughly east, while the Furiádhin chose the other road, tending toward the south.

"I know a third way we might take," offered one of the Skyrran riders, after a careful study of the marks in the dust. He had been a hunter before the war and one of Prince Kivik's scouts since, and was chosen as part of this company because he knew the hill country well. "Not an easy trail but much more direct, and it should bring us through the hills and back to the road again in half the time."

"Then by all means, Orri, show us that way," said Prince Kivik. "If we can gain a day on the villains who have taken my cousin, let the path be as hard as it will!"

Back in the saddle, the scout led them through what looked like an impenetrable wall of brush to a trail no one would have suspected from the other side, it was so thoroughly screened by boulders and shrubbery. At first it took them on a meandering course over the shoulders of the hills, then the path narrowed and made a sudden plunge, down a slope so steep it was necessary to dismount and lead their horses.

To call it a trail at that point would have been too generous, it was so poorly marked and the footing so treacherous. Sindérian lost her balance before she reached the bottom and slid the rest of the way, but Aell was beside her almost immediately, offering a hand up. She was quickly on her feet again, with scant loss to her dignity and only a few shallow scratches where she had grasped at thorny shrubs on her way down.

Back in the saddle, they urged the horses into a brisk trot. They were in a deep cleft between the hills, which turned out to be a very good trail, keeping to a nearly straight course for miles and miles. Yet as the day went on it became uncomfortably warm in that airless pocket between two slopes, until Sindérian found herself longing for a breath of wind.

It was still early the following day when a sharp bend in the trail brought them out of the foothills, into an open country vivid with wildflowers and short, springy turf. The weary, plodding horses became frisky and eager. It seemed to raise the spirits of the men as well.

Eventually, they came back to the same road they had

abandoned in the mountains, where the scouts discovered evidence of a camp along the verge, cold ashes where the Pharaxions had lit a fire and cooked a meal.

"They were here the night before last," Orri reported to Prince Kivik. "We *have* gained on them, but not so much as I hoped."

"The Furiádhin will be taking fewer and shorter rests than we do," said Sindérian. "They make little of discomfort themselves—and their guards and acolyte-servants have no choice."

"Then we have no choice either. We must ride harder and longer too," said Skerry, coming up just in time to hear this exchange. "We followed this same road before, in the other direction. It has many windings, but we can cut across country some of the time."

Under his raven-dark hair, his face was pale and set in lines of pain as well as determination. Long days in the saddle could only be torture on newly healed wounds—Sindérian wondered if she had done the right thing, encouraging him and Prince Kivik in the belief they were strong enough to ride. Yet would they, under any circumstances, have consented to stay behind?

They rode due south all of that day, where the grass grew higher, thicker, and greener, and the short turf gave way to beardgrass, foxtail, and wild oat. Once they left the road it became obvious the land was not nearly so flat as it looked from a distance. There were dips and hollows, dells and gullies, streams and wetlands; sometimes the fields were divided by sharp spines of stone, rising up like natural barriers.

Sindérian sensed desolation and a deep sadness through

all this land. Travelling in the Autlands on the way to Tirfang there had been countless deserted farms and villages along the way, but little actual destruction. The Haestfilke had another tale to tell: charred ruins of manors, farmhouses, and settlements dotted the countryside; vast grain fields and orchards had been burned to the ground; crops that had somehow escaped the Eisenlonders' attention lay untended in the heat. Occasionally, a great cairn of stones marked a mass grave; more often they rode past battlefields where acres and acres of bones lay bleaching in the sun.

Late on their second day of riding through this lonely country, one of the scouts pointed out a thread of silver smoke rising like a warning in the sky ahead of them.

"There are none of our farmers and herders left in this part of the realm," said Kivik. "And while it might be a company of our own warriors, it will probably be more of the cursed Eisenlonders. We are too few to challenge a large band of them, so we will go around on the west and try to avoid meeting them." Yet he took his sword out of its sheath and carried it naked across his saddlebow in case of trouble, and the other men did the same.

They rode on for several miles in the gathering twilight, veering toward the sunset. After they turned south again, a smudge of light grew on the horizon directly ahead, and brighter flares bloomed in the darkness to the east and west.

Kivik called for a halt. "This is as close as we dare go, until we learn whose fires those are."

"I don't understand why they have spread out over such a distance," said Skerry, peering through the darkness. "No single encampment could be so large."

It was decided Faolein should fly ahead and scout out the encampment, whoever it belonged to. The hawk launched himself into the sky and set off in the direction of the distant fires. It did not take long for him to disappear in the dusky air.

While the others awaited his return, they made a camp in a little hollow behind one of the bony ridges, kindling only the smallest blaze so that the light could not be seen by hostile eyes.

Sooner than anyone might have expected him, Faolein was back again. He landed in the grass at Sindérian's feet, ruffled his feathers, tilted his head, and looked at her out of one firelit yellow eye.

It is not at all as we thought, he told her. *They* are *Eisenlonders, but not roving bands. They are felling trees in a little woodland to the south. Elsewhere, they are digging ditches, hammering together stockades and pens for their horses; the next step, it would seem, will be building houses and planting crops.*

Her eyes widened as she absorbed the news. This was not information she was eager to relay to Kivik and Skerry, but it had to be done.

"There are the beginnings of farms and villages up ahead," she told them. "It appears that some of the Eisenlonders have made up their minds to stay."

"It is good land here, despite their depredations," said Kivik, his fingers curling into fists. "And maybe we shouldn't be surprised that having come so far, having murdered or run off the rightful inhabitants, they mean to live on that land themselves."

"But how could they have settled in so quickly?" asked Skerry. "Those creatures out of Phaôrax are hardly more than a day ahead of us, and even if they *have* been spreading the word that Ouriána is severing her ties with Eisenlonde, that's no time for the barbarians to put aside their murdering ways and take up farming!"

Prince Ruan was the first to guess. "It might be that they heard the news earlier, as the Furiádhin rode north. Or perhaps they simply grew impatient of wanton destruction and decided to take something of value for themselves." His brows came together and his extravagantly colored eyes glittered in the firelight. "In the end, what does it matter? There they are, and there it would seem they intend to stay."

In the days that followed, Prince Kivik's riders were often obliged to turn aside from their chosen road as more and more of the new settlements sprang up ahead of them. *So much for any last lingering notion that the war might be over,* Sindérian thought unhappily. In all likelihood Skyrrans and Eisenlonders would be disputing this territory for the next hundred years.

Summer was wasting away toward autumn; the nights were getting longer and the days had lost much of their heat. These reminders of the passage of time, along with the detours and delays, only increased the crushing sense of dread that pressed on her. Day after day, and mile after mile, a thousand fears took shape in her mind: Camhóinhann would sacrifice Winloki as soon as he came to the shores of the sea. Or he would do it out on the water, where Ouriána's influence was most potent. Or he and his cohorts had only been waiting for an auspicious hour or phase of the moon, which had finally arrived; the knives were already being sharpened.

But they can't have harmed her yet. I would know if she were dead, Sindérian told herself over and over.

Faolein said the same, though with more assurance. *Such a momentous event would never pass unnoticed. Too many webs of cause and effect, probability and circumstance, would unravel with the Princess's death—and the downfall of the prophecy would be the very least of it.*

Sindérian knew that he spoke the truth. Such was Winloki's latent power that her violent passing must send shock after shock along the ley lines.

Yet none of that served to diminish her fears until Faolein began to give her thoughts a new direction by teaching her some of the lessons in magic she had missed by leaving the Scholia so early. *War called you away too soon,* he told her. *We both know that you would be capable of more, much more, if you had stayed to study longer.*

Other healers made that same sacrifice, she protested. *How could I have stayed behind, when so many went out before me?*

But few, very few, with natural gifts to match your own. Oh, the need for healers is great, I cannot deny it, said Faolein. *But there may come a time of greater need when more will be required of you.*

And so the lessons began, most often during the quiet hours of the night when only the men assigned to guard the camp were awake: first those things she already knew, but always in such a way that even the most basic principles of magic led on to a deeper understanding of greater mysteries. Thus he led her, step by step, through the Wizard's Runes—so different from the runes of ordinary writing—then on to the various spells of white magic: the *lledrion, béanath,* and *shibeath.* The last two were already old friends, for these were the charms of blessing, protection, and healing. Now he taught her other applications, equally benign.

Of the darker spells, the *waethas,* and the curses, *aneiras* and *aniffath,* she learned only enough to understand their dangers. *Of all spells,* said Faolein, *curses are the most difficult to undo. Only Master Wizards may attempt it, and rarely with any success.*

The *lledrion* had its basis in knowledge of the eight elements. *Each element carries within it some basic intention, the thing which distinguishes it from primal matter: in mist, mutability; in light, illumination; in wind, movement; and so forth. All things have intention, but only animals and the speaking races have will. It is through the power of will that the magician imposes his or her intentions on the material world.*

There came a time when it became necessary to put some of these lessons into practice. Then Sindérian insisted on taking her turn alone for the late-night vigils, that she might work in peace and not startle the men with displays of magic. "Not truly alone," she told Prince Kivik. "My father watches with me. And it is only fair that we take our turn." Her other reasons she kept to herself. Faolein's keen senses would be always alert and the camp would be safe—that was all that the others needed to know.

Those spells are easiest which encourage things to do what is already in their nature, he told her on the first of these nights. *To make a breeze into a great wind is not so difficult, for even the faintest breeze already carries within it the intention of movement. To call up a wind in a dead calm, that is a greater mastery. The air is still, it intends to remain so. In convincing it to do otherwise you must change its very nature. As for fire, because it is already fluid it is easily shaped, but to make it cool enough to handle you must perform the elemental spell, the* lledrion. *You speak the spell, and if your will is strong enough, the fire answers in the way that you wish.*

So Sindérian spent all the rest of that night, until it came time to wake the Prince's men for the dawn watch, learning to hold fire in the palm of her hand without being scorched by it. In the beginning it was difficult, and more than once she was burned. *But if you are wise you will leave one small scar,* said Faolein as she worked a healing spell, *to remind yourself never to take your power over fire for granted. Like all of the animate elements, its intention—in this case heat—is very strong. As you have seen, if you let your will or your attention flag for a single instant, it will have its way.*

That lesson learned, she spent the next night shaping fire into one form after another: flowers, birds, wheels, sunbursts, shields, towers. On the third night she wove it into long, shining ropes. Implicit in all this, but never spoken, was the knowledge that fire might also be used as a weapon.

They passed from open country into a region of scattered woods and meandering watercourses. Riding past a stand of low oaks and dense brush, late one afternoon when the shadows were long and the shade of the trees lay full across their road, Sindérian felt a sudden tingling at the base of her skull, a prickling across the skin. She had only time enough to shout a warning to the other riders, at the same instant that Faolein rose screaming into the air, before chaos came hurtling at them out of the woods.

A dozen Eisenlonders, ahorse and afoot, had them half-surrounded in seconds. Knives flashed as the barbarians closed in, going for the vulnerable legs and bellies of the horses. Two horses were hamstrung immediately, throwing their riders to the ground, where the Eisenlonders quickly finished them off. By then the Skyrrans had whipped out their swords and rallied their defenses, and the battle began in earnest. One barbarian fell, ridden down by Lord Skerry. Another was impaled by Kivik's sword. Prince Ruan cut to left and right in a blur of motion, killing one man after another.

But an arc of riders appeared out of nowhere, sweeping in from the other side. Horses went down screaming. One man was decapitated, and another cut almost in half as blood spattered everywhere. The hawk entered the fray, swooping down again and again with slashing beak and talons. Sindérian had been so jostled and pushed aside that she was outside the circle. So she could only watch helplessly, knowing herself useless in a fight, until one of the barbarians spotted her, broke away from the melee, and whipping up his rawboned grey bore down on her. She tried to turn her horse and make for the woods, but the mare was fighting the bit and would not budge, dig in her heels and pull on the reins as Sindérian might.

She could see Prince Ruan, silver-blond hair and red cape flying, as he spurred his horse and rode into a wall of swords and spears, trying to reach her. One spearman fell; Ruan slashed at another, reined back, and whirled on a third who was threatening his flank. He broke free, scattering the barbarians before him, and was out of the circle.

By then, the Eisenlonder was already on her. The mare had finally consented to move, but she was far too slow compared to the grey coming in at full gallop. Sindérian ducked and just avoided a whirling axe. She fumbled for the knife at her belt, knowing all the time that it offered no defense against an armed man twice her size.

But as the blade slid out from the sheath, an unexpected instinct took over. The knife seemed to move of its own volition, and her mouth formed the words before she even thought them: *"Cyllig tinar domha! Tinarach llathan!"*

With the strength of Sindérian's spell behind it, the backhanded thrust took the Eisenlonder in the gut—and kept right on going, up through the stomach and into the heart, coming to a grating stop only when it hit a rib. Her fist on the hilt followed after the blade, shearing through flesh, muscle, and the organs beneath. She managed to jerk the knife loose just as he toppled from the saddle, and her hand came out covered in blood and trailing viscera.

The skirmish was over. The wounded and the dying were scattered on the ground in all directions. Sliding down from the saddle, Sindérian managed to make it as far as the bushes before she dropped to her knees and heaved out the contents of her stomach. It seemed she would never be done gagging and retching, even after there was nothing left but burning bile.

She had *known* why it was that healers never carried arms into battle, but the reality was infinitely worse than anything she could have imagined: to be slayer and slain at the same time; to feel the shock along the nerves as the knife went in, the last convulsion of the heart; to hear the shriek that leaped from his mind to hers as the soul was ripped from the body in a white blaze and hurled out into eternity. As for the incredible butchery of how she had done it . . . She began to shake so hard she could not catch her breath.

Through the grey haze, the shuddering and heaving, she had only a confused impression of the sounds and movements around her.

"Is the Lady injured?"

"Not, I think, in any way the rest of us could possibly understand," said Prince Ruan's voice very close to her ear. She realized, with vague surprise, that his was the strong arm supporting her, his the hand that held back her hair as she vomited again and again.

After a time the tremors became less, the screaming inside her head subsided, and she found she could breathe again. Her vision cleared and she became aware of her surroundings. Aell was kneeling in the leaf mold beside her, offering a flask of water to wash out her mouth, but after only a tiny sip nausea clawed at her stomach.

"I'm sorry" was the first thing Sindérian could think of to say.

The man-at-arms shrugged. "I've seen men taken worse after a first kill—and with less reason than you, maybe."

Embarrassed by her own weakness, she struggled to her feet. "There must be men who were hurt, men who need healing," she whispered hoarsely.

Prince Ruan did not withdraw his support—which was fortunate, for when she caught a glimpse of her hand and arm, bloody to the elbow, the world turned as transparent as water for a moment, and she could neither see nor stand. "It doesn't look as if any of the injured men are in immediate peril of dying," he said, helping her to sit again. "Let their comrades look after them until you are feeling more like yourself."

Sindérian nodded wordlessly. It did not appear she had any choice in the matter, as wave after wave of dizziness passed over her.

Over by the horses, she could hear Orri and one of the other scouts reproaching themselves. "It shouldn't have happened that way. We should have noticed the woods were too quiet. We should have *seen* something—"

"No," she said from her place on the ground. "There was a spell on the wood—they had someone with them, a warlock or a hedge-wizard, but I sensed him too late."

Footsteps crunched on dry leaves as Prince Kivik came up beside her. "One of their barbarian shamans? But that isn't one of their usual tricks. They call down curses and other mischief; they don't bother with illusions."

"We've all been changed by the war and its aftermath—the Eisenlonders no less than ourselves," said Skerry. There was a bloody cloth wrapped around his hand where someone had inexpertly bandaged it. "The world we knew doesn't exist anymore."

They buried their dead and continued on the next morning, more warily than before, some of the men riding double to support injured comrades. Within a few more days they left the Haestfilke and came into marshy lowlands: a vast wilderness of reeds, cattails, and queer spiky grasses, stretching as far as the eye could see.

It was a wild, unfriendly, and nearly uninhabited region where the war had never come. And even though it fell within the boundaries of King Ristil's realm, it was unknown country. It did, however, give promise of abundant game—duck and heron and blackbird and otter—a welcome prospect to empty bellies, since the provisions they brought with them from the mountains were now so low that meals were few and meager. Some of the riders carried bows with them, and Orri in particular had never been known to miss his shot, so everyone began to look forward to meat for supper.

While two men dismounted and went stalking game, Kivik, Skerry, Ruan, and Sindérian held a brief consultation. The two Skyrran princes searched through their memories, hoping to dredge up vague recollections of maps they had seen.

"The rivers Nisse and Sark converge somewhere to the east of here," Skerry remembered, "so the land in that direction will only get lower and wetter. Going around would take many days. But men do live here, so there must be a road or trails to take us through. I suggest that we look for one."

This seemed sensible, and after the hunters came back (with their bag of four fat ducks and an unidentified waterfowl), the company turned their faces west. After a few hours riding along the outskirts of the marsh, they came upon a trail, or something very like one, which seemed to promise a way through the fens.

It had now been so long since they parted with the King— and they had no way of knowing how close he and his army followed behind, or whether his scouts had been able to track their course so far—there was a strong possibility that once they entered the fens he would never be able to find and catch up with them at all. The only remedy seemed to be to send Faolein winging along their backtrail until he met the King—

after which it ought to be easy, from his aerial viewpoint, to locate the Prince's company again and bring both parties together.

The wizard consented to this plan—rather more readily than Sindérian, though why she should feel such a pang of misgiving she did not know. She watched him so long as he remained in sight, then gathered up the reins and followed the rest of the company as they headed deeper into the marsh.

For several hours, the trail took them through acres of sedge, willow, and osiers, and if it never quite failed them, neither did it entirely win their confidence. For just when they thought they had lost it in a mire, it reappeared on the other side. And as soon as they began to feel sure of it, it ended on the banks of a muddy stream. One of the scouts waded gingerly across, expecting at every step to be swallowed by quicksand or drowned by bog monsters, but on reaching the other side he motioned to the others that it was safe to follow him. They splashed through the water, and there on the opposite bank, hidden by a clump of cattails, was their wayward little trail again.

Sometimes, as the day wore on, they saw puffs of smoke rising in the distance, which Sindérian took to be evidence of hearth fires and the haunts of men, though the track never brought them within sight of any houses, and the marshlanders continued to be purely conjectural.

Toward evening, the path wandered into a maze of watercourses and murky-looking pools. The ground became unstable; in places, to their horror, the riders could feel it moving under them. Mud sucked greedily at the horses' hooves, and one of the extra mounts managed to stumble into quicksand. It took four of the men more than an hour to pull the poor, panicky beast out again.

Sunset had turned all the dark pools into melted gold and deepened the shadows within the reeds and sedges when Sindérian chanced to catch a flash of bright color, so far distant and so swiftly gone she could not even be certain what she had seen. She twisted around in the saddle to ask if Prince Ruan had spotted it, too.

He nodded his head, urged his sorrel stallion to a faster walk until he came abreast of her leggy bay gelding. "There *are* riders up ahead: men in black and men in scarlet. But the way that this trail meanders back and forth, we are probably hours and miles behind them."

It took a moment for Sindérian to truly take it in—that Winloki and her captors could actually, finally, be so near. Her heart gave a great leap, battering against her ribs, then resumed its ordinary rhythm. "And do you think they have seen *us*?"

"Our own colors are not so showy, and the light is fading. Even if they're keeping an eye on their backtrail, I doubt they have spotted us." He leaned a little closer. "If we should overtake them, what will you do? *Delay them*, that is what you said before, until King Ristil and his army could finally catch up to us. But how do you mean to accomplish anything of the sort—and without Faolein?"

Sindérian shook her head, having no answer to give him. After a fortnight on the road, and every day of it living toward this moment, she was still caught unprepared. But then, she had been depending all along on the hour and the place to show her what she must do.

And so it will, she told herself. *When we have closed the distance a little more.*

In the meantime, it seemed advisable to tell the others what she and the Prince had seen. A thrill went through the entire company as the word spread. Men loosened their swords in their scabbards; all signs of weariness fell away. Even the horses caught some of the excitement and began to dance and shake their heads.

It now seemed imperative to press on as long as they were able, which unfortunately meant putting off the meal everyone had been anticipating—a small consideration, but difficult not to think about as night fell and stomachs began to rumble.

It was a clear sky, with the moon an almost perfect circle of incandescent silver, casting a light so bright they could see their shadows moving on ahead of them. To Sindérian's heightened senses, the night was touched with mystery and wonder. Owls swooped overhead; frogs sang shrill, insistent songs in the rushes; every pool reflected back a galaxy of stars.

Finally reaching higher and safer ground, they had to stop for sheer weariness. They made a fire out of dried reeds that they braided into sticks, and for a time some of the men were busy dressing and cooking the birds, while others looked after the horses.

Sindérian woke, cramped and shivering, to a misty grey world, and sounds of the camp stirring back to life around her. She sat bolt upright, realizing with a shock of dismay that like everyone else she had drifted off to sleep almost immediately after eating. If there had been any discussion of who should stand watch, she could not remember it.

Scrambling to her feet, she made a hurried survey of the camp and was relieved to see that all were present and unharmed. No one looked any the worse for a few hours of sleep. And though Faolein had not returned, she had not really expected to see him again so soon.

On this morning there was no breakfast, just saddling up the horses, tightening their girths, then forcing cold, stiff limbs back into the saddle again. As the company set off, mist continued to rise from the ground in veils, wreaths, and twisting serpents.

It *smelled* like an ordinary fog, Sindérian decided, sniffing the air. It felt like one, too. Yet her intuition told her it was no such thing, even if she could sense no immediate harm in it.

After an hour's ride, the trail simply ended at a wide expanse of ominous, dark water. Prince Ruan said he could just make out the other side, but the keen-eyed scouts could not, defeated by the fog and distance. Faced with acres of cattails barely able to keep their heads above a scummy surface, not even Ruan wanted to attempt to cross.

"Perhaps we went astray among the pools and quagmires yesterday," Prince Kivik suggested. "Or maybe we missed a fork in the trail, riding after dark."

They turned and backtracked for about a mile until one of the scouts, beating back the high grass, uncovered another path branching off from their own, which no one had noticed before. It was even more narrow than the one they had followed and was probably only a game trail, but it did head roughly south.

At first it seemed to be the right choice; the trail ran more or less straight, and much of the time on high, firm ground.

The fog lifted. A faint salty breeze blew in their faces, promising a glimpse of the sea before nightfall. Then they came to a place where the path divided—or two trails met—presenting them with the choice of three different directions. After some consultation they chose the right-hand turning—only to be disappointed a mile or two later when the path brought them up short at a particularly nasty-looking bog.

By the time they had returned to the fork they were all missing Faolein, and his ability to soar aloft and take accurate bearings. Overhead it was bold, bright noon, and suddenly no one could remember which way was south.

"We will stop here a while," Kivik decided at last, "and wait until the sun gives us back our sense of direction."

Long before evening, everyone knew that they had been riding in circles most of the day. Trails had divided, looped, run into each other, ended at streams or at standing water, sometimes just *ended* for no reason at all. The one thing that no path ever seemed to do was bring them any closer to finding a way out of the fens.

Even knowing that she took a risk in doing so, with Ouriána's powerful High Priest not far distant, Sindérian had twice been desperate enough to extend her senses outward and ahead, trying to discover what awaited them farther down a trail—and each time she had succeeded only in becoming disoriented. In a maze like this one, she thought sourly, a person might go mad with frustration, with the winding trails and the endless gurgling and trickling of the waters.

Then, quite suddenly, she understood—truly, she must have been addled not to see it before! She drew rein and fell back, letting the others ride past her, before she dismounted.

She stooped down by one of the sluggish streamlets. Scooping up a handful of water, she raised it to her lips. It was brackish, definitely brackish. To anyone else it was only water, but to a wizard it was more, much more: it tasted of salt and seaweed, sharks and shellfish; it carried more than a hint of ocean depths, for it was almost three-quarters seawater. There was water here that whales had swum in and ships had crossed—the very same water that she and her friends had nearly drowned in not so many weeks ago.

A waxing moon and a high tide. She sat back on her heels, grinding her teeth in vexation. *And channels and currents and arteries of seawater running through the marshes, mixing with the fresh water.*

But most of all it was the *aniffath,* Ouriána's curse. Every last bit of ill luck that Sindérian left behind when she had travelled inland, it was all flowing back to her the nearer she approached the sea, carried on those same currents of brackish water. *And now the others are caught up in it as well, simply for riding in company with me.*

She knew the spell might release them eventually; she was reasonably confident it would. It might even lose its grip on *her* in a day or two, when the moon decreased and the tides lost a little of their force. It would not be the first time she had somehow managed to survive in spite of Ouriána's ill will.

But long before that happened it would be too late; the Furiádhin would have reached the coast, where they could buy, steal, or conjure up a boat. They—and Winloki with them—would have already set sail.

16

*

Winloki stood on a low bluff overlooking the sea, watching the waves advance and retreat, fascinated by their constant motion. Winds swirled around her: that from the land pushing her forward, that from the sea cold and stinging with salt. Beyond her vantage point there was nothing but air and water so far as the eye could see. She felt as if she were balanced at the end of the world, on the edge of forever: behind her everything she knew, directly ahead an unknown and unfathomable future.

When she turned to look over her shoulder, back toward the land, she caught another tantalizing glimpse of a tiny town situated across the narrow inlet: an irregular line of gabled roofs, stacked-stone chimneys, and untidy storks' nests, partly screened by sand dunes and dune grass.

A party of guards and acolytes had been dispatched to replenish provisions and to look for a boat capable of carrying fifteen people in reasonable comfort and safety across the channel. Though hardly more than a fishing village, this was the largest settlement they expected to find within hundreds of miles—and in all likelihood the last little bit of Skyrra and the Skyrran people Winloki would ever see. Her wish to be there was so intense, she could almost smell the woodsmoke and boiling cabbage, hear the washerwomen gossiping over their soapy cauldrons and the creaking of cart wheels in the streets.

The winds blew a lock of red-gold hair into her eyes, fluttered the ragged skirts of her gown. When she reached up to brush the hair from her face, she felt a familiar tug on the silver chain joining the manacle bracelets, constricting her movements, preventing her spells—most of all reminding her that she was a prisoner. Time and again she had tried to break the bracelets or force them open, but as delicate as they looked, they remained impervious. Nor could she ever learn the knack of removing and replacing the chain, no matter how many times she saw Camhóinhann perform that action.

She glanced at the armored youths standing to her right and left, her guards, her shadows: Marrec and Efflam, Lochdaen and Kerion. They were, she had learned during these last weeks of captivity, simple men and not unkindly, pledged to the temple in Apharos since they were boys of fourteen or fifteen, in order that their families or their villages might gain dispensations, with no choice in the matter at all. One might call *them* prisoners too, except that they had no desire to better their situation. They worshipped Ouriána, so far as Winloki could tell, with a pure and simple faith, but her white-haired priests they feared and obeyed—and no amount of proximity could lessen that fear or call that obedience into question.

Well, she admitted with an inward sigh, *no reasonable person could fault them for that.* For her part, she was growing accustomed to the Furiádhin in this much only, that sometimes when she looked at them she saw men, not monsters. Yet they were just as terrifying in what remained of their humanity as in what they had become: Goezenou, that bottomless well of hunger and devouring need; Dyonas, fierce, brilliant, and utterly heartless; and Camhóinhann, the enigma, the riddle she had no wish to unravel.

They had eldritch powers, did Ouriána's priests. They could do uncanny things. But the worst by far, in Winloki's estimation, was an ability to inflict frenzy or paralysis, to compel the temple guards and acolytes to absolute obedience, without lifting a hand or saying a word.

With that thought, the wind suddenly felt colder and sharper; the Princess shivered and hugged the tattered brown cloak more closely around her. No one had seen fit to chastise *her,* but she felt the threat of it always. She countered that fear by resisting the priests in every way that she could, though her gestures of defiance had so far been met with perfect indifference. Sometimes she did sense strong passions moving between them, for which she was the apparent source—but it seemed that she roused those emotions merely by *being,* not by anything she did or said.

At sunset, the wind dropped, the sea turned a sullen red, and those who had visited the town returned. "We looked at many boats," said Rivanon, the chief acolyte, "and some were large enough and sound enough to suit our purpose, but none that the fishermen were willing to sell."

Which means that they are going to steal somebody's boat,

Winloki thought bitterly, watching the men break up their temporary camp and prepare the horses for the short ride into town. It was not to be supposed that Camhóinhann and the rest would allow the wishes or the rights of mere fishermen to stand in their way.

By the time they reached the outskirts of the town, a huge lopsided moon hovered over the housetops, and the peaked roofs made long shadows on the ground. Winloki rode through the narrow, unpaved streets breathless and watchful. Bats squeaked, swooping overhead; a door slammed in another part of town; yet the way to the harbor seemed strangely quiet. No light leaked out between closed shutters or glowed behind windows made of glass or horn. Even a little tavern they passed—which ought to have been overflowing with business at this early hour—was as silent as a graveyard.

Winloki swung around in the saddle to accuse Dyonas. "What have you *done* to the people who live on these streets?"

"The people in these houses will sleep until morning," he replied carelessly. The acolytes riding before and behind him were mere blots of darkness, but the robes of the priests had turned a deep wine-red. "Why should we wish to harm them? They are less than nothing to us."

Stung by the utter indifference in his quicksilver eyes, she could not resist challenging him. "Then why meddle with them at all? It can't be that you *fear* these people."

"If the whole town rose up against us they could not stop us. But were they to cause us any inconvenience—that would be *their* misfortune."

The words she had been about to say froze in her throat. The image of Camhóinhann riding down Haakon and Arvi at

Tirfang remained painfully clear in her mind; she knew that just as the Furiádhin had killed to take her, they would surely kill to keep her.

At last they came to the little harbor. In spite of her fears Winloki looked eagerly around her. Though she had no actual memories of sailing vessels, she dreamed of them often. Yet her first glimpse of the fishing boats brought a stab of disappointment. These shabby wooden tubs, with their weathered hulls and fishy odors, fell far short of her expectations—and the way they rose and dipped with every movement of the water made her stomach feel queasy.

After a brief inspection, Camhóinhann singled out one of the larger boats. She had two masts and was nearly as broad in the beam as she was long, but he seemed to think her seaworthy. Several of the men jumped lightly on board, where they began doing things with ropes and canvas that Winloki could in no wise understand. The rest unloaded the packhorses, unstrapping bedrolls, saddlebags, and knapsacks.

Through all this activity, Winloki sat with her hands clasped together under her cloak, struggling with a sickening panic.

I simply can't do it, she told herself, terrified that once she left Skyrran soil she would never find her way back again. *If they mean to kill me, let them do it here.* With such thoughts running through her brain, when Marrec reached up to help her down from the saddle she instinctively thrust out both hands to stop him.

"Walk or be carried," hissed a rough voice, and looking back over her shoulder, she saw Goezenou watching her with malign satisfaction. "Either way, you *will* go aboard."

The idea of being touched by his snakeskin hands made

Winloki physically ill. She plucked up her courage and slid down from the saddle—disdaining the young guard's offered assistance—and stood on unsteady legs, willing them not to give way.

"You are robbing some family of their livelihood." She tried to say it haughtily, but her voice wobbled and came out much smaller than she had intended.

"And enriching their neighbors," said Dyonas, coming up beside her. "We have no time to become horse traders—it could be weeks before we found anyone with the price of so many fine horses in a town the size of this one. We will leave them behind, along with their saddles and bridles, for whoever finds them in the morning."

At last everything was ready. Tents, food, and other supplies had been transferred from the horses to the boat, and Winloki had reached the point where she had no choice but to follow them on board.

Not like a coward and not *like a prisoner,* she decided, squaring her shoulders and lifting her chin. She accepted the offer of Efflam's hand getting over the gunwales, allowed somebody else to guide her to a seat. The remaining men scrambled over the side after her and found places for themselves in the bottom of the boat.

Someone moved between her and the moonlight, and Winloki looked up to see Camhóinhann standing over her, with his white hair floating on the wind and his legs braced against the pitching and tossing of the boat. The light made a halo around his head.

"Where are we going?" she asked, over the frantic drumming of her heart. "Will we be sailing to Phaôrax?" She had little idea of geography, and only the vaguest notion of distances.

"No. The seas have lately become perilous, even for us. It would be folly to attempt a long voyage, and doubly so in a fishing boat."

Folly however you look at it, Winloki thought. Yet she could see that the men were pleased and excited, as if they were quite at home in this preposterous vessel, as if the ocean might be something more to them than a watery wasteland.

Catching her eye, Marrec smiled encouragingly. "We are islanders all—and islanders know the sea like shepherds know sheep, or farmers the soil. Have no fear: we will take you safely across."

As the boat slid silently away from the dock, the lights burning in distant parts of the town gradually receded until they were nothing more than yellow sparks shining in the dark. Long before they reached deep water, Winloki had already resigned herself to drowning. The way the boat groaned and protested, it sounded as if she were being battered to death by the waves. One moment a great billow would lift her up, up, up, under that tipsy moon. The next there was nothing beneath her but air, and the boat would drop, hitting the milky water with stunning force, sending up fountains of drenching spray. The sensation of falling was so unnerving, the Princess was convinced each time that the boat would be pitched with all on board into some deep abyss of the sea.

Instead of creeping inside the tent some of the men erected for her use in the stern, Winloki sat up all night. Yet by the time dawn crept like a shadow over the ocean—and the boat had not been swamped or sunk—she began to share, tentatively, some of the confidence the others felt. And when the rim of the sun rose up from the waters, setting the entire ocean on fire, she had to allow that there was something rather fine in this battle the men fought with wind and wave.

But in daylight the ocean appeared much wider, the horizon less defined, as if sea and sky were all one element. Without landmarks she was unable to gain any true idea of their progress; it seemed they might hang suspended forever in this vast blue nothingness.

Then Camhóinhann moved past her, his red robes whipping in the wind, and there was a flash of silver as he drew one of his long knives.

And so it comes, she thought on an indrawn breath, bracing herself for the worst, closing her eyes so as not to see the blow when it fell. Long moments passed, during which she counted each heartbeat. But the blow never came.

When she could no longer bear the suspense, she opened her eyes. She realized (as her body should have told her, even with her eyes closed) that the boat was no longer moving, except for a gentle up-and-down motion with the almost imperceptible rise and fall of the water. The air was utterly still, a dead calm that some part of her understood could not have occurred naturally.

The High Priest stood in the prow, looking out across the water. Once—twice—three times he cried out words in that language she almost understood, and each time he spoke, Winloki had a sense of warring elements, an intolerable strain.

His withered hand sketched runes on the air; she could see them written there like silver fire. The air turned dark, and she could see it *move*—not as any ordinary wind, invisible but for its effect on what it passes, but as a thing in motion itself. She realized with a thrill that he was working a powerful spell, instinctively recognized magic on a scale she had never experienced, had scarcely even imagined before.

The turbulence increased until Camhóinhann stood at the center of a great vortex of dark winds. Chaos roared around him, yet he remained there unmoved, immovable. The only light in that unnatural darkness was he himself, a lurid glowing figure that it almost hurt the eyes to gaze on.

Then, as quickly as it had begun, the disturbance subsided. It was broad daylight again. In the sudden deafening silence, a low wave hit the side of the boat, and then another. In a moment she was moving again, up one great billow and down another, plunging her prow into the water so that the spray flew. All was as it had been before—but for Winloki the whole world had changed.

"What did you do?" she asked, just above a whisper.

He turned and stepped away from the side. The awful glamour of his spell-casting was still on him. "There is a line just here on the bottom of the sea. It is one of many—some on the ocean floor, some on the surface of the earth—and we call them ley lines. They are the veins and arteries that carry the Blood of the World. And the Blood of the World is *power*. Wind and fire, storms, earthquakes, tidal waves, these are but a few of the ways that power expresses itself. All things would exist in a state of perpetual stasis without it.

"I have tapped that power, as a miner taps into a rich vein of ore. And with it I have created a line of my own, just under the surface of the water. Anyone who follows after us will call up a great storm and gale as soon as they cross that line."

Winloki felt a flare of indignation; she did not believe for a moment that anyone was actually following to rescue her, but she could not be so careless as he was of the lives of strangers. "That might be *anyone;* you might catch anyone in your trap. You could sink a hundred ships!"

The glamour around him was beginning to fade. His face looked more haggard and hollow than ever, the flat golden eyes even more remote. "The line will exist for a few days only. There is very little chance that anyone who is not pursuing us will be harmed; traders do not sail these waters, and fishermen rarely come out this far. In truth, a large ship and an experienced crew might even be able to ride out the storm."

Winloki twisted her fingers in the coarse brown wool of her cloak. This was the power she had yearned for, the inheritance so long denied her—turned to mindless destruction. As he used it, it was a wicked thing. Yet having seen, how could she forget; remembering, how could she not wish to experience that power again, if only at second hand?

"You might, for all that, kill innocent people, people who have no idea of interfering," she insisted in a small voice.

Something in his face changed, something moved behind his eyes—she did not deceive herself that it was regret, or grief, or any such human emotion, yet it was more than she expected.

Then he shrugged his broad shoulders and turned away. "That is, unfortunately, a risk we will have to take."

For two days and two nights, one or the other of the Furiádhin kept a steady wind in their sails. On the morning of the third day they landed on a forested shore, where a little creek flowed into the Necke and the trees came down almost to the water. From the sea, they had spotted a town of considerable size, with a fine harbor behind a substantial breakwater, but Camhóinhann had chosen this isolated spot a mile or two to the east instead.

Having no further use for the boat, they ran her aground in the shallows and waded in knee-deep water up to the beach. After that, the men made themselves busy establishing a camp, just above the tideline where the woods began. Winloki settled down on a fallen log and watched the acolytes help the guards to unload the boat: kilting up their coarse black robes, splashing back and forth through the water while the tide flowed in and out. Afterward, some of them gathered firewood and kindled a blaze, and before long preparations for a meal were well under way. Winloki had no idea what they were cooking, but it promised to be more delicate fare than the dried fish and hardtack they had all subsisted on for two days.

But what place is *this?* she wondered. Taking stock of her surroundings, she was suddenly appalled by her own ignorance.

She might have excused that ignorance by reminding herself that she had never been interested in maps or geography, her thirst for knowledge being amply satisfied by the things she had learned in the Healers' House. But if she was honest—and what use now being anything else?—Winloki knew she had been very careful to learn no more than she must about distant lands, fearing that knowledge might lead her away from Skyrra and the people she loved by providing her with a name and a history she had no wish to claim.

A strategy that has proved singularly unsuccessful, she admitted with a sigh. For the greater world had reached out to claim *her,* and her carefully cultivated ignorance had protected her not one whit!

She ransacked her memory, trying to remember names of places: Arkenfell, Pehlidor, Weye. Thäerie, Malindor, Rheithûn. Oh . . . but what was the *good* of remembering the names when their proximity to Skyrra and to each other was what she needed to know—and the very thing she did not. Finally, she was forced to swallow her pride and ask.

"Mistlewald," said Efflam. "At least by my reckoning. Though we may be just over the border in Arkenfell."

Then Winloki was even more ashamed. That much, at least, she *should* have remembered, that Mistlewald and Arkenfell were just across the channel from Skyrra.

Would the people here aid me if they knew I was a prisoner? Would the ancient kinship and friendship between Skyrra and Mistlewald be strong enough, their distrust of strangers out of the south deep enough, to rouse them to action on her behalf? She knew there was little chance she would ever have the opportunity to find out. The Furiádhin would keep her away from towns and villages, in order to avoid "inconvenience."

Camhóinhann's long figure moved across the camp to join her. He was followed by one of the acolytes, who placed a large bundle of cloth in her lap. She frowned up at him, startled, suspecting . . . she scarcely knew what she suspected, only that it could hardly be anything good.

Still, her curiosity had been piqued, and she could not resist unwinding the wrappings. Inside, she found a gown and a cloak: the former of a dull gold velvet, the other of a rich brocade. She stared at these things for several minutes, dumbfounded, before she realized such beautiful garments were meant for her.

Then the priest bent down and deftly removed the chain from the silver manacles. "I believe this will no longer be necessary. And it is time we began to treat you according to your rank. As a princess of Phaôrax, it is hardly appropriate for you to be taken there in rags and chains."

At first she was only bewildered, trying to make sense of his words. Despite her abduction by Ouriána's priests, she had never imagined that she herself might have any connection to Phaôrax—because if that land had a legitimate claim to her, what need for kidnapping? Besides, if she were a Pharaxion princess—

Understanding came like a physical shock. "But that would mean—that would—that would mean some near kinship with . . ." Try as she might, she could not get the words out.

"With the Empress Ouriána, yes. Her sister was your mother."

A thousand new questions, a thousand wild speculations and suppositions jostled for space in her mind. Incredible to believe she could actually be related by blood to the woman most hated and feared in all the world—and a self-proclaimed goddess at that! She cudgeled her brain, trying to remember everything she knew about the Dark Lady of Phaôrax. Again her knowledge was far too scant, and none of it encouraging.

"But then why was I taken to Skyrra? Why was I raised *there* and never told anything about my mother or father?"

"Your mother was sister to the Empress, but your father

was a Thäerian prince. Not of the Pendawer line; of the house that ruled there before the fall of Alluinn, when the High Kings made Thäerie their home. That is where you were born, on the isle of Thäerie, almost twenty years ago."

"But Thäerie and Phaôrax are at war. They've been at war since—" Truly, she did not even know how long. It might have been a century, it might have been forever. What had that war ever meant to *her*, half the world away on Skyrra?

"Your father was killed fighting that war, and your mother . . . indirectly." Camhóinhann hesitated, so briefly Winloki almost failed to notice it. "When she died, there was some question where you belonged, who should take charge of you. The King on Thäerie and his allies on Leal decided to hide you away, so that your mother's people would never find you."

Lies, he is telling me lies, she thought. *Or at least, he's not telling me all of the truth.* How many of those omissions concealed a threat? Certainly, there were no answers to be had from studying his face.

The eyes are windows to the soul: she had heard that said many times. But the eyes of a furiádh admitted no light; they only reflected it, so that you could never see in. The dead white skin was similarly opaque; even the lips and the rims of the eyes were void of color, apparently bloodless. That there *was* blood in his veins she knew only from the powerful beating of his heart that first day, when he snatched her up in his arms and carried her before him on his horse.

She looked down again at the fine clothes he had given her, and the silver she wore on her wrists caught the light. Without the chain she could move more freely—but so long as the bracelets and her guards remained she was still his prisoner. That hardly argued that his Empress's intentions were wholly benign.

And if I am half of Thäerie and half of Phaôrax—which half is it that Ouriána wants?

17

✳

The rescue party, muddy, disheartened, and weary after three days wandering, came out of the fens, leading their horses, and walked into a world of wind and empty sky, so flat and featureless it might have been the world unmade and waiting to be created again. To the east and west, there was only silt and sand, unmarked except for occasional bird tracks. To the south the salt flats ended at a glittering sheet of water.

For a time nobody spoke; the sickening sense of failure was simply too great. All possibility of fulfilling their avowed task—to delay Winloki's captors until King Ristil and his army might arrive—came to an end at the sea. The Necke was a barrier the King and his riders would never cross, not while half of Skyrra remained in Eisenlonder hands.

Sindérian was the first to break the silence. "Camhóinhann and the rest can't fly to Phaôrax; neither can they swim." Though her words were clearly intended to encourage the others, she spoke in a dull voice, entirely lacking the vitality and determination Prince Ruan had come to expect of her. "There may be news of them somewhere along the coast. Let us at least make certain they are no longer on Skyrran soil."

They mounted and rode east into that vast emptiness, while a bitter-tasting wind off the sea tried to blow them back into the marsh. Sometimes they splashed through shallow saltwater creeks running inland; sometimes they could hear the muted roar of the sea, faint but threatening, like thunder heard at a distance.

In the afternoon they came into a village: about twenty houses gathered together on two crooked streets, and another half-dozen straggling along the beach. Most were only drift-wood shacks, but a few of the better sort were of wattle and daub with seashells showing through the plaster. In Ruan's experience, the great cities, the larger towns, they each had their distinctive character whether you travelled north, south, east, or west, but coastal villages were much the same everywhere. He saw little to distinguish this one from hundreds like it on Thäerie and Leal. There was even a ramshackle pier staggering out into the water, and a slatternly little tavern with a starfish tacked up over the door. He saw no boats, not even a sail on the horizon, but then, at this hour the fishing boats would be about their business far from shore.

Hunger and a desire for news drew the weary travellers inevitably toward the alehouse. Once through the door, the interior was smoky and unwholesome, so small that half of the riders chose to sit outside on the porch instead. The host served a surprisingly good thick soup, along with beakers of a dark local brew tasting strongly of seaweed, which made a sat-isfying meal. And before he moved on with his pitcher of ale, he regaled the princes and Sindérian with a tale that had been amazing people up and down this stretch of coast for the past three days: how some odd-looking foreigners had been seen in the town of Havneby thirty miles away, how a fine, large fishing boat had disappeared that same night, all of which had been followed by a mysterious gift of thirty-five riderless horses the townsfolk discovered grazing in their gardens or running wild on the beach the following morning.

"But why a *fishing boat*?" Kivik exchanged a bewildered glance with Skerry across the scarred plank table. "I always thought they would have a ship of their own waiting for them. If they are planning to sail to Phaôrax—"

"They have no such intention," said Ruan. "They will be travelling overland most of the way, as they did before—although this time almost certainly not through the coastal principalities." He took out his knife, began sketching out a map on the table. "The waters along Weye and Hythe are full of warships they won't want to meet. And no one ventures into the empty reaches of the Thäerian Sea—or at least, no one has tried in more than a century. Those waters are known to be deadly perilous."

Skerry turned toward Sindérian with a hopeful look. "Given luck and ingenuity, you said, a small party might do what a greater force could not—that is still true, isn't it?"

She sat at the end of the bench, a little apart from the men, with her rough crockery bowl of soup untouched and an air of not listening to anything they said. But when directly addressed, she flushed and answered in a low, intense voice. "Yes. There was never much chance to begin with, yet what chance there was, it was never a matter of numbers."

"But we have to *be* there to take advantage of any favorable circumstances that might arise," Skerry insisted, leaning across the table to speak to her. "We have to *be* there—just in case."

Her dark, abstracted gaze flickered briefly in his direction and then away. "I can't advise you what to do. I hardly feel qualified to choose for myself." Which was, in Ruan's opinion, an answer so uncharacteristic as to alert every instinct for trouble he possessed.

He had watched her grow increasingly silent, increasingly remote, these last few days, and he thought that killing the Eisenlonder perhaps weighed on her mind. Sometimes he had seen her lips move, shaping words he could neither hear nor quite make out despite his keen eyes and quick ears. At other times she would shake her head emphatically, as if holding some internal debate. And if Sindérian in one of her stubborn, reckless moods gave him ample reason to fear for her safety, to see her so subdued as she was now was absolutely hair-raising. Wizards, to Ruan's way of thinking, were all a little mad—his ten years of tutoring by Eliduc notwithstanding—and healers were the worst by far, liable at any moment to turn volatile and emotional and self-destructive.

Skerry, however, did not seem to notice anything amiss. "Our minds are already made up: Kivik and I will be continuing on. We made a vow before we left Tirfang that we would do everything in our power to rescue or avenge Winloki. If Ouriána's priests had chosen to sail to Phaôrax . . ." He shrugged and made a wry face. "Well, there is no saying what we would have done, or tried to do. Something foolish, in all likelihood, for we know no more of ships and the sea than we do of wizardry. But you say they will be travelling most of the way by land, and that at least is something we know how to do."

"To the land's end and no farther, that is what my father said before we left," added Kivik. "Which is why we never told him, Skerry and I, of the oath that we swore between us. But that vow binds no one but ourselves; I can't in good conscience ask any of my men to continue on, not when the King has ordered otherwise. And by what you say, five may do as much, or as little, as a larger company might. That is—I suppose there will be five of us?"

"Our way lies south in any case," Ruan said absently, half of his attention still on Sindérian. "And unless you can find a fisherman willing to take you across the Necke, you'll need someone with you who knows how to sail a boat." Then the Ni-Féa part of him flared up, and his eyes kindled. "Nor do I have it in me to refuse a challenge."

Sindérian's response was a long time coming. Almost, Ruan thought, as if she were afraid of saying too much. "I will follow Winloki, too," she finally answered in a colorless voice. "Wherever that takes me."

Evening brought the fishermen home, two or three boats at a time. If the Furiádhin had been reduced to stealing a boat, that was not to be the case with the King of Skyrra's own son. Once word spread of Kivik's presence at the alehouse, nearly every boat in the village was offered for sale, "if the Prince would deign to look at it." Fortunately, he had carried a pouch of amber and ivory coins in his saddlebags ever since Lückenbörg, and having had little occasion to dip into it since, he could afford to pay a fair price and still retain a sufficient amount for the journey ahead.

But the actual choice of a boat he left to Ruan and Aell. While they made their final selection and paid out a handful of his coins, he and Skerry said farewell to his men. Orri and the rest had insisted they would accompany their prince to the ends of the earth if he should ask; nevertheless, they were all of them obviously relieved when he refused them.

In the confusion of their departure, Sindérian found an opportunity to slip away and wander along the shore beyond the houses, still debating within herself.

My fault, she thought. *Without me, everyone would have made it out of the marshes days ago. Why didn't I warn them I was under a curse? And how can I possibly justify continuing to expose them to* my *danger?*

Ahead of her, the last level rays of sunlight turned the beach to dull silver; driftwood lay scattered above the tideline like the runes of some forgotten spell. Yet even as she watched the little green waves come in with a hiss and go out again, dragging sand with them, she was keenly aware of other, invisible tides that would shape the rest of her journey.

The power she feared most was ebbing as the moon diminished, but it was still formidable. And who was she to set her own limited experience against Ouriána's will, linked as it was to the primal forces of the sea? Indeed, where was safety, where was refuge for *anyone,* if Ouriána could subvert the very elements?

With the inner Sight, she saw her own death in a hundred different guises: crushed under stones, shattered by a fall, strangled in her own hair—so vivid was that image, Sindérian put a hand to her throat—but most of her deaths involved drowning. She could see herself sinking, sinking through fathoms of clear green water, the surface of the sea like a shining roof overhead. She could see her own bones lying on the sandy ocean floor.

The sea flicked out a narrow tongue and licked at her boots. At the same time, she felt something nudge at her mind, the very lightest touch. Startled, and then alarmed, she gathered up her skirts and backed away from the water.

But the second time Faolein's voice spoke more clearly. Sindérian swung around, her head tilted to the skies and her heart lifted at the sight of a single pair of dark wings speeding over the marshes, coming closer and closer with every wing-beat. When he was over the beach, the sparrowhawk began descending in a long, beautiful glide. Then she felt the familiar prickle of his talons as he landed on her upraised arm.

I bring greetings from King Ristil, he said. *He hopes that his son will understand why he was unable to keep his end of the bargain. When I last saw him, he was in the midst of a skirmish with Eisenlonder settlers.*

Sindérian received this information without surprise; it was no more or less than what she had expected since encountering all of those new settlements along the way.

Turning back toward the village, she gave him a brief account of what they had learned in the alehouse, what the princes planned to do next. She had wandered farther down the beach than she had realized, until the village was only a dark smudge against a sky that looked like it had been powdered with gold leaf. She had a long trudge back in the loose sand; even so, she did not tell her father everything that was on her mind.

There was no need, for he sifted through her words with uncanny precision, swiftly drawing his own conclusions from what she had *not* said. *You have no intention of going with the others. You intend to find your own way across the channel— alone.*

Reluctantly, Sindérian admitted it. And once she confessed to that much, the rest came out in a rush, everything she had been concealing since they were wrecked on the coast: the *aniffath*— the ill luck she carried with her—the revelation that came to her while she was wandering through the marshes. This time she held nothing back. But if she meant to unburden herself, there still remained a cold lump of guilt and fear. *My company will be even more perilous in a boat out on the water. Unless I am much mistaken, Prince Kivik and Lord Skerry can't swim a stroke.*

The hawk walked up her arm to perch on her shoulder. *I wish you had told me these things before. Such matters are— complex. An aniffath is not like any other curse: it grows and changes, reaches out to engulf others for whom it was never intended. By this time we are all of us almost certainly hopelessly enmeshed.*

Sindérian caught her breath, came to a sudden stop. *My fault, then, for keeping silent. At the very least, I might have saved the Skyrran princes.*

Do you think you could have dissuaded them from accompanying you, whatever you said? her father asked gently. *And Prince Ruan, what would he have done? How long will you pretend not to know what he feels for you? He would never allow you to face this danger alone. As for the curse: that came about through no fault of your own. What were you to Ouriána before we left Leal? There can be little doubt we have Thaga to blame that she even knows you exist, and if I had not been supposed dead, her curse would have fallen on me. Think of that, when you feel inclined to blame yourself for anything that has happened.*

The knot in her chest began to unclench; her breathing came a little easier. How comforting it would be to believe what he told her! But it was always his way to think and hope for the best, hers to question and doubt.

Faolein swiveled his head around to look her in the face. The hawk's fierce yellow stare was nothing like the mild glance of the wizard. And suddenly she found herself wondering, as she had not wondered for many months, what changes he had experienced during that time they were apart after Saer. What had he seen and known when Thaga unmade his body and cast his spirit out into eternity, in these moments between unmaking and transformation? *We are caught in a web of Ouriána's weaving, and we can't break free. But while she has chosen the threads and selected the pattern, be sure of this: hers is not the only hand on the shuttle: she may not be the one who determines the ultimate design. She has not grown so great that the stars or the seasons obey her; they are not hers and never will be. And there are other sorceries in the world, forces more potent than any our enemy knows or commands. Become their instrument.*

If you wish to save the others, Sindérian, you can't be like the weathercock, changing your direction with every wind. Be the lightning rod instead. At the very least you can draw the danger away from our friends—at the best, you may take the power and direct it where you will.

Long before midnight, they had loaded up the boat with supplies they bought in the village, and by the time the tide turned in the small hours, they were ready to depart.

"I was beginning to think you would not be coming with us," said Prince Ruan when he looked up from his place in the boat to see Sindérian standing on the pier, her face blazing like the moon.

She swung over the side, landed softly in the boat beside him. "You are the one who always had doubts," she replied, flashing him a bright, challenging smile. "I've always believed that chance or the Fates would throw some opportunity in our way. Why should I think any differently now?"

Why indeed? thought Ruan, watching her take a seat near the bow, while the hawk landed on the gunwale beside her. The change in her was remarkable: all the color and light restored to her face; her eyes clear and confident. Yet, there was a steely edge to her smile, a hard brightness to her glance he had never seen there before. He would have given much to know what had passed between her and Faolein on her father's return.

Kivik and Skerry boarded next, one after the other, making valiant (but unsuccessful) attempts to hide their trepidation. Observing how they unconsciously flinched at every slight dip and roll, Ruan could only hope that neither would be sick once they reached rougher water.

Aell loosed the rope and leaped into the boat; then he and Ruan took up the oars. For a time all was silent except for the gentle slap of water against the hull, the splash of oars breaking the surface. When the village was only a faint, dark blur in the distance, Ruan took charge of the tiller while Aell put up the weatherbeaten sail. They sailed for what remained of the night, always with a light, following wind.

Morning dawned wet and misty grey, though the fog burned off quickly and they continued on at a good clip for many hours over the sunlit waves. A meal of cold fowl, hard biscuits, and seaweed-flavored ale put heart into everyone, and as no one, so far, had shown any disposition toward seasickness, it began to look as if the the voyage would be a short and uneventful one.

But in the early afternoon, more ominous signs began to appear. Clouds began to boil up on the horizon; the wind increased and the light darkened. Gulls whirled overhead, caught in the vortex of the air.

Even so, the storm caught them unprepared, it hit so suddenly and with such force. Within minutes, the wind was screaming in their ears. Rains lashed at them, and greater and greater waves battered the hapless little boat. No natural storm could possibly have moved so swiftly. There was barely time to take down the sail.

Struggling with the rudder to hold a steady course, Ruan tried to pierce the curtain of rain up ahead. But it was too dense, like a solid wall of falling water; even the far-seeing eyes of the Faey could not penetrate it. The boat reeled, now leaning so far to one side that it seemed she would capsize, then tipping the other way. With every wave that washed over her, with the weight of water that she had already taken on, he thought that she must surely sink. He believed it was only the will of the two wizards that had kept her afloat so long.

Sindérian stood upright in the bow, shouting back at the wind; how she maintained her balance, he did not know, nor how she kept from being flung over the side. At one point, Ruan saw Faolein fighting the air and almost being blown away, before finally landing on his daughter's shoulder. Poor Skerry had finally succumbed to seasickness; he was down on hands and knees retching helplessly into the bottom of the boat. Aell and Kivik were frantically bailing.

Giving up his battle with the rudder, Ruan went to help

them. Once or twice, he looked back toward Sindérian to see how she was faring. Her hair was streaming with water, the green cloak clung to her like seaweed; she looked more like a mermaid than anything belonging to the land. He thought he could hear her chanting the same *lledrion* over and over, and had just enough knowledge of the Old Tongue to guess what she was doing: not trying to command the elements but wooing them, not adding to the turmoil with a counterspell but trying to create a safe passage *within* the storm.

The boat bucked and rolled; she fell into a trough between the waves and hit the water with stunning force. Between the hammer of the wind and the anvil of the sea, it seemed they would all be flattened. Somehow they stayed afloat. In between singing her *lledrion* to court the elements, Sindérian must have been working spells to keep the boat from breaking up.

But by now she must be hoarse with shouting, exhausted with her efforts to bring them safely through; Ruan doubted she could keep it up much longer.

18

✳

In Apharos on Phaôrax, the Empress surprised everyone by grieving nine days for the son she had never seemed to value while he was alive.

It was not a desperate grief, and not, perhaps, a very deep one, but it was *human,* and therefore a revelation to those around her. Sometimes, it appeared, the goddess within gave way to the woman and the mother.

The funeral ceremonies were elaborate. The entire court went into black, the women covering their faces with gauzy veils as though they had all been simultaneously widowed. Indeed, some of them *had* taken a tender interest in the gallant and handsome young Prince, a passion none had dared to express during his lifetime, considering he was more often than not out of his mother's favor. While Ouriána herself spent most of her time brooding in an upper chamber, or else sitting in the throne room—dry-eyed, inscrutable, the tresses of her auburn hair coiling like serpents—a golden coffin (minus, of course, a body) was paraded through the streets, and rituals and additional sacrifices were performed each day inside the sprawling monstrosity that was the New Temple. At night torchlit processions trooped through the city, and the lights in the streets made patterns as complex and various as the Hidden Stars.

Even before the Prince's death, it had been a season of curious omens and bewildering portents. Unexpected manifestations appeared throughout the city and across the island kingdom: ghosts and phantom music and stranger things besides. The three acolytes who had gone into seclusion many weeks before were seen in public for the first time, their transformation complete. They emerged white-haired, tallow-faced, garbed in priestly scarlet. It had been twenty years since the Empress last had twelve Furiádhin to do her bidding, and the fact that they were restored to their original numbers was one even the most devout found somehow disconcerting.

But on the tenth day, Ouriána began to recover, her very natural bereavement giving way to a vast irritation at what she was beginning to regard as a monstrous inconvenience.

"Two sons dead. Guindeluc and Cuillioc gone, and only that fool Meriasec remaining," she said to Noz, her Lord Chancellor. The grotesque little hunchback had known and served her in the days of her relatively obscure youth—when she was not even a king's daughter, but only a royal niece waiting to be displaced in the succession by male cousins as yet unborn—and she occasionally confided to him things she would never have spoken in public. It was no part of her policy to acknowledge that sons of hers might have proved unsatisfactory—though acknowledged or not, everyone always knew.

As for Meriasec, if Cuillioc had been but a pale copy of his brilliant, dazzling older brother, her youngest son was even less than that. A bully with a streak of cowardice, he was spineless and compliant in the presence of his mother. Meriasec's servility, meant to please her, had just the opposite effect, and Cuillioc's questioning mind, his struggles to reconcile his somewhat misguided principles with his obedience to her, had been, she realized belatedly, much more to her taste. His loyalty, so painfully genuine, *meant* something, and now that Cuillioc was gone, she discovered in him something irreplaceable.

In her rage and confusion she began to pace through the palace. Such was the force of her personality that when she was angry, her presence filled a room until all those present felt crushed by it. Waiting women blanched at the sight of her; the young squires and pages, suddenly discovering they were needed elsewhere, went scurrying off to unnamed duties on the other side of the palace; and Prince Meriasec, with rare discretion, absented himself altogether.

But on the eleventh day she put her three sons, living and dead, from her mind and turned her green-eyed basilisk's gaze elsewhere.

"How can it be, with five hundred of the city guard and half that many spies scouring the city for a single drunken juggler, the man nevertheless continues to elude them?" She turned her baleful regard on the six red-robed priests she had summoned to one of her private chambers.

"It is possible that he is no longer *in* the city," said six-fingered Vitré tentatively. He and his companions smelled strongly of smoke, and there was a subtler odor about them of religious fervor and superstition. Stains of a darker crimson marred the hems of their robes and their hanging sleeves, for though Ouriána had put aside her grief, the official period of mourning was to last a fortnight and the sacrifices continued. "Possible that he left before the search for him even began."

"If that is so," she replied ominously, "the sorcerers and seers you have no doubt employed to look for him should have learned at least that much by now."

Vitré and his companions shifted uneasily. "There has been an—unforeseen difficulty," he said. "It appears that Maelor, as he was known in the city, was not the name he was given at birth. Even *he* does not seem to have known his true one, and you will appreciate the difficulty of casting a seeking spell where the name is unknown."

Ouriána ground her teeth. "The task is beneath me, but I am beginning to think if I want the man found I will have to look for him myself. His possessions, if he had any, whatever hovel he lived in—these things were searched thoroughly for any clue to his whereabouts?"

"Searched and scryed by your own seers. And there is this." Vitré took a hesitant step forward, knelt at the Empress's feet, and offered her a worn and dirty rag of fabric. "A scrap of the blanket he slept in, in case you might wish . . ."

Ouriána wrapped her long, smooth fingers around the threadbare bit of cloth. Her nostrils flared, as though taking some scent. "He was not much of a magician, if he knew no better than to leave something so personal behind."

Scioleann cleared his throat. "They say the old man had a habit of misplacing more than his name, and especially what-ever knowledge of magic he once possessed. No one seems to know whether or not he was ever a true adept, although the spells he performed that day in the marketplace—" A slicing movement of her hand chopped the sentence short.

"His spells that day would argue there is more to the man than anyone suspected, yes." As her glance moved from one face to the next, each of the priests in turn had the uncomfortable sensation that there was not nearly enough air in the room. "And the disruption he caused has not yet dissipated. Quite the opposite. Noz tells me that his spies hear far too many whispers of former days and the Old Religion. These things *will not be allowed to continue.*"

The Furiádhin prostrated themselves at her feet, signifying their obedience.

In the palace at Apharos there was a chamber at the top of the highest and most isolated of the nine towers, where even Ouriána's priests were never permitted to go. To enter, it was necessary to pass seven stout doors, locked and sealed and bespelled, which required seven different keys, and seven different names, and seven different charms to open.

In that many-sided room full of strange devices, she kept the greatest treasure of her house and lineage—which in former days, before her apotheosis, had also been the source of their temporal power—the *Talir en Nydra*, the pearl-grey Dragonstones. They rested, each one in an intricately worked silver stand, directly in front of the twelve windows. On the tiled floor was a map of the known world with a great lurid stain at the center, the mark of Ouriána's most ambitious spellcasting, when she broke the Thäerian fleet twenty years ago and crippled her own power for many seasons in doing so.

The place reeked of magic; the scent was so strong that

even she, who was accustomed to the atmosphere, detected it immediately on entering. Though the room was open to the air, no breeze ever freshened it; the miasma was always there. Sometimes, stray tendrils would drift down to the nearest houses, or to the ships anchored in the bay, causing the inhabitants to dream strange dreams or experience vague, irrational fears.

As soon as she closed the last door behind her, locking it with a curiously constructed key like a tiny fingerbone, Ouriána moved purposefully toward the largest of the stones. They were not quite spherical, and when not in use, the *Talir en Nydra* appeared dull and opaque. But as soon as she placed her hands on one of them the stone would begin to glow with uncanny lights and became translucent, while a well of darkness appeared at the center. There was peril in gazing too deep, but a strong mind and a resolute will could conjure images in the heart of the well. Then, if that was her desire, she could see the inner fires of the earth, or the upper reaches of the air where the stars shone even in daytime; she could see kingdoms so far distant that their names, even the bare rumor of their existence, had never reached Phaôrax.

There were limitations. The stones lengthened sight but they did not sharpen hearing. You could catch the thief with his hand in somebody else's purse, but you could not hear the patter of the mountebank three feet away; you could spot a gathering of conspirators met together in secret, but you could not hear them plotting. And with distance came lack of clarity: the images became like figures seen through water, flattened and distorted, their movements crablike and hideous. Moreover, the world was so wide it was almost impossible to locate any single person or any specific place within in, unless you had something—a strand of hair, a handful of soil, or a scrap of cloth—to bridge the gap. For that reason, each stone was linked in some way to a specific location, like the streets outside the King's house in Pentheirie on Thäerie, or the town of Baillébachlain on Leal, below the wizards' Scholia. The largest, the one she chose now, she used to spy on her subjects in Apharos and the surrounding towns and villages.

The sun was sinking. Little grey bats flittered outside the unglazed window, but they would not come in. From this dizzy height, looking back from the promontory, the city was a shadowy landscape of spires, peak-roofed houses, and towers whose conical roofs as looked as sharp as thorns from above.

When she looked into the depths of the stone, the city and its inhabitants gradually became more distinct: tiny people in the market squares, the shops, and the gaudy palaces of the nobles. For a time, she allowed her attention to wander, spying out all the places where her people were gathered. And when her thoughts turned at last toward the man she sought, it did not take long for a bent grey figure to swim into view. Though his exact location was unclear—all she could see was wood and stone, dimly illuminated—now that she had found him she had only to watch his movements until he came to some other place that she could recognize. Ouriána felt a surge of satisfaction. Almost, it had been too easy.

Then something wiped it all away: the face, the figure, along with her satisfaction at finding him so easily. It was the sort of resistance she had not experienced in years—in decades. She stepped back from the stone, the breath hissing through her teeth, her brain seething with indignation. Truly, it was too much: first that mum-show in the marketplace, the unrest he had fomented ever since, and now this!

She felt a momentary tremor of doubt, an unaccustomed pang of fear, wondering if the deity within might have abandoned her. Yet how could she suffer such a loss—a severing of flesh and spirit far greater than any mere death—and not know of it?

Swiftly, she cast off the woven silver that bound her hair, let the rich auburn tresses tumble down her back. She unclasped the gem-studded belt that girdled her waist and allowed it to fall to the floor. Rings and bracelets followed, until she stood there with no other adornment but her own beauty and raw power, with no net or chain or fetter to impose any limits.

Reaching deep inside, she eventually found what she was seeking: the Darkness coiled at the center of her being, the ancient thing that sometimes looked out through her eyes, that spoke to her with the dull booming of the tide or came to her with the cold salt smell of the ocean floor. It was still there. How could it ever leave her, when it was her second self?

Gradually, her panic subsided, her confidence returned; she knew herself a goddess. What had happened, she concluded, must be something quite different from what she had feared, some interference from outside. Yes, yes, that was surely it. It could not possibly be through any gift of his own that the old man defied her. There must be some person or entity far greater than he was, who for reasons yet obscure was protecting him. Indeed, it was probably a consortium of magicians, for there was no single mage or wizard of such power still living who was not in her thrall.

Once she had *him,* she would discover who was responsible, and destroy them too, one by one. She smiled to herself, once again sure of her power.

In a cave by the shore, not a league from the city wall, the object of her search waited, cold, cramped, and utterly miserable.

The cavern was a large one, the abode of smugglers. When the moon was dark, they regularly brought in shipments of illicit goods, but they also occasionally smuggled desperate men out of the country. At the moment, a number of boxes and bales occupied most of a narrow ledge running the length of the cavern. During a low tide that ledge was dry; during a particularly high one it was apt to be submerged, as the presence of sand and shells attested. From the ledge, steps of water-rotten stone led down to an equally rotten wooden pier, where the smugglers moored their boats.

It was on the pier that Maelor sat, awaiting a man who had promised to aid his escape from the island. It was a risk to go out on the sea, which was Ouriána's ally—of this he was well aware—but the island was hers, too, and her spies too numerous to count. In any case, he had grown weary of hiding, weary of the fear that hunted him day and night.

The cave was dank and dim, lit only by a pair of green glass lanterns. From the sea that light could easily be mistaken for the glow of phosphorous in marshy places along the shore. Dampness trickled like snails' tracks down the rough stone walls. There were bones under the green water, for there was only the one entrance, and on certain days of the month the place became a death trap. In a rare moment of prescience, Maelor knew that someday soon one of the wild, lawless men who frequented the place would drown; with equal certainty he knew that any prediction of his would go unheeded.

Rather than waste his breath on warnings, he sat in the sickly light, scratching the waterlogged wood with a rusty knife over and over, creating the patterns that had obsessed him for all the years that he could remember: the same figures he had painstakingly formed of sticks and bones, or written in chalk, charcoal, and red paint on the walls, floor, and ceiling of his cluttered attic chamber.

He had performed the same useless and frustrating ritual a thousand times before. He expected nothing to come of it; it was merely habit—less than habit by now, it was mindless instinct. Yet his thoughts were swarming with strange fancies, with bright, many-colored shadows of realities that had been or might be; another identity and another life were struggling to emerge. The familiar exercise was a welcome distraction.

Maelor the Astromancer was a fabrication, not even his own, he had always known that much—but the real man had been buried for so long, the old juggler and sometime magician had never allowed himself to believe it might be possible to bring him back into the light. Now he was beginning to hope, and that hope terrified him, almost as much as the knowledge that Ouriána's soldiers, Ouriána's spies, were seeking him. Indeed, the two fears fed each other—because what if they should find him before he learned the truth?

As he gazed down, with a puzzled frown, at the symbols he had carved in the wood, something happened. Perhaps it was Ouriána's probing, the brief touch of one powerful mind against another whose power was only latent, bright steel striking dull flint to make a spark and ignite a fire. However it came about, the spark was lit and cold ashes stirred to life.

The slap of water against rotting pylons gradually receded, along with the rumbling voices of the men loading the boats. In a growing excitement, he drew a new line here, scratched out another there. The symbols began to make sense—why had he not recognized them before? They were runes, images of power that wizards studied and used in their spells.

A sudden trembling came over him, and the words seemed to speak themselves: *"Duenin. Désedh. Güwelen. Theroghal."*

As soon as he named the runes aloud, all that had been confused and mysterious became orderly and familiar in his mind. A whole train of memories trooped through his brain until he knew his entire history, both before and after the disaster that had changed him so grievously; he knew his name and the purpose that had driven him. And with that knowledge, power welled up inside of him, filling him from the soles of his feet to his fingertips, to the roots of the hair on his head. He buried his face in his hands and wept for joy.

Even when the tears had passed, for a time he remained oblivious to all around him, and therefore failed to notice when the man he had been waiting for finally arrived. It was several minutes before it even occurred to him that a harsh, impatient voice was speaking to *him* and not to somebody else.

"We won't dally here to miss the tide. If you mean to come with us, old man, it must be *now.*"

The old man—no longer so old, so feeble or befuddled— glanced up with a bright, lucid, wide-awake gaze. He was weighing very carefully his own situation.

One thing he knew for certain. Broken, as he had been before, he had managed to pass Ouriána's wards and reach this island—where otherwise he might never have come at all. He had, in fact, successfully penetrated defenses that, if he should ever decide to return as a whole man, would undoubtedly defeat him.

It was not, in the end, such a difficult decision.

"I thank you," said the wizard Éireamhóine in his deep, calm, powerful voice, "but I think I am not ready to leave Phaôrax as yet."

19

✳

For Winloki, Mistlewald was as another world. The land spoke to her, at first in snatches and whispers, gradually growing more distinct and comprehensible: voices of earth, wind, and stone, the long, slow dreams of trees—she had never imagined that trees could be so eloquent. Raised in a country where wizards and great magicians were only a distant rumor, she had never suspected this brimming life in the landscape, and many days would pass before she finally realized that none of this arose from any special qualities in the place; it came of a profound change in herself.

In the meantime, her material circumstances had altered, too. The three men who had gone into the nearest seaside town to buy (or steal) horses and supplies returned with an elegant little cream-colored mare, complete with a lady's saddle. Unable to conceal her own delight, Winloki saw a corresponding pleasure briefly add color and animation to the pallid face of the young acolyte who handed her the reins, and the same emotion even more fleetingly (but just as unmistakably) reflected on the faces of his elders. Spirited yet gentle, the mare was a joy to ride and a vastly superior animal to the sturdy but undistinguished horses assigned to the rest of the party. Even Camhóinhann's great grey stallion was of lesser breeding. This gift—for it was impossible to view it in any other light—along with her fine new clothes, made it clear to Winloki she would henceforth be treated as a privileged individual, a princess of Phaôrax in truth. Yet far from reassuring her, these marks of status only served to emphasize that the barrier of the Necke had placed her, once and for all, beyond any hope of rescue or escape.

As though I needed any reminders, she thought wistfully, *of how very far I am from home.*

And indeed, it was a very different country from Skyrra, more forest than meadow or farmland, and exceedingly flat. If there were any hills in Mistlewald they were either too far off to be seen, or so lowly and humble they never held their heads above the trees. Oak, elm, ash, cowan, and other species she could not identify until they whispered their strange but beautiful names in her ear crowded on either side of the road. For the better part of two days she spotted no farms or villages, nor even the smoke of a single hearth fire rising in the distance. It was not, perhaps, a land for men. The roots here went deep, the trees were very old, and the woods—of which these were only the latest generation—far more ancient than any wood in Skyrra. She thought she had never met a living thing of like antiquity.

One evening they stopped long before sunset to set up camp in a little dell of green grasses, and Winloki detected a stir of excitement and anticipation among the priests and acolytes unlike anything she had seen in them before. Immediately after a hasty supper, the Furiádhin and their particular servants among the acolytes all left the camp at once, disappearing among the trees.

"What is it? Where are they going?" she asked—not wishing to show too much interest in their private rituals, but so curious and apprehensive that the questions slipped out.

"By all the signs, the Empress has performed a Summoning," said Lochdaen, who happened to be the nearest guard. "They hear her calling, and when the full moon rises above the trees they will be in deep communion with her. When this happens," he added, dropping his voice and casting a wary glance over his shoulder, "they will often have speech with her the rest of us are not intended to hear."

"They can speak with her across such a distance?" Winloki was frankly incredulous. She had been told that more than a thousand miles of land and sea still divided them from Phaôrax. The night suddenly turned close and breathless as she tried not to imagine what sort of rite they masked with this lie.

"She speaks to them, that is all I know," the young guardsman replied, with another backward glance. "Who can say what an incarnated goddess can or cannot do?"

Before the priests returned, a harvest moon the color of brass, tiger-striped with dark clouds, stood high in the sky. Finally, about midnight, they came striding into camp with the acolytes following behind them, more subdued than ever. Then it was very hard for Winloki to maintain her belief in some blatant deception meant to fool the temple guards—it was so obvious the Furiádhin had received momentous and disturbing news. Yet even when the information began to spread, moving from one campfire to the next, no one saw fit to enlighten the Princess.

By the time they were ready to break up camp the next morning, she had already decided that Camhóinhann was the one most deeply affected; his expression, ordinarily solemn and aloof, had become so grim and terrible. Dyonas, hitherto imperturbable, seemed vaguely troubled, and she could see that Goezenou harbored some gloating satisfaction.

"It is an interesting situation," she heard him say to Dyonas. "We knew, did we not, there was little enough chance she would choose Cuillioc to rule after her—but no chance at all for Meriasec. What use will she have for the girl now? I had imagined it would be either a wedding or a knife—"

"You imagine too much!" Dyonas cut him off with a severe look. "And you would be wise to say none of it to Camhóin-hann."

This conversation occupied Winloki's thoughts for many days. *A wedding or a knife*—except something had happened to the supposed bridegroom. She knew very little about Prince Cuillioc. That he had not, apparently, stood very high in his mother's favor ought to be enough to commend him, and he and his brother Meriasec would be, she supposed, her own first cousins. So while she would never have married him, of course, she would be very sorry to hear that he was dead—and more so if it happened that his death had sealed *her* fate too.

It was about that same time that she began to notice Goezenou watching her more avidly than ever. If they stopped in a clearing to rest the horses or to set up camp for the night, he had a habit of hovering somewhere nearby whenever she dismounted, of never being very far off when she moved among the black tents.

She found him indescribably loathsome: his wide, sneering mouth and aggressive nose; the thick fingers, curving nails, and silvery fish-scale backs of his hands. Yet, it was more than physical deformity that made him hideous. Had that been all she would have pitied him, but every instinct told her there was mental and spiritual deformity as well. The liquid quality of the metallic eyes, which in the other Furiádhin suggested mirrors, in him reflected a bottomless hunger, a monstrous craving. He was like one being devoured from the inside out, seeking to devour others that he might assuage his own emptiness. Had he, Winloki wondered, chosen to serve Ouriána hoping she would fill him up? If so, then why did he continue to serve her when she had done no such thing?

Again and again she had seen how the guards and acolytes tried to avoid attracting his notice—he was so liable to find fault with even the most instant and complete obedience. His magic was formidable, he could command the elements, yet he seemed to gain greater satisfaction from petty displays of power over his own servants.

In his eyes she saw a rage of envy and desire—not an ordinary desire of the flesh, but something darker, more obscure—and why either of these emotions should center on her she did not know.

When she could bear it no longer, she began asking her guards, one after the other, "What does he want of me? Why does he look at me in *that* way?" One after another, they shook their heads. If they knew, not one of them dared to say so. Finally, she appealed to one of the acolytes.

Longest in service to the Furiádhin, Rivanon was of them all the most like his masters: wan, hollow-cheeked, angular, with ash-white hair. Yet he had no deformity that she could see, and his eyes were dark and utterly human. There had been times when she had seen him shield the younger men from Goezenou's wrath and she thought he was a kind man, for all his silence and reserve.

When she asked her question a series of emotions crossed his face inside his hood of coarse black cloth. A thought or a memory seemed to be simmering just below the surface. For a moment she thought she was about to receive an honest answer. But the moment passed. All she could see in his face, in his eyes, was the same closed, secretive expression she knew so well. "If you are afraid, or if you believe anyone has insulted you, you should speak with Camhóinhann."

Bitterly disappointed, she turned away without even thanking him for his advice. She had not yet grown so desperate as to seek Camhóinhann's protection. Untutored in magic she might be, but she knew enough to understand: when it came to someone as powerful as Ouriána's High Priest, one did not go asking favors. A favor asked, a favor granted, no matter how trivial, was a dangerous proposition. Let him once place her under the least obligation and there was no reckoning the consequences.

How many days they rode Winloki did not know, for she had stopped counting. With nothing to hope for at the end of her journey, days and distances hardly mattered. But after perhaps a week, the trees started thinning out, until most of the country was farm or grazing land. They no longer had the road to themselves: they passed farmers in carts piled high with fruit or grain; herdsmen driving their flocks to market; peddlers riding on donkeys, or on foot dragging their wares on sledges behind them. She and the guards had fallen into an easy way of things in the wilderness, but now the men turned watchful again, surrounding her in a close circle whenever they approached a village or came near other travellers. Then she was doubly bound to silence, knowing that a reckless word from her would endanger innocent strangers, knowing also that it would certainly result in heavy punishment falling on one or more of her guards.

So I become my own gaoler, Winloki thought ruefully. There was, perhaps, a fine line between wisdom and cowardice, between complicity and common sense, and how to tell the difference she did not know, but she had seen enough bloodshed in Skyrra.

And it was a strange sort of captivity, after all, with her mind opening up to so many new experiences. On clear nights, she thought she could hear the stars humming, a thin, tuneless drone. She could sense the pulse of the tide as it rushed in and out all across the world, and envision subterranean rivers and streams spreading out beneath the lands like a net of shining silver. The beauty of these things would sometimes tear at her heart, bring quick tears to her eyes. She could not know that young wizards on Leal, and at the few remaining schools of magic elsewhere, learned to control these perceptions at an early age, to summon them or banish them at will, lest they lose touch with the human world altogether.

She could spend a timeless time in dreamlike communion with nature, then come suddenly back to herself, her ears filled with the jingle of harnesses, the dull beat of horses' hooves on a packed-earth road. In her dream, the trees had been straight and shapely, clothed in leaves like living jewels; they drank in the sunlight like wine. Here the air was cold, the trees gnarled and bent under a weight of years, clad in faded rags of autumn; sad drifts of leaves covered the ground. All the voices that sang in her mind so recently were stilled. How long had she been so absorbed? It felt like half the day—though in truth, by the position of the sun it had been practically no time at all.

And with these glimpses came a hunger for more knowledge, more understanding. She feared that she never would know, never would understand. It was Camhóinhann's spell on the boat that had expanded her senses so wonderfully, and she knew that he might, if he chose, open her mind to even greater mysteries. But then she would remember to what uses he had turned his own powers—and Ouriána, whose name had become a byword for atrocities! Oh, there were times when she could have wept for all she had missed over the years, for all that she might yet have in years to come, and would not—must not.

There was, too, another danger beyond the lure of power. It was growing harder and harder to view the men she travelled with as an alien, incomprehensible breed, the embodiment of wickedness. It had begun, of course, with the guards, those earnest young men in their shining, dark armor, but by now even the acolytes, only superficially identical in their drab black garments, their silence and pallid looks, had emerged as distinct personalities.

How easy it was to hate an abstraction. The Eisenlonders, whom she knew only by their terrible deeds, who had never come close enough to look in the face ... But with *these* men she had looked too closely and too long.

Rivanon, Morquant, and Lasaire, the three eldest, could work small magics, lighting fires, calming nervous horses; perhaps they could do more than that but refrained out of humility. Adfhail, Uinséan, Féhlim—though scarcely older than she was herself they had travelled far; they had seen so much that their worldliness put her ignorance to shame, yet for all that, they were not proud. And all of them practiced a passionate celibacy, an unremitting discipline of mind and body. "Every sacrifice we make is a sacrament," Adfhail told her. "As surely as anything done in the Temple."

As for the three priests, she could not help seeing that Dyonas was as far above Goezenou as Camhóinhann was above him. Where Goezenou's personality was distilled from many small cruelties and petty hatreds, Dyonas was as lacking in malice as he was in pity. All his passion was for his goddess and his religion. When he performed the rites, when he sang hymns of praise in his beautiful voice, it was impossible for Winloki not to see, with that new vision of hers, how Dyonas burned with a bright inner flame, impossible not to accept that he, at least, had an unshakable belief in Ouriána's promise of a world transformed.

More than once she had glimpsed under his robes of velvet and silk brocade a garment of coarser stuff, likely to chafe, and she had been surprised to discover that he wore bracelets similar to her own—although his were made of iron, with tiny barbs inside that scored his flesh. Skyrran religion did not demand, would not have approved, these excesses of devotion, yet she could not help feeling a grudging admiration for the terrible certainty that informed his faith. He was, she reminded herself, just the sort of man who drew other men into evil and misguided causes. He could turn right and wrong upside down, he could make black into white and white into a muddled grey.

Yet even so, he presented no danger to her compared to Camhóinhann.

Too often, her eyes were drawn to the tall, charismatic figure of the High Priest, to his face, white as bleached bone, gaunt, yet alive with power. He was a constant threat to her peace of mind, for it was impossible to recognize what he had become without being reminded of what he must once have been. Marred by whatever terrific experiences had transformed him, he remained the embodiment of sufficient tragic grandeur to stir her blood.

She knew—she had always known—that he had the ability to bind her to him. Such was the force of his personality that he might have willed her to love, obedience, adoration—to anything. That he did not do so argued an admirable restraint—yet there was a subtle seduction in that very restraint. An uneasy suspicion would sometimes intrude, stifle it as she might, that Camhóinhann was, even in his ruin, some kind of vindication for Ouriána's new religion.

Yet with that thought came another, equally confusing: What kind of woman, what kind of goddess, could Ouriána possibly be, if she could command—and accept—the devotion of men so utterly different as Camhóinhann and Goezenou?

At last Winloki saw hills and highlands rising up in the distance. There was something troubling and forbidding in their very outlines massed against the sky. She could not have explained it even to herself, but she dreaded approaching them.

Several days passed, days of watching those hills grow taller and craggier, before she finally recognized them for mountains and was able to make out the real hills, bare, brown, and unmistakably desolate, huddled at their feet. By that time, she and her Pharaxion captors had the road to themselves again. Whether it was the fading year, with its threat of bitter weather in the high passes, or simply the nature of the mountains themselves, *something* up ahead discouraged ordinary travellers.

She was in the hills before she quite knew it, the land rising so slowly that only when she looked back and saw the fields lying faint and misty below did she realize that the road had been climbing all that day. Fragments of stone wall began to appear at intervals on either side of the track. There were weird outcrops of rock, and ledges that had been honed by the wind until they looked sharp as daggers.

Her dreams that night were disturbed. More than once she started awake, convinced that someone had been leaning over her as she slept: a face as seamed and folded as the hills themselves, staring down into hers with dry, lidless eyes. Sometime before dawn she woke, trembling, ghost ridden, and clammy with sweat, to hear a patter of rain on the roof of her tent.

By the time everyone had breakfasted and mounted up, it was still raining: a sad, slow, continuous drizzle. The road, which until now had had few windings, divided into many crooked paths, continually running back on themselves until it became difficult to tell whether they were making any progress. When a track took them to the summit of a hill higher than any of the rest, Winloki saw that all the countryside around was scarred with ruins.

Between the stones grew a coarse, dry grass. Burned brown by the summer just past, it was disintegrating in the rain. Animals there were none, and she sensed no birds but hawks and carrion crows. Yet men had lived in those hills, as the ruins bore witness. There was *something* there, ancient and malign; it went so deep that it permeated the very earth, the very stones. She had a dim perception that perhaps it was of the earth itself.

Twilight came early under that heavy grey sky, and the Furiádhin lit spinning globes of werelight to illuminate the way; in their unearthly glow, the faces of all the men became corpselike and terrible. Meanwhile, the rain never let up, and the wind blew colder and colder. Her teeth chattering, Winloki locked her arms across her chest under the brocade cloak and allowed the mare to set her own pace.

That night, lying under canvas sagging with the weight of water, she feared to sleep, but for all her resistance slumber came in on dark, smothering waves and swept her away. Then her dreams were far more terrifying than the night before. She heard the music of flutes and tabors as processions of maidens went to be wed and buried in the same day. Men she saw with the eyes of beasts, and beasts with the souls of women. It seemed to her on waking that an entire history of the race that once inhabited that country had played out in her tired brain.

These ruins spread out across the hills were remnants of their cities. All their buildings they made low to the ground; even their mansions and palaces sprawled with rooms and corridors added on at random, for the people had worshipped the earth in its darker aspects and their eyes were always turned down. Refusing to look to the sky for portents, they made bonfires of bones and read omens in the flames, listened to the feverish mutterings of dying men, read auspices in the entrails of slaughtered beasts; so the stars were nothing to them, and the rites of death and the tomb came to be everything. In time, they made a cult and a fetish of death itself.

Even by day, she could not entirely erase the frightening images from her mind: ritual suicides and poisoned cups, wolf-headed priestesses in bloody garments, jewel-skinned vipers worn as living ornaments. Lost souls shrieked and gibbered on the wind; they fluttered around her like bats, or birds with broken wings; they swarmed like flies and stinging insects. Then, indeed, she wished for less magic instead of more, wished she might move among those ancient things as an ordinary girl, ignorant and untroubled.

But on the third night, her dreams changed abruptly from foul to fair, and she slept through until daybreak without waking even once. When she left her tent and went out in the damp blue dawn, the first thing she saw was a line of faint, silvery figures etched on the ground outside.

"Your guards told me they heard you cry out in your sleep," said Camhóinhann, appearing beside her as she stood, clammy-haired and shivering, scowling down at the marks in the dirt. "And this land is known to breed nightmares. Therefore, I put a ward around your tent to keep them out. You need not frown—the symbols are quite harmless. They are Wizards' Runes, the same ones your mother learned as a young healer on Leal."

Intrigued but still suspicious, she studied the figures more carefully. The runes, if that was what they truly were, did seem benign. *Even so, it would be foolish to make too much of this,* she admonished herself. *With all the power at his command, that he should know one innocent charm among so many spells that are wicked and destructive, it means very little.*

An hour later, when the tents were folded and the horses saddled, when everyone mounted up and continued on, a vague and formless oppression settled over her—a depression perhaps born as much of physical discomfort as the psychic attack on her senses. The wind blew back the hood of her cloak and threw gusts of rain in her face. Her fingers on the reins were turning blue. Sodden, chilled, dejected, fearful, despite her earlier resolve she found herself looking more and more to the High Priest, finding something in his tall, broad-shouldered figure that offered reassurance in a world that seemed shrunken and cold.

The voice that warned her against doing so was growing very faint.

There came a time when all the sky was filled with mountains, jagged peaks crowned with grey vapors. The clouds had thinned, but the air remained heavy with water. The road began to climb at a steep angle, and a sharp blast of wind came skirling down from the heights.

With hooves slipping in the mud, the horses struggled up the slope. Winloki saw Goezenou dig in his spurs, though his sturdy bay was doing the best that it could. "We are almost there," she heard Rivanon say to another acolyte, and she wondered what he could possibly mean. But for a scattering of beeches and pines, a few hardy shrubs rooted in the scree, the mountain was as barren as the hills below. She found it difficult to imagine any destination this empty country might offer. By nightfall the road had narrowed to a trail.

Late the next morning, they were riding through a region of rocky pinnacles and giddy precipices when a sudden turn in the trail brought them to a narrow defile littered with tumbled boulders. A little black rill trickled down on one side of the gorge and disappeared into a crack in the earth. They had not ridden far when the trail ended abruptly at a sheer rock wall.

Craning her neck, Winloki tried to see what was happening. What place this was she did not know, but the urge to turn the mare around and ride away as swiftly as possible was all at once so strong, she would certainly have done so had there not been so many horses and riders blocking her way.

From his seat in the saddle, the High Priest began to sketch signs on the air. They were *not* like the runes of the warding spell and were none so wholesome. Mazelike, convoluted, they suggested the writhings of serpents or the movements of scorpions.

For a moment it seemed to Winloki that the bones of the mountain were shifting, that the face of the cliff would crumble, that all its great weight must come tumbling down and bury them—until the rock wall wavered like a reflection on water, and the illusion concealing a pair of immense doors at the base of the cliff dissolved.

The doors were like nothing she had ever seen before: tremendous in scale, of a hard, crystalline substance cut but not polished, with scrollwork hinges of sun-bright metal. Instinct told her the doors were immeasurably more ancient than the ruined cities, yet unlike the cities they had defied the ages.

"Where do they lead?" she asked in a hushed voice.

"Into a catacomb," said Rivanon. "Behind these doors of adamant and gold are the tombs of ancient kings—the fathers of the fathers of the people who lived in the hills. But just as they were hidden by a spell, the doors are likewise sealed."

She felt caught in a backwash of time, sucked back through the centuries. The world was far older than she had ever imagined, and its history more terrible.

"Then how will we enter—or *are* we to enter?" Her heart lifted at the thought that it might be impossible, then sank with his reply.

"The doors will open for Camhóinhann. He and Dyonas passed this way once before, eleven years ago, and learned the secret. Morquant and I were with them."

But instead of beginning to work the necessary spells, the High Priest ordered two of the men to dismount and unload one of the packhorses. Halfway guessing what he intended, Winloki felt a cold sensation of horror creep over her skin.

"What is he waiting for? Why does he delay?"

"No king went into these tombs alone," said Morquant. "Wives and concubines went with them—whether the women met death here, or previously, I do not know. But slaves were sacrificed outside these doors. It takes a death to open them from the outside."

The lost souls that had haunted her all through the foothills seemed to press in on her, darkening the air. The mare, sensing her distress, took several skittish sideways steps. Winloki made a low sound in her throat when the dun gelding, stripped of its gear, was led before the iron doors, where Camhóinhann waited with his long knife already drawn.

"It seems cruel," she said, just above a whisper, "when the poor beast has come all this way, carrying our supplies—trusting our kindness."

"Do not grieve yourself. It will be swift and painless. It would be different," Rivanon added under his breath, "if Goezenou had the slaying of the unfortunate beast."

She gritted her teeth and forced herself to watch. This magic of blood and death was the very reminder she needed of who these men were and of what they were capable. She was hating them all now, hating herself for not hating them enough these last weeks. Had she really forgotten how many of her countrymen they had slain? *Let the lesson not be wasted. Let me remember this moment to the last drop of blood.*

By a great effort of will she neither flinched nor turned away, determined not to show them any weakness. And yet, as promised, the death was humane. Camhóinhann put a hand over the gelding's eyes, whispered a few words in one nervous ear. Then the front legs collapsed and the horse fell over on one side, lying so still Winloki was half convinced it was already dead. In one movement, so swift she scarcely saw it, the priest bent down and cut its throat. Blood bubbled out in a crimson stream, smoking on the cold air.

An acolyte knelt to catch it in a little earthen bowl. When the bowl was full, he handed it on to Camhóinhann. Moving toward the doors with his powerful stride, the High Priest dashed the basin against the stone, calling out as he did so:

Améroda, clüid boédhen na briénhani.
Néas dennath émi yllathos,
Émiras denna esora gôndhal!

Very slowly, and with almost no sound at all, the doors swung open. What waited on the other side was veiled in shadow, but Winloki thought she could see a broad, high-roofed passage: not level, but ascending into darkness.

Some of the men lit torches. Those who were afoot mounted up again, preparing to enter. Then, in truth, the Princess might have refused to follow, but Camhóinhann guessed which way her thought was tending even before the idea was fully formed. At a signal from the High Priest, one of the guards closed in on her left, while on her right Rivanon took the reins out of her hands.

Leading the mare alongside his own long-legged sorrel, he brought her across the threshold and into the stale darkness of the catacombs.

20

✳

The tumult and fury of the storm continued unabated. Flames raced across the surface of the waves, fires of emerald and opal; lightning tore open the sky. As the embattled little craft plunged down an almost vertical slope, Prince Ruan could feel the boards groaning and buckling under his feet. In a moment, he knew, the entire bottom of the boat would shatter. Even if Sindérian's voice did not give out, no spell could bind it together against such intolerable strain. The boat bucked, dived, and rolled; every moment those on board were pitched in some new direction; every moment they seemed on the verge of a watery death.

And then, quite suddenly, they broke through the wall of rain; the wind slackened. The sea remained agitated, but the wizards' *shibéath* on the boat needed to hold only a short time longer. Perhaps, thought Ruan, it actually would. Faint with exhaustion, her voice worn to rags, Sindérian sank to her knees. Her eyes were closed and her lips were white, but she was still muttering spells.

Gradually, the waves settled into a more gentle motion. The clouds parted, revealing an eastern sky purple and gold with sunset. A wet and windblown Faolein perched on the thwart, preening his feathers, while Kivik and Skerry leaned wearily against the side, their faces as green as something dredged up from the bottom of the sea.

Ruan touched Sindérian lightly on the shoulder. "Rest now. You've brought us safely through the tempest. Leave the rest to Aell and me." Then he went to help the man-at-arms step the mast and raise the sail.

Already he thought he could smell land. The storm had nearly killed them, but it had also helped to speed them across the channel. He thought they might even see Mistlewald by morning, for there was just enough wind, and it was blowing from the right quarter. Unless it changed direction, they would hardly have to tack at all.

They sailed into the harbor of a little seaside town with the dawn tide. After a long nap, Sindérian had revived enough to sit up and wring the water out of her hair, which was as lank as seaweed. They all had as much salt in their clothes and their hair as if they had swum, not sailed, across the Necke.

As they rounded the breakwater with Aell's steady hand on the tiller, Ruan sat down cross-legged beside her. "Do you think Camhóinhann knew that someone was following, or did he call up the storm simply as a precaution?"

"Whatever he knew or guessed," she said, "he can't have known that we were following with two wizards on board. If he had known, the storm would surely have been much worse."

In the shadow of the mast, Skerry gave a weak, incredulous laugh. "I don't see how it *could* have been worse."

Ruan was inclined to agree. Nor did he believe that Faolein, hampered by the shape he was forced to wear, had played much part in keeping them afloat. Sindérian might be too modest to say so, but she had performed a feat of which a much older wizard might be proud.

They tied up their craft among other fishing vessels above the town and stepped out on the dock, haggard and exhausted, but on the whole jubilant. No one had expected such a brief, eventful voyage.

"Nevertheless," said Sindérian, "I am afraid the gale blew us many leagues east of any place the Pharaxions might have landed."

"They will head south, as much as the roads allow them," Ruan answered. "We have only to adjust our own course a little to the west."

It took most of the day to find a fisherman willing to buy the boat, and to locate a man on the outskirts of town with horses to sell. Even then the Skyrran princes, unimpressed by the animals bred in Mistlewald, took a long time selecting mounts for themselves. By the time they found horses to suit them it was so near dark, no one protested when Ruan suggested they seek out an inn and enjoy a rare night's rest in real beds.

They rode out the next morning before anyone else in the town was stirring. The roads in that region were good, and they made swift progress all that day and for many days afterward. Yet Sindérian felt the same urgency that had pressed on her while crossing Skyrra. At times, she thought she could smell the smoke of sacrificial fires rising in Apharos, carried a thousand miles on the world's winds. And, linked in some way by the *aniffath,* she believed she could sense a growing disquiet in Ouriána's mind—although what that meant for herself and the success or failure of the quest remained uncertain.

She woke one morning to find a white owl staring sleepily down at her from the same branch where the sparrowhawk had perched the night before. Faolein had gone through another transformation while she slept. *This evening, I will begin to scout ahead after dark,* he told her. *In that way, I may be able to spot the Pharaxions' campfires.*

That night, Sindérian and her companions set up their own camp under the eaves of a great wood. There was abundant deadfall, so it took very little time to gather enough for a good fire. As they sat warming themselves around its cheerful blaze, Skerry posed a question that must have been on his mind—and Kivik's, too—for many weeks.

"You've explained to us how Winloki was born on Thäerie, and how the High King and the wizards of Leal decided to hide her from Ouriána—but what we don't know, for I suppose we never asked, is how her mother came to live on Thäerie in the beginning, or how Nimenoë and the Empress, being sisters, came to be mortal enemies."

"Oh, but they never were that, not really," said Sindérian, with an emphatic shake of her head. "Their feelings for each other—their entire history—were far more complicated. Nimenoë spent much of her childhood on Thäerie and Leal, while Ouriána remained on Phaôrax; that was how their estrangement began. But I see I must tell you the entire story, as my father told it to me.

"There was a treaty made between the High King on Thäerie and the King of Phaôrax, to patch up some minor dispute. Of course all the ruling houses of the old Empire lands have Pendawer blood"—she glanced sideways at Prince Ruan as she said this, and then away again—"but in spite of close kinship, Phaôrax had often been the source of trouble before."

Sindérian stopped, shrugged, and then continued on. "Well, it is enough to say that this latest quarrel had been amicably settled, and as a gesture of good faith the King of Phaôrax sent his youngest niece to Thäerie to be fostered, and a little Pendawer prince went to Apharos. But *he* is not important to the story, for he lived a thoroughly unremarkable life and died an old man in his bed.

"As for Nimenoë, she was only a child of seven or eight, and no one suspected when she arrived in Pentheirie that she was magically gifted. It was the Old Queen, Prince Ruan's great-grandmother, who discovered the truth. *She* was a great lady, and might have been a great wizard, had she been allowed time to develop her own gifts. As it was, she was determined to give the child the opportunities she had lacked. Nimenoë was sent to the Scholia on Leal to study for several years, and then returned to Pentheirie as apprentice to Elidûc. It was a long time before anyone suspected that Ouriána was also gifted. There were wizards in Apharos in those days but not very powerful ones, and it seems they were none of them capable of recognizing her talents. Perhaps that was the beginning of the rift between them: Nimenoë was learning so many new and remarkable things, which she dutifully wrote about in letters to her sister, and Ouriána . . . Ouriána was not even heir to the throne then. I am afraid she was rather neglected until the King, her uncle, died without issue."

Sindérian threw some sticks into the fire and watched it briefly blaze up before she returned to her story.

"Nimenoë did go back to Phaôrax to see her father crowned, but I'm told she was not made very welcome. As Ouriána was then the heir, I think no one liked the confusion of having her twin at court. And they were growing into beauties by that time, you see, and perhaps Ouriána, who was finally beginning to receive the attention she craved, felt a little diminished by the presence of her sister. There was no quarrel, but from that time on there was a certain coolness between them, and the letters that went back and forth became less frequent.

"I should have mentioned that Nimenoë did not go to Phaôrax alone. It is, in its way, a most important point. Naturally, a seventeen-year-old princess, no matter how magically gifted, could not travel such a distance unaccompanied. She went with a party of noblemen and ambassadors from Thäerie, and they were joined for most of the way by a like embassy from Leal. My father was part of that embassy, and Éireamhóine and Camhóinhann—" She broke off speaking as Kivik exclaimed loudly and Skerry half rose from his seat on the ground.

"Your pardon," said Kivik with a shamefaced look. "You took us by surprise with that name. For a moment I thought—we thought—but I see now that it can't have been the same man."

"Oh, but it was the same man. You didn't know that Ouriána's High Priest was at one time a Master Wizard on Leal?"

"We did *not* know," said Skerry. "But how—? No, we will be
silent and let you finish your story, and perhaps our questions
will be answered in due course."

"Camhóinhann was one of the Nine Masters on Leal: the
oldest, the wisest, by far the most powerful. Éireamhóine was
his apprentice, more than a century and a half ago, but as great
as Éireamhóine would become, the pupil would never com-
pare to the master. They said Camhóinhann was the greatest
wizard since Mallion Penn. He was also a prince of the old
Thäerian line, who refused a crown in order to devote himself
body and soul to the magical arts he loved so well—but that
was before the fall of Alluinn.

"I have said he was the oldest wizard on Leal, but being also
the most powerful, he looked—and was—a man in his prime.
And Ouriána became infatuated. Another reason, perhaps, to
envy her sister, for Nimenoë had been very briefly the great
wizard's pupil. But what attraction could a beautiful, willful
child have for him, when he had lived almost two hundred
years and known so many great beauties? He was flattered,
he was amused, he was very, very kind. Perhaps, having been
raised long ago in a royal court, he was a little *too* courteous, a
little too gallant. Her infatuation became an obsession, though
nobody knew it then.

"After the coronation, Nimenoë went back to Thäerie, and
she did not return to Phaôrax to see Ouriána crowned two
years later. Only one invitation to that coronation went to Leal,
and of course it was Camhóinhann Ouriána sent for. He could
hardly refuse. To insult the new Queen of Phaôrax—to let the

whole world gossip and speculate as to the reason—would have been unthinkable. In any case, he told Faolein, she would surely outgrow her inconvenient attachment when kings and princes started suing for her hand."

"But he was wrong?" said Kivik, across the fire.

"When he arrived on Phaôrax it seemed he had not been wrong. It was almost as though their positions were reversed," said Sindérian, brushing back a lock of dark hair. "He wrote once to Éireamhóine to say that the Queen was very cool to him—but changed, wonderfully changed! Her small gift—so minor the Pharaxion wizards had not even seen it—had grown into a prodigious one, and she was radiant with power.

"He wrote a second time to say that she had gathered around her a circle of magicians, and they were experimenting with fragments of Otöwan sorcery she had dredged up from somewhere. The dangers she faced were obvious, and so he had warned her, but he was in no position to dictate to her in her own kingdom, no matter how young and inexperienced she might have been. That was the last letter that Camhóinhann sent back to Leal. No one knows what happened between them after that. But later, when Ouriána announced her 'apotheosis' and named him as her High Priest—then you may believe there was astonishment and great consternation on Thäerie and on Leal. Even so, it was not until word came of his terrible transformation that the wizards at the Scholia abandoned all hope of his return and named another to take his place among the Nine Masters.

"But I have strayed from the tale that I meant to tell you," said Sindérian. "We were speaking of Ouriána and Nimenoë. When Ouriána declared sovereignty over all the old Empire lands—when the High King on Thäerie, and all of the kings, princes, and dukes who owed him allegiance, refused to pledge her their fealty and she declared war on them—Nimenoë did lend her strength to the wards around Thäerie and the Lesser Isles. But not then, and not ever after, did she oppose her sister in any other way. When the prophecy became known, when it came into the minds of a dozen seers at once, when it was repeated again and again over the years, no one—not anyone who knew her—thought of Nimenoë, it was so certain she would never attempt to depose her sister. It was only on the day Nimenoë wed Prince Eldori that Ouriána cursed her to barrenness, fearing a son or daughter of that union as she would never have feared Nimenoë herself.

"But it is a dangerous thing, a spell of that sort, particularly when both parties involved are so very powerful. Things get twisted. So Nimenoë died giving birth to Guenloie. Yet even then, I can't say that the sisters were truly enemies. I was there when Nimenoë died, and she did not seem to bear her sister any hatred or think Ouriána had willed her death. She might have cursed Ouriána in return, you know—a deathbed curse can be very powerful—but she took no such revenge."

Her story concluded, Sindérian sat gazing into the flames, trying to catch a memory, trying to remember a tower room and a dying princess. Might there not have been forces at work that a twelve-year-old apprentice healer, so young, so ignorant, had failed to detect? *Things get twisted,* she had said it herself. And with a dying wizard of Nimenoë's power a final turn was not impossible. Had there not been, after all, some last spell, some final magic . . .

"It is a tangled history," she heard Skerry say across the fire, and the memory she had been trying to conjure became faint and faraway again. The white owl, returning from his evening flight, settled on her shoulder, and the memory receded even further.

"A very tangled history," she acknowledged with a deep sigh. "And it may be a long time before all of the knots are untied."

As they journeyed across Mistlewald, Sindérian's lessons in magic resumed. Sometimes it seemed to her that Faolein was as urgent to teach as she was eager to learn, and though nothing was ever said, she felt that he believed as she did: events were everywhere hurrying on toward a crisis of catastrophic proportions.

When you make the werelight, he said during one predawn vigil, *you do not* create *illumination out of nothing, but gather together in one place all of the light that is present, no matter how faint. This you already know. But even in total darkness we carry some light with us: sunlight, starlight, moonlight, firelight, we are absorbing it all of the time. That light, too, you can draw upon, but it is a finite quantity. If you were locked away in darkness for many days or weeks, you would soon exhaust it.*

Likewise, he went on, blinking his round yellow eyes, *you can draw water that is mixed with air and gather it in a cup, or in any vessel you choose. Mist to water and water to mist are the easiest transmutations of all, for both are already inclined toward change. It is a useful skill to have if you are ever at sea and the fresh water runs out. In the same way, you can gather water out of the soil. But you can perform these spells only where earth and water are already mixed. To the ignorant it may appear that you change one into the other, when all that you really do is summon whatever moisture is present.*

So Sindérian practiced gathering water out of the air, separating water out of a handful of soil. Once learned, the spell was easy for her to perform. *And as you grow more skilled,* said Faolein, *you may find you can summon water from a greater distance: from that rain cloud a mile away or the underground river that passes beneath us.*

She knit her brows, working that out as far as imagination would take her—for she had learned by now that every lesson, every spell, foreshadowed another. *And the force that runs along the ley lines?*

Yes, he answered, after a brief hesitation, *you can summon that power in much the same way that you summon light or water. But that is a spell better left to the greater adepts. A momentary lapse in concentration could fill you with such power you could never hold it.*

Whenever they met other travellers they asked the same question: had anyone seen a large party riding south or west? Again and again the answer was no—until one day they met a man with a cart full of casks and a story of "white men in red robes, and a beautiful lady riding with them." It had been two days, he said, and almost fifteen leagues. That meant that the Furiádhin were still well ahead.

"But at least," said Skerry, "we know for certain we are on the right road. And that is encouraging news."

Four days later they reached the foothills. No more than Winloki did Sindérian care for that country. Though better able to ward herself against voices in the night, she could not entirely shut them out—and if no ill dreams haunted her sleep, the ruined cities had enough tales to tell during daylight; the ghosts who haunted that region were so present, so voluble.

They had believed in an endless cycle of reincarnation, viewed time as a maze of many twists and turns, so that they were always looking to the past or the future, with little thought for present joys or sorrows. Many had lived only to die, making elaborate plans for the life to follow, or dreaming strange dreams of a life before—which might lie ahead when they turned the next corner. So their minds had become like mazes, too, continually running in crooked paths. In their memories Sindérian saw shadows of an old, old power, neither of the Dark nor of the Light, but pitiless, greedy; slaves to that power they had enslaved others. In their history she saw omens of things to come: what had been in ages past, what might be in days ahead, if bindings broke and ancient evils were let loose in the world again.

Meanwhile the year was withering around her. In the mornings, frost tingled in the air; in the evenings, she saw the moon as if through a thin haze of ice. So much time had passed, and she had hoped by now to be returning with the Princess to Thäerie.

Then one night Faolein returned much later than usual, just as Aell was waking Sindérian for the predawn watch—and this time he had news that sent everyone's spirits soaring. He had flown as far as the camp of the Furiádhin and he had seen the Princess.

If the rest of you could grow wings and fly as I do, you might overtake them before sunset, he told Sindérian. As it was, given the nature of the terrain, she knew it might take two or three days.

Yet the gap between them and the Pharaxions had narrowed. Relieved of all urgency since crossing over from Skyrra, Camhóinhann and his party must have been travelling at an easy pace, while she and her companions continued to press themselves.

"They don't know that we are here," said Kivik as they ate a hasty, cold breakfast and sipped lukewarm tea.

"It is certain they do not, or we would never have been able to travel so swiftly and so safely," answered Sindérian. "But even if they did know, I doubt they would consider a party the size of ours a threat, or hurry themselves because we were following."

"Yet you continue to think that we *can* hinder them in some way?" said Prince Ruan, with a lift of his brows. "Four men and two wizards—one of whom has no voice or hands to work spells?"

Sindérian turned away rather than meet that keen gaze of his. "The world is full of many unfathomable chances," she said, "and even the Furiádhin can't always predict where lightning might strike." Yet a desperate plan was beginning to form in her mind, she was beginning to understand what she must do. And it was not a plan she was willing to share with him— or anyone.

Though the smell of rain was often on the air, they had continued to travel dry, with the weather always ahead of them. The mountains were now so near, it looked as though it might be possible to reach out and touch them in the clear air. So when Faolein failed to return at all one night, Sindérian tried not to think of the updrafts and the downdrafts that would make flying in the high country up ahead so perilous.

She was not prepared for the news he brought with him when he finally landed on her saddlebow late the next morning. *They have disappeared.*

Her first joy at seeing him rapidly faded. *What do you mean?*

I cannot find them. And I have spoken to every bird within miles. They are not the most reliable source of information, as you may know, for their minds cannot hold a thought for very long, but they all say the same thing: Camhóinhann and the rest disappeared yesterday morning. They went under the ground— gone to earth like foxes.

She tried to make sense of that and could not. There might, of course, be caves in the mountains ahead, but she could think of no reason why the Furiádhin should go into one of them and stay for a day and a night. *Perhaps,* she said, *the birds are confused. Or perhaps Camhóinhann has cast some spell of concealment.*

But from whom would the Furiádhin be hiding? She shook her head, for it defied explanation. It had been a long time since she had believed in benevolent powers, powers that took a kindly interest in the affairs of men. At best, the Fates were indifferent. But she had never imagined they could be so cruel as to allow her to come so *close,* only that those she followed might disappear, without reason, without sense. Even now she could not—or would not—believe it.

I will not tell the others just yet, she decided. *It may turn out that the birds are mistaken.*

Until now, Sindérian had been careful to move quietly through the world, using as little magic as possible, hoping in that way to avoid attracting Ouriána's attention, to go undetected by those ahead. But with the disappearance of the Furiádhin and their prisoner she grew reckless, throwing her senses wide, soaking in all the influences of the countryside around her.

The ghosts and their dark history she already knew. Otherwise, it was an ordinary record of suns and moons and passing days: the flight of a hawk, a dim memory of some traveller bolder than the rest who had braved the hill country until night terrors drove him back. She searched through it all, found the thread she was looking for, and followed it to the lower slopes of Penadamin, in the Fenéille Galadan. Her companions, not quite understanding what she was doing, allowed her to lead them on.

All this brought her to an ascending track, where it did not take a scout or a tracker to see that a party of twenty or more had passed in the last few days, the prints were so clearly marked where mud had dried and captured them. And when they came to the cleft in the mountain and entered the rocky gorge, the stench of black magic, the smell of recent bloodshed, were unmistakable.

But when the trail abruptly terminated at the base of a cliff with the carcass of a dead horse, four puzzled faces turned in her direction.

"They can't—they can't have walked or ridden through solid stone," said Kivik.

"No," she answered grimly. "I am afraid that the mountain opened up to receive them."

There was a long, dumbfounded silence, during which she fervently wished she had warned the others what to expect. Then Prince Ruan said, "You think there is a hidden entrance?"

"I *know* there is an entrance. A pair of doors—I can't see them but I can feel them—just there." She indicated the place with a weary gesture.

"And you can open them?" Skerry asked with a hopeful look.

"That I don't know," she answered, swinging down from the saddle and skirting the body of the horse. In warmer weather, the smell would have been unbearable, yet it was not the carcass that made her stomach twist into knots or her scalp crawl. "But I mean to try."

There are magics here it would be unwise to meddle with, said Faolein's warning voice in her mind. *And look at the horse: there ought to be scavengers somewhere about, but nothing has touched it. That isn't natural. We should be away from here.*

Sindérian was scarcely paying attention. A reckless mood was still on her, and in that mood good advice generally fell on deaf ears. *Those spells are easiest that encourage things to do what is already in their nature.* Faolein had said so himself. And it was the nature of doors to let people in, as much as keep them out.

But hours later, sitting on the ground and glaring at the place where she knew the doors to be—having run through every likely spell she could remember or devise on the spot— she was finally forced to admit defeat. A series of runes and other signs were scratched in the earth before her, where she had been drawing them and rubbing them out for what felt like weeks. "The spell that seals these doors is far too ancient. No one studies that sort of magic on Leal—we haven't for hundreds of years!"

Blinking back angry tears, she tried to think what she

ought to do next. But she was physically exhausted, her mind a tangle of charms and spells—all of them quite useless—and the effort required to form even the simplest plan suddenly seemed far too great.

"I suppose," said Kivik, rising from his seat on a nearby boulder, "that it will take us weeks to go over the mountains in the ordinary way?"

Without looking up, Sindérian nodded, one short, sharp motion of her head.

"Then I think we had best begin. It is not so late, and surely we can ride for at least an hour before dark overtakes us."

There was a rustle of movement and a clink of mail rings as the other three men stood. Hooking a strand of dark hair behind one ear, Sindérian raised her eyes to look at them. One after the other, the faces of her companions were hardening into lines of determination.

"After all," said Skerry, "we have come this far with very little hope. I can think of no reason why we shouldn't continue on in the same way a while longer."

Prince Ruan offered her his hand. Too tired to refuse him, she allowed him to pull her up into a standing position.

His turquoise eyes were blazing. "As Lord Skerry says, from the very beginning we've had very little hope and no real plan. I don't see that anything has changed, do you?"

21

✴

The tunnel was so broad, four could ride abreast without crowding the horses. At intervals, other passageways intersected. Then Camhóinhann, who was leading the way, would raise his torch high and examine the walls. Each time he seemed to find markings no one else could see and chose his direction accordingly.

The granite of the tunnels had been chiseled and smoothed until floors, walls, and ceilings were like dressed stone without any joins. Sometimes there were archways sealed by stone blocks, which Winloki took to be the tombs. But these were so very plain, without inscriptions or other carvings, that she had difficulty reconciling them with the diamond doors. Where she had expected mansions and palaces of the dead, she found only these dank and humble dwellings.

Though most of the passages were level, occasionally they followed one that ascended or descended, and every time Camhóinhann took them deeper Winloki's heart misgave her. Ever since the doors had closed behind her, she had remained silent, building a wall of resentment around her to keep the others out. But at last, the question that was pressing most heavily on her mind demanded an answer. "How long will we be here?"

"When we came here before we spent an entire fortnight exploring these tunnels," said Morquant. "But if memory serves me, it will be a journey of four or five days to the Doors of Corundum on the far side of the mountain."

Then Winloki wished she had not asked. The very idea of four or five days moving through this dead weight of air was simply intolerable. Sometimes she thought she caught a whiff of corruption coming from the vaults. Even the stillness was unnerving: a silence as vast as the mountain itself, it made nothing of their little disturbance clattering through on horseback.

Sometimes the ceiling soared high overhead; sometimes the passage dipped so low, the torches left trails of smoke on the roof. Once they entered what must have been a natural cavern, where a river flowed through in a deep channel spanned by a narrow bridge.

"Do not touch the water," said Camhóinhann. "There are many things here that have strange properties; the water may be one of them."

At last they came into a series of passages where stonecutters had lavished their art in friezes of intricate pattern: pictures of gardens and flowering vines chiseled in high relief, so real she was half convinced she could breathe the heady scent of the flowers. Veins of silver and gold ore ran through the floor. These, then, were the mansions of the dead that Winloki had been expecting all along. Yet there was a subtle wrongness, as of something hidden: faces in the foliage she could not quite see, figures of men and women whose proportions hovered on the edges of deformity.

An archway rich with carvings led into a chamber filled with stone tables laid out in exact rows. "Effigies," said Efflam in a low voice, for on every table rested a marble image, lying with arms crossed and eyes closed, dreaming the centuries away in imperishable serenity.

"No," said Rivanon, "not effigies, not statues. These are the dead themselves. By some ancient process of alchemy unknown today they were able to transmute the matter of living things into stone."

And when Winloki leaned down to take a closer look, she saw that it was so. No statues had ever been so perfectly modeled, complete down to the tiny lines on an upturned palm, the eyelashes resting on an alabaster cheek, or the intricate embroidery on the edge of a sleeve. Yet all was of the same milky whiteness: hair, skin, gowns, sandals. Nausea clawed at her stomach.

"Only royal burials were preserved in this way," Morquant explained in a dry whisper. "This is the first room of the queens. In chambers to either side lie the lesser wives and concubines. The kings rest farther in."

From that hall they passed through many like it, where they saw hundreds more of the petrified bodies. In the women Winloki saw a cold perfection of feature she had never encountered in the flesh; the men, too, looked noble and splendid. Yet for all their beauty her revulsion grew. There was a subversion here of the natural order of things; and in the delicate veining of marble faces and marble limbs, she discovered a horror like leprosy. By comparison, the three priests seemed vivid with life: the bleached skin and colorless hair of the Furiádhin revealed a warmer tint, like ivory beside snow, or linen next to salt. Winloki was glad when they passed beyond the last burial chambers, even though it meant a return to the stifling passageways.

After a wearisome journey of unknown duration, Camhóinhann ordered a halt to set up camp in one of the tunnels. And there everyone settled down, on bedrolls and folded cloaks, to sleep for what she could only assume was the night, all hours being the same under the mountain.

The next interval began with a meal of dried meat and dried fruit, with water passed around in a leather bottle, before they all mounted up for another torchlit journey.

To Winloki's relief, it seemed they had seen the last of the stone figures. But in a corridor lined with the unmarked tombs, they began encountering vaults that had been disturbed, the blocks that had sealed them violently cast down—as if some tremendous force on the inside had hurled them outward. At the first, second, and third, Camhóinhann hesitated a moment before riding on. Not a word did he speak, but each time he pushed the pace a little harder, so that a grim sense of urgency began to infect everyone who followed after him.

And all that day, if day it was, Winloki experienced a growing claustrophobia. Walled about with earth, above, below, on every side, she felt her craving for sunlight and pure air grow more and more insistent. It was then that she felt the true horror of deep places, became giddy when she thought of the vast number of underground passages spreading out still ahead of her, of the remaining hours and days of this dark journey.

Most of all, the incalculable weight of the mountain, the

tremendous mass of it, preyed on her mind. She felt crushed and suffocated, wondering how it was that the roof of the passage did not come crashing down under so much weight, so much pressure. And if, by any mischance, she were to be separated from the others, unable to find her way out . . .

These dreadful thoughts so occupied her that she had no warning of anything amiss until she happened to hear Adfhail, the youngest acolyte, speaking with the guard Kerion. They were leading the horses down a descending corridor more precipitous than any they had encountered so far, and because they were a little ahead of her she caught only fragments of the conversation.

"—a shuffling sound and a dull rattle. I *did* hear it. And there was something I could smell, colder and staler than the air, and it made the hair on the back of my neck stand—"

"Your imagination—it must have been. Nothing could live inside these tunnels. And do you think those *things* we saw could rise up and walk in their marble?"

There was so long a pause, Winloki wondered if *she* had imagined the whole exchange. Then Adfhail spoke again. "Look to the Furiádhin. Dyonas is uneasy, and that is unlike him. Mark my words: he and Camhóinhann have seen things here they never expected."

Winloki felt a noose of fear around her heart, drawing tighter and tighter. Was that the sound he spoke of now? But no, it was only the rattle of a harness, the clink of spurs on the cavern floor. She had been holding her breath, but now she relaxed and let it out.

Then there came a sound impossible to ignore or dismiss: a deep groaning under the earth, followed by a sound like rock shattering, and a repetitive clatter in the passages behind them. As one man, the entire company came to a halt.

"Look to the Princess," said Camhóinhann sharply from somewhere up ahead. Swords came hissing out of their scabbards as the guards drew their weapons and moved into a tight, protective circle around Winloki.

At another order from the High Priest, everyone began to move, this time at a much swifter pace than before. At first it seemed that they would easily outdistance whatever it was that followed them, particularly when they reached a place where the passage leveled out, enabling them to mount up and ride again. But they had been riding only a short time when they were assailed by a stench so foul it wrenched at the gut and turned the knees to water.

All of the horses erupted into madness at once: squealing and bucking, bending nearly double in their efforts to savage their own riders, rising up on their hind legs and beating at the air.

Winloki was one of those thrown. Stunned by the fall, for a moment she could only lie on the cold stone wondering what had happened, why her head throbbed so, what this commotion of stamping hooves and shrilling horses swirling all around her could be. By some miracle, she was neither trampled nor crushed before she collected enough of her wits to roll over, lever herself off the floor, and scramble to her feet.

Trying to make her way out of the press she stumbled over a body—by his armor one of the guards, though his hair was matted with brains and blood, his face reduced to an unrecognizable ruin. Struggling for balance in that battering confusion, she had it, then almost lost it again, tripping over a fallen acolyte.

Those of the men still mounted fought for control of their panicking horses; those who had managed to regain their feet were engaged in a furious battle with a horde of creatures who seemed to consist mostly of bone and shriveled flesh. Armed only with broken teeth and long hooked nails, they were literally tearing their way through her guards.

It was very dark. All but a few of the torches had been extinguished and those few lay guttering on the ground. She searched for Camhóinhann or Dyonas but could not find them. She knew they had been somewhere near the head of the column when the horses went mad, but she had been so pushed and jolted and turned around ever since, she was no longer certain which way to look.

And the men around her, they were putting up a valiant fight, but even as swords swiped off bony hands, skinless arms, or heads with stringy hair and carious teeth, the separated parts went on snapping, slashing, and crawling. Bones cracked and splintered, tendons snapped, rotten flesh sloughed away, yet still the severed limbs continued to bunch and move with wormlike writhings.

An eyeless head came bouncing toward Winloki with clashing jaws. Despite her efforts at evasion, it attached itself to the hem of her gown—until one of the horses kicked it aside and sent it flying into darkness. All around her there were shrieks and groans. Two of the guards were beaten down trying to defend her. Seeing one of them move, she tried to reach him, but something or someone knocked her aside and spun her around, so that on regaining her balance she could not find him.

Someone tossed her a knife, which she snatched out of the air and used to skewer a crawling hand that was pawing at her boot. Held in place by the point of the knife, the fingers continued to squirm until the hand tore itself apart in its efforts to get loose.

Then there was a flash of crimson, a smell like lightning, and all three Furiádhin broke through the wall of bodies around her, spitting out spells, crushing severed limbs underfoot, causing the horrors to sizzle and burn.

When it was all over, those who had survived rekindled the torches and looked about them, counting up their losses.

Six men had died: two acolytes and four guards, Merrac and Lochdaen among them. In spite of everything, Winloki could not help grieving. They had been so young; they had treated her always with as much kindness as their duty allowed; she was sorry she had been angry with them. Two geldings and her beautiful cream-colored mare had been killed as well, their throats bitten or their bellies slashed. The remaining horses had retreated down the passageway, where they stood shivering and sweating.

"We dare not ride," said Camhóinhann. "The horses are not to be trusted if the ghouls attack again. And we will leave the bodies of the men behind, for we would be foolish to encumber ourselves. Therefore, let them lie here entombed with the kings."

No one protested; they simply gathered up weapons and gear from their fallen comrades and stripped the saddlebags from the dead horses. Yet Winloki could feel the fear radiating off every one of them as they reckoned up all the grim possibilities of their situation. They had reason to be afraid. Not only had the journey turned unexpectedly perilous, it was likely to take longer, walking, than anyone had anticipated. *And every extra hour adds to our danger. We may all end up lying "entombed with the kings."*

Sometime in the hours that followed she heard two of the Furiádhin talking, their voices echoing faintly in the dark passageway.

"A mistake," said Goezenou in that gloating voice of his. "One for which Camhóinhann is likely to pay dearly."

"For which we are all likely to pay dearly," Dyonas answered coldly. "Or do you really imagine you will escape your share of the blame if anything happens to the Princess?"

She heard Goezenou laugh, but this time she thought she detected a note of uncertainty. "Ironic, surely, when hers was the presence that attracted the ghouls in the first place."

"It may be so," said Dyonas, in the same level voice as before. "The ghouls were not here eleven years ago, or if they were they never troubled us. And that much latent power *can* bring about unexpected effects—especially when it is beginning to unfold."

22

✳

The road Sindérian and her travelling companions followed was an old one and not well marked—it was more like the memory of a road than a road itself. But they had left the ghosts and haunts of the hill country behind, and if the air was thinner, it was also cleaner. Falcons and eagles nested on the cliffs high overhead; she could hear their far, lonely cries, see them soaring with wings dark against the pale sky. Wind boomed between the ridges and sang among the pines, but it spoke with its own voice and no other.

Still, it promised to be a difficult ascent. This time of year there was always the danger of snow in the high passes. *But it can only delay us, not defeat us,* she told herself whenever her spirits began to flag. *The worst blizzards are still many weeks off.*

She believed the Furiádhin had chosen the underground journey only to avoid weather in the passes up above. Camhóinhann was in no great hurry, that much had already been proven. Beyond the mountains there was all of Lünerion, Alluinn, and Rhuadllyn still to cross before they came to the ocean; surely, over such a distance, it would be possible to overtake them. And then . . .

Her heartbeat fluttered and her mouth went dry. Better not to dwell too much on journey's end, on what she had resolved to do no matter the cost. If she thought too much about *that* she would lose her nerve.

It rained during the night, but they found a hollow place at the base of a cliff and managed to avoid the worst of the storm. In the morning, the sun whitened a cloudbank to the east, then burst forth in glory.

They had not ridden far when Prince Ruan's quick ears caught sounds he had not expected: a rattle of pebbles, followed by a regular patter like footsteps on one of the ridges above. He scanned the mountainside. "I think there is someone up there following us. Or at least observing us."

"It is the wind," said Sindérian. "What else could it be? If anyone was spying on us, Faolein would have spotted them, or the birds would have told him."

Whatever it had been, it was silent now. And though he continued to listen, the sounds were not repeated.

Sindérian had been animated all morning, but she now turned somber and introspective. Ruan would have given much to know what she was thinking. By this time he was well accustomed to her fluctuating moods, to the rise and fall of her spirits a dozen times a day; they were the inevitable result of her ardent nature. A richer blood flowed in her veins than that of any woman he had ever known; he would not alter her in that respect if he could. No, what troubled him now was a desperate resolution he saw in her eyes, as of some set purpose that remained through all her mercurial changes.

She had reached an important decision, he was all but convinced of that, and her silence on that point was a very bad sign.

"There is something I wish to tell you." Sindérian's offer came so suddenly, it caught him off guard. She stole a glance at the others, then pitched her voice so that only Ruan could hear. "Something I would rather not say to Prince Kivik or Lord Skerry."

But if he expected some personal revelation, he was soon disappointed. "I have often wondered why the Furiádhin keep Winloki alive. What use could they have for her living, when her very existence is a continuing threat to their Empress-Goddess? Now I think I have found an answer, and it is not . . . not an encouraging one.

"We know," she went on, "that there was a time when Ouriána meant to circumvent the prophecy by passing the crown to her son Guindeluc. He would rule Phaôrax, but she would rule him. But Guindeluc is dead these two years, and she has never shown much favor to her younger sons. Oh, there can be little doubt of her intentions when the Princess was born, but now . . ." Her voice trailed off.

"You think she is looking for an heir rather than a sacrifice?" It was a possibility he had never considered; he was not even certain he was prepared to consider it now. "Yet why Winloki and not Prince Cuillioc? She may not favor him but he *is* her own son, while the Princess—Ah, I see. Winloki has great magical gifts; Prince Cuillioc none at all." Now he too stole a glance at the riders up ahead. "But would she *allow* herself to be bent to Ouriána's purpose?"

"Our friends, I think, would say no. But living in Skyrra all of these years, what does the Princess know of us or our wars, what does she know of Ouriána except rumor and reputation? And Ouriána would offer her an empire—she has seduced *many* over the years who were far older and far wiser by offering them less.

"And I," she added, in a much lower voice, "have an idea of the temptations she might offer. I cannot say I would not have found them . . . beguiling, when I was Winloki's age."

They rode on together in a thoughtful silence until Sindérian spoke again.

"And there is something else. I have asked myself again and again: if I were Ouriána, and I meant for Winloki to come to Phaôrax already half persuaded, who, of all the Furiádhin, would I choose to bring her? Perhaps you can guess the only answer that ever made any sense."

"Camhóinhann—perhaps Dyonas, by what one hears of him. Yes, those two before any of the others," said Ruan. "Although it's difficult to see why she would choose Goezenou, if those were her intentions."

Sindérian shrugged. "Perhaps only because he was in Mere with the others when they first set out. Or maybe to frighten the Princess, so that when she arrives in Phaôrax and finds Ouriána gracious and welcoming, she might turn to her as a kinswoman and a refuge."

Ruan narrowed his eyes, considering what followed from that. "Then you are afraid if we don't rescue the Princess very soon, she may not *wish* to be rescued, she might not choose to come with us." It was a disturbing idea, yet one that was all too plausible. He began to understand the urgency driving Sindérian all of these weeks. Nevertheless, he did not think that she had told him everything that was on her mind.

They camped that night in the shelter of a ridge topped with wind-writhen firs. When they started out at dawn, the sky was overcast and the air smelled of snow. Unless he was much mistaken it was falling already on the peaks above. But Faolein, flying ahead by moonlight, had discovered a trail and a pass. Speaking through Sindérian, he had assured the others they would not have to climb so high.

By *érien,* the midpoint of the day, the sky had cleared. And the road—curiously—had become more like a real road, as though it had seen recent and frequent use. He could see no tracks but those of bear and lynx, but the rain two nights ago would have washed away evidence of men and horses.

A sudden change in the direction of the wind brought a scent that was musky and earthy; at the same time, there was a rustling in the heather to either side of the road. He reached for his sword, but before it was free of the scabbard a dozen squat figures sprang out from the bushes, and it was all that he could do to control his horse.

Then a pair of gnarled brown hands reached up and took a firm hold of the harness. The gelding stopped in its tracks, suddenly turned so meek and compliant that Ruan could scarcely believe it was the same animal. Within seconds, the other horses were caught in a similar fashion and the entire party brought to a halt.

Sindérian looked down at the dwarves, and the dwarves stared steadily back at her. This was a meeting she could hardly have expected. The *Corridon* were a secretive, reclusive race. So far as she knew, they had not had contact with Men for more than two hundred years.

"Courtesy would dictate that you dismount," said the dwarf attached to her bridle. He wore a circlet of gold in his dark hair and had an altogether lordly manner. "For we mislike craning our necks in order to speak with you." As he spoke, some of the rocks up on the slope began to move and became more dwarves, in grey cloaks.

It seemed to Sindérian that they had no choice but to comply, for they were assuredly outnumbered. All of the dwarves carried weapons; two held crossbows cocked and aimed. And whatever influence they had exercised on the horses still seemed to hold.

"We have no quarrel with your people," said Prince Ruan, his turquoise eyes glittering and his chin jutting out at an uncompromising angle. Nevertheless, he dismounted along with the rest. "It is to be hoped that you have no quarrel with us."

"That remains to be seen. If you resist us you will die. If you put yourselves in our hands, it may—just possibly—be to your advantage."

On equal footing, none of the dwarves appeared quite so small as they had from the saddle. Big boned with short thick limbs, it was not, Sindérian realized, that they were ill proportioned, their proportions were simply . . . different. They wore belted tunics of green, grey, or brown and high leather boots that turned over at the top in wide cuffs. Some were ferociously bearded, none were clean shaven. Broad-shouldered and sturdy, they looked tough as old tree roots.

She spoke to the men in a low voice. "It seems we have trespassed without even knowing it. Let us try to make amends."

*   *   *

Winloki walked until she saw everything through a grey haze of exhaustion, and still Camhóinhann allowed no one to rest. The cold of the tunnels had numbed her feet, but miles of walking over hard stone floors caused a dull ache to climb her legs and lodge in the small of her back. Though her world had grown dim and narrow, she could hear the men panting, their feet stumbling. She was not the only one whose strength was failing.

At last the High Priest took pity on them—or simply realized they had reached the outermost limits of their endurance. They all sat down on the floor of the passageway, some with their backs to the wall, others reclining against gear they had dropped when Camhóinhann gave the order to stop.

Winloki rubbed her eyes with the heels of her hands. Nothing had been said about eating or sleeping, so she supposed it was only a temporary rest. *Could* anyone sleep after the horror of the ghouls? But it would be days before they were safely out of this place, and they would *have* to sleep long before that.

When she lowered her hands and looked up, she saw Camhóinhann looming over her in his scarlet robes. He crouched down beside her, and from somewhere in the heavy folds of his outer garment, he drew out a leather flask. "Drink this. It will put heart into you."

"I am not afraid—nor in any danger of swooning away." It was a lie and perhaps he knew it. Fatigue had dulled only a little the sharp edge of fear.

Under his level, dispassionate gaze, she found she could not, after all, refuse what he offered her. She accepted the flask, unstoppered it, and took a swallow of honey cordial. It felt cool going down, but became warm as soon as it reached her stomach. That warmth diffused swiftly through her veins, until she began to feel, if not braver, at least a little stronger.

He had not moved from his place beside her. "Though you ask no reassurance, still I will offer it. If anyone leaves these tunnels alive, it will be you. There is not a man here but will lay down his life on your behalf."

"I don't want anyone here to die for me!" She realized even as she said it how petulant, how childish she sounded. "I want nothing from any of you, except my freedom. I want to go home."

The priest rose smoothly to his feet. "We *are* taking you home, home to Phaôrax. You may not understand that as yet, but you will."

After too short a rest, they were up and walking again. Winloki had thought they had seen the last of the burial chambers, the last of the petrified bodies, but she soon discovered her mistake. After stumbling through a dozen more rooms, she felt she could not possibly bear another sight of them.

When they did stop to eat and to take a longer rest, Winloki found that she could sleep after all. Despite fear, aching muscles, and the hardness of stone floors, the body made its own demands. While she slept, with her feet tucked up inside her cloak and a blanket to warm them, the pain woke again in her insteps and ankles.

She soon stopped counting the intervals of weary trudging punctuated by short snatches of sleep. As miserable as she was, she knew there were those who suffered far worse. Two of the men who had sustained minor scratches during their battle with the ghouls had grown weak and feverish. Their comrades supported them as they walked.

Wherever they went, the horses followed at a short distance, sometimes in a straggling line, sometimes in a tight little herd. They would not come too near; neither would they drop far behind. And though they ate the grain the men scattered for them, they would suffer no one to touch them. Even when she slept, Winloki could hear the horses stamping the ground and shrilling their distress.

In time, water ran low, all the leather skins and bottles they carried with them empty or nearly so. The horses still carried water, but it was impossible to get at it. Only the injured men were allowed more than a sip during their brief periods of rest. Though food was a little more plentiful, the priests rationed that out carefully, too. With mouths so dry, eating became a chore; Winloki chewed and swallowed only because it was necessary to keep up her strength.

As for the men, she had given up hating them for who and what they were—it had been a pretense anyway, a lie she told herself and never entirely believed. They were so brave, so cheerful in adversity, so generous and considerate to her that she would have been ashamed to despise them.

"We will not drink any of the water we find here," said Camhóinhann when they came to a place where moisture trickled down from a crack in the ceiling and formed a little pool, "not unless we are forced to do so."

The water *did* smell of minerals, and remembering the stone men and women in the burial chambers, Winloki was content to go thirsty a good while longer. "But the horses—"

"It would be difficult to prevent them. And since we have

not enough to share with them, we must hope for their sakes that the water is wholesome."

There was another attack by the ghouls. This time, coming up near the back of the party, where Camhóinhann kept watch, they were quickly repelled, but not before three men had been viciously slashed by the ghouls' long, curving nails.

The cuts were very deep, and they continued to bleed even after Dyonas bound them up with strips of linen from one of the reclaimed saddlebags. "I could help them if you removed these silver bracelets," Winloki said to him. "I could help the others, too, the men who are sick. I *am* a healer."

"A healing would cost you strength you cannot spare," he answered shortly. "In any case, none are seriously injured— and the pain will pass."

There came a time when Camhóinhann announced they were only a short march from the Doors of Corundum, which would provide them a way out of the catacombs. "We may yet win through to safety."

Heartened by this announcement, they continued on with renewed strength and hope. All other considerations aside, this news came none too soon. They were running out of torches, and Winloki thought she might have gone mad if forced to continue the rest of the journey by werelight.

Yet they were all beginning to flag again by the time they saw the faint flicker of blue in the passage up ahead that told them they had reached the final gate. It was Dyonas who knelt down by the sapphire doors and began to chant a spell, while Camhóinhann and Goezenou kept a watch on the tunnels and everyone else waited in a fever of impatience.

Yet the doors did not open, and an unaccustomed look of strain appeared on Dyonas's face, great beads of sweat on his pale forehead.

"What is it?" said Goezenou, leaving his post and coming up behind him.

"I am not . . . entirely certain," he answered, his jaw tightening. "I believe the darkness lies here so thick and deep, it is almost becoming earth. You know what that means: it is growing in intention. And that intention is apparently to hold these doors in place."

In the tunnels behind them, there was a fierce clatter, followed by a rolling rattle coming steadily closer. Scenting danger, the horses scattered down intersecting corridors, their hoofbeats echoing off the walls. Winloki turned along with the men, her heart pounding furiously, her eyes straining in the dim light of the guttering torches, searching for the source of the continuing rattling noise.

And then she saw it: a great mass of decaying and putrefying bodies melded together into one huge creature, inside a coat made of bones and armor. It was not possible to count the limbs, they were so many and various, but it moved on its body like a snake, and the parts had been joined together so badly she could hear bones grinding and the intolerable soft squelching of the fleshy parts rubbing together. In the hollow sockets of the great eyeless head something moved: an unlight, blacker than black, a rudimentary intelligence that Winloki could sense—and knew with a thrill of horror that it could sense *her*, that it was seeking *her*.

There was a soft hiss of steel as all the guards and acolytes drew their weapons. But scarcely had swords cleared their sheaths before the hands that gripped them lost all strength and they went clattering to the floor. For the reek of the thing was beyond all corruption, and wherever it spread, minds grew confused, limbs were chained. Winloki felt a cry rise up in her throat, but her tongue was a stone; the sound shriveled and died while it was yet inside her. Around her, the men made frantic, incoherent noises.

Of those closest, only Camhóinhann retained sufficient willpower to move. Whipping out his sword, he stepped quickly between her and the lurching monstrosity, raising the other hand in a commanding gesture. For a moment her courage rose—until he opened his mouth, no sound emerged, and the spell died on his lips.

Outside the ring of silence, she could hear Dyonas chanting the door spell with increasing urgency. "*Érodach! Érodach! Riholar ém néma—érodach!*"

The creature had now crept so near the stench of it nearly choked her. But Camhóinhann leaped to the attack, scarlet robes swirling, sword flashing in the last of the torchlight. Once, twice, three times he struck—impaling one of the putrefying bodies, wrenching out his blade, then striking again—yet still the thing continued to creep forward. Lifting his blade, he slashed downward, shearing off portions of decaying flesh—yet the horror lurched on, veering only a little and heading straight for the Princess again.

When she felt a bruising grip on her arm, she knew without looking that it was Goezenou. *If Camhóinhann falls,* she thought dazedly, *Goezenou will sacrifice me to save himself.*

Like a snake preparing to strike, the thing rose up, and a hideous mouth stretched open. Winloki could only watch in helpless terror as that mouth gaped wider and wider, two rows of bony teeth came closer and closer—And Camhóinhann flung himself between, thrusting his sword into the mouth and down the throat, with all of his weight and strength behind it. The teeth clashed together, imprisoning his arm, but the entire mass of the thing shuddered, and there was a high-pitched squealing, agonizing to hear.

Then it began to melt, the separate parts falling like a hideous rain, drying to dust as soon as they touched the floor. Released from its grip, Camhóinhann dropped to his knees, letting his sword fall to the floor. A dark stain—a darker shade of crimson—spread across the sleeve of his robe.

Winloki struggled frantically in Goezenou's grasp, freed from the spell that had held her immobilized, forgetting she still wore the silver bracelets and intent on helping the man who had just saved her.

The earth shuddered, and there was a loud grinding. Finally responding to Dyonas's spell, the Doors of Corundum swung open, letting in a sudden blaze of sunlight. Then a rough arm encircled Winloki's waist. Despite her efforts to resist him, Goezenou dragged her across the threshold and into the dazzling light of day.

23

✳

Reluctantly, Sindérian and her companions gave up their horses and weapons, and allowed an escort of dwarves to march them off the road and along a meandering path through the heather. Then she had ample time to reflect on whether it had been wise, after all, to yield without a fight. Foolish to shed blood, to make enemies without good cause, but so little was known about the *Corridon*—were they friendly or unfriendly? And why had they chosen *this particular moment* in time to come out of their centuries-long isolation?

The dwarf in command, he of the golden circlet, was called Prince Tyr. So much she had gathered from hearing the others speak to him. He walked with a tremendous air of self-importance, though surprisingly light footed. In that he reminded her a little of Prince Ruan. Otherwise, they could hardly have been less alike, the sturdy dwarf with his broad, brown face and the slender, light-skinned Faey.

When they came to a fork in the path, the dwarves chose the

uphill turning. It was a well-marked trail, running straighter than the other except when it skirted a stony outcrop or a pile of rocks. Every moment, Sindérian expected to see a cave mouth or crack in the earth opening into their underground kingdom, but none had appeared by the time the slope leveled out and the path ended. If there was spell or illusion hiding such an entrance, it was too slender and subtle for her to detect.

In the middle of the flat area stood a great boulder—too large and heavy, she would have thought, for a dozen men to shift it. Yet it was so cunningly balanced, a single dwarf rolled it aside, uncovering a door in the ground: a single slab of iron less easily moved, for it took two dwarves, straining against the weight, to lift it. The opening dropped down into a shaft so deep it was impossible to see all the way to the bottom. But there was a series of narrow shelves cut into the side of the pit one above the other like a ladder, and iron rings had been hammered into the rock on either side. By this means, Sindérian realized, they were meant to descend.

"The Lady goes first," the dwarf prince said.

Prince Ruan stiffened and his eyes narrowed. For a moment she thought he would do something foolish. "*I* should go first."

"I am not afraid," she assured him hastily, though in all truth she did not relish trusting herself to those narrow footholds, particularly not in the dark of the shaft. "First is no worse than last." *And better down than up,* she added silently. That way, at least, her skirts would not hamper her nearly so much.

A red-haired dwarf with a forked beard reached out to take

Faolein. "I will see to the owl." Silver rings glinted in his ears; like the others, he had a bold, buccaneerish look about him that went far beyond the pair of knives he carried in his belt.

Words of protest were already on her lips when Sindérian suddenly thought better of it. Wiser, perhaps, not to reveal just yet that the owl was a wizard and her father. Besides, she would climb more easily without his weight on her shoulder. She sat down on the edge opposite the ladder, dangling her feet. "How far *down* does it go?"

When the dwarves made no answer, she put a tentative boot on the first step and reached for the handholds.

"Count the steps as you descend," said Prince Tyr. "When you have counted one hundred and two, look for a ledge on the right-hand side. Step off there and wait for the rest of us."

Feeling her way and counting, there was less time to wonder about the depth of the pit. Twice she almost missed her foothold, but by holding firmly to the iron rings she avoided a fall. The shaft became wider as she descended, but it went down at such an angle that the rectangle of sky grew narrower and narrower and the light dwindled. Fifty steps down and her hands were slick with sweat. Seventy-five and her legs began to shake. By the time she had counted one hundred and two, her eyes had adjusted enough to the dark that she could just make out the ledge.

In the dark of the shaft it was impossible to see how far the ledge extended, but it was very narrow. Once she was there, she stood with her back pressed up against the rock wall, waiting for what seemed like a very long time before another body blocked out the narrow band of light and she heard the scrape of booted feet on the steps above.

First to climb down was a dwarf, and then came another, moving past her confidently on the slender shelf. Prince Ruan came third. He too edged past, so that rather than lose him in the dark she was obliged to sidle farther along the ledge herself. More dwarves descended before Aell, Kivik, and Skerry were allowed to climb down, one after the other.

By that time, the first dwarf had produced a lantern from a niche in the wall. When lit, it gave off a feeble blue glow, so dim that daylight would have washed it out completely; it would have been no light at all. Here, it was barely enough to see by after someone up above dropped the door into place. She heard hinges creak and iron groan as the boulder's weight settled on top.

"Where is my fa—Where is my owl?" she asked indignantly, for the last dwarf had stepped off the ladder and Faolein was nowhere to be seen.

"Your bird has been taken to the cave where we will stable your horses," said Prince Tyr. "No harm will come to it there." Taking charge of the lantern, he set off along the ledge.

With dwarves ahead and behind them, Sindérian and the men had no choice but to follow. The cavern—she supposed it was that—proved to be larger by far than she had imagined, and the ledge much longer.

"Take my hand," said Prince Ruan, in that composed, faintly arrogant voice she knew so well. "The stone is damp and the way is slippery. Also, it grows a little narrower just ahead."

It would be unpardonably foolish, she decided, not to take advantage of his sure feet, his ability to see in the dark like a cat. So she swallowed her pride and put her cold, moist hand into his warm, dry one. His clasp was light and in no way intimate, but his grip tightened each time her feet slipped. She lost track of the time, concentrating on each step, trying not to think about the unknown depths below.

"Can you see the bottom?" she asked when the suspense of not knowing became unbearable.

There was a long pause before he replied, which was all the answer she needed. "No," he said at last, "but I see an opening in the rock up ahead. I don't think we will have to continue on this way much longer."

When the light disappeared, Sindérian's heart dropped.

Prince Ruan's voice came to her out of the dark. "He has passed through the opening with his lantern. But it is only a few yards more—as you see, we are already there."

Indeed, on the right-hand side the light, such as it was, shone out again, and there was a tunnel in the rock. She stepped into the passage with a heartfelt sigh of relief, and Ruan released his grip. There was only time to catch a brief glimpse of his face before he turned away, just enough to see the grim set of his jaw, the frown between his eyes. She realized that he was not so unmoved by their plight as he had sounded on the ledge.

The passage was long and winding, and it led into an intricate maze of caverns, tunnels, and shafts. Sindérian soon lost track of all the twists and turns. She could see very little by the dim glow of the lantern, moving like a firefly up ahead, but she had a vague suspicion that some of the turns were unnecessary, that Prince Tyr frequently doubled back to make the route even more confusing.

They did not intend that we should be able to find our way forward or back again without a guide. She wondered drearily if it was her own bad luck, the result of Ouriána's ill-wishing, which had brought them all there.

At several places there were shallow steps cut into the rock, always leading down. Sometimes there were faint, faraway footsteps or the glimmer of lights in distant passages. Sometimes the lamp would briefly illuminate something in passing—a pinnacle of white limestone, a pendent curtain of crystal like a lacework of ice.

Once she heard the Skyrran princes speaking together in low voices just behind her. "If they meant to harm us, I think they would have done so already," said Kivik.

"I would not depend on that," answered Skerry. "By all the old tales that ever I heard, they don't readily admit strangers into their underground kingdoms. Will they be any more ready to allow us to leave again?"

Meanwhile, the dwarves were silent. It did not seem to be a hostile silence, but how could she tell? It had been hard to read their faces when she could see them clearly, and trying to sense their emotions now was like trying to pierce stone. They were manlike, but they were not Men.

"You will begin to find the way more difficult just ahead," said Prince Tyr. "Only a few feet of rock divide us from the catacombs."

Sindérian could already feel it: an increase in the weight of the air, which created a resistance like moving through water; a pressure of darkness that made every step a labor to be accomplished only by a concentrated act of will. Her eyes felt gritty; the taste of earth was in her mouth. She realized they had come to a place where the density of darkness was increasing, in the process of altering to something more solid. As a natural transmutation, it was supposed to be the work of centuries, of eons—if it was palpable here, something had occurred to hasten the process.

We are truly in the belly of the earth, she thought. It was a region whose mysteries wizards did not wholly understand.

But at last the pressure of darkness grew less. There was a faint pallor of light, which became stronger as they drew nearer, as if it were spilling out from some brighter place, and there was a low rumble as of many voices.

An archway loomed up out of the darkness: dressed stone of a greenish hue, carved all over with complex figures that might have been ancient runes, long forgotten in the world up above. Even without the symbols she would have known there was a gate spell, one so powerful she sensed it even before the first dwarves passed through. Sindérian wondered if she would be able to follow them.

But the ward opened to admit her, and she walked under the arch without any impediment. It was not a weakness in the spell; neither had it been Prince Tyr's doing—of that much she was certain. She had felt herself weighed and measured, identified in some way, then *allowed* to pass. It seemed that someone of greater authority was already expecting them, or, if not aware of them before, would be expecting them now.

"This is the fortress of King Yri," Prince Tyr announced. "His kingdom of Reichünterwelt extends from Penadamin to Min Rhuidain, and goes nearly a mile deep."

The prospect before them was truly awe inspiring, a cavernous hall of vast extent rising hundreds of feet above their heads.

Doors, archways, cross corridors, passages—a bewildering number opened out on three sides, leading on to further immensities. There seemed, too, to be an infinity of staircases ascending and descending, landings and galleries joining those staircases, balconies looking down on the hall from dizzying heights. In the regions above there was a great traffic of dwarves coming and going by the light of more of the glowworm lanterns, and there were glimpses of more brightly lit spaces beyond and farther in.

"We have entered my father's palace by a back door," said Prince Tyr, "for I hope to bring you before the King without creating a disturbance. Your presence among us unannounced would surely cause an uproar."

He set a faster pace, crossing the great expanse of floor, then passing through an opening on the other side and down a long corridor. From there they threaded a path through kitchens, sculleries, storerooms, and pantries, all of them showing signs of long disuse. Sindérian was reminded of the great hill fortress at Saer, where she and Prince Ruan had wandered long through subterranean chambers much like these. The reminder was not a pleasant one, and stealing a sideways glance at Ruan to see if he was thinking the same thing, she read tension in every line of his body. Aell, too, appeared troubled and wary. But at Saer they had walked unknowing into a trap, believing they would find friends; here at least they were on their guard.

"*Put yourself into our hands,*" the dwarf prince had said, "*and it may be to your advantage.*" Yet that offered cold comfort, for he had made no promises.

They climbed a broad stone staircase with shallow steps

to accommodate the short legs of the dwarves. Rich scents of cooking came down to meet them, as from a kitchen nearby that was still in use. Her stomach growling, Sindérian wondered if the dwarves intended to feed them when they reached whatever place they were heading. It had been so long since her last meal, even bread and water would be welcome.

At the top of the stairs they passed into a small, square chamber and stopped before a massive wooden door. Silver bolts and silver scrollwork hinges seemed to promise a chamber of more than ordinary importance on the other side. "You will remain here until the King sends for you," said Prince Tyr, handing the lantern over to Kivik. "I do not think you will wait long." Then he and his band marched off before the prisoners had time to ask a single question.

There was a soft creak of metal, and for the second time a door swung shut, closing Sindérian and her companions in—except that this time they were left alone, and in an unpleasantly confined space.

"We ought to have put up a fight to begin with," hissed Prince Ruan, "rather than allow ourselves to be taken in this cage of stone."

"They took us by surprise," said Sindérian, too tired to argue. "But now we have a little time to plan. If we are questioned, as I suppose we will be, it would be better not to tell them too much—though where we wish to keep something hidden I think we should simply remain silent, making no attempt to deceive them. They may have heard us speaking together on the mountain, and if they catch us in any lies we will only convince them we are up to no good."

"Good or ill, what are our *human* plans or ventures to

them?" Skerry exclaimed, in a rare show of impatience. "For myself, I thought their race extinct. For two hundred years they have lived without meddling in our affairs or us meddling in theirs. Why should that change now?"

Sindérian shook her head. "We don't know for certain that we're the very first Men they have spoken with in two hundred years. We live in strange times, and news travels slowly."

A heavy silence fell over the room, broken at last by Kivik, asking the question on everyone's mind. "But if not us, then who?"

No one answered; nobody needed to. If not the allied lands, if not the men of Skyrra, Mistlewald, or Arkenfell, who but Ouriána, whose reach seemed to grow longer with every passing day?

"I wonder," said Prince Ruan, scowling ferociously at the great oak door, "whether we would be wise or foolish to try and find out what waits on the other side?"

As if in answer, the wooden panels began to swing outward.

At first they were dazzled by torchlight pouring out from the chamber beyond. A voice bade them enter. Once they were past the threshold, Sindérian's eyes quickly adjusted. She found herself in a large audience chamber with a stepped dais at the center. The floor was paved with rich marbles, jade, and agate, and the rafters of that hall were the bones of some colossal creature—a fossilized leviathan of ancient seas, perhaps, or one of the shape-shifting giants, like the one whose bone was in Nimenoë's ring. Upon the dais, on a throne carved from a single dragon's tooth, sat King Yri.

Bent, crabbed, wrinkled, very ancient he was, with hair and beard reaching almost to his feet, so that he seemed to be clothed in a mantle of white hair. Below and to either side of the platform a crowd of dwarf lords and ladies—if not so old, nevertheless of venerable appearance—were gathered, and the jewels they wore burned brighter than the torches. In all that throng the youngest face belonged to Prince Tyr, who had changed his plain green tunic for one of unknown weave and substance and a mantle trimmed with lynx.

"Come forward," said the King in a cracked voice. "Come forward that I may see and hear you."

Sindérian was not deceived. As she drew near the throne and sank into a deep curtsy below the first step, she saw quite plainly that King Yri's eyes, though pale as glass, were filled with light and singularly penetrating. Neither his sight nor his hearing was failing. He sat for a long time studying them. Only Prince Ruan gave him back look for look.

"It is many years since there have been Men on Penada-min," said the King in his creaking old voice. Between the wrinkles, whiskers, and bristling eyebrows, his skin was very pale and fragile looking, giving him the appearance of a wax doll. "The hills to the north do not welcome travellers, and it is wild country south of these mountains. Yet Ouriána's people were seen on the lower slopes five days ago, before they took the underground road through the catacombs, and I think it is not mere chance that brings you so soon after them."

As there seemed to be neither a question nor an invitation to speak, Sindérian prudently remained silent and the men did likewise.

"You have names, I suppose," he said abruptly.

They named themselves one after the other, beginning

with Prince Ruan and ending with Aell, and she could see by the expression in those disconcerting eyes that King Yri was far from ignorant of the kingdoms of men or of the houses that ruled them. Yet for all this recognition of the others, she was the one who seemed to interest him the most.

"Sindérian Faellanëos," he repeated. "Unless I am mistaken, it is a name from the Isle of Wizards. And I ask myself: for what reason would two princes from Skyrra, a wizard woman from Leal, and a half-blood Faey wish to cross the Fenéille Galadan, particularly so late in the year?"

His gaze moved on to Kivik and then to Skerry. "There is a lady who travels with the Furiádhin; she speaks with the accent of the north. From what we have observed, they treat her with some gentleness, yet she appears to be their prisoner. I think it is she who brings you here, perhaps with some idea of rescue. A hopeless task, it seems to me—but then I have found little wisdom in the race of Men." There was a murmur of agreement from the courtiers gathered around.

When one gnarled hand reached out to clutch the arm of his chair, it could be seen that the King wore massive rings on every finger, even his thumb. "They say the Fates intended all the peoples of the earth to live together, our very differences binding us more closely. But as the years go on, it becomes more and more plain to me that those differences only divide us." His keen glance came to rest on Prince Ruan. "As you should know better than most, Ni-Féa prince."

For a moment Ruan's handsome, colorless face was like a mask; then something flared up inside him and he flushed to the eyebrows. "You have mistaken me. I am not any prince the Ni-Féa would recognize as such."

"Do you not bear a Ni-Féa name as well as a Man's—

Anerüian Pendawer? And are you not the grandson of Gäiä, their great queen?"

"I am—or was," said Ruan between his teeth. "But that connection was severed many years ago."

"And your part in this," said the King, turning toward Sindérian again, "that I do not understand. This girl Ouriána's priests have taken—there must be more at stake than a simple abduction, to bring you here from half a world away."

Rather than meet that questioning gaze, she dropped her own. So many bewildering impulses were contending inside her, it was hard to know what to do. Common sense dictated that she remain silent, that she say as little as possible. Her heart told her that she ought to trust him. For she suddenly realized that this shrewd old dwarf would make a most valuable ally—if he were not already aligned with the enemy. *But the heart can be a terrible liar, the Sight a cheat, if one* wants *to believe.*

"Twice you have named the Dark Lady of Phaôrax," she said softly. "If I knew what you were to her and she to you—"

There were gasps from the dwarf lords and ladies, a babble of indignant voices that swelled briefly and then died. "Indeed," said the King, "who is this slip of a girl who dares to stand before me in my own hall and question my motives?" Raising her eyes to meet his, she was surprised to see a glint of amusement. "Yet perhaps I have invited the question. In any case, I mean to answer it.

"It is five years since Ouriána sent her minions—I will not dignify them by calling them ambassadors—to bargain with us for certain of our treasures. Favor for favor is what she said: She would make us mighty in the New Age to come. We should command wide lands upon the earth as well as those under them. Magic arts she had that she would teach to us. When we refused to bargain, her messengers resorted to threats." There was an angry rumble throughout the room.

But of course, thought Sindérian, looking around her at necklets, bracelets, rings, and brooches glowing with gemstones, worked with consummate artistry—in the world above, artifacts of dwarfish make were highly sought after, and their value had only increased since trade with the underground realms had ceased. *Ouriána would covet these riches. If not for herself, than to pay her mercenaries.* But that was not all: there were objects of legendary potency attributed to the dwarves whose value was far above gold or gemstones. It was said the *Corridon* had created the Dragonstones, the greatest treasure of Ouriána's house.

"But," said King Yri, as if in answer to Sindérian's thoughts, "there are some things we value so highly, we will not sell them at any price, nor yield them under any duress. For that reason Men have called us greedy, a miserly and heartless race. But in this they wrong us. For what we will not sell, we will occasionally bestow as a gift, freely given. She had done better in the beginning merely to have asked.

"And now that you know this," he concluded, "is there some boon you would ask of me?"

Sindérian took a deep breath. "We have not come here as beggars, or to haggle with you like Ouriána's messengers. How could that be, when we never guessed we would meet dwarves in the mountains? All that we ask is to be allowed to continue our journey. Unless . . ." She hesitated. "Unless you know of some way that we might cross the mountains more swiftly. As it seems you are no friend to Phaôrax—"

"Understand this: I have no intention of embroiling my people in your wars," the King answered with a fierce look. "It is for your kind to end that madness, if it is not too late. I *may* be willing to assist you in some small way, but I am still considering whether to do even that much. I am, as you say, no friend to Ouriána, but she has never yet carried out those threats she made five years ago. We have not, perhaps, been much in her thoughts since then, and I would prefer that it remain so. Though haste may be to your advantage, it may not be to ours. I will think long and carefully before I decide what is to be done with you.

"In the meantime, rooms have been prepared for your use. It is now night in the world above and you will wish to eat and rest." He sat back in his dragon-tooth chair, as if he, too, were suddenly weary. "Though we do not regard you as welcome guests, no guest of any kind has ever had cause to complain of our hospitality."

Time moves differently in the kingdoms of the dwarves, as Sindérian was soon to learn. Without those cycles of dark and light, the phases of a fickle moon, or the revolving seasons by which Men measure their lives—time flows gently. How long she and her friends awaited the King's decision, if it were one day or many, she could not have said.

Two periods of rest she spent in a closet bed, on a feather mattress under fine woven blankets. Along with the men, she ate several meals in a room where all the furniture was of carven oak, well made and of goodly proportion, though somewhat low to the ground. During the intervals between, they were allowed to roam at will through Yri's palace.

In the underground kingdom no winds stirred, and the air was heavy with the resinous scent of torches and hearth-fires, yet it was a dim world, for it appeared that the dwarves did not require much light. The presence of strangers had apparently been duly announced, for while they received many curious looks from those who waited on them and those they met in the halls, the dwarves seemed to take the arrival of human visitors in their stride, and treated them with unfailing courtesy.

Much more *than courtesy,* thought Sindérian. For the palace seamstresses had stitched for her, in what seemed a miraculously short time, an underdress and a loose flowing gown to her exact measure—which the maidservants insisted she put on while they took her own garments away for washing. The cloth was strange to her, with milkweed and thistledown spun into the wool, but very fine and closely woven, and she was not sorry to put aside the dirt of the road.

"King Yri seems to favor you," commented Prince Ruan when he first saw the gown.

She shook her head. "I think it is only that the ladies here wanted a closer look at my clothes."

Whether he accepted that explanation or not, the Prince grew increasingly moody.

"We are surprisingly complacent prisoners, are we not?" he asked, as he and his fellow travellers lingered over a meal of venison, pheasant, goat cheese, roast chestnuts, and elderberry wine. "They do not keep us confined; why then do we not even *attempt* to escape?"

Sindérian eyed him over the rim of a goblet set with cat's-eye and tourmaline. Of them all, he seemed to take their captivity the hardest, being at all times animated by such fierce unrest that it exhausted her just watching him. Was it only his wounded pride, or was there something more serious amiss? Claustrophobia was inevitable under the circumstances, and she believed they each struggled with it, but there seemed to be something in their situation that goaded *him* almost past endurance.

"Why shouldn't we just walk away?" he said when the others remained silent. "The way to the surface is dark, but you could make a light."

"Even with a light, we would soon be lost in that maze of caverns," Sindérian replied. "That is, supposing we even had time to lose ourselves before the dwarves overtook us. I think there is little that happens under or over the mountain that King Yri doesn't know about, and he would *certainly* know if anyone passed his ward."

Ruan left his seat and began to pace the room. "We escaped from Saer, despite spells and losing our way."

Hoping to turn his thoughts in a less reckless direction, she said the first thing that came into her mind. "King Yri had much to say. Far more than he needed to tell us, all things considered. I think he was watching to see how we responded."

Ruan stopped pacing, an arrested look on his face. "You believe he was testing us?"

"Yes, I am sure of it. But I think, also, there was greater significance in what he did *not* say, in things he merely hinted at. What happens in our world affects them, too. They must go above to hunt, to gather food. Yes, and they must keep domestic animals somewhere—goats for cheese, bees for honey. Some of them may spend as much time on the mountain as under it. In the end, they are no more immune to the winds of the world than we are."

With a thoughtful look Ruan returned to his seat. "They are obviously in communication with the Ni-Féa, and that I do not like."

"But if he should chance to be a friend to your grandmother . . . ," Kivik began.

"The Ni-Féa don't make friends of other races." Ruan folded his arms across his chest. "If Queen Gäiä ever had friends of any sort, they are long dead. Such friendship as hers could only prove lethal."

"Then," said Skerry grimly, "we have no possible claim on King Yri. No reason to expect that he will wish to help us. Moreover, his knowledge seems altogether too vast and comprehensive. Where does it come from?"

Sindérian shook her head. "I don't know. He is a very powerful seer, that I can tell you. Perhaps the strongest I have ever met. But he may have other ways of learning things, too."

She pushed away her cup and plate, for her appetite was spoiled. Prince Ruan's mood was beginning to infect her, and she thought she would explode with frustration if they were forced to wait much longer for the King's decision.

24

✳

Blinded by the light, shaking with the shock of her suddenly reversed circumstances, Winloki was only dimly aware of the men gathered around her. She crouched on the ground, breathing the clean air, slowly assimilating the fact that she was alive and safe. Finally, she gasped out a single word: "Camhóinhann?"

"Is here, Lady," said Dyonas's voice somewhere nearby, and a shadow moved between her and the light. Gradually, that shadow resolved into a pale face with glinting metallic eyes, inside a halo of white hair. "Nor have you any need to fear for his safety."

"He spoke the truth. He truly was willing to lay down his life for me," she said wonderingly. She had feared any obligation no matter how slight, and now she owed him her life. She ought to be appalled, not grateful, for gratitude itself was a trap, and yet . . .

"Did you think he would lie to you? What reason could he possibly have to do so?"

Stunned by a question she had never thought to ask, she had no answer to give him. She had been entirely in Camhóinhann's power, first to last—why then should he fear to tell her the truth about anything? It had only been her own weakness, her own fear, that made everything he said seem a lie.

To her surprise, Dyonas bent down, worked some secret clasp on each of the silver bracelets, and took them away. "I believe you wished to work a healing on some of the men. I see no reason to deny you that opportunity now."

She sat for a moment rubbing her wrists, bewildered as much by this as by anything that had gone before. At last, gathering her wits about her, she rose to her feet and went to offer her help to the injured guards and acolytes.

Afterward, a little unsteady from the effort it had required to purge the lingering poisons and to begin the process of knitting together torn flesh, she turned her attention to the one who had been on her mind all along: the stern, solitary figure in crimson robes who sat apart from the others in a pose of meditation or prayer.

Camhóinhann opened his eyes at her approach, but said no word when she knelt down beside him. She hesitated, unsure how he would receive her offer. "I could heal you," she said, gesturing toward his injured arm. "I need not use my mother's ring. See, I removed it even before I touched Morquant or Rivanon, knowing that to look on it causes you pain."

"You are mistaken," he replied. "It does not pain us to look on Nimenoë's ring, not in the way you mean. It merely reminds us of what we were before—and that is a memory we do not like to dwell on. As for the healing you offer, it is not for me."

She sat back on her heels. Why did she feel this pang of the heart at the sight of blood on his sleeve? Empathy was a part of healing, but this—this was something more. And was it not a betrayal of everything she had been before, everyone she had *loved* before, that she should feel *anything* but hatred and loathing? If he had saved her life, that had been duty to his Empress who for some reason wanted her alive; had he been commanded to kill her, she would have assuredly been dead. So she reasoned—but all along she knew that reason was no part of what she felt. "Is it that you mistrust me? But I helped the others—"

"What is allowed to them is not permitted to me. Even Rivanon and Morquant have not come so far down this road. Your offer is generous but may not be accepted."

"But why?" she insisted. "*Why* is it denied you? Why should you not be healed like the other men?"

"Because I renounced it long ago. Healing, and many other things besides." He rose to his feet, stood looking down at her with that unfathomable glance. "You do not understand yet— it's not necessary that you should—but I could not be what I am and accept what you offer."

The horses who had emerged through the partly open door much sooner than Winloki had expected them. She was sure the Furiádhin had called them; there could be no other explanation. Once mounted, they did not travel far that day, only until they found a little stream gurgling down from the higher slopes, where they might refresh themselves and water the horses.

On this side of the mountain, there was no stain on the

land, and the weather was warmer. "We will rest here for a few days," said Camhóinhann. "There will be game for the hunting, and forage for the horses. By that time it will be safe to ride them."

"It is only practical," Dyonas agreed. "We will travel more speedily afterward."

In the morning, when Winloki went to examine Rivanon's wounds to see if they were healing properly, the acolyte surprised her by speaking up. "You asked me before what Goezenou wanted of you, and I did not answer. I think, perhaps, that I should have done so."

She glanced warily over her shoulder, to see if anyone was listening. "In the catacombs, there at the end, I thought he would kill me."

Rivanon shook his head. "Oh no, Princess, I think that he meant to rescue you—he has always imagined himself greater than he is." Then he fell silent and the silence stretched out so long that Winloki began to fear he had decided not to speak after all.

"Few know this," he said at last, "but Goezenou was the first to hail Ouriána as a goddess. Because of that, he believed he would also be first among her servants. When she chose Camhóinhann instead—" The acolyte lowered his voice, leaned so near that his pale face almost touched hers. "He does not mean to be passed over a second time. He knows you fear him, and would ingratiate himself if he knew how."

She had been kneeling, but now she sat down on the ground, all of the breath driven out of her. "He thinks that I—that I will someday—"

"It is what we all think, Princess."

In its own way, the idea was far more terrifying than *any* of the fates she had ever imagined for herself at their hands. "Even Dyonas and Camhóinhann? They think I will be—a goddess?"

He shrugged. "Who can tell what Dyonas thinks? As for Camhóinhann, he is different from the other Furiádhin." He dropped his voice again. "The nature of his bond with the Empress is different, too."

Winloki's mind was still spinning; it was hard to form a coherent thought. "In what way different?"

"While the others glory in her worship, his bond is one of pain. I believe it is the stronger for that, but—" Rivanon frowned and shook his head. His face suddenly looked weary and very much older inside the black hood. "I should not speak of these things. I have said too much already."

"I would never betray you," she protested. She knew that it was wrong to press him—dangerous for him, perhaps even dangerous for her—but her desire to know more about Camhóinhann was stronger than ever. Returning to the task of bandaging the acolyte's hand, she could not resist saying, "You must know I would never repeat anything you told me in confidence."

"I did not think that you would. But there may come a time when, remembering I was indiscreet, you might wish to chastise me yourself."

It was, of all the things he had said, the most horrifying, the most bewildering. *What does his Empress mean to make of me? Does she think she can re-create me in her own image?* Winloki was certain she would rather die a horrible death than allow Ouriána to do any such thing.

* * *

The kingdom of Reichünterwelt was a place of ceaseless activity but very little hurry. When Prince Tyr offered to escort his father's "guests" through the workshops of King Yri's artisans, Sindérian and the Skyrran princes readily assented. To be shown what few other humans had ever seen was, they agreed, too good an opportunity to refuse—particularly under the aegis of such a guide.

"And it is not," she said, "as though declining his offer will hasten our departure from Yri's realm by as much as an hour. Courtesy, on the other hand, may gain us much."

Prince Ruan apparently thought otherwise, so they left him behind with the faithful Aell in attendance and accompanied the dwarf prince with a pleasurable thrill of anticipation.

The living quarters of the dwarves were warm and dim like burrows, but their artisans always made a bright light to work by. Forges, potteries, and glasshouses were hives of industry; in the workshops of goldsmiths, silversmiths, and jewelers were created items of timeless beauty.

"Some of these masters," said Prince Tyr, "will spend years—nay, sometimes even decades—designing, casting, and perfecting a single exquisite item."

Sindérian had seen such artifacts before, treasures of royal houses with the patina of age on them. But here the metal was bright from the fire: silver candelabra like branching trees, golden drinking vessels shaped into basilisks, mermaids, and griffons; sea serpent necklaces with emerald or ruby or diamond eyes.

They lingered longest among the jewelers. In one such shop, Prince Tyr explained, the artisans were crafting funeral jewelry. "We never bury our dead without some fine and precious thing to honor them. And the stones that embellish these grave gifts have special significance: garnet and topaz for kings and queens, beryl for a prince, amber for a princess ... the list is long, for every craft and every occupation has its own stone."

They moved on to other chambers, where dwarf women were no less busy than the males: carving delicate ivory brooches, illuminating manuscripts with letters of gold leaf, doing fine needlework. Others made musical instruments or intricate toys. And though they visited no workshops of weavers or dyers that day, evidence of such work was everywhere. Tapestries of many colors adorned the walls; floors were covered with rugs of exquisite weaving.

"Not all of these things we make for trade with the other dwarf kingdoms," said Prince Tyr. "Much is made for the love of fine craftsmanship, and that reason alone." And Sindérian had a vision of level upon level of storerooms and treasuries under the earth, all of them filled with marvelous handicrafts.

What must it be like to live only to create beautiful things? She felt, momentarily, a bitter stir of envy—not for their riches, certainly, but for their splendid isolation, for their orderly, useful lives, far from the brutality of war. *What must it be like to* not *spend a lifetime healing broken bodies—to* make *and not to* mend?

She was still pondering this question when King Yri sent for her after dinner, specifying a private audience. Much surprised by his invitation—and more than a little apprehensive—she shook her head when Prince Ruan offered to accompany her, and followed the small page sent to escort her, out of the room and down a dim hallway. Arriving at the same audience chamber where the King had received her before, the dwarf youth bowed her through the door, then left her to cross the vast expanse of floor alone.

As she approached the dais, a familiar voice spoke in her mind, causing her heart to soar. Yet her spirits plummeted again at the sight of the white owl perched on an arm of Yri's throne. As pleased as she was to be reunited with her father, there had been some satisfaction in believing him free while the rest of their party remained captive.

"The hawks on Penadamin told me of a bird that was not a bird," said the King. He gestured with a hand heavy with rings. "So I sent for your owl—or, should I say, the wizard Faolein?"

The owl fluttered up from his perch on the throne and landed on her shoulder. *You need not worry to see me here. The King and I have had a lengthy conversation. I believe we understand each other very well.*

"Perhaps," said Sindérian, biting her lip, "I should have told you before—"

"You might have trusted me with the information—but you were not to know that," answered the King, more kindly than he had spoken at any time before. "But as pleasant as it is to bring you and your father together, that is not why I sent for you. Seat yourself on the top step—you are tall enough, we may speak together quite comfortably. I mean to tell you something of those you follow."

As soon as she had seated herself at his feet, he continued: "Since taking the underground road through the catacombs,

Ouriána's priests leave a chain of disturbances wherever they go. It began when they sacrificed a horse outside the Doors of Adamant, in order to gain entry."

"So *that* was how it was done," said Sindérian under her breath. "I did wonder."

The King gave her a sharp look under his tufted white eyebrows. "And would you shed blood to follow after them—if I were to release you? For though you would be forced to backtrack two days before you came to the doors again, the catacombs *are* a swifter road than any that goes over the mountains."

She shook her head in emphatic denial. "My companions and I, we all have blood on our hands—I wish I could say otherwise—but whatever it is that opens those doors and feeds on death . . . No, I would not strike a bargain with that."

"You are wise," said the King. "In that much at least you are wise." He leaned forward, gripping the arms of his throne. "Travelling through the hill country . . . perhaps you felt a presence there, ancient and malign? Perhaps, too, you recognized what it was?"

"I think it was a *durathagh*, one of the Old Earth Powers," she answered tentatively.

"Yes. And there is another one, even stronger, within the catacombs. What do you know of them?"

She tried to remember, but there was little to recall. "They were once worshipped as gods; men made sacrifices to them. Beyond that, we know very little about them on Leal."

"When they were worshipped as gods they were very powerful," said the King. "In this age, they can do comparatively little without creatures like ourselves to serve as their eyes, ears, and hands. Perhaps it was always so. And they are particularly drawn to young people whose powers are just beginning to unfold—that combination of potency and ignorance, power and vulnerability, is naturally attractive to them. The young woman with the Furiádhin had a very narrow escape—but you need not fear," he added, as Sindérian started up from her seat. "She did escape, in full possession of her own mind and will. Others were not so fortunate—or at least not all who entered by the Doors of Adamant succeeded in reaching the Doors of Corundum and returning to the surface. Your own danger would be less; nevertheless, there are some bargains which never should be made. The road through the catacombs is not for you.

"But we were speaking of the *durathagi*," he said as she settled back on the top step. "Of the one in the catacombs I know, alas, too much. Dwarves made the tombs—not of our own will. For many hundreds of years, our stonecutters toiled there, slaves in fact if not in name. The distant ancestors of the Men of the north were also slaves, but of a lower sort, and the kings who ruled in those days squandered their lives as you or I would spend small coins, carelessly. But when the civilization that enslaved us degenerated, dwarves and Northmen joined together to win our freedom. Yet we never forgot that it had been Men who made slaves of us in the beginning."

"There is nothing of this in our own lore," she said with a thoughtful frown. "Your memories, it seems, are far longer than ours."

"That is because our records are written in stone. Then, too, we are a long-lived race. For us, not so many generations have passed. We may live as long as the greatest wizards, but not so long as the Faey. Alas, we bear few children, and our numbers remain small. It is the same with wizards, is it not?"

She shook her head. "We bear as many children as ordinary Men, though not all of them are born to magical gifts." She was beginning to suspect that there was some purpose to this rambling conversation, though what that purpose was remained obscure.

"Yet your own line breeds true, does it not?"

She glanced at Faolein, uncertain whether she ought to answer. *Tell him,* said the owl. *What harm could there be in reciting our family history? He appears to like you. He may like you better for confiding in him. Confidences win trust.*

So Sindérian took a deep breath. "When my father was young—as wizards reckon these things—he married a woman who possessed no magic. Wizards had been born in his family for six generations, but the children of that particular marriage were ordinary in every way. When the last of them died, he wished for a child who might outlive him, one who might inherit his gift.

"My mother had reached a similar conclusion. She was also a wizard, with a lineage to match Faolein's, but she had lived all her long life at the Scholia. Faolein and Shionneth wed for the sole purpose of creating a child. Not a thing easily accomplished, even by wizards, when mother and father had each lived for more than a century. Yet magic eventually proved stronger than nature, and Shionneth gave birth to me. It was, I fear, a somewhat cold-blooded union."

He ran a hand through his white beard. "Like a marriage between two royal houses, in order to produce an heir."

"I am no princess," she said, more amused by the idea than otherwise.

"Are you not? But the Master Wizards rule on Leal. And

your Pendawer prince—does *he* not view you as an equal?" he asked with a sly smile.

That sobered her. She had never considered whether Prince Ruan's intentions were honorable or not, she had been so busy rejecting him: first out of loyalty to Cailltin, later because she knew that encouraging him would be selfish, even cruel.

"It is a very small island," she said with a frown. "And the children of wizards must make their own way in the world. We inherit nothing by right of birth."

"I think you are wrong," he replied. "Like all the children of Men you have inherited a harvest of grief. Ill days are coming; what will you do to avert them?"

She almost said: *What will* you *do?* But she swallowed the words. What right had she to challenge him, when Men had brought their world—and his—to the brink of ruin?

"I will do all that I can," she said fiercely, knotting her hands into fists. "I will do whatever it is in me to do, no matter the cost."

Afterward, she spent a restless night—if night it was—unable to sleep, trying to fathom the true purpose behind her lengthy audience with the King. He was old and he was subtle. Had he meant to learn something from her, or to convey some wisdom she was too young and too ignorant to comprehend? If Faolein, who had listened to the entire conversation, knew what it meant, he did not choose to enlighten her.

She rose, heavy eyed and out of sorts, as soon as she heard the servants moving around in the room outside the bed, the sound of firewood being stacked on the hearth.

Over breakfast in the adjoining chamber, she told the men

a little of her conversation with King Yri. They had naturally been surprised to see her come in with the owl on her arm and had pelted her with questions.

"It seems you were right when you told us not to attempt to deceive him," Prince Ruan said. "With every bird—and probably every beast—on the mountain spying on us ..."

"We might have guessed when we saw how Prince Tyr and the others controlled our horses," said Skerry. "How many of them, I wonder, have this affinity for creatures feathered and furred? But at least we know now why the birds failed to warn Faolein that the dwarves were near."

"And *I* know how King Yri exchanges news with the Ni-Féa," said Ruan, his silvery eyebrows drawing together. "For my grandmother also talks to birds."

There was no time to say more, for a pair of dwarves entered the room, announcing King Yri. Appetites fled and everyone rose at once. No one doubted that the King had finally reached a decision, or that they would soon learn his intentions.

Four stout dwarves carried him in in a chair and put him down by the hearth, where the firelight lent a ruddy glow to his normally waxen features. "It could be said with some justice that the quarrels of wizards and magicians affect us all," he began. "Nevertheless, I have decided not to involve myself in yours. Your arrival on my doorstep was unfortunate, and perhaps I was not wise to summon you here, but it is too late to undo that, much as I might wish it."

His pale eyes moved grimly from one fallen face to the next. "You are to leave at once, and my son and his servants will take you to the surface. From there, it is up to you where you go and what you do."

Sindérian was sorely disappointed. She had hoped for more; she had believed it was well within King Yri's power to do more. *And if this was to be his decision, he might have reached it sooner,* she thought bitterly. The time she and her fellow travellers had spent in the dwarf realm would surely cost them dearly.

25

✳

When he died, they buried him deep. He had thought that death would be balm to his troubled spirit. He had thought that in dying he would leave behind the terrors and humiliations of the flesh. But in the necrotic darkness of the grave he experienced torments unspeakable.

In the darkness and silence, it seemed that his perceptions had expanded to take on horrifying new sensations. Thus, with organs that were not eyes he "saw" through the lid of his coffin the relentless march of the worms; with organs that were not ears he "heard" the hideous workings of thousands of tiny insect jaws. His skin, in particular, had become wonderfully sensitive, capable of receiving impressions similar to taste and smell, and through these he experienced his own dissolution—the loosening sinews and decaying brain, the swift reduction of flesh into liquid corruption. And not once, but again, and again, and again, as his bones were continually reclothed in flesh, then sloughed it off again.

At last he broke free from the torpor that held him. In a

sudden burst of agitated writhing, he cracked open the lid of his stone coffin and struggled up through infinities of earth—only to be thrust down deeper than before as soon as he broke the surface.

Someone gripped Cuillioc's shoulder and raised him up from his sweaty pillow. Where was he? His entire body was clothed in a chill perspiration; more was pouring off of him. When a damp tendril of hair fell across his face, a rough hand brushed it away. He felt these things but he could not see them, for darkness still pressed heavily on his eyelids.

The hard rim of a cup was pressed against his lips; a bitter liquid dribbled into his mouth. The odor was familiar but not the taste, which was unbelievably foul. He gagged and retched and brought it up again.

"If he will not take the medicine he will surely die," said an angry voice.

"It will be *your* misfortune if he does die," said another, cool, dispassionate; Cuillioc did not know to whom it belonged, but he disliked it instinctively. "Lord Vaz would not be pleased."

"I can only do so much." Blind as he was, the Prince sensed a seething resentment. "He will not take the medicine, and you know it is death to refuse it."

He lay in a tomb-chamber inside one of their obelisks, his body wrapped in bands of silk, preserved in musty spices. So the Mirazhites honored the deities of their bizarre mystery cults: the two-headed calves, dog-faced women, and other abortions of nature.

The spices had mummified him, tightening the skin, causing his eyes to bulge out from their sockets and his lips to draw back, baring his teeth. Silent laughter racked him, for his leather tongue and constricted windpipe would not produce the tiniest whisper of sound. He had hoped to become a hero; they had made him instead one of their thousand blasphemous gods. Was that better or worse?

Somewhere a granite slab scraped against sand, letting a gust of humid air into his tomb. Men came in with flaring torches; he could smell the smoke even before he saw the fire. When they came to his couch of stone, one of the intruders stooped down to look at him. "This one is none of ours. How did he come here?"

Someone thrust his torch so near, Cuillioc could smell the musty perfume of the spices rising from the silken bindings. Then the wrappings ignited; he felt the flames licking at his dried skin. Finally his entire body went up in a white-hot conflagration.

And he burned and he burned. For centuries he burned, and all the while he could smell his own flesh scorching,

A foul taste filled his mouth. He tried to spit it out, but a hard hand kept his jaws clamped shut, and for all his struggles he could not pull away. Weak. He was far too weak, and they could do what they liked with him.

"I had the inspiration, you see, to put the leaves under his tongue," said the voice he had come to associate with his worst moments. "In that way, even though he will not swallow them, he still absorbs some of the virtue."

"He does not wake?" There was a sound like the scrape of a chair against a stone floor.

"Never fully. His wounds are healing, but as you see, he has grown very thin. He will never eat more than a few bites, and only when the boy feeds him."

"It was clever of you to bring the lad here." The words of praise sounded grudging at best. "But if the choice was mine, I would put a knife through him and be done with it. He should be lying at the bottom of the sea with the rest of his men."

He was sinking through the water, down and down. Much sooner than expected he hit the bottom. All around him there was slime and ooze, a primal stench that seemed to go back to the world's beginning. They had not buried him at sea, as they had promised, but had flung him into the swamps outside the city.

If he had been alone it might have been bearable. But eels caressed him with loathsome wrigglings, fish nibbled at his lips and ears. He knew the abominable caresses of crocodiles, and the vampire kisses of leeches. Even the very slime was amorous, defiling him in orgasm after orgasm.

When Cuillioc woke the next time, it was to uncertainty and confusion. Where was he and how had he come there? Where had he been before that? He caught at a memory: a ship and a battle. But it was all noise and falling bodies—a blaze of sunlight on bright blue water—smoke and flames. And he was not on a galley now; he was lying on a narrow, uncomfortable bed in a cool, dim room.

"You have been wandering in your wits for many weeks. Now you are awake, we may hope for a speedier recovery." Gradually, his eyes adjusted to the dusky chamber, and the first thing he saw was a man in the black five-cornered hat and dark green robe of a Mirazhite physician, bending over the bed as if to study him more closely, a sardonic expression on his lean, bronzed face.

"I don't wish to recover," said Cuillioc fretfully. "I thought I would die. I *meant* to die."

"But that would not please my lord, the Son of the Sun."

Slowly the rest of the room took shape: walls of raw, undressed stone; an iron grille covering a single window; a heavy door with a narrow slit cut into the wood, through which someone might easily peer in from outside. Besides the bed and a chair there were no other furnishings, and the blankets that covered him were stiff and coarse under his hands, as though they might be made of sacking.

"Is this the Citadel?"

"No, you are no longer in Xanthipei. This is the palace of Lord Vaz, the Prince of Persit. By his order you were brought here after the battle in the bay." A shade of amusement crept into the doctor's voice. "You are the son of the moon goddess and he is 'First-born of the Sun.' But the moon dare not approach the sun too nearly, or she would be burned to cinders. You might have profited from her example."

Cuillioc ignored the majority of this, for it did not much interest him. "What does your Lord Vaz want of me?"

"That," said the physician, "is for the Prince to tell you himself."

In another day, Cuillioc was able to sit propped up by pillows in the bed. On that day and the days that followed, his page would appear, from time to time, for the purpose of feeding him. But they never allowed the boy to remain with him long.

"What do you do in the times between?" Cuillioc asked him once, when the boy was spooning a thin broth flavored with the vile, life-giving herb into his mouth.

The urchin answered with characteristic brevity. "Same as I did for you, mostly."

"You attend on Lord Vaz?" It was impossible not to smile at the idea of a guttersnipe from Apharos waiting on haughty Mirazhite royalty.

"I listen to people. I tell him what they say." But then he added, in a startling burst of volubility, "They think I don't know more than a word or two of their language. They think they can say what they like, and I'm too stupid to understand."

In fact, Cuillioc remembered, the boy had picked up the language with amazing facility. If not the formal tongue, at least the argot of the servants. And it was not surprising if he was spying now for Lord Vaz. His life had been such, that he had learned to find friends where he could—and discard them just as readily. "Do you spy on *me*?"

A shake of the untidy head. "No need to. He knows where you are. He knows you aren't going nowhere."

Each morning in Persit the trumpets shouted at dawn. Soon after, a noise like the gnashing of thousands of teeth came in through Cuillioc's window. It was a sound (he eventually learned) originating in the hovels of the lowest class, where the women bent over their mortars and pestles grinding the grain that would feed their families that day. In Xanthipei, his apartments had been quiet, for they were not on the city side of the palace, but here he was exposed to the clamor and stench of the streets.

Despite the physician's optimistic predictions, his recovery was slow. He continued to be subject to nocturnal sweats, alternately freezing and scalding his flesh, which drove the poisons out of his body even as he breathed more of them in. Nevertheless, the physician felt that a more drastic purging was necessary, and treated him with drenches and bleedings—for there were no natural healers in Mirizandi, and these were the methods the doctors were obliged to use. On learning that the leeches, at least, had been real, Cuillioc shuddered with horror and burned with humiliation, wondering how many of the other things he had dreamed were real as well.

Whether through the ministrations of his doctor or the healing hand of time, he finally grew stronger. Then they dressed him in somebody's cast-off garments, marched him through miles of thick-walled corridors and pillared courtyards, and at last brought into the presence of Lord Vaz himself.

The Prince of Persit gazed down on him with delicate scorn from a raised chair under a gaudy silken canopy. A slender hand, every nail of which had grown to incredible lengths, gestured toward a low, cross-legged stool. "Be seated."

"I prefer to stand," said Cuillioc, with a haughty look of his own. But a pair of slaves—naked to the waist, with coppery skins oiled and glistening, the better to display the bulging muscles of their upper limbs and torsos—took hold of him on either side and lowered him forcibly to the stool. "I understood it was an invitation, not a command."

"By which it may be seen," said Lord Vaz, "that you do not understand our customs at all. When a superior speaks, there is no invitation. He expects obedience."

"So it is among my people," Cuillioc answered. "But I am

the son of the Empress, you a petty prince. You are not my superior, nor even my equal." One of the slaves struck him hard, nearly knocking him off the stool.

With a bleeding lip and a smashed face, Cuillioc managed to maintain his fragile equanimity. The blow had neither surprised nor dismayed him. His desire for death had not diminished, and he hoped, given sufficient provocation, Lord Vaz would oblige him. "There can be no possible advantage to you in keeping me here. If you think you can hold me hostage or collect a ransom, you are greatly mistaken. I am disgraced; my mother would not lift a hand to recover me, or even to save my life." To speak was painful; he thought his jaw was broken or at least dislocated, but pride forced him to continue. "She would *never* yield to threats under *any* circumstances."

"You are not here as a hostage, but as my prisoner, to live or die at my whim. How I choose may depend on whether you prove yourself useful or not. I wish to know how Ouriána—mere mortal flesh, and a woman besides—ascended to such power she can pretend to be a goddess."

Were it not for his aching jaw, Cuillioc would have laughed; the man was so ignorant, so obtuse. "My mother *is* a goddess. And there is nothing I can tell you about her apotheosis; it is a holy mystery."

"That is nonsense. I myself am half a god, and so I know." Lord Vaz sneered, and his fingers drummed the arm of his chair. "Do you think I cannot force you to speak? I am gentle with you now"—there could be nothing less gentle than his expression as he said this—"but my patience is not long. Spare yourself pain by answering my questions now."

"I cannot tell you what I do not know. What only Ouriána

herself knows." A meaty fist drove into his stomach; another knocked him from his stool. As Cuillioc curled up in agony on the floor, the slaves kicked him repeatedly.

Yet, the beating was a surprisingly brief one. After only a few minutes they hauled him to his feet and escorted him back to his room. Such was his infirmity, to subject him to too much violence would have killed him—and Lord Vaz was willing to be patient after all.

Every two or three days, when the bruises were fading, when the ache in Cuillioc's belly began to subside, they took him before Lord Vaz again. The Prince of Persit always asked the same question, and Cuillioc always replied that he could not answer him. Then there was another beating. It would have been amusing if it were not so painful, for no amount of abuse could force him to give answers that he did not have.

"I could geld you," the Mirazhite said one day.

With a sigh, Cuillioc studied the cool marble floor at his feet. He did not discount the threat, nor was he unmoved by it. But what did that matter? "Then I would be gelded," he said wearily, "and you would learn no more of Ouriána than you knew before."

The threats continued, at irregular intervals: *I could put out your eyes. I could have you hamstrung. I could tell my slaves to break your back.* Naturally, none of them achieved the desired result. Even had Cuillioc been inclined to speak, nothing he could have said would have brought Vaz any closer to the truth.

One day it pleased his tormentor to increase his discomfort by having a woman present during the interrogation. She was standing by the Prince's chair as Cuillioc entered the room: one of the loveliest women he had ever seen, with smooth copper skin and hair like liquid shadow. A straight, sleeveless garment, very simple but of sumptuous materials, fell from her neck to her feet, and she wore a necklace of many pendant diamonds.

"I wish to know Ouriána's secret," said Vaz, coming directly to the point.

Until now, Cuillioc had felt no real hatred for Vaz or any of his people—viewed in a certain light, any revenges the Mirazhites took against him were just and right—but at this new humiliation he was enraged. So enraged that he did not even deign to give his usual answer, but stood silent and seething.

"Why are you so foolish as to defy me? Do you like being kicked and degraded by *slaves*? Or are you one who take *pleasure* in pain?"

Still Cuillioc did not reply.

This time his silence had an unexpected effect. "I have decided to be merciful," said Vaz. "You are, after all, a prince of a noble line—though not the son of a goddess as you pretend. Give me your friendship, tell me what I want to know, and I will not only grant you your freedom, I will give you my sister in marriage."

The glorious creature beside him on the dais turned toward Cuillioc with a dazzling smile. He had been so long without even the sight of a woman that he might have been enchanted, were it not for his aching wounds and his strong suspicion that it was all a trick. Was she even a princess? He did not forget the deceit they had practiced on him months ago in Xanthipei.

"Your sister is incomparable." It was one thing to provoke Vaz, another to insult a woman, be she princess or pleasure slave. "But I am, as you have said, a prince of a noble line. I have been offered wives of great beauty and high lineage many times before—and not as a bribe to betray my mother."

The slaves moved in, and he expected the usual hard blows to follow. But Lord Vaz was not finished with him yet. "Do you think I cannot make your life infinitely more unpleasant than it already is? Believe me, I can and will."

So it had come to this, as Cuillioc had known it would eventually. His stomach cramped. He hoped it was only a weakness brought on by his sickness, his injuries, not ordinary cowardice. He hoped he would somehow retain some measure of courage and dignity under torture.

Something in his face must have betrayed him. "Ah, you think I am about to hand you over to my torturers," Vaz said with a ghastly smile. "But a man may die under torture if he is stubborn—though the ordeal may be cruel, he knows it has its natural limits—and a dead man is useless. There is but one ordeal I know that will break even the strongest man: a daily taste of the lash, the unremitting degradation of slavery. I am sending you to the mines."

This time, after a beating more lengthy and vicious than any before it, they stripped him of his borrowed clothes, leaving only the loincloth to cover his nakedness, then attached heavy chains to his wrists and ankles.

As they led him off, he caught a last glimpse of the Princess up on the dais; she seemed mightily amused by his plight. Probably he thought he would not have liked being married to her anyway.

They paraded him through the streets, in his nakedness, in his chains. His bruised white skin instantly attracted attention, and everyone seemed to know who he was. People stopped what they were doing in the marketplace and turned to stare at him. There were catcalls and curses. Some of them mocked him with obscene gestures.

A stone flew through the air and hit him on his forehead; another hit him in his chest. One of his guards drew a scimitar and disappeared into the crowd. After that there were no more stones, but the rain of verbal abuse continued. He kept his head high and his eyes forward, scorning to recognize any of it. Let them see how the son of the Empress comported himself under the worst circumstances.

He was still so fragile that he believed he would not last many months as a mine slave, but he found he could contemplate that prospect with perfect equanimity. He would welcome death when it came. Dead, he could not disappoint Ouriána. The one thing he feared most was being returned to Phaôrax— and that was the one thing Lord Vaz would never do.

26

A second trip through the caverns, by the light of a pair of pale blue lanterns, was no less convoluted and bewildering than the first trip had been. If Sindérian had tried to count and remember all the turns, the ascending and descending tunnels, she could never have done it. But she made no such attempt. Once she and her companions left King Yri's realm behind, she had no plans—indeed, no wish— to ever return again.

And that was why she never guessed that Prince Tyr was taking them by a different route. Not until a door in the cavern wall swung open, letting in a draft of fresh air, and they came out in a glen on the lower slopes of the mountain, to find their horses already saddled and waiting for them.

Sindérian looked around her, trying to gain her bearings. The sun was low in a sky the color of pearl. A few faint stars bloomed near the opposite horizon where it was darker. Never, she thought, had a glimpse of the stars been more welcome.

"The day is new," said Prince Tyr. "You will be able to ride a long way before nightfall." And with a brief farewell, he and the other dwarves disappeared back into the tunnel.

The door had already closed behind them, melting back into the mountainside so thoroughly that there was no evidence it had ever been there, before she grasped the meaning of his words. If the sun was in the east and Penadamin at her back—"We are *south* of the Fenéille Galadan—on the far side of the mountains."

The faces of the others brightened immediately. "Then we are days, not weeks, behind the Furiádhin," said Kivik. "Our encounter with the dwarves was more fortunate than we knew!"

Sindérian nodded. It was far more than she had ever expected. Even at her most optimistic, the most she had dared hope for was to be shown some hidden path known only to the *Corridon*. "I think that King Yri meant to help us all along—though whatever happens as a result, he means it to take place *far away* from his own country." He had been kind, but he had also been canny.

He had been generous as well, as they quickly discovered once they examined the packs strapped to the horses. The supplies of food they had carried before had not only been restored but replenished, and there were other items as well which had not been there before: knives with the sharpest of edges for the men; a store of herbal medicines in neatly labeled packets, phials, and pots for Sindérian; lightweight but tightly woven cloaks for them all, against the cold weather ahead. And at the bottom of one of her saddlebags Sindérian found something that surprised, moved, and disturbed her all at once.

It was a silver bracelet, incised with scrollwork and set with amber like drops of honey. A cold shiver passed from the back of her head down her spine. *"Amber for a princess."* It was a delicate compliment but—if she remembered Prince Tyr's words aright—it was also a grave gift.

What has King Yri foreseen? How much has he guessed? She was beginning to understand why he had taken more interest in her than anyone else, why he had been at such pains to draw her out. She slipped the bracelet back into the saddlebag without showing it to any of the others. There would be a time to wear King Yri's gift, but that time had not yet come.

They mounted up and rode for many hours. By nightfall, they found themselves in the foothills, following a road of sorts through what was otherwise a tangled wilderness.

"Once we descend from the foothills we will be in Lünerion, which was a principality of Alluinn. After a few days more we will come into what was once the heart of the Empire." Sindérian relayed this information to the others as it came from Faolein. "No men have lived in these lands since the world was Changed. Ahead of us there are forests, marshes, lakelands, and the remains of great cities lying in ruins—but not a single town, village, or farm. There will, possibly, be abundant game for hunting, but otherwise we will have to make our food supplies last."

"No men live in Alluinn," said Prince Ruan with a grim look, "but the Ni-Féa do, in the southeastern part. I was born there and I know something of the country between. Besides the game you mention, there will be bears, mountain lions, lynxes, and wolves that hunt in great packs. Worse than wolves, one may occasionally meet creatures that have wandered in from the wastelands to the east: Tirhénian basilisks, manti-cores, griffons, snakes that are almost the size of dragons—"

"We may meet any or all of those things," Sindérian inter-rupted him, "but not all of them at once."

"No," the Prince admitted, "not all of them at once. We may even travel for days without meeting anything."

Luck was with them during the next few days, for they reached the lowlands without seeing anything more daunting than a bear loping along on all fours in the rain, and a lynx that snarled at them and retreated into the bushes. It was only after they left the hills behind that a monstrous snake crawled into their camp one evening. It would have killed one of the horses had not Aell, who was keeping the first watch, whipped out his sword and sliced the serpent in half just as it was rear-ing its head to strike.

But that wolves inhabited that region in great numbers there could be no doubt. They filled the nights with their wail-ing cries, first from one direction and then another. And when the travellers came upon a road heading more directly south, Sindérian began to notice, with increasing frequency, tracks of wolves printed in the road after the latest rain shower: dozens and dozens of paw prints, great and small, as if the road were not a road at all, but a trail the wolves had made for them-selves. Such numbers of them travelling in the same direction, like a great migration, struck her as ominous and improbable. After crossing the wild parts of Mistlewald without meeting any of the werewolves which she knew infested those lands, she fervently hoped they would not encounter them now.

The road eventually turned east, but by then they had come into a region of wide meadows and occasional woodlands and were able to set out cross-country. The mountains caught the worst of the weather; yet even though they were heading almost due south, winter would overtake them in the end—and all the sooner if they did not make haste. Once, Sindérian caught a glimpse of the river Glasillient shining in the distance. Sometimes they passed heaps of weed-covered masonry on either side of the road, all that remained of towns and villages crushed by the tidal wave of power that had swept across Alluinn, levelling the entire kingdom in less than a day. Tens of thousands had died in that disaster, and their bones would still be there under the rubble.

Then one clear morning Faolein returned from a night-time scouting expedition and Sindérian could tell immediately that something had occurred to disturb the even tenor of his mind.

There is something southwest of here I think you should see.

He led them in the direction of the river. Before they had gone far, the horses began to balk, throwing up their heads and snorting. Urging them forward, they soon found evidence of a recent campsite: the sodden, ashy remains of a campfire, some trampled grass, and that which put the horses into a sidling, eye-rolling sweat—the bodies of three unnaturally long-legged wolves, as well as the body of something midway between man and beast. The air was rank with the foul, musky odor of the skinchangers. That men with steel had killed them was immediately evident, for one head had been lopped off as if by a sword or an axe, and Sindérian could see by a wound in the belly of the man-beast that he had been impaled by the blade of a sword.

"Not many days past," said Prince Ruan, curbing his roan

gelding with a firm hand, "else even in this cool weather the bodies would be more decomposed."

But Sindérian had already noticed an ominous cairn of stones not far from the campsite. When she pointed it out to the men, the Skyrran princes both turned a ghastly shade of pale. "You don't think . . . ?" said Skerry.

"No, I don't." Nevertheless, there was a cold, heavy feeling in the pit of her stomach, because Winloki had so narrowly missed total annihilation of soul and spirit in the catacombs, and she had never guessed it. "But let us shift those stones anyway, to put our minds at rest."

The horses would not stand still within sight or scent of the dead skinchangers, so it was necessary to lead them a short distance away. That task fell to her and Aell, while the other men set to work on the pile of heavy stones. When they reached the riverbank Aell left her alone to mind the still-restive horses and returned to assist the others at the cairn.

Their grisly task uncovered the corpses of two black-robed acolytes, but nothing worse. A gesture from Prince Ruan reassured Sindérian that Winloki was not there.

"How many of them?" she asked, when the stones had been replaced and the others had joined her beside the river.

"Two men," replied Kivik. "But no telling how many of the Pharaxions might have been injured."

Prince Ruan swung back into the saddle. "There were injuries on both sides, men and wolves alike. Besides the stink of skinchangers the site reeked of blood. But you'll already have guessed as much."

Indeed, the residue of anguish and desperation had still been strong enough to sense. And as they resumed the journey south, Sindérian had much to think about. She felt as though she had been wandering a long time through a maze of possibilities, most of them fearful—but now there was the dawning of a tentative hope.

"Something is on your mind." Skerry interrupted her reverie a while later, bringing his horse up beside hers.

"Until we reached the mountains," she said, "the Furiádhin seemed to have everything their own way—any mischances were ours. But ever since they entered the tombs, they've had their share of misfortunes. King Yri said they lost men in the catacombs, and now there is this. And I've been feeling changes in the world around us for many weeks now: an energy along the ley lines, a shifting of probabilities . . ." She shook her head. "I wish I knew what was happening in the west, in the south."

"You believe the probabilities you mention may be shifting in our favor?" asked Prince Ruan, bringing his horse abreast of theirs. "In favor of all who serve my grandfather and the alliance?"

"Perhaps. But it may also be that there is no safety for anyone, anywhere. You remember the conversation we had long ago on the *Balaquendor,* before the sea dragon attacked us?"

"You said that Ouriána had been tampering with things she had better have left alone. You said that she was unleashing forces she would ultimately be unable to control."

"Yes," said Sindérian. They turned the horses' heads away from the river toward higher ground. The ground below was growing muddy; there were trickles of water and a smell of marshes was in the air. "And I also said there are things—like sea dragons—that are friends to no one. And when we were nearly drowned in the Necke on our way to Skyrra, I saw things under the water. . . ." She hesitated, for there were parts of that experience she did not choose to share with anybody.

"Tell us plainly what you fear," Ruan prompted her.

"It may be as you say," she replied. And because Kivik and Aell had drawn closer, too, in order to hear what was being said, she raised her voice to include them in the conversation. "Or it may be that we are all of us—Phaôrax, Thäerie, Leal, Skyrra, everyone—heading toward some world-altering disaster. Like Alluinn and Otöi before us, we might be on the verge of mutual destruction."

"How would we know?" asked Aell in a subdued voice.

"We can't know, not until it overtakes us," she said wearily. "That is, we can't know it all, the doom of the entire world or its salvation. But we may know the answers to more immediate questions very soon."

Days earlier, just after the battle with the skinchangers, Winloki had been numb and heart-bruised, staring at the cairn of stones the other men had piled over the bodies of Adfhail and Rivanon.

She felt Camhóinhann's presence beside her at the gravesite, even before she turned to face him. "This was my fault," she said, blinking back tears.

He did not attempt to deny it. "Why should that grieve you? You were kidnapped, snatched away from the people you call your own. Our land is not your land; you have made it quite clear that you do not and will not consider Phaôrax your home."

Winloki could not find the words to answer him. But he seemed to know what she would have said. "Your abilities as an empath are growing very rapidly, along with your other gifts. It is a dangerous time—for you as much as others."

"Teach me what I need to know," she said passionately. "Teach me how to prevent something like this from happening again."

Camhóinhann shook his head. "That I cannot promise. The world is full of many hazards. It may even be that you are not responsible for attracting this one."

"But the men who died in the catacombs," she insisted, "I must bear some responsibility for that."

"No more than I," he said. "If I had known the ancient power slumbering there was already awake, I would never have brought you there. At least not as you are now. There are many things that I might teach you, but . . ."

She bit her lip. "Perhaps you don't trust me enough?"

For the first time in all their long journey she saw the ghost of a smile cross his face, and she suddenly felt a fool for thinking she could possibly threaten *him*. "I will teach you to use your power not as a weapon but as a shield—and how to shield *it* in turn. But I caution you to think very carefully before you agree to this. Some decisions, once made, are irrevocable."

"To do nothing, that is a choice, too," she said fiercely. "And the deaths of these men, that is irrevocable too."

They moved away from the cairn, toward the campsite. Already, the tents and other supplies had been packed away and men were saddling the horses. "Then if you are not already tired from the healings you have performed, we will begin your lessons as we ride."

"Now?" she said breathlessly. "We can begin . . . so soon?"

His face had resumed its usual austere expression. "Are you, after all, having second thoughts?"

"I was merely surprised," said Winloki. "I am ready to begin whenever you wish."

A short while later they were in the saddle, following along the course of the river.

"I should start by telling you something of your own gifts and of those from whom you have inherited them." A slight breeze lifted Camhóinhann's long white hair as he rode. Afoot or on horseback, he was more than a head taller than any of the other men; yet it was more than his imposing stature that always made the Princess feel dwarfed beside him.

"Your mother," he went on, "had great gifts for healing and warding, though her other talents were impressive, too. Your father, on the other hand, had no such abilities, though he came of a line that had produced many wizards and minor magicians over the centuries. Queen Elüari, who wore the ring of bone before your mother did, had a deeper knowledge of elemental magic than anyone I have ever met."

"You *knew* these people?" Again Winloki tried to remember, if she had ever known, how long Thäerie and Phaôrax had been at war. She tried to calculate how old he might be, but the effort defeated her.

"I knew them," he said. "Like yourself, I was born on Thäerie. In truth, we are distantly related, you and I."

Startled, she turned to look up at him. "You never told me this before. Not even when you explained to me about my mother and my father."

"It seemed irrelevant," he said, "And I did not think the information would be welcome."

Winloki tried to think whether it was welcome or not. She

dearly loved her adopted relations in the north, yet there had always been a sense that she was . . . somehow alien to them. Oh, not in their behavior to her; it was merely something she felt in herself. At the same time, her recently discovered tie to Ouriána terrified her.

And now this, so unexpected—and yet, in some deep part of her soul, had she not known it all along? Blood called to blood. Had it not been some instinct of kinship that drew her to him, albeit reluctantly, from the very beginning? "I know so little about you," she said, staring straight ahead between the ears of her horse—because suddenly she was afraid to look at him again.

"My own history would make unpleasant telling," he answered. "I do not think you are ready to hear it just yet."

27

＊

L eaves were falling in the woodlands and gusting across the road in clouds on the autumn winds. Now the great peaks of the Cadmin Aernan reared skyward far to the west, their upper slopes crowned with silvery snows. In the evenings, Sindérian brewed a bittersweet green tea from among the packets the dwarves had put into her saddlebags. When the stars came out, the sky was alive with fiery signs. There were times when she could feel the world shifting around her, currents of change more potent than the winds; but of these she spoke to no one but her father.

Many nights she sat up late staring into the fire, searching for portents until her eyes ached. *You are trying too hard,* said Faolein. Yet along with much that was distant and obscure she had seen what she was looking for: runes brighter than the flames, burning in the heart of the fire. *Caet*—battle. *Eirëo*—destiny. And the rune she both hoped and feared to see: the dark rune, the nameless rune.

One morning, before they broke camp, she sketched a map

in a patch of soft earth. "This is the Fenéille Galadan, this the Cadmin Aernan," she said, drawing two lines with the point of her knife. She drew a curving line representing the Glasillient. "This, I believe, is where we are just now. You seem to know more of this country than any of us, Prince Ruan. Can you tell us what lies ahead of us?"

"The Whathig Wood is here." He added something to the sketch. "Not a place we would ordinarily want to visit, but to go around would take too long. And here is the ruined city of Ceir Eldig, where the Emperor had his palace. If I am not mistaken in my bearings, it is almost directly south of us. East of that, on the lower slopes of the Cadmin Aernan, is the realm of the Ni-Féa. If the Furiádhin are heading for Rhüad-llyn, as we suppose, we will come very close to Queen Gäiä's borders."

"And because of this estrangement you mentioned," said Skerry, "you would be reluctant to ask for her aid? But are there not great magicians and warriors among the Faey?"

"Not magicians as you think of them. And I would have thought you had enough of that sort of thing at Tirfang. The place reeked of Faey enchantments."

The Skyrran princes exchanged a glance. "You are saying that the witch-lords—" Skerry began.

"Were Faey, yes—distantly related to either the Ni-Ferys or the Ni-Féa. But as for asking aid of my grandmother's people . . ." He laughed, a short, sharp sound without any humor in it. "They care for nothing but their intrigues, love affairs, and revenges. They scarcely notice even the most cat-astrophic events in the world of Men. I doubt they are even aware we are fighting a war."

"They must notice us—some of us—sometimes," said Kivik under his breath.

Ruan gave another bitter laugh. "Or else how should I be here? They do take notice of individual humans, occasionally. They are highly susceptible to beauty, even in Men. But such affairs always end badly, and the children of these unfortunate unions come to be regarded as . . . an embarrassment." He rose to his feet and dusted off his hands. For a moment, his eyes were veiled under his silvery eyelashes, then a fierce look shone out. "Suffice it to say that I would not ask—or expect—any help from my mother or grandmother, not if my life were in direst peril."

Even at a short distance, the Whathig Wood had an eerie, unwholesome appearance. It grew on a range of humpbacked hills, where spidery upper branches seemed to scratch at a bloody sunset sky. In the language of the ancients the name might be interpreted in two ways: the wood of knots or tangles, or the wood of bindings, of dark sorceries. Neither one was reassuring.

"It will take two days to ride through—if we are lucky," said Prince Ruan. "I would rather not spend more than a single night there, and I suggest we wait until morning before we approach any nearer."

No one protested, not even Sindérian, for all her desire to press on. They stopped and made camp at once. But the near presence of that place of ill omen made for a restless, uneasy night. They woke at dawn not much refreshed, saddled the horses, and strapped on the baggage. A short ride brought them to the eaves of the wood, and it did not take them long to find a path that would take them deep inside.

Most of the trees had shed their leaves, but the limbs and branches overhead were so tightly woven that they blotted out much of the sky. Even after several hours of riding, at a time when the sun surely rode high in the heavens, the light remained murky. There were trees like ancient crones with twisted limbs and birds' nests in their hair; oak and cowan with the bark cracked and peeling, sap dripping or clotted like blood; rotting stumps crawling with insects. Poisonous plants grew where the shade was deepest, and bramble brakes cut across the path so that the men were forced to dismount, draw their swords, and hack a way through. Before long, their cloaks were ripped and torn from repeated battles with the thorns.

They stopped at what might have been noon to eat a hasty meal. The forest floor was no place they cared to linger long. Leaves were rotting into humus underfoot, but instead of a clean, earthy smell they gave off a faint whiff of graveyards. Pale, whiskery roots pierced the soil from below—somehow, no one wanted to touch them though they seemed harmless enough. Was that a breeze stirring the heaps of dead leaves, or did an army of tiny, unseen presences cause that rustling and fluttering?

Near nightfall, they found a clearing to set up their camp. After passing around a whetstone to resharpen their blades, the men stretched out to sleep in the bright moonlight while Sindérian and Faolein took the first watch.

Twice she she saw things moving in the shadows under the trees. The first one she thought was a deer; the second appeared to be a giant black hare. Her heart began to thud in her chest, for the hare was a form associated with witches. Witchcraft was weaker than wizardry, but to meet such here where even the trees were hostile . . . Whatever it was, it did not disturb the horses and disappeared back into darkness.

It was nearing the end of her watch when she started up from the ground with a cry so loud it woke the others, and brought them staggering to their feet.

Two figures, as translucent as glass, had walked into the camp. They were men well known to Sindérian, Prince Ruan, and Aell—men who had died on the journey from Leal. Something had eaten Jago's eyes; there were crabs in his beard and he smelled strongly of brine. Even more ghastly was the sight of Tuillio. Sindérian put a hand to her mouth to hold back the rising bile. His hair had been replaced by wriggling sea worms; bones pierced his skin where the sea dragon had splintered them.

The phantoms passed through the clearing without saying a word, leaving a strong residue of fear and horror behind them. And whether they were genuine specters—or tormenting delusions conjured by the wood—there was no possibility of sleep after that.

Sitting on the ground waiting for sunrise, Sindérian and her companions saw ghost after ghost appear and vanish. There were warriors of Skyrra and Thäerie, showing their seeping wounds and broken limbs. Of her own dead in Rheithûn there were many: boys pierced by arrows; women and children dead of starvation or disease. Some had died in fire or had been crushed by stones, and these were the worst of all.

But no Cailltin of Aefri, she thought with a guilty pang, when dawn finally broke and the last phantom faded. *Have I truly put him out of my heart so soon?*

She slanted a look in Prince Ruan's direction. *Have I re-placed him?*

After a halfhearted attempt at breakfast, they discovered that the path which had brought them into the clearing was no longer there, that new trails leading in new directions had appeared between the trees.

"This is not uncommon," said Prince Ruan. In the shadow of trees his eyes were leaf green. "The paths *do* shift about, but usually stay in place once you are on them."

With that in mind, they chose the one heading most nearly south and this time they set the horses to a quicker pace. "I would rather not spend another such night," said Skerry under his breath, and the others could only agree.

It proved to be a good path; by late afternoon, the tangled growth was thinning out. Because they had pushed the horses hard—and with open meadowlands visible ahead between the boles of trees—they decided to dismount and lead their weary horses the rest of the way.

Wading ankle-deep in the black and stinking leaves, Sindérian was already beginning to regret this decision when something—some presentiment of danger, or a sound or scent just below the level of conscious perception—caused the hairs on the back of her neck to stand up. She craned her neck to get a glimpse of Prince Ruan and learn if his keener senses had detected the same thing. He was glancing from side to side, his nostrils flaring and his eyes dilated.

Then his hand flew to the hilt of his sword and he shouted out a warning. "Something is following us!"

The horses sensed it too. Sindérian's mare tugged at the

reins so hard, the leather cut through her hands as she struggled to keep hold of them. Then there was a loud hiss, followed by a sound from higher up the hill, one that was somewhere between a yowl and a screech. Whirling around to discover the source of the noise, she scarcely noticed when the mare finally tugged the reins out of her hands and broke free. A monstrous catlike creature was bounding down the slope.

Manticore, said Faolein inside her head, but Sindérian had already recognized it.

It moved so swiftly, there could be no thought of escape. Sindérian blinked and Prince Ruan's sword was in his hand. The other men were almost as swift to draw. But the manticore, after covering most of the distance between them with tremendous leaps, went belly-down in a crouch, shifting its leonine head from side to side. One batlike wing shifted, began to unfold, then snapped shut again; the great bulbous tail with a scorpion's stinger at the end swept a row of saplings aside as it lashed the air.

It is in no way daunted by the sight of four armed men, said Faolein. *It merely calculates when and where to strike first. It has an intelligence far beyond that of any ordinary beast.*

Choosing Aell for its first victim, the manticore launched itself into the air—barely missing him as he leaped aside and swung his sword. He was only able to graze the flank, as the creature turned with uncanny agility and swiped at him with an enormous taloned foot. Just in time he dodged behind a tree, where claws as long as a man's hand scored deep trails in the bark of the trunk.

Meanwhile, the other men had moved around to come

at the beast from two sides. Again it crouched, swinging its head from left to right. Then it threw back its head and roared, showing three rows of dagger-sharp teeth. The stench of its breath was nearly overwhelming: a hot, meaty, murderous smell.

Despite so much lethal energy, Sindérian could see that the manticore was old and ill: its wings were cracked and dry as old leather; one eye half scabbed over, the other bright with fever; foam dripped from its jaws. And gazing into those mad eyes, she tried to cast a sleep spell—but was repelled by a will and sentience of such malicious force it left her mind feeling bruised.

Continue to try to distract it, said Faolein just before he rose into the air. Diving at the snarling face, he swerved at the last possible moment when the creature's tail swung round and almost struck him.

By this time the men had closed in. Prince Ruan and Skerry had each landed a blow: one to a leg, the other at the base of the tail. Blood seethed and bubbled in the wounds, yet neither was very deep. The skin beneath the tawny fur seemed to be almost as tough as dragon scales. The manticore dodged, swiped, and caught Aell with a blow that would surely have ripped off an arm had it not been for his mail shirt. As it was, Sindérian could hear the bone snap in his arm. He fell to his knees, then was on his feet again almost instantly, whipping out his dagger.

When the manticore beat its wings, it was like a wind off the desert. Skerry's sword, flashing in a beam of sunlight, sliced through one leathery pinion—a blow that cost him dearly, for the creature rounded on him at once, caught him up in the crushing grip of its enormous jaws, and lifted him into the air. The other men all waded in, hacking with swords and daggers, while Faolein took another dive at the eyes. Under their combined attack, the manticore dropped Skerry and leaped into the air, passing over Ruan's head and landing almost directly behind him.

It twisted with the same uncanny agility it had shown before, rounding on Kivik, bending its back in a manner that should have been impossible for any creature with a backbone, and striking at him with its tail, scorpionlike. An overhead swing by Ruan connected with the tail, but not before the sting struck Kivik in his sword hand. As the Skyrran prince toppled to the ground, instantly paralyzed, the manticore took another swipe at Aell and sent him flying through the air. He slammed into the earth with such force that he was knocked unconscious.

Alone but for the owl beating its wings overhead, Ruan faced the manticore. Sindérian felt her heart drop. She did not see how he could possibly prevail. Yet, without the others to impede him, he was able to move more quickly, swing his sword more freely. Dancing aside from what could have been a killing blow from one clawed foot, he lunged, slashed, connected twice.

Once, the sword stuck fast until he ripped it free. Already his dagger was lodged between the ribs. Sindérian knew that the creature was growing weaker, but it still had three weapons—teeth, claws, and tail—to the Prince's one. A clever thrust cut through the bristling mane and left a deep wound in the neck, so that more blood gushed out.

Again Ruan danced aside, again the manticore spun

around to meet him. Rearing up on its hind legs, it flung its entire body at him, jaws agape and claws slashing. He threw himself to the right, attacking at the same time with an over-hand cut that met the manticore's skull with a jarring crack. As his blade clove straight through to the brain, the monster dropped.

Though Sindérian was stunned by this unexpected turn of events, it took only moments to collect enough of her wits to think of the other men. Knowing that Kivik—if he were not dead already—was the one in most immediate peril of his life, she ran to the place where he was sprawled on the ground, and threw herself down on her knees.

Feeling for a pulse in his neck, she detected the faintest possible beat of life. The color in his face told her that he still breathed, but the rise and fall of his chest was too slight to be seen. His hand was black with poison, spreading like a bruise under his skin, halfway up his forearm already.

"You will want this," said Prince Ruan over her shoulder, and looking up, she saw that he was offering her a narrow length of cloth he had apparently ripped from his own cloak.

"Yes," she said, taking the strip of velvet and knotting it into a tourniquet just below Kivik's elbow. With the cincture in place, she unlatched the clasp of Kivik's cloak. "Help me, if you will, to remove his mail, and then see what needs to be done for the others."

By the time the shirt of linked metal rings had been re-moved, his pulse was almost too faint to detect; his face had turned a dull, leaden hue. Fortunately, the padding under his armor was no such impediment as steel had been. Putting both hands on his chest, she used all her power of mind and will to keep pushing air into his lungs, to force his heart to keep on beating. So much poison had already entered his blood before she had tied off the limb that she could feel his muscles growing increasingly rigid.

"No," she ground out between her teeth. "*No,* you will not *die.*" Too many had perished under her hands over the years because she could not save them; she was not going to allow it to happen again. *Not while there is blood and breath left in my own body.*

Yet Sindérian had almost given up hope when the muscles in his arms, legs, and chest began to soften. A shudder passed over his body, and he began to drag in breath without her assistance. His heart started beating of its own accord. She sat back on her heels, weak and dizzy, realizing for the first time that her face was wet with tears. She had been crying without knowing it.

Aell is awake and in some pain, but not in immediate peril, said Faolein, landing on a bush nearby. *Prince Ruan has been making a largely inadequate attempt to stop Lord Skerry's bleeding. You will need to go to him next.*

She wiped her face with her sleeve and took a deep breath. Gathering what strength remained to her, she rose to her feet. *Watch here, and tell me if he stops breathing again.*

Many hours later, when she felt it would do them no great harm, she allowed Prince Ruan to carry first Kivik and then Skerry out of the woods and onto safer ground. Meanwhile, she lent her own support to Aell, who leaned heavily on her arm as she helped him to reach the starlit meadow. Drained by her efforts to save Kivik, she had had little to offer the others but rough battlefield healing. For now that would have to be enough.

"How quickly can you heal them, at least so they can ride again?" asked Ruan when they had settled the wounded men as comfortably as possible on the grass. "Without, that is, doing serious damage to yourself."

"In a day or two—with Faolein's help. The skill will be mine, of course, but he can lend me some of his strength." Indeed, he had already done so, or she would never have been able to walk out of the wood.

"And I can do nothing to assist you?"

"You can spend the time bringing back our horses," she said, sinking down into the grass. "My father says that none of them have gone very far, but they've scattered east and west."

28

Day after day, there was rioting in Apharos. Though guards from the temple and the palace arrived each time to quell the disturbance in an orgy of bloodshed, the riots continued. Nothing like this had happened in all the years of Ouriána's reign. Even now, the rioters did not appear to act in any spirit of rebellion but because a madness, a panic, swept through the streets.

A plague of hallucinations had the city in its grip, and most of the island. Fishermen reported that they had seen sea serpents sporting in the shallow coastal waters. In the inland towns, bells were said to peal out with iron voices many times a day—bells, which had been stripped from the fanes and shrines of the Old Religion and melted long ago. In Apharos itself, beggars declared they had seen temple guards briefly transformed into knights of a vanished chivalric order, and acolytes into votaries of the Seven Fates. The mass hysteria spread and spread, and there seemed to be no way to stop it—short of capturing and killing the man Ouriána held responsible.

After a week during which matters grew steadily worse, two of her priests found the Empress pacing like a lioness in the shady palace gardens. It was not, perhaps, the most auspicious location. The sun came there rarely, yet by some means or another her gardeners were able to nurture the growth of plants like nightshade, henbane, and sow's-tongue, as well as some so poisonous that it was necessary to wear gloves and masks while harvesting the leaves to avoid being blasted by them.

"There remains some question," said Vitré, after he had been obliged to report no success in finding the man, "whether the astrologer—mage—whatever he may be—actually causes these prodigies, or merely attracts them."

"Or," added the red-robed figure who had come with him, the furiádh Scioleann, "whether the *magician* is drawn to *them*. Occasionally, they do appear to precede him."

Her breath came out in a long hiss. "And *no one* has been able to learn who he truly is—or how or why he contrived to live here in such complete obscurity for so many years?"

Vitré flinched. There was that in her face that might have killed a more timorous man with a single look. "That very point, your seers and magicians surmise, is the heart of the matter. Was it all a clever disguise, or have forces already at work restored him to . . . whoever and whatever he was before?"

The priest hesitated, gathering his courage before offering what might or might not have been welcome news. "A name has been suggested."

"And that name is?" Her voice throbbed with emotions barely held in check.

"Several of our older citizens have said they recognize him

as one of the emissaries from Leal who attended your father's coronation. Indeed, he seems to be seeking out individuals who were attached to the court during that era, and asking them questions. And because the movements of the *other* two wizards have been accounted for all during the years since, that would leave—"

"Éireamhóine." Her teeth clenched so hard, Vitré was almost certain he could hear them rattle. "Who should have been dead these twenty years!"

Scioleann cleared his throat once, twice, as if preparing to speak—and then refrained. Again it fell to Vitré. "It is not absolutely certain that the man we are seeking is he. If Camhóinhann were here, I think the matter could be quickly settled."

Her restless movements had taken her from one end of the gardens to the other. Now she whirled around and started back. "I do not *need* Camhóinhann. Now that the name has come to my attention, it will take very little time to learn the truth. And if it *is* Éireamhóine I will crush him!"

Struggling to keep up with her, Vitré spoke swiftly to make amends. "Naturally I never thought otherwise. I only meant that if the High Priest were here you would not be inconvenienced—"

"There will be *no* inconvenience. He has caused me so much annoyance already, I look forward with pleasure to the prospect. By tomorrow morning, he will be dead."

"If that is your will," said the priest, "there can be no doubt of it."

But late that evening, when her little hunchbacked chancellor opened the door to the chamber where he kept all his records and interviewed his spies, he found her waiting for him there, white-faced and trembling with fury.

"He is not dead," she said. "This upstart magician has defied all my spells. Those who thought they recognized him were mistaken. Am I to be served only by fools and incompetents?"

"But perhaps there *was* no mistake," said Noz, fingering his white beard. "Perhaps—"

"No," she replied fiercely. "Not on my own island—not if I had his true name—he could *never* turn my spells."

"I was about to say, he may no longer *be* on Phaörax. He was last seen two days ago, and many ships have departed since then. If we send men to all the ports to ask questions, we may learn where he has gone."

She glared at him with her cat-green eyes. "And in the meantime he may pass out of easy reach. No. I will sink every galley and sailing ship on the ocean within a two-day voyage. That way we can be certain."

"But your own ships—" the hunchback protested.

"Must unfortunately be sacrificed," she said briskly. "I will not be thwarted in this. The wizard will die, and these annoyances will end."

Noz limped across the room on his crooked legs, a deep frown furrowing his brow. It had not, after all, been absolutely proven whether the transformation from mountebank to magician had precipitated any of these troubling occurrences— or was merely another result. Nor could he be easy with the notion of sinking so many Pharaxion ships.

Yet he had sense enough to recognize when it was impossible to reason with her. He had known her too long to be mistaken about that.

* * *

Her decision made, Ouriána wasted little time ascending to the isolated rooftop where she sometimes worked her spells. Elemental magic, most particularly on the scale that she planned, was best worked in the open air. The last time she had attempted such a spell-casting indoors, the results had very nearly been disastrous. But she had been younger then, and was wiser now.

She had delayed only so long as it took to send some of her most trusted servants on before her with the apparatus of magic. By the time she arrived, they had already arranged everything according to her instructions, then made a silent departure. Of all the nine towers, this was the only one with a flat roof, or stairs that offered access. An ancestor of hers with lesser gifts had commanded that it be built so. It offered an unobstructed view of the night sky.

Overhead, wheels, spirals, vortexes of stars spun in the black vault of night. Even the plodding ordinary stars in their fixed constellations seemed to shine with extraordinary brilliance. And while the moon was slender and still very young, she knew that its light would be sufficient. The omens could not be more favorable.

Why look to the sky for portents? said her other self. *You drive the stars. By your least deeds they are influenced.* Even after so many years, a delicious thrill passed through her at the thought.

And already she could tell that the deity within approved what she was about to do. There had been a time when temple sacrifices had mostly appeased its hunger; now it urged her more and more often toward death and destruction. Its appetite seemed to grow with what it fed on. Once that would have daunted her, but she was not so easily dismayed now.

A brazier filled with coals, as yet unlit, stood in the exact center of the roof. From her bosom she drew a silver phial set with precious stones. Breaking the wax seal and pulling out the stopper, she tipped the phial over the brazier and spilled out a few grains of red powder. They ignited at the first touch of moonlight and set the coals ablaze.

Stirring the fire with a wand tipped with crystal, she began to sing, to weave signs on the air. Calling forth mighty natural antagonisms, she set element warring against element. As she worked her spell, in the sweet intoxication of so much power, her breath came and went in an uneven rhythm. Around her, the very air quaked; it tasted of iron and ashes; it hissed and moaned. Under her feet, the stones of the tower writhed.

Then she sent the power on its way, with screaming winds and thunderclouds pulsing with the tumultuous forces building inside them. She stirred the seas to fury; she piled waves like mountains. Drawing frigid air down from the north, and hot air from the south, she brought them together with a mighty concussion.

In Apharos, doors were torn from their hinges; shutters went whirling off into the sky. A monstrous wave crashed on the western side of the island, with such force that the spray was felt a mile inland. It engulfed two fishing villages, and then sucked them out to sea when it retreated again.

Farther out to sea, lightning slashed open the sky. On ships as far away as Erios, winds ripped sails from their masts, cracked spars, dashed dozens of ships to atoms on rocky shores. A fleet of Ouriána's own galleys, rowing hard against the pull of a great whirlpool, were swallowed one by one. The captain of the last to go died cursing the enemies of the Empress, little knowing that she herself had worked the ruin of so many good ships.

The gale raged for a day and a night before it blew out. The silence that followed was like a mighty shout, so accustomed had the ears of the islanders become to the noise that had preceded it.

29

⁕

The hour being well after midnight, Sindérian lay down to rest while Prince Ruan kept watch. Although she was convinced that anxiety and exhaustion would keep her awake, she sank at once into the oblivion of utter fatigue and woke with the morning sun in her face.

There was no breakfast, because their food supplies had disappeared with the horses. She spent the rest of the morning purging what remained of the poison in Kivik's blood, while Ruan went off to the east to recover some of the horses. Aell remained in the camp with an aching head and one arm in a sling, refusing further treatment, and Sindérian could not help but glad of it. Meanwhile Skerry slept through the morning. She knew that when he woke there was still much to be done on his behalf.

Ruan came back shortly after noon, riding one horse and leading another. They made a hurried meal from the supplies he had recovered, before he went off to bring in the other horses while Sindérian and her father tended her patients.

Skerry, she soon discovered, was burning with fever. There were purple weals where the puncture wounds in his chest had been, and she feared that whatever sickness infected the manticore had passed into him. But in the cool of the evening his fever broke, proving her fears were groundless.

It was obvious by the next morning that none of her patients were strong enough to ride. They would require at least another day to rest. *Ill fortune continues to follow us wherever we go,* she said to Faolein. *Our entire party might have been killed.*

And yet, he answered, with his usual calm, *nobody was killed. The outcome could have been very much worse.*

Even so, the delay might well prove fatal to all their hopes. *I almost believed,* she said, flinging herself down on the grass, *that the winds of the world were beginning to blow in our favor.*

Neither for us or against us, I think, he replied. *I believe we have come to a period in time, however brief, when it will be possible to choose our own course. Let us choose wisely.*

They rode out the following morning, setting a gentle pace for the sake of their wounded. As if in answer to their need, there were several days of mild, bright weather, almost springlike, during which Aell and the Skyrran princes rapidly recovered.

Then the weather turned again, and the wind blew colder. They spent one night in one of the ruined villages, in a building that was miraculously little damaged: three walls left standing, and most of the roof remaining. Another night, of savage winds and smothering darkness, they spent in the inadequate shelter of a knot of trees. The next two days were wholly occupied skirting a morass of black, oozing mud and wet green mosses.

"We are a little to the north of Ceir Eldig," said Prince Ruan, after a week's travel from the Whathig Wood. "Another day and a half should bring us there, if we don't turn west and pass it by."

"Let us wait until tomorrow to decide," said Sindérian. There was something in the mention of that fallen city that set her heart racing, that sent an undercurrent of excitement racing along her nerves. As they topped a rise, a ray of sunlight struck through the clouds—and suddenly the Sight which had eluded her these many months returned to her, strong and true.

A great panorama of the earth spread out before her; distances were compressed; mountains proved no barrier. From the ground below to the vault of the atmosphere above, there was no impediment. She saw into the sumptuous chambers of palaces, and into the huts of peasants, into ships and cities, and into the nine underground kingdoms of the dwarves. Yet no mind could hold so much, and it passed so quickly that she could never hope to absorb or remember it.

Nevertheless, that brief vision left clarity behind it.

Be the lightning rod, Sindérian. So Faolein had said on the shores of the sea, and ever since then her resolve had been steadily growing stronger. *Don't be like the weathercock changing direction with every wind that blows. Be the lightning rod instead.* She had known for many weeks what she must do. But now she knew the place and the hour.

When, at Sindérian's suggestion, they stopped well before twilight, Prince Ruan saw no reason for concern. Everyone was weary of travelling, wounds were still aching, and they had reached a little grove of linden, birch, and hawthorn with a stream running through, where they could water the horses and set up a camp sheltered from the wind.

It was only after supper, when he realized that Sindérian had slipped away without him noticing it, that his suspicions were aroused. "Where has she gone—did anyone see her leave?" he asked the others.

No one had. Catching some of his uneasiness, they were all about to go out searching for her when she reappeared. Her dress was damp and her hair dripping wet; she had apparently found a spot, farther down the stream and screened by bushes, where she could bathe. Without a word to anyone, she sat down by the fire to dry her gown and comb out her hair.

The other men, sensing nothing amiss, returned to their seats on the ground and to the conversation that had occupied them before Ruan raised the alarm. But there was something about her—a strange, fey air—that continued to disturb him.

As the sun went down the western sky and the moon climbed above the trees, Ruan kept an anxious eye on her across the fire. She was humming a song he could not quite catch. And he knew, he *knew,* as he watched her throw herbs on the fire and plait her hair into a braid of seven strands, that there was something afoot that she was telling no one. Her eyes, ordinarily so candid, were full of hidden things, of wizardly mysteries.

Something she wore on her wrist caught the firelight, a glitter of silver and a glint of deep amber-gold. "I've not seen that bracelet before!"

Startled by his raised voice and abrupt question, the others swiveled their heads to look at him, and then, following his glance, at her.

"It was King Yri's gift," she answered quietly, sliding the silver band further up her arm until it disappeared inside the dark sleeve of her gown.

"Isn't that . . ." Skerry began.

"What?" said Ruan, rounding on him. It seemed for a moment as if revelation hovered on the air. "What were you about to say?"

"Something Prince Tyr said about the jewelry the dwarves make." Skerry shook his head. "I thought I recalled, but it escapes me after all."

Disappointed, Ruan looked to Kivik. "As it seems that *I* was not there at the time, do *you* remember what he said?"

But Kivik remembered nothing. "It was so many weeks ago, and so much has happened since."

Turning back to Sindérian, the Prince narrowed his eyes. "What reason had King Yri to give you such a gift?"

For a moment there was an answering spark, a swift rush of color into her cheeks. "You must ask him the next time you see him," she said with something of her old defiant manner. "He said nothing about it to me. But it was there in my saddlebag when we left Reichünterwelt, and as it is beautiful, I choose to wear it."

And hide it under your sleeve, so that the rest of us might not see it, thought Ruan. Yet for all that his suspicions were so thoroughly aroused, he could find no obvious threat in King Yri's gift of a silver bracelet.

The first watch of the night being appointed to Aell, the others arranged their bedrolls around the fire and settled down to sleep. Ruan had insisted on the early morning vigil, with some idea in his mind that Sindérian might attempt to strike out on her own at dawn. Lying on his back, concentrating on the dark behind his eyelids, he willed himself to sleep. He thought that he succeeded, for it seemed a long time later that he rolled over on his side, opened his eyes, and saw that Sindérian had risen from her bed.

She sat alone at the edge of the camp, cradling something in the palm of her hand: a little black, fluttering thing, like a moth or the shadow of a moth. Watching that mothlike fluttering made him feel drowsy and curiously languid. So drowsy, indeed, that he could scarcely keep his eyes open. So drowsy that a dark wave of sleep swept over him, and . . .

He came awake again when someone shook his shoulder and spoke in his ear. It was not like him to wake confused and disoriented, yet this time it was an effort to drive the mists from his mind, to focus his eyes on Kivik's face. "Is it my watch already?"

"No, it's mine," said Kivik. "I hardly know how to tell you, I am so ashamed. I nodded off. One moment I was sitting on the ground staring up at the stars, the next I found myself lying flat on the ground."

Ruan levered himself up into a sitting position. A swift glance around the camp told him that Aell and Skerry were already up. He knew with a cold sensation at the pit of his stomach that something was seriously amiss.

Reading his face, Skerry nodded. "The lady is gone—not just wandered off, but truly gone. She has taken her horse with her."

Ruan sprang to his feet. "Where is Faolein?" No one had thought to look, and it was Ruan himself who finally spotted the white owl asleep on a branch. "Take comfort," he said to Kivik, as he strode across the camp to rouse Sindérian's father. "You did not 'nod off.' She put a spell on us all."

Ruan scooped up his sword belt and buckled it on. His mind was reeling with conjectures, with memories; things he had never connected before were falling into place—too late. He spat out a string of oaths. "Fool that I was, why did it never occur to me that she would do something like this? She has gone to do battle with the Furiádhin, leaving the rest of us behind."

"But we are nowhere close to them," said a bewildered Kivik. "She will not even know where to find them."

"Will she not?" There was a flash of white and a beating of wings overhead as Faolein took off from the branch and disappeared into the night. "Do *you* know what passes between her and her father when they speak mind to mind?"

"But why?" said Skerry. By this time Ruan was saddling his horse, and the others hastened to do the same. "What possible reason could she have for going alone?"

Leaving his bedroll and all else behind, Ruan vaulted into the saddle, took up the reins. "Because she knows that we— that I—would prevent her from doing the thing she intends to do."

He rode south, following the tracks left by Sindérian's mare, which he could just make out by moonlight. Before long, he could hear the hoofbeats of Aell's horse directly behind him. But it was only when the moon went behind a cloud, and he was forced to dismount and search the ground for hoofprints, that the Skyrran princes finally caught up with him, bringing with them all the things he had left behind. Swinging back up into the saddle, Ruan was confident now that Sindérian was heading for Ceir Eldig.

"Tell us what you think she means to do," said Kivik as they all rode south together. "And why she would even imagine we would try to hinder her."

"She *knows* that I would do everything in my power to stop her," Ruan said grimly. "As she also knows that I, having been tutored by a wizard, could not watch her do what she means to do without understanding it.

"Before ever I left Thäerie to begin this journey," he continued, "Elidûc said to me, 'When you meet Sindérian Faellanëos, observe her well, for then you will be privileged to see the most gifted young wizard of her generation. She was born with such talents that if she had even the most distant left-handed connection with the royal house of Phaôrax, the wizards on Leal would have reared her from childhood to challenge Ouriána in fulfillment of the prophecy. As it was, they allowed her to pursue her own inclinations and devote herself to the healing arts. They let her go off at an early age to break her heart on the battlefields of Rheithûn, leaving all her other talents lying fallow.

"But I," said the Prince, "have seen her grow in knowledge and in power all during our long journey. Yes, and I have seen what she does late at night when she thinks no one is watching—the ropes she weaves out of fire, the lessons in magic her father has been teaching her. She is far, far more than she was when we first met."

"Strong enough that she feels she could survive a test of her own magic against *three* Furiádhin?" asked Skerry. It was clear from his tone that he did not believe it.

"No, not so strong as that. But then, she doesn't intend to survive. When a powerful wizard or magician dies before his or her time—and particularly if he or she should be struck down by magical arts—a great power is released. It is as though a shock passes through the entire world of matter. All that he or she might have accomplished in the course of a lifetime, all the potential for good or evil, explodes into the world as a burst of energy. The effects can be felt by wizards across the world, and the effect on *anyone* in near proximity can be devastating—if spells are not already in place to contain that power. That is why wizards and mages so rarely confront each other in open battle. The outcome can be as unpredictable as it is terrible."

"But if there is no way of predicting what will happen," said Kivik, "why—"

"Because it sometimes happens that a dying wizard can seize the moment and imprint his or her own intentions on that burst of power," said Ruan. The moon came out again, and he dug in his heels, urging his horse to a faster pace. "There is a rune they use to accomplish this—a rune so sacred that wizards never speak its true name—but they refer to it sometimes as the Rune of Unmaking. To make use of this spell is a desperate act, for it requires that the magician accept death willingly and make no last effort to survive, for which reason it is also known as the Rune of the Great Sacrifice. Elidûc told me that any least doubt, any fear of death that intrudes on the magician's final thought, and the rune loses its power—worse, the spell could be reversed, doing harm where it means good, good where it means harm."

"The bracelet," said Skerry suddenly. "It is the kind of gift that the dwarves bestow on their dead. If only I had remembered that before!"

"If only *I* had recognized what she was doing all evening long," said Ruan. "I see now that she was purifying herself, preparing herself for the ordeal ahead."

"And you are very certain that she means to make this sacrifice?" asked Kivik.

Ruan's hands curled into fists on the reins. "The spell is all but forbidden. Until tonight I never thought she would do this thing, but now I am convinced of it. Her plan, as I take it, is simple enough: to challenge Camhóinhann and the rest openly, suddenly, recklessly. She believes they will strike her down in the same fashion. They don't know her, they don't know who she is—how could they know when she hardly knew *herself* half a year ago? They will see a young, inexperienced wizard, overconfident, throwing down a challenge. And if she were truly no more than that, they could slay her with magic and take little or no harm from it." He hesitated. "I have, as she has repeatedly told me, no shadow of a right to prevent her from doing anything she chooses to do, however my own heart might urge against it. But my greatest fear . . ."

When he did not continue, Skerry prompted him. "Your greatest fear?"

"My greatest fear is that she will do this and Camhóinhann will not be provoked into any ill-considered action. That he will take her prisoner and kill her some other way. In which case she will be just as surely lost to us—but she will gain nothing of what she hopes to accomplish by sacrificing herself."

30

✳

The dark hour before dawn found Sindérian on the outskirts of the ruined city. Her pulse was throbbing like a drum; her heart seemed to have expanded until it filled the entire cavity of her chest. Dismounting and sending the mare away, she began to beat her own path through the brush and tangled growth. Finally, she came to what must have once been the main road cutting across Ceir Eldig: a broad cobblestone pavement, much disturbed in places where the earth had cracked or folded back on itself and a rank growth of grass and weeds had grown up in the gaps between the stones. It made for slow and treacherous going, but always ahead of her, awash in moonlight, she could see her goal, the great eminence on which the wreckage of the Emperor's palace stood, rising above the chaos of tumbled stone and mounded earth.

It took longer than she had thought it would to reach the base of the hill and begin to climb. By that time the moon had dropped below the horizon and the only light came from the shoals of silver stars swimming far to the south. She knew the Furiádhin would not break camp before sunrise, but she had hoped for a chance to rest and to gather her courage before it came time to act. Unfortunately, the side of the hill was so steep and overgrown—and whatever road led to the top had so thoroughly disappeared—it seemed to be hours before she finally struggled to the summit. There the devastation was just as great: shattered buildings, cracked pavements, a park full of trees grown wild, massive blocks of stone half buried in the ground, piles of dirt and rock where the earth had geysered up. And one lone roofless tower, broken at the midpoint.

She climbed a fragmentary staircase that wound around the tower. It ended abruptly, at the brink of a long drop. From that vantage point, Sindérian had an unimpeded view into the city below—and the camp of Ouriána's priests, just where she had known she would find them, in the garden of a ruined mansion. They had built fires at either end of their camp, so it was possible to make out their shadowy tents, the picket line of their horses, the two armored guards standing watch. But now a faint flush in the eastern sky heralded the dawn. Time was running out. *My* own *time is running out.*

Her mouth was dry after the long climb, her limbs shaking, yet she found she was eager for the contest ahead. All the years of her life had merely been leading up to this one night. For what else had she been born, to what other end had she been trained? Not for the endless, futile struggle on the battlefields of Rheithûn, not to wear out her heart and her talents with the endless grind of years—oh, surely not that. Daughter of a long line of wizards, she would go out instead in a white-hot blaze, like a dying star.

She began to prepare herself for what she knew would be her greatest—and last—spell-casting.

The king—for there had been no emperors in those days—who first instructed his architects to erect a palace for him at Ceir Eldig had chosen this eminence for a reason: it was the place where no fewer than four different ley lines met and crossed. Using the power generated by those lines, that king, his wizards, and generations of his descendants had driven back the Dark for a long age and built an empire so mighty they had believed it would endure to the end of the world. No one had tapped that power for generations, but the force that pulsed along the lines was still there, in no way diminished.

So now, one hand gripping the other, she bent her head, concentrating all her will and desire on one object: calling the power of the lines to her. Sweat broke out on her forehead; she felt mind and body straining with the strength of her intention. For a terrible moment she thought the task was too great, that she was too weak—Then the power answered and surged up to meet her.

In the beginning there was agony, such agony as she had never imagined. It pierced her like thorns, it burned in her veins like molten metal, it singed her like fire. It was too much to bear, yet she endured it. It devoured her, yet she was not consumed by it. And gradually, the unbearable became bearable; the first raw bolts of energy were replaced by a half-pleasurable warmth. Like the salamander, she was learning to live within the fire, as though it were her native element.

And still the power poured into her, still she soaked it up, until her skin tingled and glowed with it and her hair crackled and gave off sparks. Stars danced at her fingertips; fascinated, she drew constellations on the air. She felt that she might level mountains, stem the flow of mighty rivers, turn planets in their courses. Almost she forgot her purpose in the fierce joy of it—until some movement down in the ruins, a shout as someone caught sight of her incandescent figure, recalled her and sobered her.

So she turned her mind to shaping the power to her own ends. As it fed her, so she fed it with her own fierce will. Spells whirled in her brain; patterns formed, a complex web of mental forces strong enough to catch lightning. Then she gathered as much energy as she could hold in one hand, molded it into a javelin of fire, and hurled it into the camp below.

In response to the guard's warning, Camhóinhann and Dyonas emerged from their tents just in time to see Sindérian's javelin streak through the air, then explode in a rain of sparks as it hit the ground. By the time Goezenou had joined them, another missile had landed in their midst, and then another. In the chaos of men and horses that erupted in the camp, the three priests were unable to do more than shield themselves and scramble for cover behind sections of broken masonry.

Goezenou and Dyonas met behind a low, fragmentary wall. Scanning the hilltop, from which the barrage seemed to originate, it did not take long to locate a glowing female form, etched against a brightening dawn sky.

"What fool is that who challenges us?" hissed Goezenou.

Though it was not possible from this distance to see her face, Dyonas's memory was long. "At a guess, it is the girl

Thaga was supposed to dispose of at Saer." As he spoke, he sent a spell to divert one of her more accurate casts.

"And she has followed us all this way? So much the worse for her! A mere fledgling, with no name or reputation."

Dyonas gave him a contemptuous glance. "Do you claim to know all the wizards on Leal, their names and abilities? Whoever she is, she appears to be no mere dabbler."

"She is calling up power from the leys," Goezenou said with a sneer. "Otherwise—" A tree burst into flames behind them, and they broke in opposite directions.

Moments later, Dyonas met Camhóinhann behind an overgrown pile of stones. "The Princess?" said the younger priest.

"I have shielded her," answered Camhóinhann. "Naturally, that was my first thought."

A bolt of energy went sizzling past, only inches from Dyonas's head. "Whoever she is, she must feel she has some chance of defeating us—or else she has been sent to distract us while others approach us from behind."

"More likely," said Camhóinhann, "she is one who has just enough inherent power to think she can win by losing. Have a care," he added as the other hurled an answering bolt in the girl's direction, narrowly missing her. "If you had hit her . . . !"

"I am not *quite* a fool. I understand that much." There was a loud crash when a wall fell, followed by a curse as Goezenou crashed through some bushes to the left and joined them behind their rampart of stone. "While we draw her fire, what will you do?" Dyonas asked Camhóinhann.

"I will weave a net of spells to hold her," said the High Priest. "Once we have her fast, we can decide what to do with her."

* * *

Stone erupted at Sindérian's feet as Dyonas's searing bolt of energy crashed into the staircase, sending flying shards of rock in all directions. One grazed her temple, another passed through the palm of her hand and out the other side. Reflexively, she closed both wounds; with so much power surging through her, it took but a thought to heal them. A fiery axe spun through the air, barely missing her head. By now, all the trees on the hill were burning—but she gathered light and heat out of the air, shaped them into balls of flame, and threw them, one after the other, into the camp below.

Then the Furiádhin changed their tactics. The first spell nearly took her by surprise. She felt her bones begin to melt, her body fraying, growing thin and insubstantial. Struggling to remain solid, she slashed runes on the air, forced out their names in a dry whisper—for she courted death, not transformation. Spell after spell they threw at her, trying to warp her out of human form: she was furred; she was feathered; her skin turned warty and amphibious; she had the slick, scaly body of a fish. Each spell she countered, returning to her own shape. Then came a blast of magic more devastating than any that came before. The breath in her lungs turned to smoke, her blood to sand; something drove her out of her body and into the wind.

Blinded, disoriented, she lost all sense of self and nearly dissipated. Then someone down below shouted her name and it pulled her back into her body as a lodestone draws iron. The next spell that came her way she snatched out of the air and sent hurtling back again.

A mile from Ceir Eldig, Prince Ruan spotted Sindérian's mare grazing under a tree. This he took as a very bad sign—

one that she had no intention of leaving the ruined city alive.

"It seems that she was less willing to risk the animal's life than her own," he muttered under his breath.

The sky was rosy with dawn before he finally found the track she had made for herself on the edge of the city. "Perhaps we aren't so very far behind her," he heard Kivik say behind him. "Perhaps we woke before she meant us to. Surely her spell was meant to last until morning."

But Ruan was not to be deceived by any such false hope. "We slept exactly as long as she intended we should. We are meant to arrive too late to interfere, but not so late we're unable to take advantage of any opportunity she makes for us."

When they came out on the road, they made better progress, though still so slow that Ruan was cursing his horse in impatience long before they came within sight of the palace on the hill. The trees on the eminence were all aflame, like a fiery crown; had the wind not been in the wrong direction he would have smelled the smoke long before.

Between the smoke and the flame, he could barely make out Sindérian atop the tower. "We will never reach her from this direction, not through the fire. May the Fates grant us a way to the top on the other side!"

He tried to keep her in sight as they circled the hill, but coming around on the other side it was hard to see through the turmoil of magic roaring around her. Only now and then could he catch a glimpse of her face, very white and strained. For a terrible moment she disappeared, seemed to melt into the chaos of the air; and without even realizing he was doing so, he shouted her name. He felt a cold shock of relief when she reappeared again, swaying unsteadily, but still alive and on her feet.

He scanned the slope, searching for the quickest way to the top. Below the tower the face of the hill was almost sheer, but a little to the west there appeared to be a path, not much overgrown. Swinging down from the saddle, he tossed the reins to Aell and began to climb. He heard Kivik and Skerry crashing heavily through the dry brush behind him. More agile than either of them—and more determined—he soon outdistanced them.

In the camp below, thread after thread of shining silver spun out from Camhóinhann's hands. But before he could bind them together they faded, and it was all to do again. "There is too much magic in the air; it is distorting the spell," he told Dyonas. "I cannot hold her this way. I must try something else."

Rolling a furious eye in the High Priest's direction, Goezenou scrambled atop a pile of rocks. "Let us have done with it then. It has gone on too long already." Making signs on the air, he called out a word that crackled like lightning, and a slender column of light appeared in his hand. Too late, the others understood what he was doing.

As he drew back his arm to cast his weapon, Camhóinhann and Dyonas both cried out warnings at once—but Goezenou's spear of elemental fire had already left his hand.

On her precarious perch above, the young wizard took the full force of the spear. If she called out in agony as it pierced her, no one heard her, for there was a loud concussion in the air like two thunderstorms crashing together, and the tower on the hill rocked. For just a moment she remained standing, silhouetted against the morning sky, illuminated by the fire of Goezenou's spell.

Then the fire died, and there was only a broken body falling. Falling from the tower in a shower of stones.

Ruan was nearly to the top of the hill, craning his neck to get a better look, when something streaked through the air, heading straight for Sindérian.

She *might* have moved, she *might* have dodged it. She did neither. Ruan watched, raging at his own helplessness, as the spear impaled her, the air boomed, the tower rocked. He watched her body tumble more than a hundred feet to land among the jagged stones below.

There was no hope, no hope at all. If the spear had not killed her, the fall had surely done so. There was no reason for him to turn as he did and start back down the hill, stumbling into Kivik and Skerry along the way. In his haste, he slid almost to the bottom before he was beaten back by a wall of force: a mighty wind that seemed to rise from Sindérian's broken body, scattering leaves, rocks, and bushes, and almost knocking Ruan himself off his feet.

As the wind grew in violence, it went roaring toward the Pharaxion camp. On every side, the forces of nature began to run wild. Goezenou was the first to die, thrown to the ground and buried under a rain of stones. Two guardsmen standing outside Winloki's tent were swept away by the turbulent air. Trees were ripped out of the ground. Any of the horses that had not already pulled up their pickets and fled did so now.

For a moment, it seemed that Dyonas would ride out the

storm, until a tremor passed through the earth under his feet, opening a wide crack. Unable to save himself, he dropped into the fracture, and was crushed to death when another tremor brought the walls clashing back together again. Only Camhóinhann continued to defy the fury unleashed by Sindérian's death: he stood chanting spells, buffeted by wind, stones, tree limbs, even the flying body of one of the acolytes. Battered and bloody as he was, he still stood.

Then, as suddenly as it had risen, the wind fell again, and all was silent.

From their vantage point halfway up the hill, Kivik and Skerry had seen the devastation in the Pharaxion camp. They, too, would have climbed down had the wind not pushed them back. And when it was over they could only stand, stunned, as Winloki emerged from her tent and ran to Camhóinhann's side. They watched her slip her hand into one of his, speaking urgently.

His other arm dangled at his side, and blood dripped from his forehead. But even injured he still retained sufficient power of will to call back one of the horses. The great grey gelding returned: agitated, dancing and sidestepping nervously, but obedient. It stood just long enough for Camhóinhann to mount, offer his good hand to Winloki, and pull her up into the saddle with him. Then he gave the gelding its head, and it leaped into motion, heading south.

Only then did Winloki's kinsmen recover from the surprise and grief that had held them motionless. Running and sliding as Ruan had done, they stumbled to the foot of the hill. And there they found him, along with Aell, kneeling beside Sindérian's body.

He had moved her from the sharp rocks where she had first landed. Blood was spattered everywhere. One sleeve of her dress was soaked with it; the hair on one side of her head was matted with it. There could be no doubt that bones had shattered in the fall, though her gown covered the worst of the damage.

As they approached, Ruan glanced up. He had been in the act of feeling for a pulse in her throat, but one glimpse of his face was enough to confirm what they already knew.

"So she is gone then," said Kivik.

Ruan only nodded wordlessly before bending to imprint a kiss on her ice-white brow, her cold lips.

Then there was a sound overhead like an enormous heart beating. Looking up, they saw Faolein descending in a flurry of white wings. Instead of landing, the owl hovered in the air just above Sindérian's face, with his wings beating and his yellow eyes glaring. As the men watched in pity and horror, Faolein gave a shriek like a dying man and rent his own feathery breast with his beak—

—and Sindérian, standing at the gate of death, between the immense pillars of light and shadow that mark the threshold between one world and the next, and wholly intent on the glory that lies beyond—the cities of burning gold, the rivers of molten silver, the immense figures with rainbow-colored wings who stand sentinel outside the city walls—felt the lightest of touches, as if it were hardly more than a breath, and heard somebody calling her name.

Turning, with great reluctance, from the light ahead of her to the shadows behind, she found herself face-to-face with Faolein:

back in his own form, as she had known him for most of her life, the great wizard, the wise and gentle teacher.

"Father," she said. "You have come to comfort me, even here on the threshold of death. But it wasn't necessary to follow me. Do not think that I am afraid, or that I relinquish my life with any regrets." She laughed softly, joyfully. "In truth, I have seen what waits for me on the other side, and I am longing to go there."

"Nevertheless, you are overhasty in your departure," said Faolein. "When Nimenoë died, she linked the threads of your life to those of Winloki's. She meant it for her own child's protection, knowing how strong you were, how strong you would become. But that is why the aniffath was ineffective against you. It was the one thing Ouriána needed to take into account in weaving her spell—and did not know. This I learned when I stood where you stand now, many months ago. But even before that, I knew this hour would come. That is why I died at Saer, that is why I turned away from the gate when I might have passed freely. That is why I allowed myself to be sundered, one half existing in the world of the living, one half remaining here all of these months. It has been an uncomfortable existence, but it was necessary to give you this message: you may cross over the threshold if you choose, but that would be an act of cowardice."

He held out a hand. "Do not turn fainthearted now, you who have always been so courageous. Let me show you the way back."

Her elation began to fade. In its place came bewilderment and the beginning of fear. "But there will be pain there, heartache and loss. I don't wish to return to any of that. And my body is broken. Perhaps it can never be repaired."

"Perhaps not. I cannot tell what awaits you—that vision

was not granted me. You may live only a day, or a week, or for many years. You may spend all that time crippled in mind and body—or worse."

Her confusion only deepened. "And to that you urge me to return?"

"When I made my choice at Saer, I thought as a man and a father. My understanding is greater now. The Fates are compassionate; when they allow us to suffer it is only that we may learn and grow, that we may be purified and better suited for the world beyond."

She gazed at him doubtfully. "Not all are purified."

"Some do refuse the gift," he said. "They die with many hard lessons still unlearned."

"Am I, then, so weak and faulty?" she protested.

But she knew that she was. Her impatience, her tendency to act on impulse, these were the least of her faults. Instead of rejoicing in her strength of mind and body, her many rich gifts, she had struggled with despair all this last year. And despair had led her to misuse the rune, to choose the sacrifice—not out of necessity, not in the spirit of acceptance—but as an escape from her own fear and confusion. At the least, that had been presumptuous; at the worst, wicked and cowardly.

But Faolein was none of these things. "You will not be able to return with me," she said.

"I can go with you only part of the way. My life is done. What yours will be I do not know." He held out his hand again. "But short or long, joyous or agonizing, I ask you to choose life."

The touch of his palm was like the resumption of pain after blessed respite. Yet with it came a dread sense of inevitability. With one last regretful glance back over her shoulder—at the *glorious city, at the shining river and the glimmering plain—Sindérian took a reluctant step in his direction, reluctantly allowed him to lead her on.*

And going back was worse than dying; it was like passing through white fire, it was like being crushed and compressed and molded to fit back into the broken shell of her body. She did not know how huge she had become until the confines of the flesh required her to become small again. Nor did she fully comprehend what she was giving up, until the darkness washed over her and blotted out the light.

31

Out of respect for Faolein's grief, Ruan turned away. Feeling numb and drained as he had never felt before, he rose slowly to his feet. Beside him, Aell did the same. It was only when he caught sight of Kivik and Skerry's stricken faces that a vague memory of what brought them here, what they had hoped to accomplish by their long journey, surfaced in his mind. "Winloki?"

"She was unharmed. But ... she had a chance to escape and she chose not to." Skerry, like Kivik, had a dazed and bewildered look. "Two of the Furiádhin died; the others—the others were either killed or injured. And in all the panic and confusion, no one would have stopped her. But she never—she never even tried."

"Yes," said Ruan wearily. "Sindérian thought that might happen. She told me if we didn't rescue the Princess soon enough, she might not want to be rescued. The Pharaxions are, after all, her mother's people." Then his glance sharpened. "You do mean to go after her? She won't have seen you, she won't have known you were here. Perhaps that would have made a difference."

Kivik frowned. "But she went right to him. There seemed—there seemed to be some confidence between them."

Ruan did not need to be told who *he* was. "Why would she *not* turn to Camhóinhann in the midst of death and confusion? You know something of who and what he was—and now that you have seen him, with all his rags of glory still about him, do you not understand? He was a great wizard, a noble prince—and still something of that high nobility shines out. That is what makes him dangerous. Perhaps most of all to someone like Winloki."

As he spoke, Ruan saw eyes that had been dull take fire, faces that had looked sick and bewildered gain courage and determination. "Our horses," said Skerry, glancing around him, as if wondering how he had managed to misplace them.

"Safely tethered under some trees," said Aell with a gesture. "By good luck, just where the bulk of the hill will have shielded them from the worst of it."

"Then we should not lose any more time," said Kivik. He took several strides in that direction, then turned back with a shamefaced look. "I was forgetting—we can't just leave her here unburied."

"I will see to her and catch up with you later," answered Ruan, kneeling beside Sindérian again. He never noticed the body of the owl lying stiff and still under a bush. "I would not leave her here for the wolves and wild beasts—" Then his body tensed, his breath caught in his throat. Had he seen her move? Or was it simply the edge of her cloak, a few tendrils of dark hair, lifted by the breeze? It could not be, and yet . . .

He put his ear to her chest; he placed a hand lightly over her mouth to feel if she was breathing. The others, who had just been turning to leave, were startled by the sound, half exultant, half disbelieving, that was torn from his throat. "She still lives! I don't know how, but she lives."

"Impossible," said Skerry. He looked at Ruan—then back the way he had been about to go—then at Ruan again. "The fall alone—"

"Her heart beats, her breath comes and goes. I don't say how long that will continue." Then, seeing how the other men still hesitated, he waved them off. "Go. Go after Camhóinhann and the Princess. But be cautious. Even wounded, he is dangerous."

"But what will you do?" said Kivik.

The stubborn set of Ruan's jaw wavered, and then solidified. "I will take her to the Ni-Féa; there are healers among them, some of them extraordinarily gifted. It is only a two-day ride. If she can survive that long."

"But you said—"

"I said I would not ask them for aid if my life depended on it. Hers is another matter. And yes, they will not be much interested in helping her, but I will find a way to convince them. It is her only chance." He made another impatient gesture. "As you are Winloki's only chance. Don't delay a moment longer."

But as Kivik and Skerry went off, almost at a run, Aell still lingered. It was plain that he was uncertain where his duty might lie.

"Do not follow them just yet," said Ruan. Lifting Sindérian very gently, he moved in the direction of the horses. "Hand her up to me once I am mounted, and then go."

And a little while later, when he was in the saddle: "Try to prevent our Skyrran friends from doing anything foolhardy. If they do—and I don't catch up with you later—do what you can and then go home to Thäerie. Tell my grandfather all that has happened."

Looping the reins around one hand, he reached down and took Sindérian's limp body out of Aell's arms, resting her in the position he hoped would do her the least harm, in his own.

"The Ni-Féa *will* help her," he said fiercely. "They do not love me, my mother's people, but there are those among them who would be very glad to see me at a disadvantage. And I—I will humble myself to the dust, I will give them my heart's blood in a silver goblet, if that is what they ask."

Then, with a flick of his reins, he was on his way.

GLOSSARY

People & Places

Adfhail   the youngest acolyte to accompany the Furiádhin to Skyrra.

Aell ("air"; *ale*)   son of a fisherman, a common soldier under Prince Ruan's command.

Aethon ("furze")   itinerant wizard, educated at the Scholia on Leal, who brought word of Guenloie/Winloki's survival to the council.

Alluinn ("many lakes"; *al-oo-WIN*)   kingdom at the center of the northern empire. The name was also applied to the Empire itself. Pendawer kings and emperors ruled Alluinn for approximately a thousand years. Her downfall was the war with Otöi, in which wizards and mages made such reckless use of their magic that both empires fell and the world was Changed.

Anerüian ("midnight"; *an-eh-ROO-yon*) **Pendawer**   full name of Prince Ruan. The youngest grandson of High King Réodan, human on his father's side and Ni-Féa Faey on his mother's. Named for the hour at which he was born.

Apharos (*af-FAY-rows*) Ouriána's capital city on Phaôrax.

Arkenfell a northern kingdom, originally of the same tribal stock as Skyrra and Mistlewald, with whom they continued to be loosely allied.

Arvi Skyrran rider in Kivik's army; Winloki's bodyguard for a time.

Aurvang a town in Arkenfell, from which Sindérian, Ruan, and company sailed for Skyrra.

Autlands northeastern region of Skyrra, closest to Eisenlonde.

Baillébachlain ("town of bees, beehive") the largest town on Leal, and the site of the wizards' Scholia.

Brielliend a heavily forested region south of Rhüaddlyn. Although Ouriána's troops were able to win much territory there, the eastern portion continued to resist.

Brihac a knight in the household of Prince Cuillioc.

Cadmin Aernan ("iron mountains") a great range of mountains west of Alluinn running more or less north-south.

Cailltin ("hazel") **of Aefri** nobleman and captain of a small troop of Rheithûnian fighters. He was betrothed to Sindérian. They parted just before the fall of Gilaefri, one of the last three Rheithûnian fortresses to be captured by Ouriána's armies.

Camhóinhann ("still waters"; *cah-VHOYN-ahn*) enslaved and corrupted by Ouriána, he eventually became the High Priest of her cult, and the most powerful of the Furiádhin.

Ceir Eldig ("city of princes") the capital of Alluinn and the seat of the Emperors; ruined and deserted after the Change.

Citadel the palace-fortress at Xanthipei, in which Cuillioc made his headquarters on his arrival in Mirizandi.

Corridon ("stone folk") another name for the dwarves. Many humans believed the dwarves originally were generated from a stony matrix.

Cuillioc ("pledge" or "word of honor"; *QWILL-ee-ahch*) Prince of Phaôrax, Ouriána's second-born son, sent by her to conquer Mirizandi. An honorable but conflicted man.

Cuirarthéros one of the last three fortresses to be conquered in Rheithûn. Sindérian was close enough at the time to psychically experience its downfall, and the death throes of hundreds of its inhabitants.

Curóide ("hero") a wizard, formerly Éireamhóine's apprentice, who later took his place on the council of the Nine Master Wizards of Leal. His most notable talent was as a weather-worker.

Deor Skyrran warrior, one of Kivik's captains.

Drakenskaller ("dragon's skull") **Mountains** a high range in the northern part of Skyrra and the western part of Eisenlonde. Winters in the Drakenskallers were very harsh, and inhabitants were few.

Dreyde lord of Saer. He welcomed Faolein, Sindérian, and their companions into his fortress and then betrayed them.

Dyonas (*dye-OH-nahs*) youngest of the Furiádhin, but also the most powerful after Camhóinhann.

Efflam in Apharos, one of Ouriána's temple guards. He accompanied the Furiádhin to Skyrra.

Éireamhóine ("noble eagle"; *AIR-ah-vhoyn*) at one time the most powerful wizard on Leal, he disappeared while trying to smuggle Guenloie away to safety.

Eisenlonde a region east of Skyrra, occupied by a loose confederation of barbarian tribes, given to border raids and horse thievery. The formation of a vast Eisenlonder army took the Skyrrans by surprise.

Elidûc High King Réodan's court wizard, close friend, and valued counselor. Because he was also a great scholar, he acted as a tutor to Réodan's sons and grandsons, including Prince Ruan.

Erios ("shining hills") an island in the sea of Orania, invaded by Pharaxion forces.

Faellanëos ("dark hair") family name belonging to a long line of wizards, including Faolein and Sindérian.

Faey a long-lived nonhuman race. Divided into two sub-races, the Ni-Ferys and the Ni-Féa. Each branch regarded the other with unfailing suspicion, for though they came of similar stock they were temperamentally opposite. The Ni-Ferys often intermixed with humans, but the Ni-Féa remained extremely insular.

Faolein ("sea-lion"; *FAY-oh-LINE*) Master Wizard and Sindérian's father. Adept in all aspects of wizardry, though his particular gift was the ability to divine the name of anyone he met.

Faol-Mora ("the ocean sea") in one sense, all the oceans of the world, more commonly applied to the uncharted waters beyond the named seas.

Fenéille Galadan ("crown of the north") a high range of mountains roughly describing an arc from east to west, north of Alluinn and south of Arkenfell and Mistlewald.

Furiádhin ("the changed men" or "the mutated ones"; *FOO-ree-AHD-in*) Ouriána's warrior-magician-priests. Singular: furiádh.

Gerig a knight in the household of Prince Cuillioc.

Gilaefri a fortress that long held out against Ouriána's invading forces, until the Furiádhin overthrew it with magic. See *Rheithûn* and *Cailltin of Aefri*.

Goezenou furiádh who served as one of Ouriána's generals in Rheithûn.

Guenloie (translation uncertain; may be a variant of *Guinalli*, "lily," or a combination of *guin*, "white, clear," and *hloë*, "aura, halo") Princess of Phaôrax, daughter of Ouriána's twin sister Nimenoë, and therefore regarded as the child of the prophecy. Hidden away in Skyrra for many years, she grew to womanhood under the name Winloki.

Guindeluc ("unblemished honor") Prince Cuillioc's late brother. Ouriána's eldest son, and a dazzling figure to whom Cuillioc was always comparing himself, to his own disadvantage.

Haakon young rider in Kivik's army, briefly Winloki's bodyguard.

Haestan Skyrran warrior, one of Kivik's captains.

Haestfilke an eastern region of Skyrra.

Heldenhof ("the house of heroes") King Ristil's palace at Luckenbörg.

Herzenmark the most central province of Skyrra.

Hythe coastal principality. Part of the alliance headed by the High King Réodan. Ruled by Prince Bael.

Iobhar ("yew"; *EYE-oh-vhar*) furiádh, sent to Mirizandi with Prince Cuillioc to counsel and spy on him.

Jago ("younger son") a common soldier under Prince Ruan's command. After surviving most of the journey to Skyrra, he was killed during the crossing from Arkenfell.

Kerion one of the temple guards who accompanied the Furiádhin to Skyrra.

Kivik (*KIV-ick*) Prince of Skyrra; King Ristil's middle son and a general in his armies.

Lasaire ("flames") acolyte-servant to Dyonas.

Leal (*leel*) a smaller island off the east coast of Thäerie, the location of a great school of wizardry. For all intents and purposes, Leal was ruled by the Nine Master Wizards, but the island had long been so closely allied with Thäerie that there was a sense of shared national identity.

Lochdaen ("swarthy man") a temple guard in Apharos, he was chosen to accompany the Furiádhin on their journey to Skyrra.

Lückenbörg a town in Skyrra, site of King Ristil's palace.

Luenil (originally a diminutive of *Meluine,* "color of the sun") young Thäerian widow who was chosen as Guenloie's wet nurse after her own child was stillborn. Believed to be lost in the Cadmin Aernan with Éireamhóine.

Lünerion (*LOO-nair-ee-ON*) principality of Alluinn, formerly a rich and populous region; a hundred years after the Change it was an uninhabited wilderness.

Maël　acolyte-servant to the furiádh Iobhar.

Maelor (*MAY-lore*) **the Astromancer**　a befuddled old man reputed to have once been a great magician.

Malindor ("the wide realm")　kingdom at the very southern tip of the northern continent. By the time of Réodan's council, so much territory had been lost to Phaôrax that Ouriána held more of Malindor than its own king.

Mallion ("clover") **Penn**　legendary wizard. The most powerful of his own era, and generally regarded as the most gifted wizard ever.

Marrec　one of Ouriána's temple guards, who accompanied the Furiádhin to Skyrra.

Meraz　city-state in Mirizandi, between Xanthipei and Persit.

Mere　coastal duchy just to the north of Rheithûn. The Duke of Mere's sudden change of heart—his decision to foresake his former allies by declaring his neutrality—was widely regarded as an act of betrayal.

Meriasec　a Prince of Phaôrax, the youngest and in every way the least of Ouriána's sons.

Mirizandi (*meer-ah-ZAHN-dee*)　a nation of city-states on the southern continent, ruled by "semidivine" nobles and

princes. It was reputed to be a fabulously wealthy region because of legendary mines somewhere in the interior.

Mistlewald (*MIST-el-vahld*) a northern kingdom, originally
of the same tribal stock as Skyrra and Arkenfell, with whom
they continued to be loosely allied.

Morquant acolyte-servant to Camhóinhann.

Necke the channel between the subcontinent of Skyrra/
Eisenlonde and the northern continent.

Nephuar a kingdom on the southern continent, unfriendly
to the city-states of Mirizandi.

Ni-Féa Prince Ruan's mother's people, a sub-race of the Faey.
Little was known of them, though they were rumored to be
glamourously beautiful and masters and mistresses of enchantment. Ruan himself, who had long been estranged from
his Ni-Féa kin, painted a less pleasing picture. They were ruled
by Queen Gäiä. See *Faey.*

Nimenöe ("bright mist, shining cloud"; *nim-en-OH-ee*) a
Princess of Phaôrax, Ouriána's twin sister, and Guenloie/Win-
loki's mother. Trained in wizardry at the Scholia on Leal, her
most notable talents were warding and healing.

Nimhelli ("place of great fogs") a smaller island southwest of
Thäerie, traditionally under Thäerian rule.

Noz the little hunchback with a battered face and seemingly everything else against him, who nevertheless managed, by virtue of a keen mind and unquestioned loyalty, to rise to the position of Ouriána's Lord Chancellor. Most of her other servants, and particularly the Furiádhin, considered him a despicable upstart.

Old Fortress see *Tirfang*.

Omair ("amber") acolyte-servant to the furiádh Iobhar.

Orri one of Kivik's scouts.

Otöi (*aht-OY*) empire ruling over much of the southern continent until it was destroyed in the same cataclysmic battle as Alluinn. Reputedly a realm of black magics and even blacker rites, since the Otöwan rulers and magicians were themselves enslaved to powers of Darkness and Unlife.

Ouriána (*oh-ree-ON-ah*) Queen of Phaôrax, self-declared Empress and Goddess, and mother to Guindeluc, Cuillioc, and Meriasec. A sorceress steeped in the black arts, she was also known as the Dark Lady of Phaôrax.

Pehlidor ("the far realm") this is the name that appears on maps of the period indicating a land in the northeast. Believed to be Éireamhóine's intended destination when he left Thäerie with the infant princess.

Penadamin (literally "the only high mountain") a mountain in the Fenéille Galadan range. It was not, in fact, the highest mountain in the world, or even in the Fenéille Galadan, but its onetime inhabitants must have thought it was.

Pendawer ("land ruler") family name of the imperial house of Alluinn. After the fall of the Empire, the last surviving heir found refuge on Thäerie, where his descendants ruled as High Kings.

Pentheirie ("high place of the eagles") Réodan's capital city on Thäerie.

Persit (*per-SIT*) a city-state in Mirizandi, a short distance from Xanthipei. Ruled by Lord Vaz.

Phaôrax (*FAY-oh-racks*) island kingdom ruled (some might say enslaved) by Ouriána. Though the Pharaxions were once known as a proud, strong, honorable people, Ouriána's rule and her endless wars eliminated too many of the best and promoted too many of the worst.

Regin Skyrran warrior, one of Kivik's captains.

Reichünterwelt (*rike-OON-ter-velt*) one of the nine underground kingdoms of the dwarves. Ruled by King Yri.

Réodan ("ice man," originally a nickname given to those with very fair skin and hair; *RAY-oh-don*) **Pendawer** High King, ruler of Thäerie, and leader of the alliance against Ouriána.

Rheithûn ("where the water comes down from the hills") kingdom south of Mere and north of Rhuadllyn which put up a long and courageous resistance against Ouriána's invading armies, but was finally overrun. When the last three fortresses fell to the Furiádhin, it was said that Goezenou gave the order to execute all the leaders of the "rebellion" against the Empress.

Rhuadllyn ("red rivers") the first nation to be conquered by Phaôrax. Because of the two nations' long-standing political ties, there is reason to believe the issue was already decided before Ouriána's troops ever invaded, and that the very slight resistance the Pharaxions met was only a token effort meant by the Prince of Rhuadllyn to appease the populace. Within a decade, the people had come to identify themselves as, essentially, citizens of Phaôrax.

Ristil (*RIZ-till*) King of Skyrra, father of Kivik, adoptive uncle of Winloki, husband of Sigvith.

Rivanon acolyte-servant to Camhóinhann. One of the eldest acolytes at Ouriána's temple, he was privy to many of the High Priest's secrets.

Roric Skyrran warrior, one of Kivik's captains.

Ruan (*rune*) see *Anëruian Pendawer.*

Saer hill fort in Mere. See *Dreyde, Thaga.*

Sea of Orania the waters between Thäerie, Phaôrax, and the continent.

Shionneth ("like a fox," a name denoting either cleverness or red hair) Sindérian's late mother. This elderly and reclusive wizard became Faolein's second wife.

Sigvith Queen-Consort in Skyrra, King Ristil's second wife and Kivik's stepmother; her past was a mystery to her.

Sindérian ("star maiden" or "bright daughter"; *sin-DAY-ree-on*) daughter of Shionneth and Faolein, descended from seven generations of wizards on either side. An instinctive healer and seer.

Skerry (rhymes with *ferry*) as the great-grandson of a Skyrran king, he was accorded princely rank, but not the title. He and Winloki made a childhood pact to marry.

Skørnhäär a race of ice giants.

Skyrra (skee-RAH) northern realm, ruled by King Ristil. Once allied to the Empire of Alluinn, after the Change they threw off all southern influences and returned to an earlier way of life, only maintaining ties with the kindred nations of Mistlewald and Arkenfell. An essentially peaceful people, they could be the fiercest of fighters when threatened. Their only indigenous magic-workers were healers and runestonereaders.

Syvi a Skyrran healer, second only to Thyra in age and experience.

Thäerian Sea the waters north of Thäerie, west of Mere,

Hythe, and Weye. The point where the Thäerian Sea ended and the great ocean began was a matter of some dispute.

Thäerie (roughly translated, "home of the eagle-hearted men"; *THAY-ree*) island kingdom ruled in former days by their own native princes, later by the Pendawers. The realm of the High King Réodan. As the sea formed a natural barrier, and because of strong ties with the wizards on Leal, Thäerie had never been invaded.

Thaga ("bat") an Otöwan magus in service to Ouriána who attempted to kill Faolein. It was he who corrupted Lord Dreyde and played some part in the Duke of Mere's decision to forsake the alliance.

Thyra a healer in Kivik's army who had seen many campaigns.

Tirfang a valley in the Drakenskaller Mountains, site of an ancient, reputedly haunted city-fortress built by the legendary witchlords. Sometimes synonymous with the Old Fortress itself.

Tuillo ("mistletoe") a common soldier under Prince Ruan's command. He was killed by a sea dragon on the voyage to Mere.

Tyr (*teer*) Prince of the dwarf kingdom of Reichünterwelt and son of King Yri.

Varjolükka (singular and plural) a type of skinchanger. Skinchangers were a race of humans capable of transforming themselves into bearlike creatures, although some sources claim the reverse: that they were bears who could take on the shape of humans.

Vaz ruler of Persit. One of the lords of Mirizandi, who considered themselves semidivine.

Weye coastal principality, the most northern nation in the alliance against Ouriána. Ruled by Prince Gwynnek.

Whathig Wood ("tangled wood" or "wood of dark sorceries") forest in Alluinn, believed to be haunted by witches, ghosts, and dangerous wild animals.

Xanthipei (*zahn-thip-EYE*) a large city in Mirizandi, on the Bay of Mir. When Prince Cuillioc arrived with his fleet to invade the realm, the citizens of Xanthipei gave up without a fight.

Yri (*eerie*) King of Reichünterwelt. This dwarf of immense age (far in excess of two hundred years) was a powerful seer whose other gifts included the ability to talk with animals.

Ëanor—Time
Ëanoris—Times of the Year

lüenien—year, solar cycle

lüerin—month, lunar cycle

    Oerinora* ("cold time")

*the last month of autumn

> **Néosora** ("dark time")

> **Réomiora** ("ice time")

> **Siôdora** ("storm time")

> **Weridanni** ("roots")

> **Syviri** ("stems")

> **Duilligor** ("leaves")

> **Ariénora** ("bright month")

> **Uenora** ("heat month")

> **Ffarwid** ("fruit")

> **Grianë** ("grain")

> **Séarnid** ("withering")

> **Wisigiri** ("rains")

illüerin half-month, fortnight

gäeä winter

cormath spring

samhrad summer

hafen autumn

Ëanoril—Times of the Day

elüi daytime

nëos night, darkness

elio a day and a night, the time between one sunrise and the next

noë brightening, dawn, morning

érien brilliant, noon

yffarian waning light, afternoon

anoë dimming, twilight, evening

anërui absence of light, midnight

malanëos utter darkness, the time between midnight and first light

lüenodi sunrise

ellüen sunset

lüerodi moonrise

ellüer moonset

MAGIC

Níadhélen

Níadhélen ("the language of the ancients") was the first language; according to religious and magical texts, it was the language given by the Fates to all sentient creatures, so that all living things might live in harmony and perfect communication. As time went on, and the races and nations became more and more estranged, more and more distrustful, they began to create their own languages as a way of hiding their secrets and keeping their knowledge to themselves. Eventually, there were hundreds of different languages, some having their roots in Níadhélen, some having no relation at all to this most ancient of tongues.

By the latter days of the Empire, no one spoke Níadhélen in everyday speech, although an incomplete lexicon was still in use as the language of scholarship, diplomacy, magic, and prayer.

Its association with magic was this: In the animistic worldview held by most magicians, animals (*béodani*) had a sentience only a little below that of Men, dwarves, Faey, etc.; plants (*pléanhir*) were sentient to a lesser degree, and even some of the elements (the *éolfani*) and metals (*ora*) had the bare beginnings of sentience. As all these had an instinctive understanding of Niadhélen, the magician, in commanding or communicating with them, framed his or her spells in Niadhélen.

It was a belief widely held that the children of Men and other speaking races (the *dhin,* people) were born with an instinctive understanding of Niadhélen, but lost most or all of it by the time they were able to speak. For this reason, lullabies were often sung in Niadhélen; infants were supposed to understand the words even if their nursemaids did not. One indication of a gift for magic was a young child's retention and understanding of a few words or phrases in the ancient tongue. Yet no one retained more than that, and young wizards and sorcerers were obliged to study Niadhélen in order to reacquire, by painstaking effort, a fragmentary version of the language they had understood (but were unable to use) perfectly and completely at birth.

Which leads to another, nonanimistic theory (held only by a few) about the use of Niadhélen in magic: that the words of the spell were used not to communicate or command, but to create a higher mental state in the magician, by opening up a part of the mind that still knew and understood the first language—and was therefore in communication with the higher powers, or Fates, by whom Niadhélen had been given in the beginning.

Magicians who practiced the black arts were the exception. They could hardly invoke powers of Darkness by using the language of the Servants of the Light; another language was therefore used to invoke the Dark and its creatures. However, while white magicians never resorted to the dark arts, black magicians were perfectly willing to use the elemental magics practiced by wizards, any time that it suited their purposes. Even Ouriána and the Furiádhin spoke most of their spells in Niadhélen.

The Elements

Magicians believed there were eight elements: four *anelfani* (inanimate elements) and a higher form of each of these, the *éolfani* (animate elements).

It should be noted that in the case of darkness and light, the elements by those names are not to be confused with the greater Darkness and the ultimate Light of religion, to which they bear only the faintest shadow of a resemblance.

Anelfani—Éolfani

nëos (darkness)   **daer** (animate darkness, earth)

erüi (light)   **féal** (animate light, fire)

ael (air)   **anad** (animate air, wind)

nim (mist)   **uinn** (animate mist, water)

Spells

aneirëo   a destiny altered by ill-doing or black magic.

aneirias   a curse, a plea to higher powers to strike down an enemy or an oppressor. This was regarded as a deplorable act by truly pious people, though it was occasionally employed by the overzealous and self-righteous.

aniffath a doom, a curse, or an ill wishing against a person or a group of persons, or on some purpose or enterprise they might enter into together (for instance, a marriage or a treaty). It was, however, a very specific and complex kind of curse. Unlike an *aneirëo,* which could be spat out on the spur of the moment or on one's deathbed, an *aniffath* took time, care, and considerable power to create. It was the very blackest kind of sorcery. In theory, it could be undone, but its complexity and its ability to mutate and to take a new (though equally malign) direction whenever steps were taken to block its effects made this almost impossible.

béanath a charm of blessing. A spell meant to protect an individual or group of people against a specific danger, or to wish them well in some endeavor.

eirias a prayer to the Light or to Servants of the Light; a plea for the Fates to intercede.

eirëo "destiny" In particular, an individual's personal destiny. As this was something assigned by the Fates at the beginning of one's life, it was believed to be always beneficial—or at the very least tending toward enlightenment—but it could be altered for the worse by bad acts or by sorcery.

illedrion literally, a little spell or enchantment. A verse, a poem, or a riddle.

lledrion a charm or a spell, generally used to mean magic practiced on nonliving objects or to control the elements—to light a candle, for instance, or to call up a wind. Placing no limits or bindings on sentient creatures, these spells were regarded as White Magic.

shibeath a healing charm or a protective charm without the element of blessing.

waethag a black sorcerer's familiar spirit, or any undead or immaterial thing under a sorcerer's spell. Also, a sorcerous illusion.

waethas a spell of binding or enslaving. Loosely used of any sorcerous act done with bad intentions. Black Magic.

Runes

Loosely, alphabets, pictographs, hieroglyphs, or writings. All writing, as a symbolic form of language, was regarded as quasimagical. For the purpose of understanding this account, it is necessary to describe only two kinds of runes: 1. The ordinary "Tree Runes" that were used in writing throughout the former Empire lands, a phonetic alphabet with each letter given the name of a common tree or plant. These were also the runes used by runestone readers and occasionally by petty magicians; wizards and mages alike accounted them of little significance or power. 2. The "Wizard's Runes," which were the patterns used to contain and channel energies in order to produce specific effects. They might be written in ink, scratched in sand, etc., or merely drawn on the air, depending on the circumstances. They were also used in meditation. Opinions differ on whether the first runes were divined by wizards or simply devised by them.

New runes sometimes came to wizards in the way of visions; it was said that several wizards might be granted the same vision at once. In times of catastrophe and great upheaval, an existing rune might simply cease to work—simultaneously, all across the world. No one quite understood how this was so, yet instances of this happening are recorded in numerous accounts. Many runes lost their potency after the Change, but several new ones appeared at about the same time. Runes were sometimes forgotten, only to be rediscovered.

CHRONOLOGY

Before the Change

c. 3100: foundation of the northern empire; kings and princes of subject nations swear fealty to the Pendawer family, rulers of Alluinn

4010: Phaôrax, Erios, and then Rhuadllyn declare independence; the long struggle known as the First Pharaxion Wars begins

4016: Erios and Rhuadllyn surrender, a treaty is signed without reparations, and their rulers again swear fealty to the Emperor; however, the war with Phaôrax continues with the help of the Dragonstones

4020–4030: rise of sorcerer-kings in Otöi; many smaller nations of the southern continent are conquered and subjugated

4031: the Pendawers make peace with Phaôrax; a marriage is made between the two houses to seal the treaty

4040: Otöi makes a first incursion on Empire lands in the form of a raid on Tirhéne; though the raiders are repelled, the Pendawer emperor now perceives Otöi as a threat

4067–4069: Otöi sends out a full-scale army of conquest; Tirhéne falls; Malindor is invaded

4070: Otöwan armies driven out of Malindor

4072: Alluinn reclaims Tirhéne

4073–4075: the sorcerer-king of Otöi consolidates his power on the southern continent, declares himself Emperor of the South

4076: to maintain his interests, the Pendawer Emperor arranges the first of many marriages, this one between a Pendawer princess and the heir to the throne of Thäerie

4078–5000: the Pendawer Emperor arranges more political marriages, with Hythe, Weye, and Rheithûn

5004: Otöi attempts to invade Phaôrax; the King of Phaôrax wards off invaders with the help of the Alluinn

5012–5037: a princess of Phaôrax marries the Emperor's oldest son; twenty-five years later, their second son is crowned as Emperor in Ceir Eldig

5090: a dispute between the kings of Thäerie and Phaôrax almost escalates into war, but the Emperor mediates; however, the Pharaxions feel they have not received their due, and ill feelings continue to rankle for another five years

5098: Otöi makes another incursion into Malindor; later that same year there is an attack on Brielliend

5099–5108: full-scale war between the empires of Alluinn and Otöi; gradually, the armies of Alluinn begin to prevail

5010–5011: in a tremendous (and ill-advised) battle of magics, the wizards of Alluinn quickly gain the advantage, but not before the Otöwan mages summon up forces that neither side can control; approximately six hundred mages and four hundred wizards are killed almost simultaneously; their deaths send such a shock through the world of matter that the path of the moon is altered, and there are earthquakes, floods, and other disasters in every land of the known world; the destruction is worst in Otöi, but much of Alluinn is levelled as well, and what remains descends into a state of anarchy; Tirhéne becomes a desert wasteland

After the Change

1: a new reckoning of years is begun; unable to restore order in Alluinn, the Emperor takes sanctuary with his kinsmen on Thäerie; this is regarded as a slight by his kinsmen on Phaôrax; the effects of the new elliptical orbit of the moon are felt everywhere in the form of destructive tides that rise higher than ever before and increased seismic activity; scholars begin to divide the history of the world into two epochs, *Silüenne* ("the subsolar world") and *Silürené* ("the sublunar world")

2–88: a period during which nationalism combines with isolationism; everyone is so absorbed in repairing the damage wrought by war and sorcery that it is an era of peace between nations; the natural world, however, remains in a dangerous state of flux; midway through this period, the King of Thäerie dies and his heirs offer the throne to the Pendawer; he consents and marries a Thäerian princess to seal the agreement

89: a brief war between Thäerie and Phaôrax—their quarrel lasts less than half a year; a treaty is signed, and Princess Nimenoë is sent from Phaôrax to be fostered on Leal, while a minor princeling from Thäerie goes to Phaôrax

99: Nimenoë's elder twin sister, Ouriána, makes a secret pilgrimage to the ruined capital of Otöi

102: Ouriána ascends the throne of Phaôrax

103: Ouriána establishes a new religion centering around the Devouring Moon; shortly thereafter she declares herself an incarnation of the moon goddess

108–115: Ouriána and her twelve priests immerse themselves in the blackest of magics, and so begins her reign of dark sorcery; in 110 she gives birth to her first son, Guindeluc

116: relations between Thäerie and Phaôrax become increasingly strained; Ouriána declares herself the heir to the Empire and sends out armies to recover her lost territories; her invasion of Rhuadllyn is almost immediately successful; she nextt sends armies to Brielliend

118: the Prophecy comes into the minds of many seers at virtually the same moment; this event will be repeated many times in later years

121: Ouriána's armies enter Malindor; an alliance is made between Thäerie, Rheithûn, Hythe, Weye, Mere, Gonlündor, Leal, and Erios to oppose the expansion of Ouriána's territories and expel her armies from Malindor and Brielliend; as leader of the alliance, Réodan Pendawer assumes the title of High King.

130: Nimenoë marries Eldori, a minor prince of the Old Thäerian line; Ouriána weaves a curse to render her sister barren; later that same year, Ouriána gives birth to her second son, Cuillioc

139: Ouriána's priests take command of her armies, entering the war on many fronts; it becomes evident that what had only been rumor before is true: dark sorceries have altered them beyond recognition, and they begin to be known as the Furiádhin

141: Eldori dies; later that same year, in spite of Ouriána's curse, Nimenöe gives birth to Guenloie, but dies in childbed;

in order to distract Ouriána while Éireamhóine spirits the infant away, Réodan sends a fleet to attack Phaôrax; the invasion is a disaster, but in defending her island Ouriána works spells that leave her so weakened, she does not regain full use of her powers for several years; Éireamhóine and Guenloie are apparently killed in an avalanche in the Cadmin Aernan

160: word comes to Leal that Guenloie is still alive